'When it comes to dishing up lusciously sensual,
relentlessly readable historical romances,
Laurens is unrivalled.'
—*Booklist*

'Laurens's writing shines.'
—*Publishers Weekly*

'One of the most talented authors on the scene today…
Laurens has a real talent for writing sensuous and
compelling love scenes.'
—*Romance Reviews*

'Stephanie Laurens never fails to entertain and charm her
readers with vibrant plots, snappy dialogue and
unforgettable characters.'
—*Historical Romance Reviews*

'Stephanie Laurens plays into readers' fantasies like a
master and claims their hearts time and again.'
—*RT Book Reviews*

No.1 *New York Times* bestselling author **Stephanie Laurens** began writing as an escape from the dry world of professional science, a hobby that quickly became a career. Her novels set in Regency England have captivated readers around the globe, making her one of the romance world's most beloved and popular authors. *A Match for Marcus Cynster* is her sixtieth published work. All her works remain in print and are readily available. If Stephanie isn't writing, she's reading and, if she's not reading, she's tending her garden.

Visit Stephanie's website at www.stephanielaurens.com.

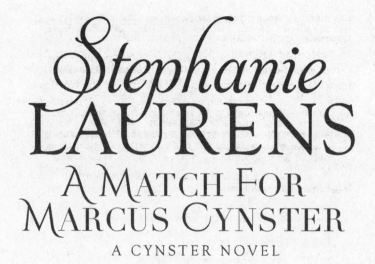

# Stephanie
# LAURENS
## A Match For
## Marcus Cynster
### A CYNSTER NOVEL

Harlequin MIRA is a registered trademark of Harlequin Enterprises Limited, used under licence.

Published in Great Britain 2015.
Harlequin MIRA, an imprint of Harlequin (UK) Limited,
Eton House, 18-24 Paradise Road,
Richmond, Surrey, TW9 1SR

© 2015 Savdek Management Proprietary Limited

ISBN 978-1-848-45374-6

59-0515

Harlequin (UK) Limited's policy is to use papers that are natural, renewable and recyclable products and made from wood grown in sustainable forests. The logging and manufacturing processes conform to the legal environmental regulations of the country of origin.

Printed and bound by
CPI Group (UK) Ltd, Croydon, CR0 4YY

# A Match For Marcus Cynster

# *Prologue*

*April 1849*
*The Carrick Estate, Dumfries and Galloway,*
*Scotland*

"Miss Niniver? Are you there?"

Niniver Carrick looked up from the silky head of the deerhound she was stroking. Recognizing the speaker's voice, she inwardly sighed.

Crouched in a pen halfway down old Egan's barn, she was hidden from Ferguson's sight. For one fleeting instant, she was tempted to stay where she was, safe in her refuge surrounded by her hounds, but as ever, duty called. Called, hauled, and had her straightening, brushing pieces of hay from her riding habit's skirts. The pens' walls had been raised to keep the hounds contained; she lifted her head and peeked over toward the front of the barn. "I'm here. What's the matter?"

Ferguson, the butler at Carrick Manor, saw her and strode deeper into the barn. A middle-aged man, upright and sober, he was one of the clan elders. "It's Mister Nolan."

Although Niniver's older brother Nolan had succeeded to the title of Laird of Clan Carrick on the death of their father, Manachan Carrick, some ten months before, clan members had yet to change the way they referred to Nolan—a telling point, to Niniver's mind.

Ferguson halted before the pen in which she stood and fixed his gaze on her face. "Sean sent word that Mister Nolan's worse than ever. Ranting and raving like one possessed. Bradshaw, Forrester, Phelps, and Canning are there, too. They all think you need to come."

Niniver stared at Ferguson while she absorbed his words and what they really meant. Shortly after their father's death, Nolan had ridden up to a narrow ledge on the western side of the Coran of Portmark, one of the minor peaks in the range to the west of the Carrick lands. As that area was uninhabited, Sean, the head stableman, had followed at a distance; he'd reported that Nolan had sat on the ledge and stared out. As the ledge afforded a wide view over Loch Doon and the Rhinns of Kells, everyone had assumed Nolan had gone there to relax and think.

Initially, Nolan's visits to the ledge had been infrequent, but when he'd started riding in that direction every week, and then twice a week, Sean had followed him again. The side of the ridge was ruffled with folds, making it easy to get close enough to watch Nolan without being seen—and to hear what he said when his visits became a daily occurrence and he'd started rambling aloud.

Then he'd started ranting.

Eventually, he'd taken to raging and raving.

The target of his fury was their eldest brother, Nigel—he who had been convicted in absentia of poisoning their father, and who was also suspected of killing two clan women. A hue and cry had been raised, but Nigel had slipped away without trace; it was believed he'd taken ship for the colonies and had escaped beyond reach.

"All right." Niniver unlatched the pen's gate. Carefully keeping the questing hounds back, she slipped out, then reset the latch.

She could guess why she'd been summoned. Like the others named, she'd been up to the ledge before and had heard the tone of Nolan's ranting. He spoke to Nigel as if their brother was there, and he clearly blamed Nigel for all the difficulties the clan currently faced—the difficulties that, as laird, it was now Nolan's responsibility to deal with. To improve and rectify.

Nolan had accepted the mantle of laird readily. If anything, Niniver would have said he'd been keen to show that he was up to the task. But as the weeks and months had passed… If she had to describe what she'd seen in Nolan, she would say he had crumbled under the weight.

She and Norris, the youngest of her three brothers, had never been that close to Nigel and Nolan, who were older by more than five years. Yet over the last eight or so months, Nolan had retreated even further from them, much like a crab backing deeper into its shell. The gulf between her and Norris, and Nolan, was now a gaping chasm, impossible to bridge. She'd given up trying.

Walking out of the barn, she glanced at Ferguson. The heads of four clan families—Bradshaw, Forrester, Phelps, and Canning—were already at the ledge. Ferguson was another clan elder. Five votes on the clan council constituted a majority. Niniver had a strong suspicion over why they wanted her there.

She pulled her riding gloves from her pocket. "Are you returning to the manor, or will you come, too?"

"The others asked me to come," Ferguson said, "so I'll ride along with you."

And that, she thought, confirmed it. Unsurprisingly, the clan had grown skeptical of Nolan's ability to manage and lead; they were preparing to confront him, possibly to take the lairdship from him, and they wanted her—his sister, but also the next oldest member of the main Carrick line—there as a witness.

Pausing to lift her face to the spring sun, she closed her eyes, breathed in, then out. All she felt was a sense of inevitability, of being on a road from which there was no turning aside. With an inward sigh, she opened her eyes. Setting her lips, she strode for her big bay gelding, Oswald, waiting placidly by the fence. "In that case, let's go."

* * *

After leaving Oswald tethered with the other horses a little way away, Niniver joined her clansmen in the fold to the south of the narrow ledge on which Nolan was pacing.

Bradshaw, Phelps, Canning, and Forrester greeted her politely. Phelps and Bradshaw had brought their sons. After exchanging quiet hellos and nodding to Sean and the young groom he'd brought with him, she joined the others in studying Nolan.

The rock ledge on which he paced was a little way down from the ridgeline, at an elevation slightly below their position. He strode agitatedly back and forth, half the time turned away from them. They only saw his face when he swung around, yet his attention remained elsewhere; he never looked their way. A stiff breeze was blowing from the northwest, making it unlikely he would hear them even if they called, but the breeze carried his words to them clearly.

She hadn't set eyes on him for the last week; he'd taken to eating his meals in the library and avoiding all contact, not only with her and Norris but with the household in general. Now, as she looked across the shoulder of the ridge that lay between them, what she saw shocked her.

Over the last months, Nolan had been growing more furtive, his expression more hunted—more haunted. Now he looked like a caricature of a madman, his eyes wild and staring, his hair—once as fair as hers but now lank and dull—standing out from his skull at odd angles. His complexion, normally as pale as hers, was red and blotchy.

Previously, he'd always dressed well—not just neatly but expensively. Now his clothes looked as if he'd slept in them for days.

Even more disturbing was the way he walked—jerkily, abruptly, like a puppet whose strings were being manipulated by some amateur puppeteer, with Nolan himself no longer in control.

As for the words that spewed from his lips…

"You bloody *bastard*! How was I to know it would be like this? But you knew, didn't you? You *knew*, and you never said anything! So now I'm here, trying to cope, and they're all watching and expecting me to be like Papa and make it all work—and it's *hopeless*! There's nothing there!" Nolan clutched at his hair, gripping and tugging, his face contorting with effort and pain. "Aargh!" He released his grip; Niniver saw several pale strands drift from his fingers.

Nolan's voice lowered, darker and grating. "I can't do this. This wasn't what I planned. I can't go on pretending, and I'm trapped! *Trapped*, I tell you!" His jaw set. He ground out the words "This wasn't how it was supposed to be."

His tone was ghastly; none of those watching could have had any doubt they were witnessing a descent into madness.

Niniver swept up her skirts and swung toward the path to the ridgeline. The path to the ledge lay ten yards further on.

Ferguson looked at her. "Where are you going?"

She glanced at Nolan. "I'm going to talk to him."

"You can't do that." Canning looked appalled. "He's beyond reasoning with."

"I know, but I have to try." Niniver met Canning's gaze. "We all know where this is leading, but he is my brother. If I can calm him down, we can all leave and ride back to the manor without a struggle."

None of the men liked it, but none of them had the right to gainsay her.

She took another step.

Sean moved to follow her. "I'll come with you."

She glanced at him. "No. If he sees you, he'll erupt—you know what his temper's like. Bad enough he's in this state—we don't need that, as well."

Sean stared at her stonily, every bit as stubborn as she. "We can't let you face him alone. I'll hang back if you promise to keep your distance from him."

She grimaced, but then nodded. "All right. I'll keep out of his reach." She turned to the path. The others returned their attention to Nolan. Niniver, along with Sean, glanced at Nolan, too.

Abruptly, Nolan clutched his head with both hands. He pressed hard, the tendons in his hands and wrists sharply defined as he pressed in, his features contorting. Then he hunched, curling in on himself as if in unbearable pain—

He released his head and straightened. Throwing his arms wide, he screamed, "You bloody fool! You should have killed me, instead!"

He took one step forward and flung himself off the ledge.

Below the ledge ran a deep, narrow, granite-sided crevasse—one of the occasional fissures that, like rocky gashes, scored this landscape.

In the sudden silence, they instinctively froze, then the breeze wafted and they heard a muted thump.

It was the most chilling sound Niniver had ever heard.

Shock held them all speechless.

Until Sean murmured, "Bugger me. The bastard's killed himself."

\* \* \*

Phelps was a sheep farmer; he and his son, Matt, always carried ropes on their saddles, as did Sean.

In a group, they walked to the ledge. They peered into the crevasse, but small bushes and grasses sprouting from the rock walls made it impossible to see what lay in the shadowed depths.

The opposite lip of the crevasse was lower than the ledge, but was flanked by scree; circling around to it wasn't an option. But the crevasse was very narrow, a gaping wound ripped in the side of the hill and lined with rock as far down as they could see; there was no way to walk in and no path down.

Phelps, Matt, and Sean laid out the ropes. The other men organized themselves into teams to lower Sean and Matt into the crevasse. Her arms tightly folded, her mind blank, Niniver watched as the pair went over the edge, each on separate ropes, with a third rope dangling between them.

As they descended into the shadows, she walked to the edge; she looked down, watching, but the bushes soon obscured her view.

She turned her attention to the ropes. The men slowly let the ropes play out—and out; the crevasse was deeper than any of them had thought. At last, the tension on the ropes eased as first Sean, then Matt, reached a point where they could stand.

A moment later, a yelping exclamation—both Sean's and Matt's voices raised in surprise—erupted from the depths. Peering down, Niniver frowned. Sean and Matt had known what to expect, so why had they sounded shocked?

"What did they say?" Ferguson called from where he waited with the other men to haul the pair up again.

Still frowning, she shook her head. "I don't know. The rock distorts their voices too much. They're talking now, but I can't make out what they're saying."

The third rope—the one Sean and Matt had planned to tie around Nolan's body—shifted. Phelps came to stand beside Niniver, but he, too, could make nothing of the mutterings rising from below.

Then Sean tugged on his rope, and Matt tugged his. Phelps rejoined the other men, and they hauled the pair up.

Sean reached the ledge first. His weathered, normally ruddy countenance was chalk-white.

"What is it?" Niniver demanded as he scrambled onto the ledge.

Sean pushed to his feet. "We found Nolan's body. He's dead—neck broken, among other things—just as we expected." He glanced at Matt as the younger man scrambled up to stand beside him.

Matt, too, looked badly shaken.

Sean turned to Niniver. He hesitated for a second, then blurted, "Nolan's body was lying on top of another body. Nigel's body was already there—Nolan flung himself down in the same place."

Niniver blinked. Her mind whirled. "Nigel flung himself off this ledge, too?" She couldn't imagine that, not of Nigel, but she hadn't expected Nolan to kill himself, either.

Looking grimmer by the second, Sean shook his head. "Nigel landed on his back, and Nolan's hunting knife, the one he said he lost last year, was buried between Nigel's ribs."

She felt her mouth fall open, then her mind whirled one last time, and like a kaleidoscope, all the pieces fell into place. "Ah."

The quiet sound—of recognition, of realization—was drowned beneath the men's shocked exclamations.

She looked around the group. Unlike the others, she wasn't surprised.

Indeed, just the opposite. Finally, everything was starting to make sense.

\* \* \*

It took several hours to bring both bodies up from the depths of the crevasse and transport the remains to Carrick Manor. Despite the depredations of small animals and the passage of time, Nigel's body was easily identified. His remains were garbed in the clothes he'd worn to the wedding of their cousin, Thomas Carrick, and Lucilla Cynster—the last time anyone other than Nolan had set eyes on him.

Niniver spent the rest of that day closeted in the library with the clan council. Norris was present, too. Although he was several years younger than she and therefore had fewer memories of Nigel and Nolan as children, his assessments of their older brothers matched and supported her own.

Fact by fact, she and the council assembled the true sequence of events. Recalling a statement Nolan had made at the inquest into the Burns sisters' deaths—an inquest that had reached no final conclusion but had left the suspicion of murder hanging over Nigel's head—Niniver sent Sean to Ayr to pose what were now clearly pertinent questions to certain people there.

It was the following morning before Sean returned. The clan council reconvened to hear his report. Once they'd digested the no-longer-unexpected news, Ferguson turned to Niniver. "What now? Do we summon the authorities, or what?"

Seated behind the desk her father had used throughout his long reign as laird, Niniver met Ferguson's gaze, then looked at Mrs. Kennedy, the housekeeper, seated alongside him, then at Canning, Phelps, Bradshaw, Sean, and the others on the council. All regarded her levelly, expectation in their eyes.

The vow she'd uttered over her father's grave resonated in her mind. *I will do whatever's necessary to ensure that all mistakes made by your children are put right and that the clan is made whole, strong, and prosperous again. I will do all I can, and whatever I must, to preserve your legacy and to steer the clan as you would have wished.*

It had been all she'd had to offer in reparation for her father losing his life; she hadn't known enough to save him from being poisoned by one of his sons.

The least she could do now was to ensure the blame fell on the son who deserved it, thus clearing the name of the son who had been another victim. That way, Nigel—Manachan's firstborn and best-loved child, the one who, despite his weaknesses, had been groomed to take the lairdship—could be buried next to Manachan in the family plot.

Yet her vow demanded she put the clan first. "We need to inform the authorities of Nolan's death, and of all we've now realized. But if at all possible, I think we should endeavor to keep the matter quiet. I see no reason for the news sheets in Ayr and Dumfries, much less Glasgow and Edinburgh, to be encouraged to re-visit the clan's difficulties."

Everyone was nodding. Phelps glanced around. "Clearly, you'll get no argument from us on that score. The clan have suffered enough—we don't need our dirty linen hanging out for the rest of the county to gossip about."

Seeing agreement writ large in every face, Niniver nodded. "We'll summon the doctor to examine the bodies—he'll confirm what we already know. Meanwhile, I'll send notes conveying the bare facts to…"

She paused, considering, then went on, "Sir Godfrey Riddle, Lord Richard, and Thomas, and ask them to meet here this afternoon. Let's see if we can manage things with just those three—they know the clan's situation and will most likely be willing to help us arrange matters with the minimum of fuss."

No one argued. Half an hour later, Sean took the notes Niniver had written and rode out to deliver them.

* * *

The doctor came, viewed the bodies, and promised to send his report to Sir Godfrey Riddle, the local magistrate.

Sir Godfrey arrived promptly at two o'clock. He came up the front steps, his expression grave and concerned. "Niniver, my dear." After taking her hands in an avuncular clasp, he squeezed gently. "This must be so very distressing for you."

She'd written only that Nolan had killed himself, and that subsequently they'd found Nigel's body. Her expression uninformative, she inclined her head. How to explain that, while her father's death and Nigel's disappearance had rocked and shaken her, Nolan's death and their subsequent understanding had restabilized her—had restored her confidence in her ability to read people, in her ability to navigate her world? The earlier situation, she simply hadn't understood. Now, she understood all too well.

As for grief—those who had deserved her tears had been dead for nearly a year. She had too much to do to preserve their memories to feel much over Nolan's passing.

Sir Godfrey released her as Lord Richard Cynster and Niniver's cousin, Thomas Carrick, rode into the forecourt—followed by a carriage that swung wide to draw up before the steps. Thomas dismounted, tossed his reins to Sean, and went to open the carriage door. He handed down his mother-in-law, Richard's wife, Catriona, and then, as if she were made of porcelain, Thomas assisted his wife—Catriona and Richard's daughter Lucilla—to the ground.

Lucilla was pregnant, the whisper was with twins. Only slightly taller than Niniver, even though she was still many months from confinement, Lucilla certainly looked large enough for the rumor to be true. Yet from the reassuring smile she sent Thomas and the ease with which, supported by his arm, she climbed the steep front steps, she wasn't seriously bothered by the extra weight she was carrying.

Although she hadn't requested their presence, Niniver had hoped both ladies would come; she was relieved they had. After touching cheeks, squeezing fingers, and exchanging grave and muted greetings, she steered her collection of "authorities" into the drawing room, where Norris stood waiting.

Niniver had had the footmen rearrange the furniture. After greeting Norris, Lucilla let herself down on one sofa, and Catriona sank onto the matching sofa facing her. Richard sat beside his wife, and Thomas sat alongside Lucilla. Sir Godfrey took one of the armchairs set to one side of the fireplace and angled to face the room, leaving Niniver to sink into its mate.

Norris had placed a straight-backed chair on Niniver's left. As Norris sat, she turned to Sir Godfrey. "If you don't mind, I would like several clansmen to attend this meeting, as any decisions made will affect the whole clan."

Sir Godfrey nodded somberly. "Indeed. This is a dire business for you all."

Ferguson had hovered by the door; at Niniver's nod, he ushered in Mrs. Kennedy, Bradshaw, Forrester, Canning, Phelps, and Matt. Ferguson followed, and Sean brought up the rear, closing the door behind him.

Ferguson and Sean placed the straight-backed chairs they'd earlier carried in from the dining room in a semi-circle between the ends of the sofas and the door, then with nods to the assembled gentry that were gravely returned, the clan members sat.

Niniver held Thomas's gaze for a moment, then she looked at Sir Godfrey. "It might be best if I relate recent events as they occurred, and then we can move on to what we, the clan, subsequently deduced and confirmed, and ultimately to what we now believe occurred in the deaths of not just Papa, but also of Faith and Joy Burns."

Sir Godfrey's gaze sharpened. "I see." He nodded. "Pray proceed."

Niniver drew in a breath and succinctly described the events of the previous day. Sir Godfrey questioned Sean and Matt as to what they had seen when they'd first reached the bodies; their answers were brief, but complete.

"So." Thomas met Niniver's gaze, then looked at Sir Godfrey. "It appears that Nolan was in fact the murderer, and Nigel another of his victims."

Thomas, too, was no doubt finding the new truth easier to comprehend than the previous judgment that had cast Nigel as the murderer.

"Hmph!" From under beetling brows, Sir Godfrey

regarded Niniver. "You mentioned deducing and confirming more. What, exactly?"

"At the inquest into the Burns sisters' deaths, Nolan said that he and Nigel had spent the night on which Faith and Joy died in Ayr, in a house of ill repute." Niniver hoped her blush wasn't too noticeable. "In light of our conclusion that Nolan killed Nigel, I sent Sean to ask the…er, ladies what they knew of that night. We thought…" She looked at Sean.

He came to her aid. "We thought as how if either of those two had left the ladies that night, the ladies would be likely to remember, even if it was nearly a year ago."

"And did they remember?" Richard asked.

"Yes." Sean looked at Sir Godfrey. "They remembered that the fair-haired one—Nolan—had ridden home that night. A pair of them heard Nolan tell Nigel he'd forgotten to put away some books they didn't want anyone reading, so he was riding home to put the books away but expected to be back come morning."

"And," Thomas said, his gaze on Bradshaw, "when the Bradshaws fell ill because someone put salts into their well, that salting occurred the night before, when both Nigel and Nolan spent the night here. They headed to Ayr the following morning."

Norris nodded. "So it was Nolan who put the salts in the well. Nigel would never have done that. He might have *joked* about doing it, but he would never actually have *done* it."

Niniver looked at Sir Godfrey. "No one asked us—Norris and me—what we thought of Nigel poisoning Papa. Norris doesn't remember Nolan and Nigel as well as I do." She glanced at Thomas. "And I saw them more consistently than Thomas—when he was around, Nolan always played a very careful hand."

Returning her gaze to Sir Godfrey, she continued, "Nolan resented—*deeply* resented—that Papa cared only for Nigel. That was Papa's one real weakness— he never truly saw any of us but Nigel. However, Nolan didn't hate Nigel. In his own way, Nolan loved Nigel, as much as he was able to feel that emotion. But Nolan was the clever one, while Nigel was…well, he was always easily led, and he trusted Nolan implicitly. From an early age, Nolan cast himself as Nigel's closest friend and confidant, and his most loyal and effective supporter. I remember seeing it happen, even though I didn't understand what I was seeing at the time—because, of course, Nolan never cared what I saw. I was just their baby sister, and no one would ever listen to me about them. To Nolan, what I—and later Norris—saw or didn't see was never anything to be concerned about."

She paused, then went on, "Over the last ten or so years, neither Norris nor I saw much of Nigel and Nolan. We stayed here, while they were out and about, often going to Ayr, Dumfries, Glasgow, and Edinburgh. However, I can't imagine that the relationship between them changed, nor that they, as individuals, changed. So when it seemed it was Nigel who had poisoned Papa and killed Joy and Faith Burns, with Nolan innocent of any wrongdoing, I…didn't know what to think." She spread her hands. "It seemed backward, mixed up and confused, but with Nigel having supposedly fled, and Nolan… Once Nigel was gone, Nolan buckled down and did the best he could, and I thought perhaps I *had* interpreted things wrongly and it had been *Nigel's* influence that had made the pair of them so wild before."

She drew in a breath and added, "And I never for a moment dreamed that Nolan might have killed Nigel because, as I said, if Nolan loved anyone, he loved Nigel."

Silence fell.

Catriona broke it. "That last fact—that Nolan loved Nigel—and yet, when it was clear there was a real risk of Lucilla seeing Manachan, realizing he was being poisoned, and raising the alarm, Nolan had to sacrifice Nigel to give the authorities and society a villain they would be content with… Having killed the one person he actually loved would account for Nolan's descent into madness."

Lucilla shivered. "Indeed."

"If I may make so bold," Phelps said, "if Nolan had intended to keep Nigel alive—to let Nigel be the laird, but for him, Nolan, to be the clever one managing the estate, and all else, from Nigel's shadow—if that's what Nolan had wanted, but then he was forced to kill Nigel to protect himself, that would also make sense of the blatherings Sean's been hearing for months. Aye, and what all of us heard today up on that ledge."

"It also explains," Ferguson said, "why, having Nigel's body close by, Nolan went to the ledge to talk to him—to still be close to him."

Thomas stirred. His expression stony, he said, "I agree. If we accept that Nolan wanted revenge on Manachan, and that Nolan effectively controlled Nigel, then killing Manachan and having Nigel become laird… That might well have been the sum of Nolan's intentions. He wouldn't have had to shoulder any responsibility—no matter what happened, all blame would fall on Nigel's shoulders. I can see that as being a nice revenge for Nolan. He would get to pull the strings

Manachan had intended to be in Nigel's hands, and any failures would be sheeted home to Nigel."

They revisited various matters, recasting conclusions in the light of what they now understood, but it was clear that no doubt lingered in anyone's mind as to the truth of what had occurred in the months leading to Manachan's death.

Finally, Sir Godfrey called them to order. "I believe we're all agreed that Nolan was the villain, first to last, in the matter of the old laird's death, and also the deaths of the Burns sisters." Sir Godfrey fixed his gaze on Niniver. "My earlier judgment will need to be rescinded, but I imagine you and the clan"—with a glance he included the other clan members—"would rather we accomplished what we need to do with a minimum of fuss, heh?"

Relief swept through Niniver. "Exactly." She glanced at Thomas, then at the others. "The clan has suffered through the scandal of Papa's murder, supposedly by Nigel. We would prefer not to have to go through that ordeal again." She looked at Sir Godfrey, then at Lord Richard. "Yet we need to have Nigel exonerated so he can be buried next to Papa. Is it possible to do that while avoiding more public scandal?"

Sir Godfrey arched his brows. After a moment, he looked at Richard.

Richard returned his regard. "What if we took Nolan's suicide as a confession? Which, in effect, it was."

"And," Thomas said, "there's no need for a trial, given the murderer has taken his own life. He's no longer here to be punished."

"Ah." Sir Godfrey looked more hopeful. After a mo-

ment's cogitation, he nodded decisively. "Yes, indeed.
That will work."

In the end, it was agreed that, without any fanfare,
Sir Godfrey would reopen the cases of her father's
and the Burns sisters' deaths, and exonerate Nigel of
the crimes by virtue of Nolan's confession and the
subsequent confirmation that it was, indeed, he who
had been the villain in all three cases. Catriona, who,
through her position as Lady of the Vale, maintained
a close connection with the local minister, volunteered
to explain matters to Reverend Foyle, thus easing the
way for the clan to arrange the appropriate funeral
and burials.

By the time all was settled and Niniver had waved
everyone off, exhaustion dragged at her, but she had
one more meeting yet to face.

Thomas had been the last to take his leave of her.
He was seven years older than she; they had never been
close, yet she had always seen him as a true Carrick,
a man in the mold of her father. After helping Lucilla
into the carriage and shutting the door, Thomas had
turned to her, met her eyes, then taken her hands in
his. He'd held her gaze levelly. "This is the end of a
dark time for the clan, and for the family."

She'd seen understanding in his amber eyes; he'd
foreseen the inevitable consequence of the day, just as
she had. All that was left was for her to deal with it, to
chart her way forward through whatever eventuated.

Regardless of whatever happened, she would, forever and always, be clan.

She found Norris in the library. He was standing
at the long windows looking out over the darkening

landscape. She suspected that he, too, knew what was coming, and had been waiting to speak with her.

Stifling a sigh, she sank onto the arm of one of the armchairs.

Norris turned. Through the deepening shadows, he met her gaze. After a moment, he asked, "What now?"

She straightened her spine and raised her head. "Now we call a meeting of the clan to elect a new laird." She held his gaze. "Will you stand?"

He laughed, a hollow, faintly derisive sound. "No. I have no wish whatsoever to lead the clan."

She'd expected nothing else, yet she'd had to ask and hear him state it. From the moment of his birth, he'd been ignored, not just by their father but by the clan, too. She was the only person he had ever been close to; she was the only person he didn't ignore back. He had no friends locally, no interests locally; his interests and ambitions were entirely academic, and thus had always lain far beyond clan lands.

"So what will you do?" She was still his sister; she still cared about him, and she knew that, inside his hardened shell, he cared for her.

"I didn't expect to be free to choose so soon, but there's nothing for me here. There never was." Sinking his hands into his breeches pockets, he shrugged. "Truth be told, I've always felt there was never meant to be. I don't belong here."

She said nothing, simply waited.

Half turning, he glanced out of the window, looking to the east. "I need to carve out a life for myself. I'm going to go—I need to leave, once and for all. Forever. I won't be coming back. And other than what I inherited from Papa, I won't expect to draw on clan funds—do tell them that."

She'd been expecting something of the sort, yet still… "Where will you go?"

His shoulders lifted again. "St. Andrews, perhaps. I can look for work there—as a tutor, perhaps as a researcher. Who knows? I'll leave tomorrow morning."

*So soon?* She drew a tight breath and rose. "So you'll just ride away?"

Norris brought his gaze back to her face. "Without a single backward glance."

She almost opened her lips to point out that meant he'd be leaving her behind, too, leaving her to cope with the disintegration of life as they'd known it, but… no. It was pointless to try to hold him. And, indeed, his leaving tomorrow would be an unequivocal statement of his relinquishing all claim to the lairdship. She forced herself to nod, then walked toward the desk. "Don't go without saying goodbye."

She felt his gaze on her but didn't meet it. He hesitated, then said, "I'll see you at breakfast."

With that, he walked to the door, opened it, and left.

She sank into the chair behind the huge desk. Once Norris left, she would be alone. The clan would meet and elect a new laird from another clan family. To her would fall the duty of overseeing the transfer of all the clan holdings—the estate, the manor, all except the Carrick family's personal wealth, a relatively meager amount that would be divided between herself and Norris. Everything else belonged to the clan—the furniture, the books surrounding her, even her deerhounds. Everything that made this place her home.

So what would she do once the transfer was complete?

She sat and stared at nothing as night closed in outside the windows and the shadows inside deepened.

Norris might be leaving, but in doing so, he was accepting the challenge of making a life for himself. She needed to do the same, but she was the opposite of him—she didn't want to leave clan lands. Her roots were here, sunk into the soil in a way she couldn't explain. She'd always felt connected, both with the gently rolling fields and even more with the people. She'd grown up immersed in *clan*, and she simply couldn't imagine ripping herself free—couldn't imagine any reason why she might wish to.

"So I'll remain," she murmured to the darkened room. "Whatever happens, I'll work out some way to stay—perhaps whoever moves in will let me reopen the disused wing and stay there?"

She tipped her head, considering it, then lightly shrugged.

Aside from not having any inclination to leave clan lands, there was the overriding matter of her vow to her father—a vow she had yet to fulfill.

Unlike her brothers, she believed in clan, in right and wrong, in fulfilling obligations, and in keeping solemn vows. In giving back to those who gave to her.

Placing her palms on the desk, she pushed to her feet. "One way or another, I will find a way."

Throughout her twenty-four years, whenever disruption had threatened, she'd fallen back on that tenet as her guide. It would steer her this time, too.

\* \* \*

They buried Nigel and Nolan three days later. The atmosphere was more that of a witnessing than an hon-

oring. The ambiance was strikingly different from that
which had prevailed at their father's funeral—but then
Manachan had been revered by the clan and respected
throughout the community, while Nigel and Nolan had
been tolerated purely on the basis of being Manachan's
sons. As for acquaintances within the wider community, theirs proved to be limited to young hellions of
similar ilk to themselves—irresponsible males intent
on enjoying a hedonistic life with nary a thought for
anyone or anything else.

Several of the latter unexpectedly turned up, driving curricles and phaetons, and greeting each other
raucously.

The clan ignored them.

Initially, Niniver had been surprised by how many
of the clan had chosen to attend. Then she'd realized
that, for them as for her, the somber service marked
the end of two years of uncertainty and unrest—two
years of confusion, of not knowing what was going on,
and of lost faith in the clan's leadership.

Nigel was buried next to their father and mother in
the Carrick family plot.

Nolan was buried in a far corner of the graveyard—
rejected and disowned by all.

It was she who cast the first sod on Nolan's coffin.
Stony-faced, the clan elders followed her lead.

And then it was done.

No one felt any need to linger; everyone was glad
to turn their backs and walk away.

As the gathering dispersed and the clan returned
to the carts and drays that had brought them there,
several of Nigel and Nolan's friends surrounded her

and attempted to press their patently insincere condolences on her.

She avoided society—in part because of just such men—but she'd long ago perfected one social art, that of keeping her feelings concealed and maintaining a mask of unruffled calm. Yet to be invited to join several would-be dandies on a picnic and, when she politely declined, to have her words ignored...

Luckily, Thomas intervened, and with several cutting words and a black scowl, he sent the horde packing. Together with Ferguson, Thomas escorted her away; she allowed them to lead her to her carriage, help her in, and shut the door.

Sean set the horses trotting, and the carriage pulled into the road, and finally, it was over.

She rested her head against the squabs and closed her eyes, holding in the tears that, suddenly, threatened to overflow.

Her family was gone—all of them. Thomas was her nearest blood relative, and he had his own place, his own role as consort to the future Lady of the Vale.

She...was alone. Completely alone. She had no place, no role—no life.

She was the one left behind.

But she knew the clan wouldn't throw her out; she would have a place, a role, within it, even if she didn't yet know what that would be.

She told herself to remain positive, or at least to keep her thoughts focused on what she yet had to do that day, on what lay immediately ahead.

The clan meeting to elect a new laird.

She sighed, opened her eyes, and glanced out of the window. "One way or another, I will find a way."

\* \* \*

She had accepted that, at the end of the clan meeting, she would need to witness the transfer of all clan property from the Carrick family's control to that of the clan family to which the newly elected laird belonged. To that end, she'd summoned the clan solicitor from Glasgow.

When she reentered the house, a footman told her that Mr. Purdy was waiting in the drawing room. Her mask firmly in place, she went to greet him.

Mr. Purdy was a dapper older gentleman with shrewd hazel eyes. After shaking her hand and accepting her invitation to reclaim his seat on the sofa, he asked, "Do you know to whom the clan will turn?"

Settling on the sofa opposite, she shook her head. "There are several clan elders who might take the role. I felt I should remain aloof from whatever discussions have been taking place. In the circumstances, I don't feel the decision of the new laird is one I should in any way influence."

Her family had let the clan down, and the loss of the lairdship was an appropriate justice.

Mr. Purdy frowned. "You have another brother, if I recall correctly. He must be…twenty-two years old?"

"Norris. He declined to stand for the lairdship and has already left to forge a new life elsewhere."

Purdy pursed his lips, then nodded. "As he didn't desire the position, him leaving might be for the best."

She'd come to the same conclusion. Whether he'd intended it or not, Norris's departure had eased the clan's way; that much she'd heard.

The door opened, and Ferguson looked in. He saw her, and relief softened his features. "There you are, miss." Ferguson recognized Purdy; a frown passed fleetingly over his face. He inclined his head to the solicitor. "Mr. Purdy." Then Ferguson returned his gaze to her. "If you would, miss, the clan's all gathered and waiting in the library."

She'd assumed there would be no need for her to attend the clan election, that it would be better for the clan if she wasn't present, but apparently, they wanted her there. Perhaps as the sole remaining Carrick to represent the family whose name the clan carried. She rose. "Yes, of course. I hadn't thought…" Turning to Purdy, she managed a smile. "If you'll excuse me, sir?"

Purdy had risen as she had; curiosity in his eyes, he inclined his head. "Of course, Miss Carrick. I'll wait here."

Wondering what had pricked Purdy's interest, she allowed Ferguson to usher her from the room. He led her to the library and held the door for her.

She walked in. Determined to maintain her composure, she looked around, and found every eye in the room—that of every man and woman in the clan—fixed on her. She blinked, but her mask didn't slip. Glancing around, she searched for a place to sit. Every chair was occupied and people lined the walls, several bodies deep.

Behind her, Ferguson cleared his throat. When she looked his way, he waved her on—to the chair behind the big desk.

It was the only vacant chair in the room—and, apparently, had been reserved for her. Keeping the frown in her mind from her face, she made her way down the long room. That particular chair—behind the big desk that her father, her grandfather, and all the lairds before them had used—should have been reserved for the new laird.

Ferguson slipped past her and around the desk, then held the chair for her. Perhaps they meant to have some sort of ceremonial moment to signify the handing on of the lairdship.

She sat, then looked around. To one side stood Bradshaw, a strong man who had demonstrated his willingness to act for the good of the clan. But he was a touch belligerent. Forrester, another of the clan elders, stood alongside with his wife and family; he was a quiet but solid man. Perhaps too quiet. She scanned the rest—Phelps, Canning, and all the other possible candidates—searching for some sign...

Out of nowhere came the thought that the French aristocrats must have felt like this, waiting for the guillotine to fall.

Her gaze landed on Sean, and the head stableman made a get-on-with-it gesture.

She blinked, then swung slightly to look up and back at Ferguson.

The big man opened his eyes at her, clearly expecting her to...lead the meeting?

She drew in a breath and glanced around again; everyone was waiting for her to speak. Clasping her hands on the desk, she cleared her throat; her voice sounded a trifle husky, but her memory supplied the right words. "In keeping with clan custom, we're gathered here today to elect a new laird." She glanced again at Ferguson; he had retreated to stand to the side with old Egan. "Do you have the list of nominees?"

Ferguson replied, "There's only one name on the clan's list."

"Only one?" While that would make matters easier, she'd felt sure the position would be hotly contested between at least three families—the Bradshaws, the Phelpses, and the Cannings.

Ferguson's gaze didn't shift from her face. "We've been talking for the past days, ever since your brother took his life—and, truth be told, even before that. But when it came down to it, there's only one person *all* the clan families will agree to follow—so that's the person we need to lead the clan, and no other."

Glancing around, she saw Bradshaw, Forrester, and all the others—and their wives—nodding in earnest agreement. "Well." She drew in a breath. "That's excellent. We won't even need to vote." And whoever it was would know they took the job with the unequivocal backing of the entire clan. She looked at Ferguson. "So, the name?"

Ferguson held her gaze. "Niniver Eileen Carrick."

It had been a decade at least since she'd been addressed by her full name. She blinked. "Yes?"

Ferguson's gaze bored into hers. His lips compressed, then he stated, "That's the name on our list."

She stopped breathing. She felt her eyes grow round, then rounder still. Her lips parted... She forced in a strangled breath and said, "You want *me* to be the laird...the lady?"

Emotion crashed into her; the realization—the confirmation she received as she looked once more around the room—was almost too great to assimilate. For a long moment, she let the impact roll over and through her. Given her vow to her father, given the clear support of the entire clan...

Moistening her lips, in a quieter tone, she asked, "Why me?"

Somewhat to her surprise, they told her.

She'd had no idea that all her life they'd been watching, that they'd seen not just the quiet girl-child, not just the young woman she'd grown to be, but the woman she truly was inside. They'd seen, they'd understood, and they'd chosen her.

She was touched, she was...slain by their faith, empowered by their trust, anchored by their confidence.

And she couldn't refuse them, couldn't say no.

She had no choice—and no other inclination—but to swallow the lump in her throat, summon the inner strength that had long been hers, and say clearly, "Thank you. I accept."

And with those simple words, she became the Lady of Clan Carrick.

# One

Niniver leaned low over Oswald's neck and let the big bay gelding run. The wind of their passage whipped over her cheeks and tore tendrils of hair loose from the knot on the top of her head. She didn't care; she just wanted to fly before the wind and forget about everything else.

The thunderous pounding of Oswald's heavy hoofs, the bunch and release of the horse's powerful muscles, filled her mind—and pushed out the frustrations that had threatened to overwhelm her. While she raced over the fields, she had no room in her head to dwell on the irritations, annoyances, petty nuisances, and simply idiotic behavior that had provoked her to near-fury.

*What were they thinking? Were they even thinking? Or were they simply reacting to a situation they didn't know how to interpret?*

She'd ridden east from the manor, over the flatter fields, wanting—needing—to gallop. But the clan's lands ended at the highway. Ahead, beyond the edge of the fields, the ribbon of macadam glimmered. Normally, she would have slowed at that point, drawn rein, and come around.

Not today.

Crouching low, she let Oswald thunder on.

Because today she needed more than just exercise. Today, she needed something akin to an exorcism— before she lost her temper and blasted her importunate clansmen in a way that would shrivel their manly confidence forever.

Giving Oswald his head, she let the gelding jump the stone wall that marked the boundary of the Carrick estate. Two giant strides later, the horse gathered himself again and flew over the drystone wall on the other side of the road.

Niniver heard a shout from behind her—from Sean, who, as always, was tagging along as her groom—but she pretended not to hear and let Oswald race on toward what had in years past been their favorite valley for a gallop. The horse remembered, as did she, but she hadn't ridden that way since Marcus Cynster had bought the old Hennessy property and made it his.

Usually, she avoided any chance of meeting her neighbor anywhere, much less on his lands.

But not today. Today, her clansmen had pushed her too far. She needed this run, and truly, the chances of meeting Marcus in the narrow valley were slight. She would race to the end, then turn and race back, and he would never know she'd been there.

The long, narrow valley curved and wound deep into the old Hennessy estate. Sinking into the moment, she let herself become one with her horse and galloped wild and free.

But when she reached the rise at the end of the valley, Oswald was tiring. Deeming it wise to let the horse rest before heading back to the manor, she eased up, and let the gelding slowly climb the rise. There was a twisted tree at the top, its canopy casting sufficient shade to provide a pleasant spot out of the afternoon sunshine.

She'd barely noticed the sun was shining until then. With her very pale skin, she had to be wary of freckling, and she wasn't wearing a hat.

Drawing rein in the shade, she remembered that the vantage point allowed her to look down on the old Hennessy farmhouse. Built of faded red bricks with lintels of local stone, the solid house sat nestled comfortably on a shelf of land, with the usual outbuildings neatly arrayed around it. Thin streams of smoke rose from two of the many stone chimneys.

She'd heard that Marcus had renamed the house and estate Bidealeigh.

Her eyes drinking in the peaceful scene, she eased the reins and let Oswald idly crop the coarse grass while she waited for Sean to catch up. He wouldn't say anything when he did; he knew what had sent her off in such a temper.

She'd been the Lady of Clan Carrick for almost a year. The first months of her reign, over late spring and through last summer up until harvesttime, had been intensely busy, not just for her but for all the clan as she and the clan elders uncovered and came to terms with the depredations her brothers had visited on the estate. When she and Ferguson had first sat down with the estate's ledgers, she'd wondered what all the fuss—all the worry—had been for. Then she'd stumbled on the second set of accounts—the ones Nolan had kept hidden. The ones that had shown the true level of the clan's coffers and also testified to the parlous state of the clan's enterprises.

That had been a sobering time, but under her leadership, the clan elders had rallied, and, together, they'd devised and put into place a plan to resurrect the clan's finances, one designed to get the clan back on its financial feet and heading toward the road to prosperity.

They hadn't made it to that road yet, but at least they were moving in the right direction.

But then autumn had set in and winter had followed, and the snows and storms had kept everyone indoors. The pace of work naturally slowed to a crawl, and suddenly, the younger men who'd been kept busy all summer had time to think.

Too many had chosen to think about her.

Because she was still unwed.

What the dimwits failed to realize was that, as lady of a clan—especially a clan like the Carricks, *especially* given the straits the clan was in—marriage was not in her cards. She was the only remaining member of the original Carrick line, while the rest of the clan was composed of many families who, through the passage of generations, were now only distantly related by blood, yet they were held together by common purpose and cause and a common share in the clan estate. The clan had elected her to lead them for a very good reason—namely, that she was the only one all the clan families would agree to follow.

And *that* was the critical point. The clan followed *her*.

Any man offering for her hand would expect that he would be entitled through their marriage to assume leadership of the clan.

That wasn't going to happen, because she would never allow it to happen. She'd been entrusted with the position of Lady, and it was incumbent on her to always act for the good of the clan—and the good of the clan meant *her* keeping ultimate control of all clan matters.

After all she'd seen of the weaknesses of men, she wouldn't trust any man with the clan's reins, and there wasn't a man born—or at least not one she might consider marrying—who would agree to take second place to her.

She'd accepted her unmarried state as inevitable—more, as desirable, at least for her. She still had her vow to her father to fulfill, and she would never let that go.

Unfortunately, several men in the clan, her age or older and as yet unwed themselves, had decided to vie for her hand. She'd tried to make clear that her hand wasn't on offer to be claimed, but none of them believed her. Others in the clan, wiser heads, understood, but not the younger hotheads who seemed to have convinced themselves that if they just pushed her harder—did something wilder—she'd develop a lasting tendre for them and gladly surrender her hand and the clan.

That afternoon, looking forward to a peaceful ride, she'd walked into the stable yard and had come upon Clement Boswell and Jed Canning violently wrestling in the middle of the yard. Over her. They'd been yelling insults at each other and taking liberties claiming various favors from her—favors she had never granted.

They hadn't seen her in time to shut up.

She'd wanted nothing more than to knock their heads together, to knock some sense into them, but she was a slip of a thing against their tree-trunk forms. Instead, she'd lost her temper and had screeched at them to stop.

They had, eventually, but by then she'd felt like a harridan and a shrew.

She'd clambered onto Oswald's back in a fury with all men.

Luckily, the horse was a gelding.

Sean ambled up on his black and drew rein. He sat his horse alongside her and didn't say a word.

He and the other clan elders understood, but even they were unable to help her—not in this.

She needed a champion, someone to take her side, to do what, as a delicate and fragile-looking female, she was unable to accomplish—namely intimidating her would-be suitors into accepting the truth, respecting her station, and leaving her alone.

She couldn't call on Norris. He'd settled in comfortably to a life as an assistant to a history professor, and had secured a position teaching students at St. Andrews. It was a new and promising start for him. Besides, he wasn't…man enough, old enough, impressive enough for her needs. She needed a man willing and able to fight for her, to defend her position.

Oswald shifted beneath her. Instinctively settling him, her gaze sharpened on the vista before her.

*If you ever need help, remember that you can always call…on me. If you are ever in need, please don't hesitate—just ask…*

It had been nearly two years, but she could still hear Marcus Cynster's deep voice saying those words. She knew he'd meant them.

And she could no longer pretend that she didn't need help. The sort of help he could give.

She'd avoided even seeing him for what still ranked as an excellent reason, yet if she was to do what her clan needed her to do…

Gathering her reins, she glanced at Sean. "Wait here. I won't be long."

With that, she tapped Oswald's side and headed down the rise to call on her nemesis.

\* \* \*

Marcus Cynster was peering down the barrel of his shotgun when a sharp rap fell on his front door. He raised his head; his hands still busy cleaning the gun, he waited to hear the heavy footsteps of Flyte, his majordomo, heading for the door.

Then he remembered he was alone in the house. The Flytes—Mrs. as well as Mr.—had gone into Ayr, and Mindy, the maid who helped Mrs. Flyte with the housework, wasn't on duty today.

He set down the shotgun on the canvas he'd spread over the pembroke table in his living room and headed for the door. As he ducked under the archway into the farmhouse's small front foyer, another rap sounded, sharp, distinctly imperious, the heavy knocker plied with inherent command.

Even before he grasped the latch and swung the heavy oak panel wide, he was fairly certain whoever was there wasn't one of his farmers come to report some problem.

He hadn't expected the vision of loveliness that graced his front stoop.

He hadn't seen Niniver Carrick in months, and even then, only from a distance.

Now he was close enough to see the soft color in her porcelain cheeks, the golden glints as the sun touched wayward strands of her pale blond hair, the delicate arches of her brown brows, and the intelligence in the cornflower-blue eyes beneath. The sensual promise

in the lush curves of her full, rose-tinted lips was off-
set by the stubborn determination conveyed by the set
of her chin.

He suspected few others registered either her intelligence or her stubbornness, distracted instead by the
ethereal beauty, the fairy-princess picture she made.
He saw the same—that distracting body—but he'd also
always sensed what lay within.

Once again, he was face to face with that confound-
ing reality, and more than close enough to be reminded
why being near her wasn't a wise idea. The attraction
between them…he couldn't remember when it hadn't
been there. Yet over the last years, intermittent sight-
ings notwithstanding, it had grown.

And grown.

If what he felt now, simply on setting eyes on her,
was any indication, that uncontrollable attraction had
only escalated further.

For several silent moments, she stared at him while
he stared at her.

He managed to find his voice. "Niniver?"

His implied confusion broke the spell.

"May I come in?"

"Yes. Of course." He stepped back, holding the door
as she passed before him in a glide of black velvet riding jacket and brown velvet skirts. Glancing outside,
he saw her usual mount, a big bay gelding, securely
tied to the hitching post. A frown formed in his mind,
although he kept it from his face. Had she been riding alone?

It wasn't his place to ask. He reminded himself of
that as he closed the door and followed her. She'd swept
straight through into the living room. As he ducked be-

neath the archway, he saw her pause by the table, inspecting his endeavors. She turned as he crossed the room toward her.

She was petite, while he stood over six feet tall; her head barely reached his shoulder.

Rather than tower over her, he waved her to the pair of armchairs that faced each other across the wide hearth. He sensed rather than saw her approval of the courtesy as she walked on and, with a swish of her heavy skirts, sat.

He followed and sat in the other armchair. His gaze on her face, he tried to imagine what she was doing there—why, after all these months of no contact, she'd sought him out. When she volunteered nothing, just studied him, as if trying to imagine his likely reaction to some request, he said, "I would offer you some refreshment, but my housekeeper and majordomo have gone shopping. I don't think you'd appreciate my efforts at making tea."

She blinked, slowly, and he saw her absorb the information that she was alone with him in the house. If this was a social call…

She shook her head. "I didn't come for tea. Or any other refreshment."

Definitely not a social call, then. Her big blue eyes still measuring him, she caught her lower lip between her teeth—something he'd noticed she did when uncertain, or cogitating about something that bothered her. Him? Or what had brought her there?

He sat back, attempting to look as unthreatening—as encouraging—as he could. "So, how can I help you?"

Now she was there, face to face with him, Niniver

had second and even third thoughts about the wisdom of her course, but she still needed help. She desperately needed a champion, and there he sat, the perfect man for the task.

With his black locks—not true blue-black but black with an underlying hint of red, the very deepest mahogany—framing his face, one dark lock falling rakishly over his broad forehead, sitting as he was, relaxed and at his ease, his long-fingered hands elegantly disposed on the chair's arms, his muscled horseman's thighs, long, buckskin-clad legs, and top-booted feet arranged in an innately graceful pose, he should have appeared no more dangerous than any London dandy. Instead, a tangible aura that seethed with restrained power, edged with menace, emanated from him.

As a deterrent to her importuning suitors, she couldn't imagine finding better.

Squelching all caution, she met his dark blue gaze—a midnight blue so dark it was difficult if not impossible to guess his thoughts. "Remember that promise you made to me up at the lookout?"

He blinked, dense black lashes briefly screening his eyes before they rose again, and he pinned her with his gaze. "That if you needed help, you could count on me—that you only needed to ask?"

She nodded—once, decisively. "Yes. That." She paused to marshal her words. "I need help with a particular problem, and I think—I believe—that you are the most appropriate person to ask for assistance—the person most likely to be able to help me resolve the issue."

He was now considering her exactly as she'd previously considered him. "And your particular problem is?"

"Men." The word slipped out before she'd thought. She grimaced and forged on, "Specific men—namely men of the clan who assume I must be looking for a husband, and who are putting themselves forward overenthusiastically." She couldn't hide her irritation; it underscored her tone.

To her surprise, Marcus…stilled. There was no other word for it. His gaze remained on her—he was still looking at her—yet she got the distinct impression he was seeing something else. That he was viewing something beyond her.

He barely seemed to breathe.

But then he blinked, and he seemed to draw back, pull back. He hesitated, then asked, "How…enthusiastic have they been?"

His voice had lowered, deepened. For an instant, she wondered if she was doing the right thing in setting him on her poor unsuspecting clansmen. Then she remembered the scene in the stable yard. She tipped up her chin. "I suppose you could say that, each in their own way, they've been trying to woo me, but they keep tripping over each other, and then they clash. But even worse, they egg each other on to ever more ridiculous exploits, ones that are harder and harder for me to…avoid."

Put into words, the situation didn't sound that bad, but to her, it was seriously bothersome, and more worrying than she could easily convey. "I know it sounds silly, but I have a position within the clan to maintain, and with matters as fraught as they are at the moment, having to deal with idiotic behavior directed toward me

personally, behavior that tends to—well, belittle me—
is distracting, disturbing, and sometimes unnerving.
On top of that, some of the men involved are sons of
clan elders, and that adds a certain political constraint
to how blatantly I can repel their advances." She blew
out a breath. "I need someone who will simply step in
and tell them all to *stop*. Someone they'll listen to—
because not one of them pays a posset's worth of attention to me."

The last words came out on a tide of frustration.

Marcus's instincts pummeled and pushed him to
volunteer, to leap to her defense, especially against
importunities of such a nature. But when it came to
her, he didn't know if he could—if he should—trust
his instincts; far from protecting her—their immuta-
ble goal—they might, in such a case, lead him to un-
intentionally hurt her, and that was not a possibility he
would ever willingly court. Not in this lifetime.

Protecting Niniver Carrick had become his personal touchstone, at least in guiding his actions with
her. Yes, he was attracted to her—deeply, viscerally.
So attracted that, as soon as he'd become aware of the
nature of that attraction—at her father's funeral, of
all places—he'd asked his mother and his sister to see
what The Lady, the deity their family served, could
tell them of his future. But all they'd seen was that his
fated future lay somewhere in The Lady's lands, meaning somewhere in the local area, but at that time, all
they'd been able to tell him was that his fated future
was "not yet."

Was it now? Was that why Niniver had come to
him? Why she'd finally come to call in his promise of
two years ago?

Was *she* his fated future, or…?

It was that "or" that had kept him from her through the intervening months. That, and his impossible to shake, impossible to deny, drive to protect her. If he'd approached her, if he'd wooed her as he'd wished, she might well have been happy to succumb—but what, then, if his fated future came calling, and said future was not with her?

He couldn't harm her, so he'd had to keep his distance in case she wasn't for him.

Knowing the fickleness of Fate, he'd been disposed to believe that the very last woman Fate would hand him as his destiny was the one woman he desired—at least at this time, desired above all others.

He'd convinced himself that Fate would send him some female he'd never met before.

Instead, Niniver had come knocking at his door.

Was Fate laughing at him—or testing his mettle? Testing his commitment not to harm Niniver?

Or was this his destiny calling?

Her gaze had remained leveled on his face, the expectation in her expression patently clear. He shifted, straightening in his chair as he searched for options, for what other choices he—and she—might have. "I understand…your difficulty." She was such a tiny thing, and quiet, and—as far as he knew—sweet-tempered. He knew her clan folk thought the world of her—quite obviously, as they'd elected her their lady. But she was kind-hearted and loved deerhounds; dealing with large angry men wasn't something she was well equipped to do. "You need someone your clansmen respect, someone whose statements they'll accept."

He met her eyes; her gaze didn't waver but remained

fixed on his face. "What about Thomas? They know and respect him—and, what's more, he's clan himself."

Her eyes narrowed a touch. "Thomas—as you must know as well as I do—has all he can handle with his daughters. I'm not going to ask him to come and rescue me. I wouldn't do that to him, much less to Lucilla."

Marcus inwardly winced at the implied rebuke. His twin sister had given birth to twin girls five months ago, and both Lucilla and Thomas were, indeed, fully engaged with caring for the tiny but demanding bundles of joy. "Indeed. You're right." No help there. He frowned. "What about Norris?" He leaned forward, resting his elbows on his thighs; her remaining brother was surely the right person to defend her. "I know he's younger than you, but only by about a year—which means he's what? Twenty-five?" Old enough.

Her lips firmed into a line. Her eyes narrowed further. "I'm twenty-five—he's not yet twenty-four. But he left. He's pursuing his own life in St. Andrews, and I'm not about to call him home—besides which, none of the men in the clan would pay the slightest attention to him."

Niniver paused but felt compelled to push. "I need someone with standing. With a status that will command attention at least, if not outright obedience."

She needed someone like him; that was so obvious it barely needed stating.

Abruptly, she stood. When he started to rise, too, she brusquely waved him back; the last thing she needed was a crick in her neck. She started to pace back and forth across his hearth. She only paced when she was agitated or anxious; she'd worked to break herself of the habit—it revealed too much—but in this instance, she wasn't sure she cared.

She'd *steeled* herself to do this—to hide her reaction to him, to ignore the waves of prickling awareness that washed over her skin whenever he was near. She'd told herself she could face him and ask him to honor his promise even if he wasn't attracted to her, as she, so very definitely, was to him. She'd pushed herself to do it, and she'd done it and asked, but for some reason, he was now reluctant.

The realization didn't please her at all. Now that she was there, making her case, she wasn't about to let him off any hook she could find. "I had hoped"—pausing and facing him, she enunciated the words evenly, endeavoring to remove all emotion from them—"that you would see your way to assisting me in dealing with this situation as a favor to a neighbor."

His face was all chiseled angles and planes, sharply prominent cheekbones above lean cheeks. His lips were mobile, fascinatingly so, but as he looked up at her, his blatantly squared chin left no doubt of his ability to remain unmoved. The arrogance born of supreme confidence etched his features, yet as she met his eyes, she saw that her comment had reached past his façade; even though he gave no sign, she knew she'd prodded him in a sensitive spot. Neighborly assistance, if requested, was taken for granted in the country.

She'd avoided him for months, and if her senses' preoccupation with his appearance—with every little thing about him—was any guide, that had been one of her wiser decisions. Even though she'd remembered his promise, she'd previously hesitated to ask for his help precisely because of the unnerving attraction—

avid and compelling—she felt for him. Because that attraction was obviously one sided. He was a Cynster; she knew what sort of man he was—a gentleman descended from a noble line and with all the natural arrogance and confidence that background bestowed. If he'd harbored any interest in her, he would have approached her—he would have let her know.

Just as her idiot clansmen were doing, but doubtless with more panache.

His dark gaze had locked on her. "How, exactly, do you imagine I, as a neighbor, might aid you?"

She swung around and continued pacing; she hadn't actually thought that far, but since he'd asked… "If you would come to Carrick Manor and spend time there—long enough for the others to notice, or for you to have a chance to…" She vaguely waved.

"Redirect their thinking?"

"Yes—exactly." She glanced at him as she turned. "Intimidation wouldn't go amiss, either."

Marcus pressed his lips tight, fighting a grin. Then his thoughts rolled on, and he sobered. "How long do you imagine this…communicating of your disinterest in marrying your clansmen will take?"

She frowned. "A week? Two?"

Two days would be too long for him. He understood what she was suggesting, but acting as a shield for her would, of necessity, mean spending that time all but glued to her side—and he could all too readily predict the outcome of such enforced propinquity. Blue balls wasn't a condition most men courted, and he was no exception.

She was looking at him hopefully. He hardened his heart and raised the point to which she seemed oblivious. "You said you're twenty-five. As you're now also lady of your clan, I assume you've considered your prospects for marriage. Why not simply make your choice now and be done with it?"

She halted in her pacing and stared at him; the expression on her face wasn't one he could interpret. Then she stated, "I have no intention of marrying. Not now, not later."

Something within him jerked to attention; he slapped it down. Now was not the time to go leaping on challenges—especially not challenges like that. He frowned. "Why not?" Greatly daring, he asked, albeit more gently, "Don't you want a husband and children?" His sisters, his female cousins, those of marriageable age, talked of little else.

But Niniver swung away and paced across the hearth; when she turned back, her expression was composed. "What I wish for is not the point. As lady of the clan, I can't marry."

His frown deepening, he continued to study her. "I still don't see why." He made the statement without inflection, an invitation to explain if she would.

She sighed; her luscious lips twisted in a grimace. "I'm the only one holding the clan together—if I hadn't been there to elect as lady, the clan would have fragmented. I didn't realize how near a thing it was, but Sean and Ferguson both eventually told me." She halted and looked down as if studying the flagstones. After a moment, she went on, "Papa gave his life to the clan. He held it together, and I can't, in all conscience, not make the best attempt I can to do the same." She raised her head and met his gaze. "And given I'm a female, that means not marrying, because any man I marry will expect to replace me as head of the clan, and if such a thing occurred, the clan would almost certainly break apart."

He held her gaze while he considered that conundrum. The challenge had just become even more challenging... What was he thinking? He honestly wasn't sure, and with her pacing back and forth within arm's reach, he wasn't at all confident his normal mental prowess would return any time soon.

Niniver sensed him drawing back; she couldn't have said how—she simply knew. And while casting about for arguments with which to sway him, she'd just had the most hideous thought. Too hideously awful to think about now; she bundled it to the back of her mind, but its mere existence only underscored her need—her escalating desperation to secure Marcus's help. Before she lost her courage, she baldly asked, "Will you help me?"

He didn't reply. After a second, he glanced away from her.

And her temper slipped its leash.

Sorely tried by the day's events—poked and pricked by the confrontation in the stable yard, fueled by the realization that she couldn't deal with the escalating situation by herself and truly had to plead for help, spiked by the sudden thought of what might occur if she didn't secure effective help and successfully dissuade her would-be clan suitors, and now scraped raw by the understanding that all she'd pushed herself through to be standing where she was—having revealed all she had—had gained her nothing...her temper spiraled out of her reach.

Her lips set. With a furious swish of her skirts, she

turned and paced away across the fireplace. The sound of her boot heels striking the flags testified to the emotions roiling inside her.

"Niniver."

She halted. He'd sounded weary. Bored? And resigned.

Facing away from him, she filled her lungs and raised her head. He was going to refuse to help.

Her temper boiled over.

She looked up and raised her hands to the ceiling. In a voice that shook, she implored, "Can I count on no man at all?"

She whirled, intending to look scornfully back at him—

Her hand, swinging down, powered by the violence of her turn, collected a tall candlestick that had been sitting on a small shelf projecting from the mantelpiece. The candlestick went flying.

She was still turning when she heard a solid *thunk*. She came fully around as the heavy candlestick clattered on the stone floor.

Marcus, eyes closed, sat slumped in the chair.

"Oh, *my God*!" Had she killed him?

Heart thudding, she rushed to his side. His head lolled; grasping his shoulders, she tried to press them back, but his weight was too great for her to shift. Hauling aside her skirts, she crouched by the chair and tried to look into his face.

He didn't look dead. She was fairly sure he was still breathing.

Fighting back panic, she pressed her fingers to her lips—then reached out and wriggled her fingers beneath his neckerchief, searching for a pulse…

There!

Strong and steady, his pulse throbbed beneath her fingertips.

She exhaled and, slowly, drew her fingers free.

She remained crouched beside the chair, waiting for him to stir...but he didn't.

Tipping her head, her gaze tracking over his face, examining his unresponsive features, she frowned.

After a moment, she straightened and rose to her feet.

She stood looking down at him for several more seconds. Eyes narrowing, lips compressing, she debated whether she dared...

She decided that she did—that she would.

Turning, she headed for the door.

# Two

Marcus returned to consciousness slowly. Awareness dripped into his mind, drop by drop, until at last, he was back in the world.

Eyes closed, he tried to remember…

He'd been talking to Niniver. About her problem.

He'd been about to tell her that he would think about how best to aid her, and that he would call at Carrick Manor in the next day or so to discuss the possibilities. He'd intended to ask his father's advice, although he hadn't been about to tell her that.

Then…blankness.

And now he was…lying on a bed somewhere, fully dressed, soft mattress and covers beneath him, with a feather pillow cradling his aching head…

He opened his eyes and saw Niniver sitting in a chair a few yards from the bed. Late afternoon light streamed through the window and lit her fair hair to a silver-gold. She was looking down, plying a needle, stitching something.

His arms lay above his head. He shifted and tried to lower them—and realized his wrists were bound with a fine silk scarf that had been looped around the post at the head of the bed.

The movement drew Niniver's attention. Her gaze collided with his.

"Oh, good! You're awake."

He would have sworn she added a silent "thank heavens" after that.

He watched her lean down and put her sewing into a basket, then she straightened in the chair—and looked at him uncertainly.

He narrowed his eyes at her. "Did you clout me over the head?"

Her eyes widened. "No! Well…not intentionally."

He squinted at her. "*Un*intentionally?"

"If you recall, I was angry. I lost my temper."

He vaguely recalled her increasing agitation, then memory strengthened. *Can I count on no man at all?* His lips thinned as he recalled the stark emotion in her voice; that jabbed at him now, as it had then. "I remember."

"I threw up my hands"—she demonstrated—"and whirled around, and I hit the candlestick off the mantelpiece shelf. It struck you on the head. You have a lump above your left ear." Her soft blue eyes traveled his face, her concern openly deepening. "I had no idea you would stay unconscious for so long. Are you all right?"

He grimaced. He swung his legs and hips around and shifted to sit on the edge of the bed near the bed's head. There was enough slack in his silken bonds for him to tip his head and, with his fingers, explore said lump. He grunted. "What is it with you Carricks that every time you need help, you knock me out?"

She frowned. "Who else knocked you out?"

"Thomas." He fought a wince as he palpated the tender area. "When the Bradshaws fell ill and he came to fetch Lucilla from the grove, I was keeping watch. Rather than waste time arguing with me, he knocked me out." He gritted his teeth. "In *exactly* the same spot." Apparently Fate, using the Carricks as pawns, knew the precise spot on his otherwise hard head where a sharp tap could render him unconscious for an hour or so—thus rendering him amenable to Fate's plans.

That consequence hadn't escaped his notice. Lucilla had been meant to go with Thomas. Presumably Fate and The Lady meant him to be exactly where he was. Getting knocked unconscious when he'd been about to vacillate seemed a fairly clear indication.

Lowering his bound hands—he'd get to them in a moment—he glanced around. "Where am I?"

"Carrick Manor."

He caught her gaze, then pointedly dropped his to the pale blue silk scarf knotted about his wrists. "Are you really this desperate?"

He glanced up in time to catch her "Did you really need to ask?" look, but she contented herself with uttering a terse "Yes."

He considered her for several silent seconds, but he knew better than to try to fight Fate. The throbbing in his head was subsiding; he inclined his head in acceptance and discovered that didn't hurt. "All right."

Rapidly, he canvassed where he and she were now, what they wanted to achieve, in the short term at least. He refocused on her. "How did you get me here?" With a wave of his fingers, he indicated the room and the bed. "Obviously, I didn't ride here and climb the stairs on my own."

She looked a trifle guilty. "Sean was with me—he's the head stableman."

"Strange. He always struck me as a sane, sensible man."

Somewhat to his surprise, she rose, bringing her head level with his. "Stop sniping." She folded her arms and regarded him severely. "Sean's a rock. I don't know what I would do without him. And if you hadn't been so obstreperous over keeping your promise to help me when I asked, I wouldn't have had to drag him into this."

He was impressed—entirely unnecessarily—by her immediate defense of Sean. Eyeing the martial promise in her eyes and the uncompromising set of her lips and chin, he was reminded of the conundrum she posed. Delicate, fragile, and ethereal she might be, but there was a strong streak of bloody-minded, steely stubbornness in her, too. All the surrounding gentry were quietly admiring of the way she'd handled being lady of the clan ever since the Carrick clan had done the unexpected and elected her to the role. He doubted she'd expected it, but she'd made a good fist of things thus far.

And, clearly, her position and her ruling of the clan was one element of the challenge Fate had handed him.

Was he really going to do this?

Apparently, he was. "In the interests of setting our stage, as it were, how many here know I was carried upstairs unconscious?"

"Sean and Mitch smuggled you up the back stairs. No one but them knows you're here."

"Good." He knew both men slightly from evenings at the local inn. They were sensible and practical, and they didn't gossip, even in their cups.

Niniver had been eyeing him uncertainly. "You might have a bruise or two. You're rather large and heavy, and they had trouble getting you around the landing."

Presumably that explained the pain in one hip and at the point of one shoulder. He tried to think—to plan—but his wits were still a trifle disconnected. But she was there, and he was, after all, there at her bidding. "So I'm here, where you wanted me to be." He looked at her. "And it appears that I'm helping you with your current problem."

She met his gaze. Rather than looking guilty, he sensed she was hiding her delight.

"So"—he arched his brows—"how do you propose we proceed?"

She blinked, then sank into the chair again. Clasping her hands in her lap, she fixed him with an earnest look. "As I suggested at your house, if you stay for a time, and just generally be about, then the others will see and know you're here, watching, and they'll stop pushing."

Possibly. "I live a bare four miles away. I can ride back and forth—"

"No." Her lips set mulishly. "That won't work."

He studied her expression—one hundred percent determined. "Why?" She wasn't a flighty female; there had to be a reason.

Again, she bit her lower lip; he wanted to tug it free. With his teeth. Apparently, that thought didn't show in his face. After another second of studying his features, she released that fascinatingly plump lip and said, "The manor is a clan house. Tradition dictates that the house is always open to clan members, so the doors are never locked. Not even at night." She paused, then went on, "As I said, several of the men have grown...

pushier of late. Their rivalry urges them to do things, to act in ways they normally wouldn't, and…it's an old tactic, isn't it? A sure-fire way of forcing a marriage. And it's hardly difficult for any clan member to learn which room in the house is mine—and I'm the only family member living here now, the only person with rooms on this floor."

His blood had run cold. He stared at her, but no matter how much he wanted to reassure her, to dismiss her fears—to tell her they were fanciful and wave them away—he couldn't. Because they weren't. This *was* an isolated pocket of the country, and matters like clan marriages were still—occasionally—settled in the age-old way. If her clansmen were intent on claiming her hand—and it sounded as if several believed they had a chance no matter her protestations—if they deluded themselves into believing they could get away with it and they tried to force her…

Every instinct he possessed rose snarling at the thought.

His gaze locked on her face, he slowly nodded. "All right. I'll stay at the manor." She was right; he had to be there even at night to be an effective shield, and as he was, it seemed, destined to accept the position of her champion, he damn well intended to be effective.

It hadn't escaped him that she—and Fate and The Lady, too—were not just casting him but forcefully pushing him into the role of her protector and defender. It was a role he'd been born to fill; it would fit him like a glove and seamlessly mesh with his character and personality. He'd always assumed he would play such a role—ultimately, eventually—for some woman. He just hadn't believed that woman would be she—that Fate and The Lady would be so kind.

He still wasn't sure they truly were, but his way forward seemed clear: Play along and find out.

He still wasn't thinking entirely lucidly; his focus on practicalities, on the what and how, was still hazy. Pushing concerns of fate and destiny aside, he concentrated—and one pertinent point rose above the roiling cauldron of his thoughts. "Who else lives here? In the house?" He refocused on Niniver. Did she have a chaperon, or were he and she truly alone, socially speaking, under her roof?

Niniver promptly replied, "My old governess, Hilda, has an apartment upstairs. Now that my father and brothers are gone, she comes down to have dinner with me."

He nodded. "Good enough."

She knew he meant for propriety's sake.

He glanced toward the window. "Where in the house is this room?"

"We're in the main wing—this is the room next to mine." She stated that matter-of-factly and waited for his response.

Predictably, he frowned. "That's not wise."

She could see him dredging up all he'd heard about the house.

Eventually, he said, "You have a visitors' wing. I can use the same room Thomas used when he stayed here."

"No, you can't." When he directed his rather black frown her way, she calmly went on, "The visitors' wing is on the opposite side of the house from where we are—from my room." She tipped her head, and more quietly said, "The doors of a laird's house are never locked. If you're at the other end of the house, how will you know if anyone comes for me?"

Marcus looked at her for several seconds, then he dropped his head back, stared at the ceiling, and heaved a sigh. He would have liked to have fallen back across the bed and inquired of the universe: *Why me?* But Niniver wouldn't understand, and he certainly wasn't about to explain to her how she affected him. Clearly, she had no notion of that at all, or she wouldn't equate putting him in the room next to hers with protecting her from danger.

More like exchanging one potential danger for the certainty of a more potent one.

Fate was certainly beckoning him on. Seductively whispering as she made everything fall into place… He really didn't trust Fate all that much, but, in the circumstances, he wasn't going to argue.

Returning his head to vertical, he looked at Niniver—who, whether she knew it or not, Fate was handing him on a silver platter. "All right. If I'm staying here for the immediate future, how and when did I arrive? And why am I staying?"

His brain was starting to function again.

Niniver was quick to reply, "You rode back with me. No one but Sean and Mitch saw us arrive, and they won't tell. Since then, we've been in the library discussing"—she waved—"various issues. No one will have gone into the library this afternoon, so no one will know that's not true. And you're here in this room now, and staying, because you've agreed to remain to…" Her inventiveness ended at that point; she widened her eyes at him, inviting his input.

"To ensure that nothing untoward happens to you."

His gaze remained on her for several moments, but once again, she wasn't sure he was truly focusing on her. Then he nodded as if satisfied. "Very well." He looked at the scarf she'd wound around his wrists. "Now I've fallen in with your plan, come and untie me."

That sounded rather like an order, but she was far too relieved to take umbrage. All but bouncing to her feet, she crossed to the bed. She slowed as she neared— and was thankful when he shifted along the mattress so she could bend over his wrists and pick at her knots without pressing against his legs.

Marcus hauled his gaze from her down-bent head and focused on the wall. Her perfume, a subtle blend of flowery scents, reached him; he forced himself to think of the practicalities, and not of porcelain skin he was fairly certain would be petal soft… He frowned. "I'll need to go home and fetch some clothes."

Still bent over his wrists, she glanced fleetingly up at him. "You can send for clothes tomorrow. For to-night, there are plenty of men's clothes here. Norris's are probably too"—her gaze flashed across his chest— "narrow. But Papa's clothes would fit you, and there'll only be me and Hildy here for dinner."

"Your father's clothes are still here?" Manachan Carrick had died nearly two years ago.

She responded to his real question by raising one shoulder. "I haven't had the heart to tell Edgar to clear them out." Still tugging at the knots, she sighed. "I suppose I should tell him to give away anything useful to other men in the clan."

He heard the lingering sorrow in her voice; of Manachan's four children, she had most sincerely mourned him. "Who's Edgar?" he asked, to distract her as well as himself.

"He was Papa's manservant for decades and took care of all Papa's things. He's clan."

The scarf finally fell away. She pulled it free and straightened—bringing her face level with his. She was no more than a foot away.

A visceral wave of lust swept through him; rising from the bed, he forced himself to walk away from her.

Reaching the door, he grasped the knob and looked back at her. Caught the considering curiosity in her gaze as she trailed in his wake.

Opening the door, he waved her through.

As he followed her into the corridor, his mind served up the observation that, as he'd always suspected, Fate wasn't a benevolent force; in her habitual, sneaky, underhanded way, she'd hooked him with a challenge that was shaping up to be significantly more difficult than anyone might have thought.

\* \* \*

Descending the main stairs at Niniver's side, Marcus looked about him; Niniver assumed he was endeavoring to get his bearings in the huge old house.

She felt beyond relieved that he'd agreed to stay and help, yet the continual abrading of her nerves simply because he was there, so close—so much closer than he'd been in nearly two years—left her wary and trepidatious. She didn't think she could bear it if he guessed how *infatuated* her senses were with him, but she was fairly certain she hadn't said or done anything to alert him to her weakness.

Yet.

She wasn't concerned that such a revelation might

prompt him to seek to take advantage of her; she knew what caliber of man he was—honest and honorable to the core. What she did fear was having to weather any "kindness" on his part, any gentle letting down of her supposed expectations. When it came to him, she had no expectations of a romantic nature. He was a Cynster, wealthy, well born, and of a noble house. When the time came for him to choose his bride, he would have his pick of the ton's young ladies from London to Land's End. She couldn't compete on any number of levels—not least her situation.

There really was no question of where she stood with him. She was a neighbor he'd agreed to help with a problem he was uniquely qualified to deal with.

Yet now that he was there…she wasn't really sure what to do with him.

Instinct steered her to the library; it had become her domain, the room in which she felt most comfortable. Sitting behind the big desk was where she felt closest to her father—not in the sense of emotional attachment, but in terms of insight into how he'd run the clan. That was where he'd sat throughout his years at the Carrick helm; seated in the same chair, looking over the desk at the same view down the long room, she sometimes felt she could almost hear his voice murmuring—irascibly—in her head.

But she wasn't about to mention that to the male who prowled into the room at her heels. She went straight to the desk, drew up the worn admiral's chair, sat, and pulled the ledgers she'd left open on the desk closer.

She forced her eyes to focus on the words and figures, forced her mind to read and take them in.

Marcus ambled around the room, eventually coming to a halt before the wide desk. He studied the top of Niniver's head and the portion of her face he could see as, with every evidence of deep industriousness, she seemed to sink into the tomes.

She started chewing her lower lip.

He shifted.

Fleetingly, she glanced at him. "I need to finish checking these accounts." She waved at the ledgers. "I intended to go for just a short ride, but the fight in the stable yard distracted me."

"Fight?" His instincts leapt to the fore—and as matters now stood, he didn't need to restrain them. Alerted by his tone, she met his eyes, and he demanded, "What fight?"

She hesitated, but only for a second, apparently accepting that she'd brought him there precisely for this—to deal with her would-be suitors. "It was Clement Boswell and Jed Canning—they were wrestling over which of them I favored most." She looked down at the ledgers.

He studied her closed expression and wondered how much she hadn't told him. No matter. He'd find out soon enough. He knew who Jed Canning and Clement Boswell were; they were of similar age to him, but there all similarities ended. They weren't, however, stupid. He wouldn't have thought them dangerous, either, but over a woman, men could be pushed into acting in ways they normally never would.

Regardless, if breaking up fights between the likes of Canning and Boswell was now her lot, small wonder she'd come to him for help.

He was, he realized, genuinely delighted that she had.

Knowing where he could learn more, he started for

the door, but then halted and looked back at her. "What are the names of your would-be clan suitors?"

She looked at him, then rattled off a list. Jem Hills, Liam Forrester, Stewart Canning—as well as his older brother, Jed—John Brooks, Camden Marsh, Ed Wisbech, Martin Watts, and the aforementioned Clement Boswell.

For a moment, he considered those males and how they might impinge on his best route to his personal, most-desired goal. When he focused on Niniver again, she'd returned to her ledgers, and once again, she had her anxious face on.

Some part of him urged him to dally and see what he could do to lift the weight from her shoulders—to ease that harried look. He'd been raised and trained to manage a large farm-based estate; he could almost certainly help her, but…one step at a time. Would-be suitors first, then he would turn his attention to all the other issues that bothered her.

His head no longer hurt, and his customary facility for planning was functioning again. He debated, then returned to the desk and waited until she looked up. "If I could borrow some paper and a pencil, I'll write to my people and let them know I'll be staying here until further notice."

Without a word, she handed over several sheets of paper and found him a pencil with a decent point.

He retreated to the sofa and used the low table before it to write two notes—one to his staff, informing them of his plan to remain at Carrick Manor for at least several days and instructing them to pack a bag and deliver it the next morning, and to contact him via the manor household if they had need of him. The second note he addressed to his parents in the Vale of Casphairn, which lay to the south of the Carrick lands, alerting them to his temporary change of abode, but giving no reason for that change.

His mother would probably smile knowingly, but refuse to tell his father why. If he pressed, she would most likely say that all was as it should be.

Marcus certainly hoped that was true… Increasingly, he felt it was.

Rather than disturb Niniver again, he left the pencil on the table, pocketed his notes, and quietly left the room.

\* \* \*

He found his way to the stable yard. He recognized Sean and Mitch; they were standing with two other men, one of whom Marcus thought was called Fred. The other was a younger man he assumed was a stable lad.

Unhurriedly, he approached the group. As he neared, all four men nodded respectfully; clearly, they recognized him.

Sean, Marcus noted, was watching him with a degree of wariness. Pretending obliviousness, he fished the notes out of his pocket. "I need these delivered— one to Bidealeigh and the other to the Vale."

Sean immediately reached for the notes. "Fred and Carson can take them."

Marcus smiled approvingly and stood back; within minutes, Fred and the young stable lad mounted and rode off. Standing with Sean and Mitch, Marcus watched the pair ride down the drive. Then he turned and leveled a much more intent look at Sean. "And now, if you will, you can tell me what you know of what's been going on here. Lady Carrick has asked me to assist in…"—he arched his brows—"shall we say discouraging?—any further occurrences such as the fight that took place here earlier today." His gaze still fixed on Sean's face, he added, "It would be helpful if I had a better idea of what to expect."

Sean glanced at Mitch.

Mitch snorted and waved at him to get on with it. "He's here, and he can do what she needs better than we can. Weren't any good us trying to break those two up earlier, was it? All we ended up with was getting knocked on our arses."

Both stablemen had the build of jockeys grown just a touch too tall; neither was all that large.

"Aye, well." Sean returned his gaze to Marcus's face. "The thing is, this is clan business, if you know what I mean."

Marcus did; he appreciated the loyalty that made Sean reticent to speak. He looked at the distant hills. After a moment, he looked back at Sean and Mitch. "What if, in return for the pair of you keeping quiet about the state I was in when you ferried me into the house, I pledge to do all I can to protect Lady Carrick from any further nuisance, from within the clan or otherwise, and in so doing, I agree to respect the privacy of the clan?"

Sean's and Mitch's brows furrowed as they considered his words.

Eventually, Sean glanced at Mitch.

Mitch met his eyes. "That's good enough for me."

"And me." Looking back at Marcus, Sean nodded. "Done. So what do you want to know?"

Marcus settled more comfortably. "Tell me everything you know about the incidents that have occurred, and then you can tell me about the men involved."

The list of incidents wasn't short and included several would-be suitors chasing Niniver down and pressing flowers from the garden she herself tended into her hands—something that had resulted in weeks of no flowers for her sitting room because, of course, the men had paid no attention to the finer points of flower harvesting.

"Just ripped them out, in some cases roots and all," Mitch said.

"Once," Sean said, "after she'd sent whoever it was that time on his way, I think she cried."

Marcus felt his jaw set. He'd been raised in a household where growing things were all but revered. If some man was ever idiot enough to carelessly damage any of his mother's and sister's prize plants... He really didn't like to imagine what might befall that man.

In addition, there'd been several chases on horseback, plus numerous attempts to claim Niniver's time for social engagements in which she'd had no wish to indulge. The most disturbing incident to date was the recent fight in the stable yard, which—he wasn't surprised to hear—had been significantly more violent on multiple levels than Niniver had let on.

"They was yelling about her—and she was standing right there!" Mitch softly swore. "Oblivious, they were, and her white as a sheet."

"And it's not as if she's some lily-livered miss," Sean said. "Things she's put up with, both now and while Mr. Nolan was still about... Well. Strong, she is."

Feeling increasingly grim, Marcus nodded.

Sean continued, "But some of the things they were

saying would have curdled any lady's stomach—
claiming they'd had relations with her and all. It was
disgusting—and her lady of the clan!" Sean nodded
at Mitch. "We and the others tried to break it up, but
Clem and Jed are heavyweights." Sean glanced at Marcus. "You'd be more up to their weight, but even then,
with the pair o' them whaling on each other like there
was no tomorrow…" Sean grimaced. "Wasn't until
Miss Niniver screamed at them that they stopped."

Mitch wiggled a finger in one ear. "Sounded like a
banshee, but at least it got their attention."

"She didn't like it though," Sean said. "It took something out of her to do it. She was shaking like a leaf
when she got into her saddle. If Oswald hadn't been
her mount for so long and not likely to play up, I'd have
felt forced to stop her riding out." He glanced at Marcus. "Lucky I didn't, as it turns out."

Tight-lipped, Marcus merely nodded. "So tell me
about the men involved."

Sean and Mitch obliged; both clearly accepted his
right to know—had accepted his pledge and his implied position as Niniver's champion.

The list they supplied of her suitors matched the
names she'd given him, but Sean and Mitch filled in
the details he hadn't asked her for—the men's ages
and occupations, their characters and temperaments,
and the relative standing of their families, and the men
themselves, within the clan. Accustomed to keeping
mental track of the details of the lives of a plethora of
cousins of varying degrees, let alone a massive list of
familial connections, Marcus had no difficulty slot-
ting away all the information in his mind, ready for
retrieval whenever he might need it.

Knowing the abilities of the opposition was one of the first requirements for mounting an effective defense—or, as this situation seemed to warrant, an effective offense.

When Sean and Mitch finally wound down, Marcus nodded. "Thank you." After accepting the pair's offer to assist in any way they could in sparing Niniver further upset, he walked back to the house.

In coming to him and insisting he fulfill his promise and aid her with this particular problem, Niniver's instincts had been sound. Now he'd gained a more comprehensive understanding of what she'd been facing, there was no doubt in his mind that, with respect to dealing with this, he was the right man for the job.

He strolled into the front hall and came upon the butler, Ferguson; he'd met the man on a previous visit. "Is Lady Carrick still in the library?"

In his later middle years, graying but still upright, Ferguson eyed him with restrained suspicion. "I believe so, sir."

Marcus made a mental note to discover Ferguson's standing in the clan, and whether it would be wise to enlist him in the cause of protecting his mistress. For the moment, he merely inclined his head. After several seconds' cogitation, he made for the stairs and went up.

From all Sean and Mitch had said, none of Niniver's would-be suitors had yet braved the walls of the manor itself. She should, therefore, be safe enough buried in her ledgers in the library. Meanwhile, he could use the time away from her distracting presence to review what he'd learned and, possibly, to get a better grasp of a more nebulous problem he could see looming on his horizon.

He reached the top of the stairs and stepped into the gallery. Rather than return directly to the room she'd insisted he use, he circled the first floor. She'd mentioned that only she currently had rooms on that level, so he had no compunction over opening doors and looking inside. The instant he opened the door to the room to the left of his, he knew that room was hers—he smelled her scent, unmistakable and alluring. Quickly shutting that door, he walked on.

He found the archway leading into what he assumed was the visitors' wing. After walking to its end, he had to admit that having a room there, at such a distance from hers, would never have worked. He returned to the main wing and explored in the opposite direction, and discovered the door that led into what, from the dust smothering everything, he assumed was the so-called "disused wing."

Resigned, he returned to the room next to Niniver's. He went in, shut the door, then, at loose ends, walked to the window.

The day was waning; he looked out at a small walled garden that bore all the signs of being lovingly tended. The colors of bobbing blooms stood out sharply against the foliage, darkening in the fading light. An old rusted gate had been set across the entrance, with a hand-lettered sign that read "Keep Out." Obviously to prevent further depredations from the would-be suitor horde.

Although the garden was bursting into full-flowered life, on looking more closely, he saw several ragged patches where plants should have been, but no longer were.

The sight made those instincts he was finding harder

and harder to control rise, insistent and demanding. Now he'd accepted that his fate was linked with Niniver's—that, ultimately, she was the lady fated to be his bride—the more primitive side of him saw her as his. His to protect, his to defend.

His to have.

Which was all very well, but his instincts were pressing ahead without consideration for the obstacles in his path.

And at least one of those obstacles wasn't one he'd expected to face. The complications likely to arise when marrying a lady who was the leader of a clan wasn't an issue he'd previously spent any time contemplating.

But he needed to pay due attention to those complications now—and, more, find some way to...not so much circumvent the potential difficulties as nullify them.

Exactly how to achieve that and secure Niniver as his wife wasn't yet clear. Thus far, he'd only got an inkling of the problem, enough to know it was there, lurking like a concealed pit trap waiting for him to fall into it.

A knock on the door drew him from the view and his reverie. "Come."

The door opened to reveal a tall, lean, dark-featured, and rather cadaverous-looking man. He bowed, formal and stiff. "I'm Edgar, sir. Lady Carrick informed me that you would be staying for a while, and that until your own clothes were brought to you, you might welcome some evening wear, and possibly some nightclothes."

Marcus nodded. "Thank you."

Edgar ran his eye down Marcus's length, hesitated, then said, "If you would be so good as to come to the old laird's apartments, it might be easier to select what would suit."

Marcus was only too happy to agree; he was curious as to what insights into its late owner Manachan's private domain might provide. Although he'd met Niniver's father on several occasions, he hadn't known him well. His view of Manachan relied heavily on what Thomas had let fall. Thomas was Manachan's nephew and had been close to the old curmudgeon. But if Marcus was to marry Niniver, then, given the situation, learning all he could about her late father seemed wise.

Edgar led him around the gallery and past the large door Marcus had earlier confirmed led to the master suite. Edgar opened the next door along, a narrower panel, and went through. Marcus followed him into a well-appointed dressing room.

One that, clearly, still played host to the clothes of a lifetime past.

Pausing just over the threshold, Marcus saw Edgar steel himself before opening the wardrobe doors.

Surveying the offerings thus revealed, Edgar murmured, "I believe we should find something to fit you in here."

The tone of his voice conveyed…resignation. Marcus stepped further into the room and shut the door. The uncurtained window admitted sufficient light for their purpose.

Although perfectly capable of choosing his own clothes, Marcus allowed Edgar to steer him. They found an evening jacket that fitted him well enough in the shoulders; although it was loose about his middle, buttoned up… Marcus studied the effect in the cheval mirror. "It'll pass muster, at least for one night."

Edgar sniffed as if the sight offended his sartorial standards. "At least you'll only be dining with Lady Carrick and Miss Hildebrand tonight."

Presumably, Miss Hildebrand was Niniver's old governess. "Has Miss Hildebrand been here long?"

"She came when Miss Niniver was a nipper—the old laird's wife was still alive then." Examining and discarding various pairs of trousers, Edgar continued, "We were surprised she stayed after Miss Niniver left the schoolroom—she didn't approve of the old laird's ways, and she's not clan. But she is devoted to Miss Niniver—she remained for her."

So Hilda Hildebrand was another potential ally. And he'd be meeting her that evening over dinner—reason enough to pay attention to his appearance.

All Manachan's trousers, evening or otherwise, were far too big about the waist, and not quite long enough in the leg. In the end, Edgar led Marcus to Norris's old room; there, they found a suitable pair of trousers to pair with the evening jacket, shirt, and waistcoat they'd selected from Manachan's wardrobe, and also a pair of pajamas.

Marcus examined the pajamas. "The shirt's too tight, but the trousers will do."

Edgar looked faintly scandalized. "Let's return to the laird's room. I'm sure we can find a nightshirt for you there, and you'll need a cravat."

They found the cravat easily enough, but all Manachan's nightshirts were of the old-fashioned voluminous variety. Marcus allowed Edgar to give him one, but knew he'd never wear it; it would make him feel like he imagined his sisters felt, swathed in their long nightgowns.

When, with a certain triumph, and certainly in a more engaged mood, Edgar handed Marcus the stack of selected clothes, he accepted them with thanks. Then he hesitated.

Edgar looked at him inquiringly.

"To be honest," Marcus said, "I'm rather surprised to see the old laird's clothes still here—as if he were still here. In the Vale, when anyone passes on, we distribute any useable clothes and other items to those who might benefit from them. We consider it a part of honoring our dead—that the possessions they accumulated continue to be useful to the living. A last act of kindness in their name and a memento for those who receive the items."

He wasn't entirely surprised when Edgar gravely nodded.

"Aye—the clan follows the same ways." Edgar glanced at the array of clothes packed into the wardrobe, then closed the doors. "Truth be told, Ferguson, Mrs. Kennedy, and I have discussed the matter several times, but…we don't feel we can encroach. Mr. Nolan refused to even consider the issue, and now he's gone… Well, Miss Niniver—Lady Carrick—still seems reluctant to let go of her father's memory, as it were. We don't see as how we can push."

And Niniver was, indeed, finding it difficult to make the decision, yet Marcus sensed she knew it was past time the decision was made. He considered for several seconds, then said, "If I might make a suggestion— Lady Carrick doesn't lack for inner strength. For backbone."

Edgar dipped his head. "No, indeed."

"Yet as you and the others rightly note, she is finding it difficult to come to the point of…as I suspect she feels it, dispersing the last lingering presence of her father. She made reference to the issue when she suggested I borrow these clothes." Marcus raised the stack of garments. "And while I agree that you and the others cannot, outright, make the decision for her, I do wonder if, perhaps, if you and your colleagues were to suggest that other clan members—those to whom some of the clothes would go—have need of them, it might pave the way for her to more easily give the order. I've noticed she tends to act decisively on any matter deemed for the good of the clan." He endeavored to look innocent as he said, "It might be a kindness were you and the others to recast the decision of dispersing her father's clothes in that light."

Edgar looked much struck. A moment later, his expression lightened and he nodded. "I—we—hadn't thought of it in that way, but you're right. I'll speak to Ferguson and the others. Ferguson will know how to best phrase it."

"Excellent." Marcus turned and left the dressing room. Edgar followed, something almost like a spring in his step. They parted, and Marcus carried the clothes to his room.

While laying them on the bed preparatory to changing for dinner, he was aware of feeling smugly pleased. Helping Niniver over the hurdle of dealing with her late father's things was a very minor matter, no doubt. It was, nevertheless, his first tiny success in what, if Fate and The Lady were to be believed, was destined to be his lifelong task—caring for Niniver Carrick.

# Three

Niniver studied her reflection in the cheval mirror in the corner of her bedroom and bit her lower lip.

The plum silk evening gown she'd had her maid, Ella, pull out of her armoire warmed her pale complexion, but the fitted bodice and heart-shaped neckline also showcased her breasts, which appeared somewhat plumper than she'd expected. Her waist, in contrast, looked impossibly tiny. Thank heavens her Edinburgh modiste had insisted on reducing the bulk of the skirts that spread over her hips and spilled to the floor, so that despite her being so short, the skirt's width didn't make her look dumpy.

She'd attended a bare handful of social events over the past year, and she'd worn mourning or half-mourning to all. But the six months of mourning for Nigel's death had passed, and she felt she needed a gown with more… energy to help her face Marcus over the dinner table. Or even in the drawing room.

While one part of her mind vacillated—was the color the right one for the task? Was the neckline too daring? Or not daring enough?—her more practical and prosaic self scoffed and told her to get on with her evening.

Marcus might look at her, but like all other men, he wouldn't *see* her. Worrying about her appearance on his account was foolish beyond belief, and likely a waste of time.

"This'll be just the thing to set off that gown." Coming to stand behind Niniver, Ella looped a thick gold chain from which hung a large garnet pendant, intaglio-carved with Niniver's mother's face, about Niniver's throat. The pendant was a handsome piece, distinctive yet understated; it was, indeed, the perfect ornament to complement the gown.

Lifting a hand to touch the pendant, Niniver considered her reflection while Ella fiddled with the clasp. When Ella straightened and stepped back, Niniver nodded. "Thank you. That's an inspired choice." For what she required tonight, the gown plus pendant would, indeed, serve. Together, they would be armor enough.

She turned and walked to her dressing table. Sitting on the stool, she reached for her jewel box, then waved at her hair. "You get started. I'll hunt out my garnet earrings."

While Ella unraveled the tight knot Niniver had anchored her long hair in for the day, Niniver ferreted through the pirate's hoard of jewelry jumbled together in the rosewood box. As the only girl in the family for several generations, she'd inherited jewelry from multiple sources, but as her interest in such items was transient at best, she'd never bothered sorting the pieces into any useful order.

By the time she'd located both of a pair of simple garnet drops, Ella was twisting the final curls of her creation for the evening into place. Niniver glanced at the mirror—and blinked.

Eyes widening, she drank in the sight. She so rarely thought of her appearance that she was wont to forget just how delicately fairylike she could appear. Normally, fairylike wasn't a helpful look, not when she had to discuss business matters with men. But tonight…

She raised her gaze and, in the mirror, met Ella's eyes and smiled. "Thank you. This will all do very well."

Ella beamed. "You look lovely, my lady. And if I may make so bold, it's nice that having Mr. Cynster to stay gives you a chance to shine so."

Niniver hid a wry grin; it wasn't as if she had any competition against which to shine.

Nevertheless, as she anchored the garnet drops in her lobes, she felt satisfied. Confident enough to go downstairs without too many butterflies reeling in her stomach.

She still couldn't quite believe that she'd done it—that she'd actually gone to Bidealeigh and asked Marcus for his help, let alone having, albeit inadvertently, knocked him unconscious, then more or less kidnapped him.

He'd been more understanding than she'd expected. In fact, now she thought of it, he'd seemed almost… resigned.

Not that it mattered; he was there, and that was what she needed. Even though he hadn't yet been called on to act in any way, she already felt less worried, less anxious—less fearful that one of her clansmen would step over the line and commit some irrevocable act that the entire clan would live to regret.

Having Marcus staying at Carrick Manor, occupying the room next to hers, had effectively reduced the chances of such a horror occurring to negligible.

In the distance, the sound of the gong summoning them to the drawing room resonated through the house. As she rose, she cast one last look at her reflection. Having Marcus there and keeping him there for however long it took to drill the right message into her misguided clansmen's unfortunately thick skulls was surely worth the effort of suppressing her reactions to him. Worth the effort of putting herself out to entertain him in the manner he would expect of an evening.

Walking to the door, she reminded herself that she owed him that much, at least. Despite his initial reluctance, he'd vindicated her belief in him, confirming her expectation that he was the type of gentleman— the sort of man—in whom the impulse to aid a damsel in distress was ingrained so deeply that no matter his inclinations, he wouldn't walk away.

Now he'd agreed to help her, she knew he would. More, she knew he wouldn't leave until all and any threat to her was past.

Feeling more confident, more assured, than she had in weeks, she opened her door and headed for the stairs.

\* \* \*

Marcus was tying his cravat when he heard the second gong. A minute later, as he was easing his chin carefully down, he heard Niniver's door open and shut, then her footsteps passed his door as she walked to the stairs.

He considered his reflection. He didn't have his sapphire cravat pin or any other to anchor the folds, so the arrangement as was would have to do. Hoping Flyte remembered to pack the pin along with his brushes, he raked his fingers through his hair, shook his head to settle the locks, then turned to the bed, picked up the evening coat, and shrugged into it.

His fingers went to the buttons; he swiftly did them up, critically surveying the result in the long mirror in the corner. He felt curiously underdressed without his fob watch and cravat pin, but this wasn't, after all, a major social event.

Then again, he was going to be facing Miss Hilda Hildebrand, ex-governess and now chaperon, so a certain degree of sartorial care was in order. He couldn't recall ever setting eyes on Miss Hildebrand, but if she'd accompanied Niniver to the Hunt Balls in years past, Miss Hildebrand might well know him, at least by sight, and most likely by reputation as well.

As he walked to the door, he wondered what Miss Hildebrand's current opinion of him was—favorable or…? Despite his preference for residing in the Vale, he hadn't been a monk—far from it—but in all his liaisons, he had been discreet. With luck, Miss Hildebrand would accept him at face value—which, in this instance, would be close to the mark; his intentions toward Niniver might not be innocent, but they were honorable.

As he made his way to the stairs and went down, he saw no one else, heard no one else. Stepping onto the tiles of the front hall, he saw that the door of the drawing room had been left invitingly wide. No sounds of conversation drifted to his ears as he neared; he wondered if Niniver was waiting somewhere else… Reaching the doorway, he realized she wasn't.

She was pacing back and forth before the fireplace,

not in agitation but, he sensed, with faint impatience. She saw him and halted. "Oh, good. You found your way."

*It hadn't been difficult...* His tongue couldn't seem to form the words, or any others. His mind, his senses, had seized.

Several seconds ticked past before he got them working again and he managed to draw in a much-needed breath. He hadn't seen Niniver socially, at a ball or anywhere else, for several years. In the interim, she had, in common parlance, blossomed.

Her riding habit hadn't done her figure justice, but the reddish-purple gown she currently wore rectified the oversight. Combined with her more elaborate hairstyle, it made the most of her utterly delectable charms, creating an image from a gentleman's fantasies.

His fantasies, at least.

The vision she presented was so alluring it took palpable effort to drag his gaze from her—and swing it to the severe-looking, dark-haired, hatchet-faced lady seated on the sofa. Clad in a gown of pale gray, Niniver's erstwhile governess was a large, heavy-boned female who exuded an aura of formidableness.

While Niniver was regarding him with her usual open and direct gaze, Hilda Hildebrand's eyes were narrowing, and her lips were tightening in growing disapproval.

Shaking off the impact of the vision that was Niniver, he forced his features to relax into a smile and walked forward to bow before the dragon. "Miss Hildebrand, I take it?" Grasping the hand the governess reluctantly offered, he smoothly continued, "Despite being neighbors, I don't believe we've met."

After releasing her hand, he straightened and stepped back.

Miss Hildebrand regarded him severely. "Indeed, sir. But I have, of course, heard of you. And I must admit I was surprised to learn that you are presently residing under this roof."

Marcus read the dragon's suspicions. Instead of responding, he glanced at Niniver and waited; as she was still standing, he couldn't sit.

Comprehending the unvoiced message, she moved to sink into the armchair beyond the end of the sofa. "I told you, Hildy—Mr. Cynster is here because he's agreed to help me settle things within the clan."

"Indeed." Claiming the armchair opposite the sofa, Marcus sat and fixed Miss Hildebrand with a level gaze. "It appears Lady Carrick needs support in convincing some of her clansmen that she is not interested in marrying any of them."

Miss Hildebrand's dark brows rose in poorly screened skepticism. "And that's why you're here?"

"Precisely." Marcus held the dragon's gaze and watched her digest his refusal to append the words "that and nothing else." After several silent seconds, he did, however, add, "I can assure you that Lady Carrick's safety is my principal and dominant goal, and that I will do whatever proves necessary to ensure she remains safe and untroubled."

Hilda Hildebrand's gaze remained steady on his face as she absorbed that declaration; he could almost see the arrestation of her thoughts as her calculations shifted her initial conclusion about why he was there to something significantly more palatable. Eventually, slowly, she inclined her head. "I see." Her defensive stiffness fading, she hesitated, then ventured, "I've heard you're an honorable gentleman, which is what I would expect of a scion of a family such as yours."

He hid a smile that might have appeared too predatory. If he was any judge, Hilda Hildebrand considered herself a guardian of Niniver's virtue—a dragon in truth. Having her on his side would prove helpful in the short term, and also later on, assuming Fate hadn't led him up any garden path but had, indeed, steered him in the direction he was supposed to take.

He still wasn't one hundred percent certain of that, although, thus far, all the omens were pointing that way.

"I understand you've acquired the old Hennessy property." Miss Hildebrand resettled her shawl. "What plans do you have for the land?"

Still hiding a grin that grew ever more appreciative, he replied to that and a subsequent inquisition that would have done any father interrogating a daughter's suitor proud.

Niniver frowned. Although she didn't interrupt, she grew increasingly restive. Marcus watched her clasp her hands in her lap, her fingers twisting and twining. Initially, her restiveness seemed due to nervousness; he put that down to concern that her governess's interrogation would drive him off. Subsequently, however, when that clearly wasn't going to happen, nervousness was replaced by impatience.

Impatience over what, he wondered?

Then Ferguson appeared in the doorway, and the three of them glanced his way. He bowed. "Dinner is served, my lady."

Niniver got to her feet. "Thank you, Ferguson."

Marcus rose, crossed to the sofa, and gallantly offered Miss Hildebrand his arm.

With a nod of approval, the ex-governess placed her hand on his sleeve and allowed him to help her to her feet.

He turned and, smiling at Niniver, held out his other arm in invitation.

She hesitated, but only for a second; he got the impression it was her impetuous impatience that pushed her to step to his side and slip her small hand into the crook of his elbow.

It was ridiculous, he knew, yet he felt smugly pleased as he led both ladies out of the room.

Niniver walked beside Marcus, glad that he'd adjusted his longer paces to her and Hildy's much shorter ones. She wished she could breathe more freely; she felt as if an iron band had inexplicably cinched about her lower ribs, constricting her lungs, rendering each breath shallow, tightening her nerves and leaving her a touch giddy.

Luckily, the dining room was only yards away.

Yet, apparently, that was far enough for her senses to riot. For them to fixate on everything about the tall, rangy, powerful gentleman who walked by her side, separated by an acceptable social distance, perhaps, yet nevertheless close enough for everything about him to impinge on her greedy senses. She felt his midnight-blue gaze briefly touch her face, and a wave of prickly awareness washed over her, closely followed by an equally distracting warmth. Oddly, her nerves felt more alive, more alert and energized than ever, eager to glean every last iota of experience.

Her giddiness didn't abate.

The instant they crossed the threshold, she dragged in a breath, drew her hand from the warmth of his arm, and rounded the table to her usual chair.

A footman moved to draw it out for her—but he halted, then stepped back.

From the corner of her eye, she glimpsed Marcus ambling close behind her; rather than seat Hildy, he'd elected to perform that office for her. With a negligent wave, he dismissed the footman. She reached her chair and paused; Marcus stepped past her and drew it out.

Summoning a vague smile and directing it—equally vaguely—in his direction, she dipped her head in thanks and sat.

He eased the chair in for her, then moved to claim the one beside hers.

Glancing across the table, Niniver saw Hildy happily thanking the footman who had held her chair. Her ex-governess's initial distrust of Marcus had evaporated, which was a very good thing. Despite Hildy not being clan, and otherwise living a relatively reclusive existence, her opinion held sway with both Ferguson and Mrs. Kennedy. The pair—and through them, the clan—relied on Hildy to accurately assess the effect of any happening on Niniver's social standing beyond the boundaries of the estate.

Although initially distrustful, Hildy now approved of Marcus.

While Ferguson served the soup, Niniver tried to recall the last gentleman of whom Hildy had approved, but couldn't, in fact, recall Hildy ever lowering her guard to this extent. In the aftermath of her father's death, and again after the deaths of her brothers, several friends of Nigel and Nolan's had made a point of calling on her, but she'd never liked or trusted any of them, and Hildy had been only too happy to assist her in sending them on their way.

So with respect to Hildy, Marcus was something of a first, but then he was a local, his family well known, and there was no denying he was a great deal more personable—and more understanding and ready to be accommodating over Hildy's questioning—than any previous caller.

And, as he'd said, he was there for a purpose; ruthlessly quelling her internal flutterings, she vowed to keep herself—and him—focused on that.

They all tasted the soup, then, as if he'd heard her resolution, Marcus asked, "In light of my purpose here, it would help if you would tell me more about the clan." With his gaze, he included both Niniver and Hildy. "How many families are there? How many farms overall?"

The answers tripped readily off Niniver's tongue.

Marcus continued his questioning. His inquiries had a dual aim; he did need a more comprehensive understanding of the clan and the estate, but he'd also sensed Niniver's flaring awareness—and her resulting jitteriness. The latter was something he felt sure would fade with continuing exposure to him, but he was wary enough to seek to distract her from it in the meantime.

And he'd already realized that talking of the clan—anything to do with the clan—was guaranteed to seize and fix her attention.

"So the manor itself has no farm as such?"

"No," she replied. "But the surrounding paddocks are used for horse-breeding. Sean, Mitch, and Fred manage that, and they provide as many of the horses the clan needs as they can, so we don't have to buy as many. And, of course, we have pens and barns for the stock, either for when they're collected for market, or when they're brought in for the winter."

A memory from ten years before surfaced. "As I recall, many of those on the outlying crofts come in to the manor over winter."

She nodded. "Originally, everyone did, at least for the worst of the snows. These days, only the smaller crofters stay for all of winter. It's what the disused wing used to be used for—housing all the clan families over that time."

"I believe," Hildy said, "that over the past twenty years, the larger farmhouses have been made more secure, so those families haven't needed to retreat to the manor over winter."

"I see." Marcus sat back to allow Ferguson to clear his plate; his questions had lasted over the entire meal. "But what of the household—how many live at the manor at present?"

Niniver's expression suggested she was adding up names... "Twenty. Not counting Hildy and myself, and including our healer, Alice, and her two apprentices."

Across the table, Hilda Hildebrand caught Marcus's gaze, then pointedly looked at Ferguson. While the man's impassive mien gave nothing away, he had to be wondering why, with a perfectly good house of his own only four miles away, Marcus was staying at the manor. He hadn't exactly explained that, even to Sean.

In the circumstances, Marcus held back his next question: How many of the twenty residing under the manor's roof were men? He needed to know that, and whether any of those men might prove a threat to Niniver. But he didn't want to start that hare running in her brain, so he'd wait and ask Ferguson tomorrow; he could then phrase the query so that it wasn't unnecessarily confronting.

The dessert came and went—a light trifle with a lemony sauce.

As the footmen cleared the dishes, Miss Hildebrand magisterially rose. "Lady Carrick and I will leave you to enjoy your port."

Marcus rose and drew back Niniver's chair. He had intended to return to the drawing room with her and Miss Hildebrand; he would rather enjoy their company than any glass of port. However, dallying in the dining room would give him a chance to speak with Ferguson privately—and there was one question he needed to ask someone other than Niniver.

He waited until both women left the room, then sank back into his chair. The footmen drew the covers, then retreated. Ferguson reappeared with a silver tray bearing glasses and three decanters.

Setting the tray on the table by Marcus's elbow, Ferguson said, "The master always insisted on the three—brandy, port, and good Scottish whisky."

Hiding a grin, Marcus reached for the whisky. Splashing a small amount into a crystal glass, he set the decanter back on the tray. "As I expect you've heard, I've agreed to assist Lady Carrick in dealing with the recent disturbances created by certain men in the clan." Raising his gaze, he shifted to meet Ferguson's steady regard. "To that end, I'd like to meet with you and the housekeeper tomorrow morning to discuss the situation, but for tonight, I have one point I need clarified." He sobered. "Norris. Why isn't he here? And why does

Lady Carrick feel she has no right to call on him for assistance?"

Ferguson returned his regard steadily. Marcus knew the exact moment when the stony-faced man decided to reply.

"The answer owes more to Mr. Norris than Miss Niniver. Aye—and the old laird. He was a good laird—he did well by the clan—but other than Mr. Nigel, he ignored the rest of his children. Despite that, Miss Niniver found her own path. Mr. Nolan tried to but failed, and he went mad with the trying. Mr. Norris… We, the household, always thought that he stayed sane by cutting himself off from us all. All except Miss Niniver. She knew how to reach him. I'd say she understands him. But Mr. Norris left—and perhaps he had to leave. I know that, no matter how we push, Miss Niniver refuses to call him back." The big man raised a shoulder. "And mayhap she's right."

Marcus held Ferguson's gaze for several seconds, then he nodded and looked at the amber liquid in his glass. "It sounds as if she might well be right." He was starting to suspect that, among other skills, Niniver read people rather well. Certainly those close to her.

Ferguson shifted but didn't retreat. When Marcus glanced up, curious as to why the man was lingering, Ferguson focused on the decanters and reached to re-arrange them on the tray. "The household—well, we're clan, too, so we talk. Of course we do. We might not be the same class as the Carricks, but it seems to us that all the men in Miss Niniver's life—those who should have been here to take care of her, that she had a right to expect would be here for her—all those men, every last one of them, have gone and deserted her, and left her to manage the clan all by herself. And make no mistake about it"—Ferguson's hard gaze rose to Marcus's face—"if she weren't here, the clan would fall apart. We had no choice but to ask her, slip of a thing though she is, but she took on the responsibility without flinching, and she's carried the load without complaint."

Ferguson paused; Marcus saw the pride and respect that glowed in the older man's eyes. Then Ferguson's lips twisted and he turned away. "It just seems wrong, to us, that she has to do it all by herself, and there's not one man who's man enough to stand by her side."

But there was. Marcus was there now, and that was precisely what he intended to do. But he said nothing of that—not yet.

He watched Ferguson leave the room, then drained his glass and rose.

As he walked to the drawing room, he inwardly acknowledged that, no matter how things played out between him and Niniver, the pride, respect, and devotion she commanded from the more experienced heads within the clan was something he would need to take into account—to preserve and ensure he did nothing to undermine.

*  *  *

Three hours later, Marcus lay on his back in the middle of the bed in the room next to Niniver's, and watched a shaft of moonlight slide across the ceiling. Sleep was eluding him; his mind was full of Niniver.

Hardly surprising given the events of the day, and after dinner, the hour and more they'd spent in the drawing room had brought still more revelations. When he'd joined the two ladies, Niniver had been skittish again, but this time over what she perceived to be her lack of ladylike accomplishments with which to entertain him.

He'd bitten his tongue to keep back the words that she could just sit in her chair and he would deem himself sufficiently entertained simply through being able to look at her. Instead, he'd suggested that *he* play the pianoforte for *her*—a concept strange enough to have had her blinking in surprise long enough for him to walk to the handsome instrument sitting in one corner, open it, sit, and place his fingers on the keys.

Miss Hildebrand had promptly suggested that Niniver should sing to his accompaniment. She'd hesitated, but then he'd run his fingers along the keys and asked what style of song she favored, and she'd acquiesced and come to stand by his shoulder. He'd tried the opening chords of a familiar country air. He'd been conscious of her drawing breath, then she'd opened her ruby lips and sung…and transported them all to paradise.

Her voice was unbelievably pure; he'd never heard a more perfect soprano, and several of his cousins had been very well trained. Not one could hold a candle to Niniver. Her voice held passion and the sort of soaring power that brought to mind the sweeping flight of birds…

She sang like an angel.

He'd played three pieces just to listen to her, then couldn't resist trying a duet. He'd had to mute the strength of his baritone so he didn't overwhelm the piercing, rather haunting clarity of her voice, but he'd adjusted, and so had she, until their voices had blended in effortless harmony.

Lucilla played the harp, which was why he had gravitated to the pianoforte, and because of long evenings spent with his large family, he had a ready store of country songs literally at his fingertips; he'd gone from one to the other, interspersing an orchestral piece when Niniver needed a few minutes to recover before sliding into the introduction to another song.

At one point, he'd noticed a reflection in the highly polished face of the piano. Ferguson had arrived pushing the tea trolley, but on opening the drawing room door and hearing their music, he'd paused on the threshold, listening. Other staff had heard, and had come to gather about the open door, delight in their faces.

An hour had sped by, but eventually, Niniver had called a halt, claiming she was growing giddy.

Accepting that that was quite likely true, he'd concluded with a dramatic run of chords, then had closed the piano, risen, and taken her hand. He'd turned her to the crowd at the door. He'd bowed. She'd laughed to see their audience, then had curtsied, and the staff, led by Miss Hildebrand, had all beamed and applauded.

It had been a moment of simple pleasure. He'd looked at Niniver, seen the genuine happiness in her face, and had felt…fulfilled. Distinctly and simply happy, too.

Uplifted.

If that was how he was destined to feel whenever he engineered matters so that she looked like that, it was a fairly potent incentive to devote himself to making her happy.

He was contemplating that point when the caterwauling started.

*"My fairest maid of joyful countenance! Look upon me with your bright eyes."*

The off-key rendition of the opening lines of a common country song shattered the peace of the night.

In disbelief, he stared at the ceiling as the next line, delivered in a quavery tenor, followed...

His eyes were open, ergo this wasn't a nightmare. It was real.

Then he heard a creak of floorboards from the room next door, followed by the soft patter of footsteps—then another line from the would-be serenader drowned out all else.

Marcus swore, tossed back the covers, and all but leapt from the bed. The night air stroked cool fingers down his naked chest and the floorboards were cold beneath his bare feet, but he ignored both sensations. Reaching the window, he flung up the sash. Slapping his palms on the outer sill, he leaned out—so that the moonlight reached his face.

A thin, gangly beanpole of a man stood rooted to the gravel path below, his mouth hanging open as he absorbed the full impact of Marcus's glare.

At least the idiot had stopped trying to sing.

"As you can see, I'm no fair maid, and my countenance is far from joyful. Might I suggest you shut your mouth?"

The man, still staring, snapped his jaw shut.

Narrow-eyed, Marcus nodded. "Excellent. Now go away."

The man gawked, but then his gaze flicked to Marcus's left, to the next window along—then, eyes widening even further, the man looked back at him.

Marcus growled. "I said go! And if you value your vocal chords, I strongly suggest that you never attempt such foolishness again."

The man swallowed—Marcus could see his throat working—then the man's gaze started to swing to the left again.

"Don't." Marcus's voice had dropped to an even lower register; he let quiet menace ripple beneath the words "You do not want me to come down there and help you on your way."

Eyes like saucers, the man swallowed again, then he ducked his head and scurried off.

Leaning further forward, Marcus watched him rush around the corner of the house. He waited until he heard the muted thud of hoofbeats. As the sound faded, he heard the soft scrape as Niniver's window sash slid up.

"Thank you." Her voice floated across to him.

He fought the impulse to turn and look at her—tried his damnedest not to think of how she would appear, sleep-warm and tousled from her bed. Then he felt the warm caress of her gaze as it slid over his naked shoulders.

Thanking The Lady that Niniver couldn't see below sill-level, he gripped said sill until his hands ached and forced himself to focus. "Who was he?"

His voice still rumbled like a portent of doom.

She hesitated, but then answered, "Jem Hills."

One of the clansmen she'd named. He sifted through the information he'd gleaned earlier. "One of the principal woodcutter's sons?"

"Yes."

"Has he done this before?"

She hesitated, then admitted, "Twice. But he's fairly easily frightened—I don't think he'll be back."

But Jem Hills had already returned twice, because

she hadn't been able to frighten him off on her own. Marcus snorted. "He better not come back, or he'll discover just how easily irritated *I* am."

Which was odd. He wasn't normally quick to anger, yet when it came to her…

He forced himself to push back from the sill and step away from the window. "Hopefully, we won't be disturbed again tonight."

"No—I mean, yes." She sighed, then softly murmured, "Good night."

He managed to return the words and not just grunt. He waited until her window sash slid down, then closed his and retreated to the bed.

Once under the covers, he returned to his contemplation of the ceiling—and the type of anger, the particular nature of the aggravation, still coursing through his veins.

Instinctively, he knew what it was, yet it took several long minutes before he was willing to place the correct label on the emotion. Possessive jealousy. Just the thought of what Jem Hills would have seen—the sight Marcus had denied himself, but that Jem would have been rewarded with had Marcus not been there to chase him off—set that ferocious anger spiking again.

He'd started the evening not yet one hundred percent certain that being Niniver's champion was his destined path. Now, not a shred of doubt remained. Fate had sunk her claws deep and hauled him irrevocably onto his true path.

For good or ill, there was only one way forward.

For him. For her.

For them both.

With that conclusion resonating clarion-like in his mind, he closed his eyes—and to his surprise, found Morpheus waiting.

* * *

After shutting her window, Niniver stood staring unseeing through the pane.

The vision emblazoned across her mind's eye was one she should endeavor to erase. Instead…she dwelled on every curve, every line, committing them irrevocably to memory.

He'd been leaning forward so Jem could see him. That had also meant *she'd* been able to see him. With her gaze, beyond her control, roving over the powerful muscles of his shoulders and upper arms, the corded strength of his forearms, she'd barely been able to string together two coherent thoughts.

More, when he'd drawn back, he'd shifted slightly, fleetingly giving her an even better, less impeded view of the magnificent expanse of his chest bathed in moonlight…

Her mouth was still dry. No matter how hard she tried, she was never going to forget that.

She'd heard him pad back to his bed, heard the bed creak as he'd settled once more.

Her mind served up the image of his hands, long fingers fluidly traveling the piano's keys as he'd played song after song, his voice a perfect counterpart to hers. Those same hands, seen minutes ago, elegant fingers gripping the white-painted sill, had looked much more deadly.

That, she felt, was the truth of him—elegantly sophisticated on the outside, and powerfully dangerous within.

Night's chilly fingers reached through her night-gown. She shook aside her distraction and returned to her bed. As she settled beneath the covers and again felt the tug of all she'd seen on her senses, on her too-distractible wits, she told herself not to be so foolish. Dwelling on visions like that wasn't going to make hiding her fascination with him—her infatuation with him, if she spoke true—any easier, yet hide that, deny that, she must.

Her mind drifted back over the evening, over the many smiles they'd shared by the piano, over the easy camaraderie that had flowed between them, carried on the music.

But she knew what sort of gentleman he was, which was why she'd finally succumbed and asked him—specifically him—for help. Because he *would* help, in the decisive and definite way he'd just dealt with Jem Hills.

Yet by the same token, she knew that with men like Marcus, all his many kindnesses were simply that—kindnesses. They sprang from the ingrained protectiveness taught to men like him from birth, and didn't mean anything more.

She'd be a fool indeed to imagine such kindnesses sprang from anything other than instinct.

Closing her eyes, she forced her mind away from him and focused instead on what had just transpired. He'd been so convincingly intimidating that, with any luck, Jem wouldn't be able to resist blabbing about the encounter. And then the message would get about that it would no longer be just her, alone, dealing with whatever silly actions her clansmen thought to visit upon her.

Her mind slid, once again, to the vision she'd seen, to the undeniable menace Marcus had exuded.

Looking ahead, she harbored no doubts that she could rely on him to protect her from any and all external threats.

But protecting her heart? Her silly, foolish feelings?

That would be up to her.

# Four

Marcus formally commenced his pursuit of Niniver the following morning. As he waited at the breakfast table for her to appear, he worked his way through a mound of ham, sausages, and his favorite, kedgeree, and mentally surveyed what he saw as his new battlefield.

His goal was clear—to claim Niniver's hand and the position by her side.

The hurdles? As far as he could see, the major ones stemmed from her being the lady of a clan.

Commonly in marriage, especially in his class, the man occupied a position of power, being the possessor of a title, a landowner, or having a similar position of wealth and influence. The woman brought a dowry—fortune or land or similar tangible wealth—but she stepped into a position of supporting the male; that was the accepted way.

But that couldn't be so in this case. Yes, he was a landowner; he possessed significant wealth and influential connections. But it was Niniver who was lady of the clan—she who held power via election by her clansmen. In a marriage between them, it wouldn't be a case of her becoming his supporter, but of him becoming hers.

The prospect of that being his fated destiny was strangely reassuring. It could be said that his birth and upbringing uniquely qualified him for the role.

Being the husband of a woman in power wasn't a position many men would covet, much less successfully fill. Several years ago, his grandmother Helena had pointed out to him that only men with supreme confidence could act as the consort to a female ruler— as his father did with his mother, the current Lady of the Vale, and as Thomas now did with Lucilla. Helena had commented that being a consort didn't mean being less of a man—it actually demanded being more. It required being the type of man whose identity and self-worth weren't dependent on a title, much less on his wife being subservient to him.

Thinking of the ladies within his extended family, Marcus swallowed a snort. None of the Cynster wives could remotely be described as subservient. Equal partners, yes—and their husbands had discovered that married life was immensely better that way. On every level.

He came from that tradition of men; his expectations, notions, and needs were rooted in that ethos— and that left him with no doubt whatsoever that he was up to the task of being Niniver's champion, protector, defender, and principal supporter. Her husband.

That was the position Fate and The Lady had groomed him to fill. It was the position he now wanted, the position that, with the commitment of his kind, he fully intended to claim.

How?

That was the one question remaining.

He heard Niniver's light footsteps in the corridor. He looked up as she walked into the room.

She saw him; her gaze met his and she slowed, but then she flashed him a smile and continued to the sideboard. "Good morning. And thank you again for getting rid of Jem."

"I would say it was my pleasure—and it was—but such an incident should never have occurred." He rose; he waited while she collected two slices of toast, but then, somewhat to his surprise, she elected to sit opposite him. Ferguson had arrived with a pot of tea; he set it down before Niniver's chosen place, then held her chair for her.

Once she was settled, Marcus resumed his seat, then, seeing her glance around the board, he lifted the pot of marmalade and passed it to her. Their fingers brushed, and he felt the expected jolt of awareness. He knew she felt it, too, but her guard slammed up, squelching her reaction, suppressing all signs of it.

Clearly, her choice of where to sit, with the width of the table between them rather than in her usual place in the chair next to his, had been deliberate.

So she was skittish. All things considered, that wasn't much of a surprise. He was an expert at drawing skittish animals to his hand, and, in his experience, women weren't all that different. He would have plenty of time to overcome her skittishness after he eliminated all the threats to her comfort.

Watching while she spread marmalade over her toast, he found himself wondering, as he frequently did on observing the same behavior with his sisters, how even slips of things like Niniver, Lucilla, and Annabelle could exist until lunchtime on two slices of toast and jam and a couple of cups of tea.

Niniver set aside the marmalade and reached for the teapot.

Abandoning the abiding mystery, he refocused on her and her recent problems. "You said Jem had serenaded you on two previous occasions." Those incidents had not been in the list Sean and Mitch had given him. Rather than relate that list in its entirety, he said, "I know about the fight in the stable yard. What else—what other similar incidents—have occurred?"

Niniver frowned and inwardly debated. Eventually, she offered, "I suppose the first 'incident,' as such, occurred early last summer. Carter Bonham and Milo Wignell came to invite me to go on a picnic with them." She grimaced at the memory, then glanced across the table and met Marcus's steady gaze. "They tried to insist, but I used being in mourning as an excuse. They came back later in the year—late October, I think. But I saw them driving up in their phaeton and told Ferguson to say I was out. They haven't been back—well, not yet. And then there were the others like them—"

"Wait." Marcus leaned forward, black brows slashing down. "Bonham and Wignell aren't clan, are they? And by others like them, I assume you mean gentlemen?"

She resisted the urge to chew her lower lip. "Yes."

"But I thought you said the men bothering you were all clan?"

"At the moment, yes. They are all clansmen. But the others—they were Nigel and Nolan's friends."

Marcus regarded her for a moment, then his lips tightened. He nodded. "Give me all the names."

She did. When she fell silent, he leaned back in his chair. His expression suggested he was adding all the names to some master list in his head. Then his gaze returned to her and he gestured at her to continue. "Tell me all the incidents you can remember."

Stifling a sigh, she complied.

The list was long—longer than she'd realized; she'd never set down each and every occurrence, not even in her mind.

Some of the incidents had been frightening, but many were, in hindsight, rather amusing. However, when she reached the end of her recitation and focused again on Marcus, there was not a skerrick of amusement in his face. His expression was set and unyielding, his features forbidding.

His power, and the menace and threat he could bring to bear, were readily discernible to her senses, yet, as had occurred last night, none of that deadly promise was directed at her; rather, it felt as if it were deployed as a shield, screening and protecting her.

She quelled an unhelpfully appreciative shiver.

Marcus sensed that shiver; it brought his attention snapping back to her. He studied her for a second, marveling that, despite the litany of assaults on her peace and privacy she'd weathered through the last year—ever since she'd been elected to lead her clan—she still remained… Niniver. Calm, anchored, with a practical streak that reached fathoms deep.

But the attacks—for that was what they amounted to—had to have taken a toll. At the very least, they'd added unnecessary pressure when, if he'd understood correctly, she'd already been scrambling to bring the clan about. The only positive outcome was that the incidents had finally sent her to him.

Had finally brought her to admit that she needed a champion, and that said champion should be him.

She tipped her head, her blue eyes searching his face. "Is that what you wanted to know?"

"Yes." He paused, then went on, "I need to know all those involved so I know who to watch for, and I needed to know what they've done because that gives me some idea of how determined they might be."

She set her napkin by her plate. "And how determined is that?"

He rose and started around the table. "Those like Jem are just trying their hand—they'll be easy to discourage. But some of the others?" Especially Nigel and Nolan's friends. Reaching her chair, he drew it out for her. "On them, I'll reserve judgment."

He grasped her hand and helped her to her feet.

He felt her fingers quiver, then she slipped them free of his hold. She glanced up at him, then, head rising, led the way from the room.

"I'll be in the library for the rest of the morning." Niniver was relieved that the words came out evenly enough; her lungs had locked—she felt as if she could barely breathe. Her senses were rioting, leaping and pointing out that he was close, that he was following at her heels—*stupid* things. As for the fingers he'd grasped, the skin he'd touched still burned.

With a ridiculously tempting heat.

But she was determined to ignore all her reactions; he was behaving exactly as a gentleman like him would toward a lady like her—nothing more.

"I've found that, at present, it's necessary for me

to review every expense undertaken by the estate. As I've not yet been in the position of lady for a full year, I'm still learning the ropes. And we do have so many different enterprises…but you must be used to that in the Vale." She walked as fast as she could short of running. The library door loomed; she opened it and continued inside.

He followed and closed the door.

Continuing toward the desk at the end of the room, she glanced back—and the long, wide room, the largest in the manor, seemed to shrink.

He took up so much space, not just physically but as if his very aura spread outward and dominated the area, somehow claiming it and making it his.

Facing forward, she made for the safety of her father's desk.

Marcus watched her slip around the desk and sink into the well-worn admiral's chair behind it. As he had the afternoon before, he watched her succumb to the demands of the ledgers, watched worry slowly claim her expression. But as he had the day before, he set aside the impulse to help her with the estate; she'd been managing it, apparently with passable success, for the last year, so she didn't need his immediate help on that front.

Protection and defense first, lifting of burdens later.

"Is there some other room—a study or estate office—that I could use for the moment?" He didn't say for what; she didn't need to know.

Her almost eager expression as she glanced up at him forced him to hide a too-predatory smile. As she was so skittish, he would take himself out of what was patently her favorite space and let her relax. For now.

"There's a small study down the corridor." She pointed with her pen. "Nigel used to use it when Papa was alive. No one uses it anymore."

"That will do admirably." He nodded at the books. "I'll leave you to it."

He turned and headed for the door. He didn't need to see the gratitude in her face to know he'd made the right move.

He stepped into the corridor, drew the library door closed, paused to consider his next move, then he went off to find the study and take the next step in establishing his position as Niniver's champion.

\* \* \*

The small study contained a desk with a large chair behind it, two narrow straight-backed chairs before it, and two tall bookshelves against the side walls. The shelves contained a few old journals and nothing else; the room was devoid of any ornamentation or amenity beyond the brass lamp that sat on one corner of the otherwise bare desk.

Seated behind the desk with a window overlooking the stable yard at his back, Marcus regarded Ferguson and the housekeeper, a Mrs. Kennedy, who were sitting on the chairs facing him. "As I see it, my role here is to shield Lady Carrick from any threat, physical or otherwise. She will not be molested. She will not be upset. She will not be preyed upon in any way whatsoever. I will take it unkindly if she is inconvenienced."

Both Ferguson and the matronly housekeeper looked, if anything, quietly thrilled.

Marcus studied them, then went on, "Last night, we sustained a midnight visit from Jem Hills, who thought

Lady Carrick would welcome a serenade. I spoke with him and corrected his misapprehension."

Both Ferguson and Mrs. Kennedy frowned.

"I"—Ferguson glanced at the housekeeper and received a distinct shake of the head—"*we* didn't hear anything of that."

"Precisely. Your rooms face in the other direction, so you were unaware of what was happening on Lady Carrick's side of the house. Which illustrates why I will continue to occupy the room next to Lady Carrick's. She patently needs protection night and day."

The butler and the housekeeper were less happy about that, but neither argued.

Marcus felt fairly certain that both would do all they could to support and protect Niniver; they were another pair of would-be defenders who, like Sean and Mitch, hadn't been able to act effectively. He was not above taking advantage of any lingering feelings of inadequacy to gain support for his own role. They might be constrained by clan loyalties and politics, but he was not. He could act where they would be forced to equivocate, and when it came to dealing with the likes of Nigel and Nolan's friends, he was significantly more able than any in the clan.

"After the interlude last night, I'm hoping Jem will spread the word that Lady Carrick is no longer alone, and that anyone seeking to interfere with her life will find themselves facing me. In short, I intend standing as her champion."

He paused to let that sink in, then continued, "I'm sure all the household are aware of what a treasure the clan has in Lady Carrick. I would appreciate it if all of you would also spread the word that your treasure now has a guardian. One who will take a very dim view of any further infractions."

The relief that infused both lined faces was impossible to mistake, yet instead of nodding and agreeing, the pair paused, then exchanged a long look.

Ferguson finally turned to Marcus. "We appreciate—very much—you being willing to come and act for Miss Niniver."

"We surely do." Mrs. Kennedy's gray curls bobbed, but her expression remained serious.

Ferguson dragged in a breath. "Howsoever, you're not clan, and we're all very fond of Miss Niniver, and as there's no longer anyone to ask for her, well…" Bravely, Ferguson met Marcus's gaze. "We feel we have to ask what your intentions toward Miss Niniver—Lady Carrick—herself are."

He'd expected the question; indeed, he would have thought less of them, of their devotion to Niniver, if they hadn't asked.

What he hadn't anticipated was the visceral reaction that rose through him in response—adamant and final. But snarling "She's mine," while accurate, wasn't an appropriate reply. Maintaining his relaxed demeanor, his expression of unruffled calm, he stated, "That will be entirely up to her—as it should be."

That was the true and honest answer, even if it didn't match the violence of his feelings. Those, he continued to keep well hidden.

Both Ferguson and Mrs. Kennedy exhaled and nodded, their relief palpable. They knew who he was, knew his word could be trusted. His declaration had erased their anxiety, removed all reason for resistance, and cleared the way for these two, and all the staff they commanded, to fall in behind him and support his shielding of Niniver.

Ferguson met his eyes again, then rose. The butler bowed. "Thank you, sir. From all of us."

Mrs. Kennedy came to her feet and bobbed a curtsy. "We'll be happy to do whatever we can to help—anything to ease the weight on Miss Niniver's shoulders."

Marcus smiled and rose, too. "Indeed. I'll let you know of any further ways in which you and the rest of the staff might assist."

After the pair had seen themselves out, he sank back into the chair. After a moment, he swiveled so he could stare out of the window.

He was happy with the way the interview had played out. He wasn't surprised by the result, yet negotiating to get the staff on his side might have taken much longer; he was pleased that it hadn't.

What had surprised him was just how violently his inner self had reacted to Ferguson's question. Or, more precisely, to the implied suggestion that Niniver was not already his.

His in the primal sense, which was the only sense his inner, baser self understood.

He wasn't the least surprised that he would feel that way about his fated bride, but that such a degree of possessiveness already lived inside him...*that* was a touch disconcerting.

It was less than twenty-four hours since he'd accepted that Niniver was his fated bride, the central figure in his true and fated destiny; he'd expected to go through several progressive stages of increasing possessiveness before reaching the *She's mine and no one else's* moment.

Apparently not so. Apparently, his baser self had leapt far ahead and was already at the end of that road, straining at the leash to forge on.

Which could be a problem given that Niniver, as her skittishness testified, as yet had no real notion of his direction, much less of the role she was fated to fill in his life. Indeed, while she might suspect in a distant fashion, she couldn't know, because he'd taken extreme pains to hide everything he felt for her for years.

He stared unseeing at the stable yard as the minutes ticked by. Finally, he swung back to face the room.

Given the truth both his rational self and his baser self accepted and understood, it would undoubtedly be wise to escalate his campaign to persuade Niniver to be his wife. As a hunter, he could be patient, but in the present circumstances, patience was unlikely to stretch all that far, not with his baser self already so deeply engaged.

That said, he could foresee another complication arising. Although he might convince her to be his, he couldn't, in fact, ask for her hand until after he'd dismissed all the threats against her, physical and otherwise.

If he didn't wait, his request for her hand would risk sounding like a demand for payment for services rendered…

The very thought made him squirm.

Sounds from beyond the window had him glancing outside. In the stable yard, Johnny, his groom, had just ridden in and was dismounting. One of Marcus's traveling bags was tied to Johnny's saddle.

Marcus got to his feet and headed for the door.
One step at a time.

* * *

He was in the room he'd accepted would be his, unpacking the bag Johnny had brought, when he heard
Niniver come up the stairs. She rounded the gallery
and went into her room.

He heard her moving around, heard what sounded
like a shoe hitting the floor.

Several minutes later, her door opened and, boot
heels striking firmly on the runner, she came his way.
He turned to the open doorway as she reached it.

She saw him and smiled. "I'm going to spend the
rest of the morning training our deerhounds. I wondered if you would like to come with me."

"Of course." Did she even need to ask? She knew
he shared her interest in hounds.

She'd changed into her riding habit. He was already
wearing shirt, breeches, and boots; deserting his half-
unpacked bag, he walked to the bed, swiped up the
hacking jacket he'd left there, and shrugged it over
the fresh shirt he'd donned. "Where do you keep the
hounds? I recall Thomas mentioning you'd moved them
out to some farm on the estate."

"I had to hide them or Nigel would have sold them."
She shrugged. "Or Nolan—I'm no longer sure who
was behind what."

"But you saved the hounds." He joined her at the
door and she stepped back. Side by side, they headed
for the stairs.

"I managed to hide the best of them." She strode
beside him, evincing no sign of her earlier consciousness. "The pack is still out at old Egan's place—he had

a barn he wasn't using, and as he was the kennel master in Papa's day, I've left them with him. Two of his nephews help him with the work. I think he's pleased to be able to hand on his knowledge."

They started down the stairs. "Incidentally, I can't protect you from importuning would-be suitors if I'm not with you." He caught her wide blue gaze when she glanced at him. "So, if you please, I would appreciate you agreeing not to leave the house without telling me first."

She considered him for a moment, then faced forward. "All right."

He would have preferred to extract a promise along those lines, but she seemed genuinely amenable, and as long as she consented to tell him of any outing, accompanying her on excursions such as this one was akin to killing two birds with one stone. Not only would his presence by her side be noted by all who saw them— and, with luck, commented upon far and wide—but spending hours by her side out of the house would afford him the opportunities he needed to introduce her to the notion of becoming his wife.

In the stable yard, Niniver waited in the sunshine while Sean, Mitch, and Marcus saddled their horses. Marcus's gray was proving fractious; when he finally led the big gelding out, the horse tossed his head and looked ready to race. Somewhat to her surprise, Marcus handed the reins to Fred. With a curt "Hold him" to Mitch, who was leading Oswald out, Marcus came striding her way...

*Oh, no.* She only had time to think the words before Mitch brought Oswald alongside her.

Halting before her, Marcus smiled and reached for her waist.

He hoisted her to her saddle as if she weighed less than a feather; to him, she probably did. The sensation of his hands and fingers locked about her waist threatened to scramble her wits, but then he released her and stepped back. Breathless, she ducked her head and busied herself settling her boots and skirts. Finally hauling in a breath past the constriction banding her chest, she managed a weak "thank you," and was relieved when, apparently satisfied that she wasn't about to topple off her perch, he turned and strode back to his horse.

He mounted in one fluid motion, all strength, power, and grace. Despite a half-hearted injunction not to look, her witless senses drank in the sight.

But then he swung his gray's head toward the stable yard gate, and she dragged in a deeper breath, straightened her spine, lifted Oswald's reins, tapped her boot to his side, and joined Marcus in riding out.

This was what she'd wanted, after all; he was clearly taking his commitment to repel her suitors seriously, and obviously intended to remain at the manor for a few days at least. She would simply have to get used to his nearness, and grow accustomed to all the little touches that were simply a part of polite interaction between a gentleman and a lady.

She'd suggested visiting the hounds because she knew it was an interest they shared, and that he would enjoy being with the pack as much as she would. A few hours of shared enjoyment was a gift she was able to give him in return for his help.

The steady *thud* of their horses' hooves calmed her. To her, riding was as easy as breathing—easier, at least when Marcus was near. She loved the motion, loved being outside, adored the feel of sunshine on her face and the wind tugging at her hair.

She felt Marcus's gaze touch her face, but didn't turn her head to meet it. From the corner of her eye, she saw a slight, rather satisfied smile curve his lips…

*Don't look! Don't look!*

This time, she obeyed. Keeping her eyes fixed forward, she led the way on.

\* \* \*

Two hours later, she stroked the head of her favorite bitch, then glanced up—smiling unrestrainedly—at Marcus. "I suppose we should get back." Reluctance colored her voice; even she could hear it. Hardly surprising; the past hours had been an even greater delight than she'd foreseen. Sharing her passion for deerhounds with someone who not only understood but felt the same abiding interest in the big, intelligent dogs had been…more than a thrill. It had been cathartic. She hadn't realized for how long she'd gone without sharing anything with anyone.

Marcus lounged against the side post of the large pen; he returned her smile, but instead of agreeing with her comment, said, "Tell me more about this new air-scenting trait. Do you really think it'll be passed on?"

She rose and dusted off her skirts. "I can't be sure yet." She nodded at the bitch. "Her pups are still too young to train, or even to test. On the other hand, I've only found the trait in any strength in her and her sisters, and to a lesser extent in the males in the same line, so I'm hopeful."

They'd spent an hour putting the pack—a remarkably healthy and strong group of hounds—through a series of standard trials and commands. To be useful to hunters, the hounds needed to have the appropriate commands constantly reinforced. Niniver had her own set, but they differed only slightly from those Marcus used; he'd quickly adjusted and had enjoyed helping her work with the older dogs.

He'd also been diligent in seizing every chance to touch her—a hand on her back as he moved past her, a touch on her arm to get her attention, allowing their fingers to brush when they'd been examining one of the hounds. Entirely innocent touches, although his ultimate aim was anything but innocent.

But then she'd shown him evidence of the trait she'd been working on developing—the ability to air-scent that she'd detected in one family of her hounds. Deerhounds were primarily sight-hounds; they could sight prey at a remarkable distance and, because of their speed, they excelled in the chase. In addition, the breed could track over ground quite well, as could most breeds of hound. However, only a few select breeds were known to air-scent, and deerhounds weren't one of those. Yet as far as he knew, trainers had never actively looked for air-scenters among the breeds already long-established as tracking- or sight-hounds.

Niniver's discovery was potentially groundbreaking, and he felt honored and deeply pleased that she'd shared it with him. That she'd trusted him enough to tell him of her secret.

One step at a time.

As she neared, he straightened from the post. "I can certainly see the advantages in having a mixed pack. Much less chance of losing a scent if you have dogs that can follow through the air as well as on the ground."

He reached out and took her hand, steadying her as she stepped out of the straw and balanced to free one boot from the clinging stuff. Then he released her and moved back. While she'd noticed his touch, she'd accepted it without any start or sign of sensual skittishness.

Another inch gained.

He waited in the long aisle that ran most of the length of the barn while she swung the gate closed and latched it. This wasn't a purpose-built kennel like his own facility; instead, they'd made do by converting the original barn into a series of hound-holding pens. A small arena had been left just inside the main doors, with a fenced yard beyond in which to exercise the dogs. Despite the make-do construction, as it had been Niniver and, as he understood it, old Egan, the previous kennel master, in charge, the refitted building worked quite well and had all the necessary areas to support an active breeding program.

And it was Niniver herself who ran that program. Marcus had always wondered, but earlier he'd spent a few minutes with old Egan—the 'old' seemed an accepted part of the man's name; while watching Niniver put ten of the most experienced hounds through their paces, he'd chatted and learned just how much admiration and respect the old trainer had for her.

After the last hours, he was willing to own to admiration and a healthy respect, too. While watching her work with the hounds, directing the ofttimes difficult beasts, he'd seen another side of her. She was firm, capable, and decisive, and she knew how to get the best from those she commanded. All characteristics of a good ruler of people as well as hounds.

She was a female of varied and contradictory facets, a fascinating meld of the delicate, fragile, and vulnerable on the one hand, and the strong, steely, and determined on the other.

After one last look at her hounds, she faced him.

"Can I take a look at the weaned pups?" He wondered how many she had, and how they would compare in health and vigor to his. He grinned. "I'm prepared to be impressed."

She laughed. "Of course, you can see them." She turned and started walking toward the end of the barn. "They're this way."

He followed, feeling inordinately pleased to have drawn that light, carefree laugh from her. The easy camaraderie they shared over the hounds was precisely the right atmosphere in which to dismantle her prickly walls.

Ten minutes later, they were surrounded by a mass of squirming, wriggling bodies in one of the end pens, both smiling irrepressibly and enjoying themselves hugely, when sounds of an altercation reached them. A rumble of male voices came from the front of the barn, distorted by the pen walls.

Then one man yelled. It sounded like "No!"

Marcus thought the protest came from old Egan. Then all other sounds were drowned beneath a chorus of yips and barks.

Rising from his crouch, he ordered, "Stay here." He opened the pen gate and stepped into the aisle. Swinging the gate shut behind him, he squinted into the glare streaming in through the open barn doors. Several large man-sized shapes were moving in and out of the light—then hounds appeared, milling about.

Whoever the men were, they were letting loose the older dogs in the pens closer to the doors.

"What the devil are they doing?" He started striding swiftly up the long aisle. As more hounds joined the fray, he swore and started running.

When he got close enough to see clearly, he slowed, rapidly surveying the chaotic scene. One burly man was standing just inside the door, holding back a struggling, curses-spitting Egan. Two others, also large, hulking brutes, were moving down the aisle, happily unlatching the pen doors. More than twenty hounds—all full grown—were milling in the aisle; because of their noise, the men hadn't heard him coming.

Then footsteps rushed up from behind him.

The nearest mountain of brawn was grinning inanely and lumbering toward the gate of the pen where Niniver's air-scenting bitches were housed.

Niniver flashed past Marcus and flung herself on the man, grabbing his arm to stop him from unlatching the pen's gate. "No! Ed—what are you doing?"

Ed—one of her clansmen?

Ed hadn't seen her coming; instinctively, he tensed to fling her off.

He realized who he was flinging at the last second; his face almost comical in surprise, he tried to halt the violent movement, but Niniver was already stumbling back.

Marcus swooped and caught her in one arm. Using her weight to add to his momentum, he plowed a highly satisfying roundhouse punch into Ed's jaw.

The giant grunted and staggered back, shock replacing surprise.

Still turning, Marcus swept the man's feet from

under him. Ed landed with a heavy thud on the straw-strewn earth.

Marcus realized he should have known better than to imagine Niniver would obey his order. Setting her on her feet, he said, "See to Egan and the hounds. Leave the men to me and stay out of the way."

One glance at her set face, at the fury blazing in her eyes, along with the grim nod she gave him, stated he'd get no argument on that score.

Reassured, he returned to his anointed task—taking care of her problems.

The giant had hit his head on the ground. He was groggy and blinking. His mates had only just realized they had unexpected company.

Hounds were still milling, but Niniver called and the beasts obediently streamed her way.

Marcus bent, grabbed the fallen man at collar and belt, and heaved—and sent his body tumbling into the closer of his friends.

The pair landed in a tangled heap in the space before the doors.

"Here! What do you think you're doing?" Filled with belligerent bluster, the man who'd been holding Egan came striding down the barn.

Marcus glanced into the shadows by the door. Niniver was now with Egan. The man advancing on Marcus must have seen her, but he was more interested in defending his friends.

Settling on his feet, Marcus let the fellow come.

Just before the man got within arm's reach, Marcus stepped forward and buried his fist in the man's gut.

With a *whoosh*, the man doubled over. Marcus

grabbed the man's head and slammed it down on his raised knee.

The man whimpered and, still doubled over, staggered drunkenly back.

Lips set, Marcus locked his hand about the man's nape, towed him to the barn doors, and mercilessly flung him into the dust of the fenced area outside.

He stalked back to the other two.

The second man had finally disentangled himself from Ed; he saw Marcus coming and launched himself at him.

Marcus sidestepped, then turned, and, as the man whirled back, punched him in the face.

The man howled and clutched his nose.

Marcus grabbed him by the hair, hauled him to the doors, and flung him outside, too.

Meanwhile, Ed had clambered to his feet. He stumbled all but blindly toward the barn doors. All he needed was a boot in the backside to help him on his way, something Marcus was happy—nay, delighted—to supply.

After ascertaining that Egan was unharmed, Niniver had repenned the hounds. Now she strode to join Marcus in the open doorway.

Marcus stood straight and tall, but he was working the fingers of his right hand.

In contrast, the three miscreants were sitting in the dirt, and all were nursing injuries and looking sorry for themselves; that last sent her temper spiraling. "Ed Wisbech. Liam Forrester. And Stewart Canning." She named them for Marcus's benefit as well as for effect. Eyes narrowing even further, she glared at the three. "You brainless oafs! Do you have any idea of the damage you might have done to the hounds? What possessed you to come here and let them loose?"

All three men had been looking from her to Marcus and back again, but it was Marcus they looked at with wariness and respect.

She hung on to her temper. "*Well?*"

Stewart Canning, the one who had held Egan and who was most likely the instigator of whatever harebrained scheme the three had hatched, sniveled through what looked suspiciously like tears, "We didn't mean no harm. We just had a thought that p'rhaps you was having difficulty making up your mind which one of us you'd have, because there were so many of us vying for your hand, like, so we made a pact."

Liam Forrester spoke through the hands he held locked about his nose. "We agreed, us three, that we'd make up a contest o' sorts, and whichever of us won, the other two would abide by the result and let the winner bid for your hand without interfering."

"We were trying to make things *easier* for you," Ed offered, still holding his jaw. His tone suggested she should be grateful.

Niniver curled her fingers into fists. "That doesn't explain what you thought you were doing with the hounds." *With* my *hounds.* They might be the Carrick pack, but everyone in the clan knew they were hers. She'd bred, raised, and trained each one. Had schemed and lied to protect all the ones she still had from her late brothers.

Stewart lifted his massive shoulders in a shrug. "Seemed the obvious thing to do—the obvious contest. We was each going to pick one of the beasts, and then race them, and whosever's dog won, he would be our winner."

"They were your dogs and all," Liam said. "It seemed right and fitting."

Marcus made a peculiar strangled sound; she assumed he was choking back a disbelieving laugh. In as level a tone as she could muster, she stated, "You can't race hounds. They're animals who hunt in packs—they work together to bring down prey. The concept of racing against each other is totally foreign to them. If you wanted to race hounds, you would have to get animals from three different packs, and even then… *Gah!*" She flung up her hands. "Why am I even trying to explain?"

She started to pace but pulled herself up. No pacing. Facing the three, she fixed them with a still-furious glare. "I'm speaking as the lady of your clan. I am banning the three of you from all hunting—of any sort whatsoever— for the next year. If I hear you've been out anywhere, even outside clan lands, I'll bring charges against you before the clan council. You will not—*ever*—come near the hounds, or Egan's farm and his family, again." She drew herself up and looked down her nose at them. "Do I make myself clear?"

They weren't happy. Lips tight, they stared almost mutinously at her, but then each glanced, very briefly, to her left—at Marcus—then, their eyes widening, they quickly looked back at her and dutifully nodded.

Marcus shifted closer. Very quietly, he murmured, "Don't spoil that performance by saying anything else. Just nod, turn around, and walk inside. I need a moment to speak with these three without you here."

Her gaze still fixed on her idiotic clansmen, she debated for a split second, but she'd asked Marcus to intervene, and he had, very effectively. She didn't want to think of what might have happened if he hadn't been there—she had to trust that he knew what he was doing.

So she kept her glare in place as she nodded curtly, then she turned on her heel and stalked back into the barn.

Marcus remained where he was, his gaze on the three louts, who at least had the sense to remain where they were, sitting in the dirt. They stared back at him, suspicious but wary—leery of tangling with him again.

He waited until he was sure Niniver had retreated out of their sight, then he shifted his weight—bringing the three men alert. He met their gazes, one after the other, then he smiled; the gesture contained no humor whatsoever. "I'm going to say this once, and only once. Consider it your only warning. Lady Carrick asked me to act as her champion in dealing with the problems currently besetting her, and I agreed. The clan elders are aware of this. Although I understand clan rules, I am not a member of your clan. I am, therefore, free to act for the good of your clan's lady without fear or favor, and I will not be influenced by any clan considerations beyond the single goal of ensuring her safety and well-being." He paused for an instant to let that sink in, then went on, "Consequently, if henceforth you do anything at all, however minor, to upset Lady Carrick, I will come for you. She might be forgiving. I will not be. The retribution I will visit on you is guaranteed to be uncomfortable."

He kept his gaze, unwavering, on the three men. "This is how things will be from now on. By all means spread the word to your peers. If any are unwise enough to seek to bother Lady Carrick, it's me they will find themselves answering to, not her." He raked one last, coldly scathing glance over the three. "Now, I suggest you take yourselves off, so that she doesn't have to set eyes on your sorry selves again today."

With that, he turned and followed Niniver into the barn.

Behind him, he heard mutters, but also the sounds of the three men scrambling to their feet. After passing into the barn's shadows, he glanced back. The three were staggering off to where they'd left their horses grazing beyond the arena's fence.

Satisfied, he walked deeper into the cool shadows of the barn and found Niniver talking to Egan. The old man was putting on a good face, but he was clearly shaken.

"You should go into the house and have your luncheon." Niniver had her hand on Egan's shoulder. "Mr. Cynster and I will finish checking the hounds, and we'll close up before we leave."

Marcus caught Egan's gaze and nodded. "We'll see to it."

The old man's nephews had been in the barn earlier, but they had gone back to the farmhouse to help Egan's wife. Both lads were young; Marcus could see in Egan's eyes that the old man was thinking of what might have occurred if Marcus and Niniver hadn't been there, and only he and the boys had been around when the three louts had arrived.

"I wouldn't worry about a repeat of that." Marcus tipped his head toward the doors; they could hear the hoofbeats of the men's horses fading. "I had a little

chat, and I doubt they—or any others—will try anything like that again."

Old Egan drew a deeper breath. He straightened and
nodded back. "Thank you." He turned to Niniver and
managed a smile. He picked up her hand and patted it.
"Don't worry about me, m'lady. I'm a hardy old coot.
But I think I will head in for lunch—the missus will
be wondering where I am."

Niniver smiled encouragingly. Egan shuffled off.
Then Niniver turned and walked back to the pens.

Marcus followed her. "What do we need to do with
the hounds?"

"I bundled them all in here." She halted by the
nearest pen, which proved to be packed with milling
hounds. "We need to sort them out."

She knew each dog by sight; she identified and indicated the correct pen for each hound, and he steered
the animal to its proper home and shut it in.

The occupation should have been calming, but it
wasn't.

He was conscious of a building need to reach out
and touch Niniver, to stroke her cheek, to haul her
into his arms. And the compulsion was only exacerbated by the way the recent incident had affected her.
She'd closed up, drawn in, and put up her shields once
more—but behind them she was tense and somehow
fragile. Something he himself had alluded to earlier—
that physical hurt wasn't the only harm she suffered
courtesy of such incidents—replayed in his mind, and
added to the pressure to react. To do something to tear
down her walls again and reclaim the happy, relaxed,
and comfortable atmosphere of the interlude they'd

shared, up until the three louts had arrived and turned everything on its head.

The longer he thought of it, the less inclined he was to allow those three idiots' actions to set back his own campaign.

By the time he shut the last hound in its proper pen, the need to act was crawling over his skin. Resting his arms on the top of the pen's gate, he stared unseeing at the hounds.

Niniver came up and halted beside him. She looked into the pen, then blew out a breath. "Thank you." Briefly, she waved. "For everything." She paused for a heartbeat, then went on, her tone level and matter-of-fact, "We should head back to the manor. Cook will have luncheon waiting by now, and you must be hungry."

He turned his head and looked at her. He waited until she met his gaze. "I am hungry, but not for any dish your cook might make."

She blinked.

He straightened from the pen gate and stepped toward her.

Eyes widening, she turned and shifted back. Her spine met the post between the pens.

He halted directly before her, then reached out and locked a hand on the top of the gates on either side of her, caging her, but also keeping his hands from her. He knew what he wanted—what he hungered for. He even understood why he wanted it—needed it.

She didn't know what to do with her hands. They fluttered ineffectually between them; as he moved closer still, she tentatively let them fall against his chest. Because of his stance, his hacking jacket was open, the sides spread wide; her palms landed on his shirt—and the sensation of her touch burned through to his skin.

Desire lanced through him, potent and powerful; he fought not to let it show in his face.

She was staring at him, almost open-mouthed—as if she couldn't quite believe this was happening. Her eyes searched his, then she moistened her lips, and whispered, "What's the matter?"

He breathed in, and the floral fragrance that was her wreathed through his brain. His senses salivated.

He wasn't thinking all that coherently. But she seemed to be waiting for an answer, so he put words to the feelings swirling through his head. "Protecting you comes with a price."

A discovery he'd made over the last hour. Accepting the role of her champion—a role that, by all rights, was her husband's to claim—was one thing. Acting in that role was something else again.

Something that had made possessiveness rise within him. With men like him, protectiveness and possessiveness were almost always two sides of the one coin.

He'd always known that, but he'd never met a woman who could evoke those intertwined emotions… other than her. She'd always been the exception, but he hadn't previously had to act physically to defend her…and that, it seemed, had tipped the scales and flipped his coin.

His gaze lowered from her wide blue eyes to the rich fullness of her lips, plump and sheening.

He wasn't, in that moment, sure whether he was or wasn't in debt to the three louts. If they hadn't needed to be brought rather violently to their senses…would he, and she, have come to this?

The question fell away as he lowered his head.

Somewhat to his surprise, she came up on her toes and her lips met his.

Niniver could barely believe her luck. If a kiss was what he wanted in return for his protection, she was perfectly prepared to pay. She was only too willing to grant him a kiss, to indulge in a kiss with him. Her fantasy man who was oh-so-very real—the one she'd fantasized about kissing for…years.

His lips were as firm—as commanding—as she'd imagined they would be. They supped at hers, and she grew hungry for the touch, for the teasing, alluring pressure.

Then the tip of his tongue traced the seam of her lips. She parted them, and his questing tongue slid into her mouth, and sensation flooded her.

His taste—just a hint of coffee and a strong sense of male—tantalized her. Tentatively, she sent her tongue to touch, to stroke—then, emboldened, she sent it questing to tangle with his.

He made an encouraging sound and angled his head; he sank into the exchange, apparently every bit as lost to it as she.

She was definitely sinking. Into pleasure. Their mouths melded and warmth bloomed and spread through her.

Her hands, she realized, had splayed over his chest, then slowly closed, trapping fistfuls of his shirt—the softness of the fine linen was a startling contrast to the hard heat of what lay beneath. Of the resilient muscles her fists rested against.

*Fascinating.*

He shifted closer still, crowding her with his body, with the long limbs, wide chest, and narrow hips she'd lusted after for nearly a decade. And fascinating converted to riveting.

To a panoply of sensations, of pressures and contours that all but overwhelmed her giddy senses.

Then wonder exploded in her mind as she realized what she could feel.

As she realized that, contrary to her long-held belief, Marcus Cynster was very definitely not uninterested in her.

Marcus barely stifled a groan as Niniver's hands clenched even more tightly on his chest. As if to hold him to her. As if she didn't want this engagement to end any more than he did. Then, on a rush of delicate desire—something he'd had no notion existed until she'd kissed him—her lips met his yet more boldly, in almost fiery incitement.

In something that was approaching blatant demand...

He—they—had to stop.

Which meant he had to somehow find their reins and haul very strongly on them.

Now, before matters spiraled completely out of control.

Beyond his control, anyway; in terms of control in this sphere, he wasn't yet sure she had any.

But until the last minutes, he'd had no idea a simple kiss could...*explode* like this. Could swell and grow so quickly, until it was all but brimming with the promise of red-blooded passion. Compelling beyond belief.

Yet the very emotion that had led them to this was

the same emotion that, at that very moment, was insisting he bring the exchange—glorious and thrilling though it was—to an immediate end.

Protecting her meant he couldn't ever harm her, and continuing with this kiss, with its escalating heat and skyrocketing passion, was now the definition of dangerous.

If he didn't end this soon, they would be rolling in the straw in one of the unused pens...no.

The thought was enough to have him hauling on his own reins. With soul-deep reluctance, he eased back from the kiss, from the slick, silken depths of her mouth...from her.

It took effort, but he had expertise enough to ease them both back, until, eventually, their lips parted. She softly exhaled, and he lifted his head.

And looked into her upturned face. Her eyes were still closed, but desire had laid a soft rose tint over her pale cheeks. Then her lashes flickered and rose. Eyes the color of cornflowers under the sun met his. And passion was there, a rose-gold glint in the blue.

It was enough. He told himself that as he pushed away from the gates and forced himself to step back from her. They needed to grow closer before they took things further; he wanted her to want him as he wanted her—with deliberation and need, not just momentary passion.

Her gaze held his—and suddenly, he didn't know what to say. Again, he let the words come as they would. "Thank you. I...needed that."

Her lips curved in a smile more confidently feminine than any he'd seen from her before, but she immediately ducked her head and turned for the barn doors. "We should get back—we'll be very late for luncheon."

She led the way out of the barn, then waited while he swung the doors shut and lowered the heavy bar into place.

They'd left their mounts tethered in the field nearby. He lifted her to her saddle, then swung up to his own and let her lead the way back to the manor.

# Five

For Niniver, the rest of the day passed in a mental whirl. That kiss…changed everything.

It had opened a door she'd thought closed to her forever.

A door to dreams that, a year ago, she'd resigned herself to never exploring.

But that kiss meant…

As she went down the stairs that evening, she finally admitted to herself that she didn't know *exactly* what that kiss portended.

Yet, clearly, Marcus desired her.

As a woman.

She'd longed for a man to desire her for herself—as a woman—for all her adult life. And if she'd had her choice of which man it would be, she would have nominated him.

She was still reeling at the prospect of having her most secret dream come true.

Here. Now. In the flesh.

Hard, hot, wonderfully muscled flesh.

She couldn't marry, but they could have a liaison.

The thought—the possibility—sent her sweeping

into the drawing room with more anticipation than she could remember feeling ever before.

Marcus was already there, elegantly seated in one of the armchairs angled before the fireplace. He rose as she appeared.

His dark blue eyes locked on her face. She felt her heart stutter—actually flutter—as she met that watchful, focused gaze, then she remembered the touch of his lips on hers, remembered the avidness with which he'd kissed her. Confidence welled, and she smiled and went forward to claim the other armchair.

Hildy was seated in her usual position on the sofa. Her shrewd eyes shifted from Niniver to Marcus, but then she looked back at Niniver and calmly said, "Mr. Cynster mentioned there was a ruckus of sorts at the kennels today."

"Yes, but"—she shot him a quick glance—"it was resolved quickly, and the hounds took no harm."

"Actually"—his drawl drew Hildy's attention—"I'm still in awe at the thought of air-scenting hounds." He caught Niniver's gaze. "What first alerted you to the possibility in your pack?"

She smiled and readily recounted the incidents that had first raised her suspicions.

The topic, and his genuine interest in her answers, carried them into the dining room and through most of the meal. She then had the happy thought of turning the subject back on him by asking about his hounds, and any particular characteristic he'd noted in them.

Hildy must have been supremely bored, but surprisingly, Niniver's erstwhile governess made no attempt to steer the conversation into more general spheres.

At the end of the meal, Marcus eschewed the decanters in favor of returning to the drawing room with Niniver and Miss Hildebrand. Earlier, he'd come down before the first gong had sounded, hoping to get a chance to speak with Miss Hildebrand before Niniver joined them. Fate had smiled, and he and Niniver's chaperon had had time to share several observations. Such as that Niniver loved to dance—to waltz, especially—but so rarely had the chance. Also that Miss Hildebrand was competent at the pianoforte and ensured her fingers remained nimble by keeping up with the latest tunes.

Now, his hands clasped behind his back, he prowled along the corridor in the ladies' wake, an eagerness of a sort he hadn't felt in years coursing down his veins.

That kiss—their first and as yet only—had opened his eyes. If *that* was how fast and furiously their flames were going to flare, then if he wanted them to get to know each other better in the usual way *before* they ventured further, he needed to make the most of every opportunity.

After they'd ridden back to the manor and consumed a late luncheon, Niniver had taken herself off to the library, stating she needed to work. Deeming that an excuse to think and to quiet her nerves—to come to grips with that eye-opening kiss—he'd let her go and, instead, had spent his afternoon planning.

Walking into the drawing room alongside Niniver, Miss Hildebrand declared, "Your efforts last evening were quite inspiring." She swept on toward the pianoforte. "I believe it's my turn to entertain you."

Niniver halted in the middle of the room, staring at her chaperon. Marcus drew level with her and touched her arm. When she glanced at him, he tipped his head at the armchairs. "Shall we?"

She allowed him to seat her. As he sank into the armchair opposite, the strains of a sonata filled the room.

Miss Hildebrand was, indeed, an accomplished performer; it was no hardship to sit and let the music flow over them. He kept a covert watchful eye on Niniver and saw the effect of the music take hold; her lashes lowered, and tension eased from her face, eliminating the slight furrow in her brow that, these days, seemed rarely absent.

That afternoon, he'd had another talk with Ferguson in the privacy of the study. As he'd started to suspect, Niniver had, indeed, taken on the full weight of responsibility for the clan's businesses, for the estate and the clan's finances. By all accounts, she'd been succeeding better than either of her brothers before her, but the strain on her was apparent to the clan elders, and something of a concern.

That was another arena in which he fully intended to contribute—to lift some of the burden from her slender shoulders—but, again, his role in that sphere would need to be carefully scripted so that he didn't impinge on her dignity or damage her status within the clan. Every time he saw her head for the library, he wanted to follow and ask to help, but even though he was acutely aware of the need to accelerate his campaign to win her, it was still very much a case of one step at a time.

All he could do was take each step faster.

As he and Miss Hildebrand had arranged, the third piece she played was a waltz. Smoothly rising, he crossed to Niniver. She'd heard the telltale opening chords and had turned to gaze in surprise at Miss Hildebrand. As he neared, she swung to face him.

He bowed. Straightening, he held out his hand. "If you would grant me the honor of this dance, Lady Carrick?"

A laugh bubbled up, delight dispelling her surprise. Eyes alight, she inclined her head and placed her fingers in his. "Thank you, Mr. Cynster." She rose as he drew her to her feet. "I would be delighted."

He smiled and gathered her into his arms. "Indeed, I believe you will be."

She chuckled, and he spun her into the dance, sending them revolving down the large room.

Niniver kept a bright smile on her face, but she immediately feared she would never catch her breath—would never regain the ability to breathe past the sudden constriction squeezing her lungs, not before she fainted dead away. The heat of his hand at her back was one step away from scalding—as if there weren't four layers of silk between his hand and her skin. On top of that, sensation was layered upon sensation—the grasp of his fingers firm and strong about hers, the unyielding steeliness of the arm that held her to him, the effortless way in which he steered her. All that was distracting enough, but the sheer closeness—the occasional brush of his evening coat against the silk of her bodice, the press of his thigh between hers as he drew her closer and swung them through a tight turn, the overwhelming sense of maleness he exuded, and the reality of being captive in his arms…was it any wonder she couldn't breathe?

But then instinct kicked in, and she hauled in a breath, and another, yet—although the constriction eased and she no longer felt the least bit faint but rather on the brink of exhilaration—her senses still whirled dizzyingly, intoxicated by the barrage of delights.

The simple pleasures claimed her, whispered and seduced with the promise that there was no danger here, that all could be enjoyed without restraint, that all would be well and she didn't need to worry while whirling in his arms.

She discovered it was surprisingly easy to set aside her innate caution, for not only was she waltzing, she was waltzing with *him*. With Marcus Cynster, the man of her dreams.

He was so much taller than she that he initially reduced his steps to accommodate her, but she'd never been a lady who placed much store in ladylike restraint—she was accustomed to striding about in her riding boots. He quickly realized she was willing and able to be more adventurous, and he stepped out more freely—and with a smile on her lips and a laugh in her eyes, she matched him stride for swinging stride.

They whirled, faster, more powerfully, swirling through the turns—giddy and delighted, and openly, undeniably, pleased with each other.

They egged each other on, and then he was laughing, too. They swept through one last turn, and he brought them to a swirling halt. Releasing her but retaining his hold on her hand, he executed a flourishing bow. Smiling in appreciation, she sank into a curtsy.

Straightening, he raised her, then released her hand, and they both turned to applaud Hildy.

She beamed and raised her brows at them. "Another?"

Niniver glanced at Marcus. Their gazes met for a

fleeting instant, then they both turned to Hildy and together said, "Yes, please."

Hildy obliged with another sweeping, rollicking waltz, but she followed that with a slower, more sedate piece.

The slower pace gave Niniver a chance to catch her mental breath, to refocus her senses—until then distracted by the energy of the dance—on other things. Like him. Like the intensity of focus in his midnight-blue gaze, echoed in the austerely handsome planes of his face and the assured set of his features, and in the reined-in strength of his arms, in his long, elegantly muscled frame. The grace with which he moved registered anew, a grace that underscored the inherent physical power he so effortlessly controlled, and so effectively wielded.

There was, and always had been, so much about him that spoke to her—to the real woman within. She'd always known that, but now, there, whirling slowly in her own drawing room, the reality—the physicality—of that connection wrapped about her, surrounding and impinging in ways she wasn't sure she fully understood.

Her breathing had grown slower, yet deeper; her senses were alive and so full of him.

In that moment, she felt she could set aside all the rest of the world and be, purely and simply, the woman she would prefer to be—there, waltzing in his arms.

Marcus sensed the change in her—and in him. He didn't know exactly what it was that had altered. Their gazes had remained locked for most of this last, slower dance; the depths of her cornflower-blue eyes had grown...not dreamy so much as richer, deeper. A blossoming, a flowering of some kind, one he instinctively recognized as desirable, as a part of what would come to link them—and something in him had shifted to meet that change, to match it. To connect with it, ultimately to hold and secure it.

Another strand in their deepening relationship.

And with that deepening came a wash of heat—not the rapid rush of desire they'd unexpectedly provoked earlier in the day, but a steady wave of escalating heat, of burgeoning need.

He saw the signs in her—in the luster of her eyes, the inviting softening of her luscious lips—and felt the complementary, answering changes in his own body.

He recognized the symptoms all too well, knew beyond question where this was leading—where the growing, swelling tumult in their veins would ultimately land them—and the temptation to simply let it happen, to let their passions sweep them to the inevitable end, waxed strong, yet...

*Too far, too fast.*

He knew that in his bones. He'd only agreed to stay and help her yesterday, and already they were running headlong into passion—the potential complications were simply too great to ignore.

Yet ignoring the beat already thudding through his veins took all of his resolve—not least because he didn't want to dim or deny it, not in himself and certainly not in her.

Encouraging that nascent link had been his purpose in arranging these waltzes; he'd intended to seduce her—he hadn't expected to be seduced himself, yet he couldn't now back away. And he didn't want to.

But he had to call a halt to this now, while he still could.

The instant Miss Hildebrand's fingers struck the last chord, he drew Niniver to a halt and forced himself to release her. He bowed, and she sank into a curtsy. Straightening, they both turned to applaud Miss Hildebrand.

The ex-governess smiled and inclined her head—then directed a swift glance his way.

Infinitesimally, he shook his head. *No more.*

Miss Hildebrand's smile didn't dim as she closed the pianoforte and rose. "That's enough for this evening. It's time for tea."

Niniver cast him a glance but obligingly crossed to the bellpull. Ferguson must have been on his way; he wheeled the trolley into the room less than a minute later.

Marcus sat and sipped. He could still feel his pulse in his fingertips, and from the covert, somewhat assessing glances Niniver threw his way, she, too, was still affected. That last, slower waltz had been a tactical mistake.

Then again, how could he have known that their passions—those deeper, more powerful compulsions that ultimately would land them naked in some bed—had been swimming so very close to their respective surfaces?

He hadn't expected that; he was still somewhat surprised it was so. Had proved to be so. An unexpectedly fiery kiss was one thing, but this? This was something he knew well enough was going to take effort to control.

Their tea consumed, they rose and left the drawing room.

He stood in the front hall and watched Niniver and

Miss Hildebrand ascend the stairs. From the glance Niniver threw back at him, she wanted to pursue what was growing—so rapidly—between them, but he—they—were definitely not going down that path, not yet.

On reaching the landing, she paused and looked down at him. "Aren't you coming up?"

*To the room next to hers?*

Lips tightening, he shook his head. "I want to check on a few things first. I'll come up later."

Tipping her head, she studied him for a second, then a faint smile curved her lips. "All right." Turning away, she murmured, "Good night."

He echoed the words, watched until she and Miss Hildebrand had passed out of his sight, then he shook aside the lingering threads of temptation, frowned and refocused his thoughts—and lit on just the right exercise to simultaneously cool his ardor while furthering his determination to keep her safe.

\* \* \*

Half an hour later, he leaned on the balustrade of the terrace that ran along the ground floor of the disused wing. Staring into the blackness, he considered how best to address the long-established but now unacceptable practice of leaving the doors to the manor unlocked, even at night.

He appreciated the concept that a clan house should always be open to clan members. He just didn't see why the Carricks couldn't view the doorbell as an acceptable means of gaining entry.

Regardless, the external doors needed to be locked. In that day and age, with decent highways making access to the estate relatively easy, let alone the prospect

Niniver had raised of a clan member, or even some-one else, seeking to seize control of the clan by forc-ing a marriage...

The very thought made him tense, but it was un-deniably true that the clan itself was courting a mas-sive risk in leaving Niniver so exposed, so vulnerable.

*That*, he decided, was the tack he would take in get-ting the practice revised. Altered. Reversed.

Straightening, he scanned the area around the manor, listening rather than trying to penetrate the inky black-ness of the country night. No sound disturbed the still-ness. No would-be serenaders had yet appeared, and it was already approaching midnight.

If he knew anything of country ways, the story of his intervention the previous night, reinforced by his actions at the barn, would already be making the rounds of the clan's farmhouses and cottages, passed from neighbor to neighbor, from father to son around the hearths.

*Good.*

He was conscious of a certain satisfaction that other men would know that he was now there, by Niniver's side, and that, therefore, she was off-limits—that they should stay away from her. He wrinkled his nose. Pos-sessiveness was a trait every man in his family knew well enough to mute and, whenever possible, conceal; he would need to be careful not to let that side of his emotions show.

A soft sound reached his ears. A footstep?

He turned in time to see Niniver round the corner of the house.

As she walked toward him, the moonlight paid hom-age to her pale hair and fair skin and left the svelte curves of her slender body lovingly clothed in shimmering silver, and for a moment, he wondered if his over-lustful mind had conjured the vision. But then, beneath the silver-gilt of the moonlight, he recognized the blue of the gown she'd worn that evening, the bracelet and necklace of aquamarines gracing her wrist and throat.

She was real; the moonlight simply made her appear even more ethereal, even more like some moon goddess come to earth to tempt mere mortals.

To tempt him, at least.

He felt the undeniable tug as she halted before him.

Head tilting, she studied him. "I wondered where you'd got to."

Clearly, she'd made no attempt to change and prepare for bed. He pushed that observation—and the obvious conclusion—to the back of his mind. "I've been checking the security of the house. You—the clan—need to change the tradition of leaving the manor's doors unlocked at night. In this day and age, it's too risky."

She wrinkled her nose and, like him, turned to look out at the darkness. "I feel the same, which should be no surprise, but it's been a clan tradition for so long..." She gestured vaguely.

"We don't have the same tradition in the Vale—but then, that's always been run by a lady." His mother was the current Lady of the Vale. "Even if the custom had been suggested, I can't imagine any consort would have stood for it."

"Apparently," she said, "the custom dates from an incident long ago—and not even from around here. Somewhere in the Highlands, a crofter family came to seek shelter at their clan's keep during a winter storm, but the keep's doors were barred and they couldn't raise anyone inside. The family froze to death on the steps of their clan's house. Out of that came the decree that clan doors should never be barred."

Dryly, he said, "That was before doorbells were invented."

She gave a little smile. "True." After a moment, she sighed and raised her head. "I'll speak with Ferguson—"

"No. Let me." When she glanced at him, he went on, "It's something I can do, and you have more pressing concerns—I'll speak with Ferguson, and we'll sort it out." He clamped his lips shut on a plea to be allowed to lift that burden, at least, from her shoulders. She'd either agree, or she wouldn't.

After a moment, she inclined her head. "All right. I'll leave that to you."

The surge of triumph he felt was ludicrous—entirely out of proportion to the deed. Still…

He looked out at the surrounding fields, then he looked at her. He waited until she turned and met his gaze; he briefly searched her eyes, then—compelled by the need to know—asked, "What brought you out here?"

There was no point trying to avoid the issue; aside from all else, he was coming to realize that she—and her stubbornness—wouldn't allow it.

She considered him for a moment, then said, "I realized I hadn't made any…payment for your protection last night, with Jem Hills."

He stared at her. *Payment?* Then he realized what she meant.

*Protecting you comes with a price.* His words—and oh, how tempting it was to allow her to continue to believe the interpretation she'd placed on them, but…lies never worked well, and behind everything else, this was Fate he was dealing with. The Lady alone knew what might happen if he didn't correct her misapprehension. Yet how to explain?

He hauled in a breath, held it for an instant, then said, "That wasn't what I meant. I didn't mean that *you* had to pay anything—give anything. Not at all."

She frowned at him; he could see in her eyes that she was replaying that moment in the barn. "If you didn't mean that…what did you mean?"

He pressed his lips together, closed his eyes for a second, then opened them and forced his lips to form the words "It's *me* who has to pay the piper, so to speak."

Her frown just grew blacker. "I don't see why. Or, indeed, how."

He didn't want to discuss the how. "It's an outcome—a result—of being moved to act to protect you. It's not how I feel before or during, but what the consequences are…" He fought down the urge to run a hand through his hair. "It's complicated."

Niniver eyed his closed expression. The tone of those last two words was unquestionably meant to put an end to the discussion, but she hadn't come down to the terrace just to be turned away. So she tried to see things from his male point of view. Tried to imagine what it might feel like were she standing in his shoes. "So… this price you have to pay is like a debt—a demand—that comes into being after you act to protect me—as you did with Jem last night, and even more after dealing with those three at the barn." Her gaze on his face, she widened her eyes. "Is that correct?"

His eyes had darkened. The tension in his features, that invested his whole frame, suggested he would rather she pull his teeth. But eventually, he nodded. "Close enough."

His voice had deepened and grown rougher; she wondered if he knew.

"And this price—this demand." She stepped closer, and he turned, putting his back to the balustrade as he shifted to face her. She kept her gaze locked on his. "Judging from what happened in the barn, then payment—satisfying that demand—is something that flows from…for instance, a kiss."

Instantly, she knew, from the lines of his face, from the tightness about his lips, that he wasn't going to respond to that—not yea or nay, not in any way. That didn't matter; his silence was all the confirmation she needed. And the thought that she, little Niniver Carrick, could affect him, of all men, to the extent of *needing* to kiss her to appease his own driven desires…such *power*. So tempting, so alluring.

She smiled softly, not as a challenge, then looked down. "So I was correct in saying that you are still owed…recompense for dealing with Jem." She edged closer still, placing her toes between his. "And, of course"—now at close quarters, she looked up and met his dark gaze—"there's convincing Ferguson about locking the doors."

"I haven't done anything about that yet."

"True. But"—she grasped his lapels and, using her grip to anchor her, leaned into him, tipping up her face and bringing her lips to within an inch of his—

"is there any reason we—you and I—can't make a down payment?"

The question surprised a laugh from him, but then he sobered. He raised his hands and closed them about hers, pressing them to his chest. He studied her face for a moment, then beneath their hands, his chest rose.

Quietly, he asked, "Do you have any idea what you're doing?"

"No. But I am quite certain that I want to find out." Stretching up, she closed the last inch, pressed her lips to his, and kissed him.

A heartbeat passed, then he parted his lips and kissed her back—took control of the kiss and supped at her lips, then dove deeper.

His lips were commanding, demanding, and she was only too ready to give. To surrender and tempt him to go further. To take more.

To demonstrate just how much he desired her—her, the woman she was, the woman she could be.

The woman she sensed she had the potential to be, at least when within his arms.

His lips and tongue plundered, and she rejoiced, following eagerly wherever he led. The heat of the exchange, the prelude to intimacy, beckoned and lured.

Then he muttered something unintelligible, and the warmth of his hands around hers vanished, then his arms closed around her. He straightened from the balustrade and drew her against him. Angling his head, he captured her senses in a scalding kiss, then he whirled her into the flames.

And although neither of them moved, she was whirling again, her senses spinning giddily, greedily, as they revolved through a landscape of heat and desire, of passion and yearning.

He laid it all out before her—showed her the path, the way to all she wanted—and she saw, and knew, and clung.

Then she got her mental feet under her, steadied, and observed—then she released his lapels, pushed her hands up and over his shoulders, over the strength of muscle and bone, slid her palms about his neck, and held him to her. Then she kissed him back with all the eagerness and enthusiasm burgeoning inside her.

He desired her. The hard ridge of his erection pressing against her belly assured her that was so.

And she desired him—she had forever, and now, at last, she was free to show him.

To let him know how much. How deeply she craved him and all he could show her. All she could experience with him—with him and no other.

He was her only chance to be who she could be—to learn who that woman truly was, the reality underpinning her wild fantasies.

Easing one hand from his nape, she touched his lean cheek, stroked her fingertips down in wordless entreaty, then redoubled the invitation in her kiss.

He shuddered as if her onslaught had breached his outer walls. Then one of his hands slid from her back to her side; he briefly gripped her waist, then his hand swept up, up, until his palm cradled her silk-clad breast.

She moaned softly, the sound trapped between their lips. Barely able to believe the wanton impulses coursing through her, she pressed closer yet, sinking against him, flagrantly encouraging him to claim.

He did, and she lost all ability to breathe. She certainly couldn't think, not with the sensations cascading through her—the heat of his palm over her breast, the strength in his long fingers as he gently kneaded, then the sharpening pleasure as those wicked fingers circled her nipple, then captured it and gently squeezed...

She nearly broke from the kiss as pleasure lanced through her. In desperation, she speared the fingers of both hands into his thick hair. Startled at the feel of the silky locks, she rumpled them, then clutched again, holding tight as his fingers squeezed again, and she surrendered to rapturous delight.

Marcus couldn't think. Not that he needed to; he'd been along this road before. But never before had he suffered from such an inability to control...anything. She had her own agenda—clearly. But hers seemed to subvert his. She seemed able to do what no other woman ever had and completely override all his inner safeguards—all the well-honed machinations that, with any other woman, left him in control.

Caressing her breasts should have reduced a novice like her to passionate surrender—and it had. He hadn't expected the minor advance of claiming her breast, just by touch through multiple layers of silk, to so rock *him*. To so effortlessly release the clawing, hungry demon of desire that lived within him.

She and that raw desire combined to create a ravening force.

Mere expertise had no power to stand against it—against the open ardor she so blatantly laid before him and his own driving need.

And that need—his deepest wanting—wasn't just hungry for her. It was hungry for this—for her and him together, reaching and searching, exploring their passions without restraint on either part. Without the slightest thought for safety.

Ah, gods—he *needed* her. But that couldn't be. Not yet. Not tonight.

Even as she and his desire combined to drag him deeper into the rising flames of the passion they'd mutually created, mutually stoked—as their kiss grew incendiary and he realized his other hand had slid down to cup her bottom and he was holding her, molding her, to his rigid length—in desperation he searched for something, for some anchor...and realized it had been there all along.

She was it. To him, she was a nymph of irresistible temptation, but she was also the tender, caring, devoted woman he had sworn to protect.

And protectiveness always—*always*—trumped possessiveness.

The core of him steadied. Even with the tide of desire swelling and rising around them both, clarity returned, and he knew what to do.

Gradually, bit by bit, notch by notch, he drew them back to solid earth. Not too fast, not abruptly. Not in a way that left either of them too tight, too tense, too unappeased.

They still kissed, their lips still melded; they touched, but the force that had driven them was subsiding with every not-quite-steady breath.

The vortex of their combined desires slowed, its power waning...for now.

She didn't know enough to counter him in that; she followed where he led, and by the time she realized he'd changed direction, they were too far along the path to turn back. Their flames had cooled to embers.

Smoldering, perhaps, but without his active participation, she couldn't fan them into a blaze again.

Not tonight.

When he finally raised his head and their lips parted, he looked into her face—watched as her lashes fluttered, then her lids slowly rose, revealing eyes lit by starlight and the fading remnants of their passion.

She looked at him—and there was enough question in her eyes to prompt him to offer in exculpation, "We can't go further yet."

She tipped her head slightly, those wonderful eyes steady on his.

"Not yet. Not tonight."

That was what she'd wanted to hear. Her lips curved in a small smile of feminine confidence—one so vulnerable and real it made his breath catch.

He set her on her feet and drew his hands from her.

She dipped her head and murmured, "All right."

The fine shawl she'd worn draped over her shoulders had slid to her elbows. She resettled it, then looked at him. "Are you coming upstairs now?"

The movement felt wooden, but he shook his head. "No. There's something I want to check before I do." He jerked his chin toward the front of the house and the door through which he assumed she'd come. "You go up. And…just for my peace of mind, will you lock your bedroom door—just for tonight, until I speak with Ferguson?"

Her brows faintly rose, but then she nodded. "Very well." She hesitated for two heartbeats, then murmured, "Good night."

He watched her walk away. He stayed where he was until she'd passed out of his sight.

Then he shook his head, as if he could thus clear

away the clouds of fascination that still lingered. Gads—how could he have known a siren lived inside her?

And now he'd lured her out? Her rising sexual confidence didn't bode well for his step-by-step approach.

Still, she'd gone inside, and hopefully by now she'd be well on her way up the stairs to her bed. In her room, the door to which she would dutifully lock.

So that even if he changed his mind—even if his baser self somehow overcame his wiser self—he wouldn't be able to follow her. She would be safe, even from him.

He thought about that for a moment more, then he swore beneath his breath and set off to circle the house. Clan tradition be damned, he was locking every door.

\* \* \*

Niniver was still awake, lying in her bed, when Marcus returned to his room. She heard his footsteps approaching along the corridor, then the door to his room opened and shut. She listened to the sounds of him moving across the floor. Imagined him undressing, then the bed creaked, and she heard no more.

*Not yet*, he'd said. She could live with not yet.

But not for much longer.

If they were to have a liaison—and after today, she was determined they would—then it needed to commence soon. How long he would remain at Carrick Manor was uncertain; he'd intimated he would stay until her clansmen accepted that she wouldn't be marrying any of them, and she trusted he would—but how long would that be?

However long he stayed, that was all the time they would have. She knew herself well enough to feel fairly certain that, once he returned to Bidealeigh, she wouldn't have the courage—the self-confidence—to get on Oswald and ride over there…for a few hours, or a night.

She was the Lady of Clan Carrick. Ladies of clans did not openly have affairs, and her riding to Bidealeigh—or him riding to the manor—would quickly become common knowledge.

While he remained at Carrick Manor, they could indulge, and only her most trusted staff would know—and they would keep silent.

She hadn't imagined the prospect of having a liaison with him would ever arise—that he would prove to be as attracted to her as she was to him. But he was; she wasn't such a naive innocent that she didn't comprehend just what he'd wanted to do with her—the evidence had been impossible to mistake.

And his "not yet" meant he was willing, but perhaps he'd felt as blindsided by the strength of their passions as she and had wanted to take matters more slowly.

She could understand that, but now that the chance to experience all she otherwise never would—that because of her position as lady of the clan she would otherwise have to forego forever—had arisen, she was going to seize it with both hands.

She was determined to learn everything she could about the woman she could be when she was in his arms.

# Six

The next morning, Niniver joined Marcus at the breakfast table. She swept into the room, smiling enthusiastically. "Good morning."

He was eating, and inclined his head in response.

Feeling unprecedentedly bright and energized, she went to the sideboard and helped herself to her usual two slices of toast.

Courtesy of yesterday and those moments in the barn, in the drawing room, and on the terrace, today held infinite promise—at least for her.

And, she hoped, for him. She didn't actually know how one went about establishing a liaison, but she felt confident that, between them, they would work it out.

He rose as she approached the table and drew out the chair beside his. Still smiling, she rounded the table and sat.

She waited until he resumed his seat, then sent an inquiring look his way. "I have to go to Ayr on business. Normally, Sean would go with me, but I wondered if you might prefer to act as my escort."

His dark eyes captured hers; he held her gaze for a split second, then simply said, "Yes."

Stifling a grin, she reached for the marmalade. "Excellent. We'll need to leave after breakfast."

His gaze once more on his plate—on the sausages, eggs, and kedgeree piled on it—he grunted.

Several moments passed while she slathered, crunched, and poured and sipped tea, and he made inroads into his meal. Then he said, "Incidentally, before I forget, I spoke with Ferguson this morning. Regardless of tradition, he agrees with me—with us—about the sense in locking the external doors. He's hunting up the last of the keys. He says he'll ensure that the house is locked up every night, and he's going to give Sean, Mitch, and Fred keys to the side door, in case, for some reason, they need to come in."

She nodded. "Good. I have to admit that I'll sleep easier knowing that no one unexpected can simply walk in."

Marcus was quite sure he would sleep easier, too. Just the thought…but that, thank The Lady, was no longer an issue. Instead, he turned his mind to the prospects and likely difficulties of spending a day with Niniver off the estate.

When she'd finished her toast and was sipping a second cup of tea, he pushed away his empty plate and asked, "Do you plan on taking a carriage? Or will we ride?"

Teacup cradled in her hands, she widened her eyes, transparently debating the pros and cons.

She was staring past him; he seized the moment to let his gaze rest on her face, on her fine features—to drink in all he could see.

From the instant she'd accepted the chair he'd held for her, he'd realized she'd lost much, if not all, of her earlier sensual skittishness. Apparently, the events of the previous day had burned that away, and while she was definitely still aware of him, if anything more aware than before, that awareness seemed to be encouraging her rather than inhibiting her.

Which was precisely what he wanted, yet managing their reins with a Niniver who was likely to take the bit between her teeth and run wasn't destined to be a simple or straightforward task. Especially as he'd yet to define the right ways to deal with her—to steer, guide, and protect her without resorting to edicts that dictated or dominated.

Indeed, how to deal with Niniver was becoming his primary concern.

She was still debating; he bit his tongue against the urge to suggest they ride. Spending several hours in a closed carriage alone with her was, in his experienced view, simply asking for trouble. He knew exactly what could be achieved in a closed carriage bowling sedately along a quiet highway.

Setting down her cup, she declared, "There's nothing of any weight we need to bring back, and I prefer to ride." She looked at him. "Unless you think we should take the carriage."

"No." Straightening, he set his napkin beside his plate. "I prefer to ride, too." He pushed back his chair and rose. "I'll tell Sean to saddle the horses. How much longer will you be?"

She smiled up at him. "I just need to change into my riding habit. I'll meet you in the stable yard."

He dipped his head and retreated, the better to ensure she didn't change her mind.

\* \* \*

They left in good time and reached Ayr by midmorning. The busy town on the coast to the northwest was, if not the closest as the crow flew, the easiest of any size to reach; they'd just followed the highway at the end of the drive until they'd ridden into the town.

The clock in the Wallace Tower stood at half past eleven when Marcus held the door of the Carrick family solicitor's office open for Niniver to leave. A meeting with the solicitor had been the first and most important item on her list. Although Marcus hadn't pressed to accompany her into the solicitor's inner sanctum but instead had kicked his heels in the outer office, from the lack of any frown in Niniver's eyes, much less on her face, and the solicitor's jovial air when he'd bowed her out, Marcus judged the meeting to have gone well.

It certainly didn't appear to have dampened Niniver's enthusiasm for a host of other errands, most of which involved shopping for this and that—not for her, but for the household or the clan.

"Where next?" He halted beside her. She'd stopped on the pavement to consult a list she'd pulled from her pocket.

"The apothecary's." Looking up from the list, she glanced across the busy street. "Ferguson wanted me to get more of that new powder for treating burns."

Marcus seized the opportunity to link her arm with his, then he escorted her across the crowded thoroughfare and along the pavement on the opposite side. The apothecary's lay toward the end of the street, close by the corner with Newmarket.

They went in. He stood back while she spoke with the apothecary. Both he and she were known to most of the town's shopkeepers and business-owners, so if he stood beside her, the shopkeepers instinctively addressed themselves to him. Even in the solicitor's office, although the receptionist had never set eyes on him before and Niniver had led the way in, the receptionist's gaze had traveled over Niniver and landed on him, and the receptionist had asked who he wished to see.

For much of his life, he'd been vaguely aware of the difficulties ladies like his mother and his sister occasionally faced, but in their cases, both possessed an innate imperious demeanor that, despite their gender, tended to alert people to their station and power.

Niniver, however, looked so delicate and fragile, on first glance people tended to dismiss her as unimportant—as the sort of person who could be ignored or overlooked.

The apothecary hadn't made that mistake; once people knew her, knew who she was and had interacted with her, they adjusted their view. Even so, if he stood beside her, he would…diminish her. People would almost certainly start to overlook her again.

The thought…offended him on some level he was only just beginning to comprehend—another facet of possessive jealousy.

She finished with the apothecary, who promised to make up the powder and have it ready for Sean to collect later in the week. As they stepped out onto the pavement, Marcus retook her arm. With her anchored beside him, at her direction they strolled down one of the lanes that led to the banks of the Ayr River. The fishmonger the Carrick cook, Gwen, favored operated out of one of the quayside shops not far from the Auld Brig o' Doon.

While they walked in public, Marcus kept Niniver by his side, where he could protect her from any potential threat. But after ushering her through the door into the fishmonger's shop, he shifted to stand behind her; although the fishmonger recognized them both and, after greeting Niniver, glanced at him, with his gaze he was able to direct the man's attention back to Niniver.

When the fishmonger went to find his order book, she glanced back at him, but she didn't make any comment. After she left the manor's order and they quit the shop, he looped her arm in his again and, feeling decidedly smug, allowed her to direct their steps back to High Street and on to the haberdashers.

They progressed down High Street, stopping at this store, that shop. Strolling down the pavements with her on his arm, he felt increasingly domesticated. And when his new tack of standing directly behind her continued to bring about the desired results, he felt ridiculously pleased.

One small detail he'd figured out; one small hurdle overcome.

When they neared the Wallace Tower again, he glanced up at the clock. "It's half past twelve." Looking down, he caught Niniver's eye. "Are you ready for luncheon yet? I asked the inn to hold a table for us."

The Tam O' Shanter Inn was the best in town, and as it stood at the end of High Street closest to where the road from Carsphairn entered the town, it was the inn Marcus and his family patronized; aside from all else, the inn's stable was up to scratch and deemed suitable for housing Cynster horses.

Niniver surveyed her list. "Only two more things to get, but we can get them after lunch."

"Excellent."

They continued strolling; the inn lay a little way ahead on the same side of the street. As always, the town center was busy and bustling; as well as the river traffic, there was a major seaport at the river mouth, and, consequently, a significant amount of commerce and trading went on within the town.

Marcus was studying the lines of what he suspected was the latest style of phaeton as its driver made his way up the street when Niniver slowed. He glanced around. They'd drawn level with the window of a jeweler's shop.

Obligingly halting, he followed her gaze to see what had drawn her attention; he'd already noticed she had a penchant for unusual pieces, although nothing she'd yet worn, even to the balls at which he'd seen her in the past, could be classed as significant.

It wasn't hard to guess what she had focused on; a suite comprised of a delicate necklace, earrings, and a ring lay displayed on black velvet. The settings, although fine, were relatively plain, the stones all circular yet expertly cut. But it was the color of the stones that caught the eye. At first he thought they must be aquamarines, but then he saw a small sign stating that the set was composed of cornflower-blue sapphires mined in faraway Ceylon.

The stones were the color of Niniver's eyes.

A small sigh escaped her, then she turned from the window. "Pretty." She glanced at him, smiled, and stepped out, drawing him along. "Come on—I do hope they kept us that table."

He walked beside her past two more shops, then they crossed the mouth of the alley that led to the stable behind the inn. As they reached the inn's door, he released Niniver's arm and grasped the knob. "Why don't you go in and tell Mac we're here." Mac was the innkeeper. "I'm just going to check on the horses—Ned was playing up earlier. I want to make sure he settled."

She nodded. "All right. I'll take possession of our table."

He smiled encouragingly and, with a bow, swept her inside. Then he closed the door, checked through the glass panes to make sure she was on her way deeper into the inn, then he turned and strode back to the jeweler's shop.

* * *

Mac greeted Niniver with a wide smile and, with his usual genial air, conducted her to the table he'd reserved for her and Marcus—a more private one at the rear of the inn's dining parlor, beside a window that looked onto a small garden behind the inn.

After settling at the table, Niniver drew off her riding gloves and set them in her lap. The action focused her attention on her hands.

She studied her ringless fingers. That cornflower-blue sapphire would have looked lovely on her hand, but she could imagine what price the jeweler would be asking—far more than she could afford. Not while she was still struggling to repair the damage her brothers had wrought on both the family's and the clan's finances.

"Lady Carrick—well-met!"

She looked up to see a dark-haired gentleman, handsome in a coarse, windblown sort of way, standing beside the table. His attire was a touch too negligent for her taste, and while his features were regular enough, any claim to male beauty was marred by the lines dissipation had etched about his nose and mouth. The latter gave her the clue she needed as to his identity. She conjured a weak smile. "Mr. McDougal." She knew next to nothing about Ramsey McDougal other than that he'd been a close crony of Nigel and Nolan's over the last few years; to her mind that made McDougal no friend of hers. But she had to be polite. "I take it I see you well?"

"Yes, indeed. In the very best of health." Without any by-your-leave, McDougal pulled up a chair and sat at the table to her right. "I'm delighted to have the chance to inquire how you go on. Nolan's unhappy demise, let alone all it revealed, must have quite shaken you."

When McDougal looked at her as if expecting an answer, she said, "It was nearly a year ago—I've put it behind me."

"So I see." McDougal beamed. "No more mourning, which is a happy day for us all. It's good to see you out and about, my dear. Tell me—can we expect to see you at the Hunt Ball?"

"Possibly." She had no intention of attending any ball, not with so many men showing interest in claiming her hand—and the clan.

McDougal's gaze seemed to sharpen, although his expression remained genial. "I take it your emergence from mourning is a recent thing. Do you intend moving about in society—well, what passes for society in these parts?"

This interlude was a perfect illustration of why she

eschewed society, local or otherwise. "Sadly, at the moment, I have a great deal on my plate, what with managing the clan's affairs."

"Ah—yes." McDougal nodded. "I heard about that. Elected as lady of your clan! Quite an honor, indeed."

"Indeed." What else could she say? She clasped her hands on the table and fixed her gaze on them.

Instead of taking the hint, McDougal leaned closer and lowered his voice to a conspiratorial rumble. "But if I may be so bold, my dear, such responsibility must be a heavy and onerous weight for such slender shoulders as yours to bear."

She only just managed to rein in her temper. Raising her head, she met McDougal's hazel gaze. "I don't find it so. Not at all."

He searched her eyes—then a shadow fell over the table.

She looked up, and relief washed through her. She glanced at McDougal. "Allow me to present Mr. Marcus Cynster."

"We've met." McDougal nodded rather curtly to Marcus. "Cynster."

Marcus's dark gaze didn't leave the other man's face as he inclined his head fractionally. "McDougal."

Raising his head, Marcus transferred his gaze to Niniver. The relief in her eyes as she looked at him was blatant—and went a considerable way toward easing the intense possessiveness that had surged through him when he'd walked into the parlor and seen Ramsey McDougal far too close to her.

McDougal was the definition of a cad.

He ignored McDougal. His gaze locked with Niniver's, Marcus smiled—easily, reassuringly—and reached for the chair opposite her. "Have you ordered yet?"

"No. I was waiting for you to come in."

He sat, then caught Mac's watchful eye and beckoned. The innkeeper immediately picked up his slate and came over.

Mac rattled off his dishes of the day. While Niniver and Marcus gave their orders, McDougal frowned and fidgeted.

When Mac retreated to fetch their food, Marcus turned to McDougal and arched a brow. "Was there something you wanted, McDougal?"

McDougal stared at him then, rather more pointedly, looked at Niniver. McDougal opened his mouth—

"Mr. Cynster," Niniver stated, "is assisting me in managing matters within the clan. I fear you must excuse us, sir—we have several matters of moment to the clan that we need to discuss."

Marcus felt like applauding but refrained. He couldn't have got rid of the man faster himself. Not without planting a fist in his face, which wouldn't have endeared him to Mac.

McDougal's gaze swung back to Marcus's face. "I... see." After a second's consideration, he pushed back his chair. "In that case, I'll leave you to your deliberations." McDougal rose and held out his hand. Clearly reluctantly, Niniver surrendered hers, and he bowed over her fingers. "Lady Carrick. Please know that, should you require any help at all, I will be only too happy to render whatever poor assistance it's in my power to give." He glanced at Marcus. "In memory of your brothers, as it were."

Finally releasing Niniver's hand, McDougal inclined his head to Marcus. "Cynster."

"McDougal." Marcus nodded vaguely and reached for the pint of foaming ale Mac had just set on the table.

Niniver picked up the glass of perry Mac had brought for her and sipped. Marcus noted that she didn't look up until the sound of the outer door shutting behind McDougal reached them.

Then she glanced up, confirmed he was gone, and directed a frown after him. "I don't like that man."

"You have excellent instincts." He paused, then asked, "How do you come to know McDougal?" As far as he knew, she'd been avoiding local society for years, and McDougal had only appeared on the scene three or four years ago.

"He was one of Nigel and Nolan's set. Which, of course, does not predispose me to look upon him kindly, although I don't think he quite understands that."

Clearly, he didn't need to warn her about McDougal; she'd already accurately taken the man's measure.

He hoped McDougal had taken his.

Mac arrived with two plates, one of venison pie for him, the other containing a helping of the inn's famous shepherd's pie for Niniver. They settled to eat. After several minutes of comfortable silence, he asked, "So what else do we need to do before we head back?"

\* \* \*

"We don't have to start back yet." Marcus halted on the pavement outside the hardware store the clan patronized. They'd just completed the last of the tasks on Niniver's list, placing an order for a new pump head.

Drawing out his fob watch, he checked the time. "It's only just after two."

Although the table Mac had given them had been more private than others, the inn parlor had still been a public place; while they'd filled their time with comments about this and that, there'd been little scope for more personal interaction. The feelings evoked by finding McDougal, of all men, hovering over Niniver still lingered just beneath Marcus's skin. All things considered, he was keen to make the most of the opportunity to further his pursuit of her, especially in surroundings that would hamper any overly enthusiastic foray of hers.

Indeed, she seemed equally eager to seize the moment. Tucking back the wisps of pale blond hair the breeze had teased loose from her bun, she looked to the west. "Let's walk past the kirk and the bridge, and then on along Harbour Street to the Esplanade. It's always pleasant to walk along there when the weather is fine and the sun's shining."

"Which it is today, so let's make the most of it." He offered his arm and she took it, linking their arms and allowing him to draw her close.

With her skirts brushing his boots and his senses highly aware of her slender form pacing so close beside him, they walked around the old kirk with its tall spire, past the Brig o' Doon, and out along Harbour Street where the breeze grew more brisk and carried the scent of the sea.

"I have to admit," Niniver said, "that I was very glad to have you there to help send Mr. McDougal on his way. If I'd come with Sean, I would most likely have been eating alone, and I would never have got rid of McDougal—he's a persistent sort."

"Trust me," Marcus dryly replied, "the pleasure was all mine." A second later, he tipped his head her way. "I admit I'm rather enjoying being your champion and sending importuning suitors packing." A smile on his lips, he met her eyes. "I believe the role becomes me."

She chuckled and looked ahead. "Oh, it does. It makes use of that dark Cynster menace you project so effortlessly." Three paces on, she said, "Tell me—are all your... Are they cousins? Those of your age who came for Thomas and Lucilla's wedding?"

"Cousins of sorts—some are first cousins, others second cousins, and some are close connections."

"Ah. Well, are all your cousins like you?" Swinging to look into his face, she widened her eyes. "I know they all look rather like you, but are they equally menacing?"

He looked at her, his expression implying that the answer was obvious. "They're Cynsters. We all have a very good line in menace." He paused, then added, "Even the females."

She laughed.

He grinned and decided he loved the sound of her laughter...as he registered the thought, he realized he'd never heard her laugh before he'd gone to stay at Carrick Manor. Then again, over recent years, she hadn't had much to laugh about.

He vowed to change that.

But first, he needed to change her mind about marriage. He had to convince her that marrying *him* would not carry any of the risks she so clearly—and accurately—foresaw. Any other man, and she almost certainly would find it difficult to believably hold on to her position as lady of the clan, and from all he'd gleaned from Sean, Ferguson, and Edgar, once she was sidelined, it was very likely the clan would, indeed, fracture and fall apart.

Even though he didn't belong to a clan in the same sense, he was a Cynster—he understood what family meant, and he understood what clan meant to her. She also seemed to have a deep-seated loyalty to her father's memory and his legacy; she'd mentioned that several times.

He had to find a way to make her see him simultaneously as an effective champion and as no threat. As a man who was willing to support her position, rather than undermine it.

That she viewed him as menacing…helped in one respect, but possibly not in the other.

They reached the Esplanade and started pacing southward along the paved walk above the beach. The wide sweep of Ayr Bay stretched to the horizon; today the water was pewter-blue, flecked with just the occasional white crest thrown up by the playful breeze.

"Are your brothers and younger sister at home—at Casphairn Manor—at present?"

Niniver's question drew his gaze to her face. Dozens of fine tendrils of silver-gold hair danced about it, a living frame, and the touch of the breeze had brought color to her normally pale cheeks.

"Annabelle has already gone south to stay with our ducal relatives for the Season. She and Louisa—Lady Louisa Cynster, the duke's daughter—are two of a group of four Cynster girls who…for want of a more accurate term, hunt together." He felt his lips twist in cynical but amused appreciation, then met Niniver's intrigued gaze. "I have heard that a certain stratum of the marriageable gentlemen of the ton go in fear for their bachelor state."

She searched his eyes, and correctly concluded he wasn't joking. "They sound quite…fearsome—your female relatives."

He saw the opening and seized it. "In my family, the women tend to be as powerful—in all the ways that truly matter—as the men. I can't think of a single lady in the family who is a meek and mild sort, and although our inclinations might be otherwise, we males have learned to live with that." He kept his expression open and sincere. "We've learned to accommodate ladies who insist on handling their own reins."

She looked ahead. A few paces on, she observed, "That's not the norm."

"For others, perhaps. But for us, it is." A genuinely rueful laugh escaped him. "We've learned that we really don't have a choice—it's adapt, or live a very lonely life." Truer words he'd never said.

"Hmm." After a moment, she returned to her earlier question. "What of your brothers?"

"As far as I know, Calvin and Carter are at home. I imagine they're hiding, hoping to avoid the first rush of the Season in town. I suspect they'll both go down eventually, to meet with their friends, or perhaps they might head to Edinburgh."

She glanced at him. "Now you live at Bidealeigh, do you miss having them—your brothers and sisters—about?"

He had to think before he could answer. "Not so much them, specifically—they'll always be there, close enough, dropping by, writing letters, and so on. As family, we won't ever lose touch. But I do miss having others about." He'd only just realized how much—how lonely he'd been at Bidealeigh, all on his own, and how much more comfortable—more in his natural element—he felt at Carrick Manor. "I'm used to a large household, with people to interact with. With things—events, issues, problems—occurring most of the time."

"You're used to being busy." She nodded decisively. "I've realized I far prefer to be busy, as I am now, rather than sit helplessly on the periphery, as I used to."

Several paces on, she asked, "Why did you call your estate Bidealeigh? I always wondered. That wasn't the name old man Hennessy used, was it?"

"No, but Bidealeigh was an older name for the property, from before Hennessy's time. The name could be taken to mean 'a place to wait,' and for various reasons, that seemed appropriate."

They'd reached the end of the Esplanade, and in unvoiced accord, they turned to head back to the inn by cutting through the town. After crossing the road and regaining the pavement on the other side, Marcus went on, "When Lucilla and Thomas married, it was simply time for me to move out. It wasn't that Thomas and I clashed, but rather that he needed not to have me there, distracting and confusing everyone, while he was learning to take on the duties my father performs, but which I, in the past, have carried. Me remaining in the Vale would have simply added an extra layer of difficulty—and irritation—for both Thomas and me."

She asked about the sheep he was breeding and his other activities at Bidealeigh. All were questions he could easily answer; while one part of his mind was thus engaged, he grasped the chance to rapidly reassess where exactly he and she stood. What he'd learned from the day. What he'd yet to accomplish.

While he'd originally assumed his best way forward would be to see off her suitors, and then subsequently to focus on winning her, the events of yesterday had made that simple plan untenable. First, protecting her had already escalated his possessiveness to a degree that it was no longer a simple matter reining in the impulses that possessiveness provoked. Compounding that, she'd decided to pursue a passionate connection with him. Exactly what she had in mind—how far she intended such a connection to go—he wasn't yet sure, but, in the circumstances, he couldn't rely on his own control holding, not if she challenged it. And he didn't think he could count on her drawing back.

So managing their evolving relationship fell to him. And it seemed obvious that he would be wise to convince her that she would be safe marrying him *before* their escalating passions reached the point of becoming irresistible and sweeping them away.

The notion of not being in control, of being swept away by passion, was alien to him, yet with her...he simply wasn't confident his control would hold. Not against her, not if she set her mind to overcoming it.

That was a sobering realization. He needed to convince her that marrying him would pose no risk to her position as clan leader, or to her life as she wished to live it. That he wanted to ally himself with her, to become a part of her life, not pull her into his.

As he'd intimated, while living at Bidealeigh, he'd

been waiting—waiting for the right place, his true role, to manifest. As it had, with her.

He didn't need to convince himself of that; he knew in his heart it was so.

They'd returned to the busier thoroughfares. Drawing her closer, he steered her protectively through the crowds. He thought back to what he knew of the events leading to his parents' marriage—not a lot—and what he'd seen of Lucilla and Thomas's road to the altar. Yet in both cases, his mother's and Lucilla's positions had been unassailable; those had never been under threat.

Not so with Niniver.

As the Tam O' Shanter Inn hove into view, he realized that in Catriona and Richard's marriage, and also in Lucilla and Thomas's, the essential challenge had been that of naturally dominant men finding their way to accepting and embracing a supportive role. With him and Niniver, however, he already knew the ways and was entirely willing to assume such a role.

The challenge before him—and her—was to get her to accept that he could.

To trust that, despite his strength, he would always support her and never undermine her.

He had to get her to trust him.

Niniver strolled under the stable arch of the inn and inwardly sighed. Their day was coming to an end. True, it would take several hours to ride home, but riding was an exercise she and Marcus both enjoyed; they wouldn't be talking, and she wouldn't be gaining any further insights into his life.

But she couldn't complain; the day had been *wonderful*. So much more relaxing than her visits to Ayr usually were. With Marcus beside her, she'd felt able to be entirely at ease, without keeping constantly alert for danger. For dangers like McDougal. Because Marcus had been there, McDougal had been nothing more than a momentary irritation; if Marcus hadn't been there, McDougal would have been a pest and, most likely, would have ruined her day.

Instead, she'd experienced her most enjoyable day in months, possibly in the past several years.

She and Marcus halted in the stable yard. She drew her arm from his as the stable lads went to fetch their horses. As he turned to talk to the stable master, she let her gaze drift over his face, over him.

Her senses were growing accustomed to being close to him. They no longer skittered at his nearness; rather, they thrummed with anticipatory pleasure.

That her senses saw him as a source of pleasure should be no surprise, but his impact on her went deeper. In his company, she felt comfortable and assured, far more so than she'd ever felt with anyone else.

She could ask questions of him, about him, about his family, and he would answer. Those questions he'd asked of her, he'd asked with an interest that had encouraged her to answer equally openly.

It wasn't, she realized, as the stable lads brought out their horses and she twisted to unhook the long train of her habit, simply that she didn't feel threatened by him, but that with him she felt—and, indeed, knew—that he would protect her. That she didn't need to fear others because he was there, by her side. That she could rely on him.

That he cared about her in a way, and to an extent, that few others did.

A stable lad angled Oswald beside her. Marcus

walked across and halted before her. Releasing her train, she straightened—and his hands closed about her waist.

She met his dark blue eyes.

The corners of those fathomless eyes crinkled as he smiled at her. "Ready?"

She nodded.

He gripped and hoisted her to her saddle. After steadying her, he released her.

She settled her boots in her stirrups and flicked out her skirts, and wondered if the sudden constricting of her lungs was wholly due to the effect of his touch, or whether the realization of how much, how very much he had come to mean to her, how close she and he had so easily grown, was also stealing her breath.

Raising her head, she caught his eye.

He turned his gray's head for the road, and she brought Oswald around. Side by side, they rode out, and set off along the highway back to the estate.

# Seven

Several hours later, the sun was sliding down the western sky, throwing elongating shadows across the macadam as they followed the wending ribbon of the highway back toward the Carrick estate.

Marcus rode easily alongside Niniver, reining Ned back whenever the big gray took it into his head to surge. Oswald, Niniver's raw-boned bay, was older and more mature; he ignored Ned's thinly veiled challenges and seemed content to stretch his legs in the alternating pattern of canter and easy gallop they'd been maintaining.

They were currently galloping, the horses' long legs fluidly eating up the miles. Niniver was an excellent horsewoman; Marcus didn't feel compelled to keep a close eye on her. Of course, because she was Niniver, his senses still remained on watch, yet it was pleasant not to feel the need to be hyperalert and on guard every second.

He'd intended to use the long ride to think of how to gain her trust, but the peace of the countryside, the crisp fresh air, the gentle warmth of the westering sun, and the rhythmic motion of riding combined with the simple pleasure of being with her and enjoying those things together to lull him into a mental daze where simply existing seemed enough.

Where thinking too much felt like something akin to sacrilege.

From the gentle curve of her lips and her relaxed expression, he deduced she felt the same.

They reached the northernmost edge of the Carrick estate. The entrance to the drive lay half a mile further on.

*Crack!*

Both horses reared. One of them screamed.

Ned went wild. Marcus wrestled with the gray. The powerful horse twisted and bucked.

Oswald bolted.

Marcus couldn't spare even a glance Niniver's way—not until he had Ned under control.

Ruthlessly, he hauled, all but wrenching the big gelding into obedience under tight rein.

Then he glanced around—and swore.

Oswald had leapt the low stone wall bordering the road and was thundering across the fields.

Marcus's fields; that was Bidealeigh land.

Niniver was clinging to Oswald's back, but she wasn't strong enough to rein the big bay in…and the area they were heading into was pockmarked with rocky outcrops, eruptions of granite boulders that littered the fields.

If Niniver fell…

If Oswald fell and rolled…

Marcus didn't stop to think. He'd already brought Ned's head around. Easing the reins, he drove his heels into the gray's sides.

Ned shot off in Oswald's wake. He soared over the low stone wall, then landed and raced straight on.

Marcus leaned low over Ned's neck. Riding with hands and knees, he urged the huge horse on.

Oswald was strong, but older and slower; steadily, Ned gained ground.

But not fast enough.

Marcus knew his fields, knew that not far ahead lay a narrowing where the valley turned. A place where a bolting horse would veer sharply. And where there were rocks all around.

Ned was gaining. He had settled and was no longer panicking, but he remained intent on running Oswald down.

Marcus started to hope. They might just make it in time for him to grab Oswald's reins and slow the big horse—

One of Oswald's hooves slid off a rock. The bay lurched. Nearly thrown, Niniver yelped.

Marcus suddenly had to make a decision—which side? Offside would be easier for lifting her free of her saddle, but if Oswald veered, she might fall to the onside and he might not be able to reach over the horse and catch her—

He opted for the onside.

Oswald veered. Niniver screamed. Losing her grip on the reins, she started to topple.

His gaze locked on her, Marcus pushed. Ned answered with a burst of speed.

Dropping the reins, Marcus leaned forward as far as he dared and reached—

Grabbed, and caught Niniver. With a massive effort, he pulled her up and away from Oswald; between her kicking and him tugging, they freed her boots from her stirrups. Then he hauled her up and into his arms as Ned followed Oswald into and through the narrow turn.

Niniver gulped air and clutched at Marcus.

Freed of her weight and racing out of the neck of the valley, Oswald kicked up his heels, then bolted again.

Ned followed, but the weight of two people on his back slowed him.

Juggling Niniver across his saddle, Marcus locked her to him with one arm, and with his free hand seized Ned's reins.

To his relief, the big horse responded and slowed.

Marcus's heart was thundering.

So was Niniver's; when he glanced at her, he could see her pulse pounding at the base of her throat.

She was white as a sheet. The eyes that swung up to meet his were huge, their expression stunned and dazed.

"Are you hurt?" The most important question.

Awareness slowly returned to her eyes as she catalogued her limbs. Then she grimaced. "My left ankle." She was breathless. "I wrenched it coming out of the saddle. But other than that…" Her gaze lifted to his face, animation returning to her own. "Thank you. I'm hale, whole, and alive—thanks to you."

He held her gaze for a moment, struggling to fill his lungs, battling to find his mental feet. Then he bent his head and kissed her.

He *had* to kiss her. Had to claim that much, at least.

Had to reassure the prowling, snarling beast inside him that she was there, safe, still his.

And she kissed him back, her hands rising to frame his face. He parted her lips, and she slid her fingers along his skull and clutched, and—for just that instant—they let passion reign.

She was alive, in his arms, kissing him back—essentially unharmed.

In that moment, that was all that mattered.

His chest expanding, he hauled in a huge breath and drew back from the kiss.

She blinked up at him, dazed again, but with color now tinting her cheeks.

The tumult of feelings roiling inside him made it difficult to think, let alone speak. How the devil did the men in his family remain sane if this—this overwhelming riot of feelings—was the outcome of keeping their mates safe?

Yet she was in his arms, alive and steadily breathing, the warm weight of her a primal reassurance, but his instincts insisted he needed to get her home—to a place of assured safety.

Feeling no inclination to ease his hold on her, he angled Ned back toward the highway. Eventually, the fever in his brain cooled, and logic reasserted control. He frowned. "Do you have any idea what happened?"

Frowning, too, she shook her head. "No. We were riding along, and then…there was a sound, and Oswald screamed and reared." She shifted in his hold, finally settling with her back to his chest. After several moments of staring ahead, she asked, "Was it a gunshot? The sharp crack that set him off?"

Marcus's jaw felt like rock splintering under too great a force. "I think so."

The thought that someone had been shooting so close to her… He felt barely sane.

But she was hurt, and whoever had fired the shot

might still be out there, stupidly hunting too close to the road.

She twisted to look back. "What about Oswald?"

"I'll send Sean to get him. He'll stop running soon. For now..." He nudged Ned into a canter. "I'm taking you home."

To Carrick Manor and safety.

Once he was certain she was well, safe, and protected, then he might well go hunting, too.

\* \* \*

Niniver's wits were only just settling back into place—along with her thudding heart—when they trotted into the manor's stable yard. She still felt giddy and shaky. Being held so securely in Marcus's arms was the only thing allowing her to cling to relative calm; the circling steel of his arms, the solid warmth of his chest against her back, and the powerful flex of his thighs beneath hers as he steered his horse had become her anchoring reality.

She'd come within seconds of dying.

Of being flung onto rocks and cracking her skull.

That realization had sunk to her marrow and tied her stomach in knots.

Their appearance in the yard, both on Ned with Oswald nowhere to be seen, caused an instant furor. Sean swore and came racing toward them, with Mitch and Fred hot on his heels.

Marcus drew rein at the spot closest to the manor's side door.

Sean caught Ned's bridle and held the big gray steady. "What happened?"

"Someone fired a gun far too close to the road just as we were passing. Oswald bolted." Marcus dipped his head to look into her face. His expression was grim, but his eyes were filled with focused concern. "Can you stand?"

She blinked. "I…think so." Her ankle felt rather warm, but it wasn't hurting.

Marcus gripped her about her waist and carefully lowered her to the ground. "I hauled Lady Carrick off before she fell, but she wrenched her ankle getting free of the stirrup."

Her weight settled on her feet—and she sucked in a breath and grabbed Marcus's booted calf as pain shot up her left leg.

"Stay still—just wait." He caught her hand, lifted it from his boot, and passed it to Mitch. His face filled with worry, Mitch had come to stand beside her. He took her hand and grasped her arm, supporting her.

Marcus swung out of his saddle and came striding around his horse.

"Where did it happen?" Mitch asked.

"We'd just passed the northern point of the estate." Niniver gasped as she suddenly tilted—as Marcus bent and swept her into his arms.

He straightened and caught her shocked gaze. "You need to keep your weight off that foot." Expending no more effort than if she'd been a child, he strode for the side door.

Fred rushed to open it and held the door wide.

As Marcus angled her through, she glanced back and saw Mitch following, with Sean close behind.

The thunder of boot heels as their small cavalcade paced down the corridor brought Ferguson out from the servants' hall. He saw her lying in Marcus's arms and paled. "What happened?"

Marcus answered before she could. "A shot startled her horse. She was nearly thrown, but I got to her in time. Unfortunately, getting free of one stirrup wrenched her ankle." He caught Ferguson's eye. "We need to get her boot off before her ankle swells, and then we'll need ice to pack around the joint."

"Oh, heavens!" Mrs. Kennedy had come up behind Ferguson in time to hear most of that. "I'll get a basin of ice water. That's always the best."

"We'll be in the drawing room," Marcus called as, without pause, he bore Niniver on.

As he walked into the front hall, she shifted in his hold and looked up at his face. It was stony, his expression graven; granite would have been softer. "It's just my ankle, you know," she said. "And as long as I'm not putting pressure on it, it doesn't even hurt."

The look he cast her was excessively brief and unrelentingly grim. "It's going to hurt a great deal when we cut off your boot."

"Cut?" She blinked. "No." She peeked at her toes. "These are my favorite boots."

Fred raced past.

Marcus paused to let him open the drawing room door. "The boot has to come off. Cutting it off will hurt less."

She set her jaw. "You said cutting it off would hurt anyway. Put me down"—imperiously, she pointed to one sofa—"and let me see if I can wiggle my foot out."

He did as she asked, setting her down as if she were made of porcelain. Others crowded into the room. They were so openly concerned, she didn't have the heart to tell them to go away. Ella pushed forward to help, as did Alice, the clan healer. Gritting her teeth—and trying to disguise the fact that she was—she shifted until she could easily grasp the heel of the boot and gingerly started easing it off.

With Ella's and Alice's help, she managed the feat—just. But the effort of pushing past the pain while suppressing all outward signs of it left her gaspingly weak and quivering inside.

During the process, Marcus knelt at her feet. The instant her heel slipped free of the boot, he drew it fully off, handed it to Ella, then gently supported her injured foot as Alice prodded, poked, and tested.

"Just a bad wrench," Alice finally pronounced. "Ice water is the best treatment."

"Thank you." Niniver shifted until she could lean against the sofa's back and surreptitiously catch her breath.

The sharp look Marcus sent her told her she wasn't fooling him, but he appeared to be sensitive to the welling concern of the crowd now surrounding them. Maids, footmen—even the pot boy was there.

Then Mrs. Kennedy arrived with a deep basin of ice floating in water. The housekeeper helped her roll her stocking down, then, with Ferguson and Marcus, helped settle her so she was sitting on the sofa propped up with multiple cushions with her foot dangling in the basin, which they'd raised using a stack of books.

"There now." Mrs. Kennedy stepped back. "We'll keep topping up the ice every half hour, and that should keep the swelling down."

Ferguson still looked troubled. "Perhaps we should send for the doctor."

"No." Struggling to reassert herself, she stated, "It's

just a wrenched ankle. Thanks to Mr. Cynster, that's the full extent of my injuries."

Her words didn't seem to have any real impact; everyone remained as they were, frowning down at her as if she were some child unable to accurately describe her own hurts.

Then Hildy rushed into the room; someone must have gone up to her apartment to tell her of Niniver's injury. Spotting her, Hildy clapped her hands to her lined cheeks. "Oh, my lord!" She bustled through the crowd to the sofa. "You were nearly thrown?" Hildy all but collapsed into the nearest armchair. "My dear, how many times have I said that brute of a horse is no horse for a lady?"

She frowned. "It wasn't Oswald's fault. Something startled him." It had been rather more than a simple startle. Frowning, she searched the serried ranks before her. "Sean." She found the head stableman half hidden behind Ferguson. "Will you go and fetch Oswald, please?"

Marcus glanced at Sean. "The last we saw of him, he was heading east on Bidealeigh lands. He'll probably fetch up to the east of the farmhouse, but I would check there first—he might have found his way to the paddocks at the rear of the stable where my other horses are kept."

"I'll find him." Sean nodded at Marcus, then at Niniver. Then he turned and made his way out of the now-crowded room.

Niniver looked around at the others—at the circle of worried faces—and forced a smile far brighter than she felt. "Thank you, everyone, but there's nothing more

I need." Other than space and privacy. When no one moved, she looked at Marcus.

He read her eyes. Even though his expression remained grim, he looked at Ferguson and Mrs. Kennedy. "Miss Hildebrand and I will sit with Lady Carrick. If you could arrange to have more ice brought in half an hour?"

"Yes, sir." Mrs. Kennedy appeared to reluctantly accept that she and all the others couldn't simply stand about watching Niniver just to make sure she truly was all right. To Niniver, she said, "Anything you need, my lady, you just have Mr. Cynster ring, and we'll bring it quick as a flash."

"Actually," she said, "a tea tray wouldn't go amiss."

"Of course!" Roused by having something to do, Gwen, the cook, bobbed her head to Niniver. "I'll go and get the kettle on right away."

Ferguson and Mrs. Kennedy started shooing everyone out. Marcus spoke with Mitch and Fred. The stablemen cast Niniver troubled glances, but they bobbed their heads and followed the others out of the room.

As the rest of the household streamed out, Edgar came in, carrying a knitted shawl, a lap blanket, and two of her father's old canes. He handed the canes to Marcus, then carefully draped the blanket over her knees. "It's been my experience with such injuries that keeping the rest of the body warm helps."

Now he'd mentioned it, she realized that she did, indeed, feel chilled. "Thank you, Edgar." She accepted the warm shawl and flicked it about her shoulders.

"There." Edgar stood back, then nodded. He glanced at the canes. "And those are for later, so you won't need to risk re-hurting your ankle."

She smiled her thanks. Edgar bowed and left. He closed the drawing room door behind him, and finally, she could close her eyes and let herself slump against the cushions.

She heard Marcus shift, then the soft *whoosh* of the cushions as he sat in the armchair to her right. She didn't need to see to know he and Hildy exchanged a glance. But neither of them said anything, which she appreciated. She kept her eyes closed until Ferguson arrived with the tea trolley.

Gwen had sent not just tea, but slices of Madeira cake. Niniver discovered that she was famished—and, it seemed, Marcus was, too. Between them, they put paid to the cake and emptied the teapot.

Hildy sipped her tea; Niniver felt her ex-governess's anxious gaze on her face. But when Ferguson came to take away the trolley and refresh the ice in the basin, Hildy stood and fluffed out her shawl. "I'm going to go up for the moment. As it appears you can't move and so will have to rest, and Mr. Cynster is prepared to remain and ensure you do, then I'll take the opportunity to finish my letters. If you need me, just ring."

Niniver summoned a wan smile; the aftereffects of the excitement were catching up with her. "I will. I'm just going to sit here until dinner. You'll have to excuse me, but I won't be dressing for dinner tonight."

Hildy made a dismissive sound. "As if we'd care about that. Just rest, and I'll see you at dinnertime."

She left.

Niniver inwardly sighed and closed her eyes—but almost immediately, the door opened again. She raised her lids. Sean hovered on the threshold. She beckoned him in. "Did you find Oswald?"

"Aye." Sean halted before her, but his gaze went to Marcus. Sean nodded. "The old coot was where you said he'd be, at the back of your stables, chatting over the fence to your horses."

She studied Sean's grim expression and wondered what he wasn't telling her. "He isn't hurt, is he?"

"As to that, nothing as won't heal well enough. But"—again Sean's eyes shifted to Marcus before returning to her face—"I could see why he went wild on you. There's a deep furrow gouged across his right flank—made by a ball fired from a hunting rifle, I'd say."

*"What?"* Marcus sat up. "Someone shot...?"

He stared at Sean, who looked steadily back at him, then he looked at Niniver and put into words what all three of them knew. "That section of road is open and clear, with no trees or bushes to limit the view. The land is relatively flat." Eyes narrowing, he stated, "No one could have shot at us—not to the point of hitting your horse—if they hadn't deliberately taken aim."

Marcus paused, then, feeling cold fury rise inside him, concluded, "Someone shot at you."

\* \* \*

Half an hour later, Niniver felt exhausted by her attempts to point out that there was no logical reason anyone would have deliberately shot at her.

"It *must* have been an accident," she repeated for at least the tenth time.

While Marcus didn't argue, there was nothing in his expression, much less in the hard darkness of his eyes, to suggest that he agreed. Indeed, she wasn't even sure he was listening.

She exhaled and slumped back against the cushions. Sean had left to tend to Oswald, but he'd refused to agree to her request to keep the gelding's injury to himself, or at least limit the knowledge to those in the stable, on the grounds that he couldn't not tell Ferguson of a threat that so deeply affected the clan.

And with that, Marcus had silently agreed; she'd read that in the look he and Sean had shared before Sean had left.

Marcus was now pacing, up and down, like a caged tiger. He looked equally as dangerous.

She was starting to feel cold again. Drawing the shawl tighter about her, she shivered.

Marcus halted, his gaze locking on her. "Cold?"

"Yes." And if he didn't stop pacing... She shifted on the sofa. "Perhaps if you sat beside me?"

He hesitated, but she didn't have to ask twice. He came and settled on the sofa alongside her.

Instantly, she felt the warmth his large body radiated all along one side. She'd noticed that he always seemed to be much hotter than her, as if he was running a fever, but he wasn't. Perhaps all large men were like that.

Her mind wasn't all that clear; her thoughts seemed to be going around and around, refusing to settle.

Deliberately, she eased sideways until her hip met his, then she let herself tip against him.

She sensed him looking down at her, then he raised the arm trapped between them and draped it around her, allowing her to snuggle still closer to all that lovely muscled warmth.

She sighed and let the peace and his warmth, the simple human comfort of it, sink to her bones.

He took her right hand in his. His thumb gently stroked the back of her hand.

Gradually, her thoughts steadied.

She wasn't too thrilled with what she saw. Eventually, her head resting against his chest, she murmured, "Why would anyone shoot at me?"

"I don't know." He shifted his head; his lips brushed her hair. "But we'll find out."

She drew in a tight breath and admitted, "I'm frightened."

"You needn't be. I'm here."

"Will you stay?"

He stilled. For an instant, she wondered if he would reply. She stopped breathing, but then he said, his voice low, "Whatever's behind this, there's no way on earth I would leave you to face it on your own."

She heard the absolute sincerity in his tone. Those weren't just words; they were a vow.

For once, she had someone on her side. Someone powerful enough to defend her.

And, for once, she believed she could count on him—that he wouldn't desert her.

"Thank you," she murmured. And let her eyes close.

* * *

The sun had dipped below the horizon when Ramsey McDougal returned to his lodgings in a squalid boarding house in the back streets behind Ayr harbor.

He tossed his hunting rifle onto the unmade bed, slumped into the single chair before the rickety table, and reached for the bottle of cheap whisky that, along with a single glass, sat on the scarred surface. Only a few fingers of liquid remained in the bottle; he'd drunk the rest before he'd had his bright idea and set out to await his quarry along the highway.

Uncorking the bottle, he splashed the whisky into the glass, raised it, and drank.

Lowering the glass, he shuddered and set it down.

*God. What had possessed him?*

Anger, mostly. After the setbacks of the past week, learning from his contacts that his plan had worked and that Niniver Carrick had—finally!—been brought to the point of turning to someone outside her clan for help had sent his spirits soaring. Then he'd glimpsed her through the inn's window and had felt that, at last, Fate was smiling. He'd gone inside to engage Niniver, his expectations riding high. Only to have said expectations dashed when Marcus Cynster had appeared, and Niniver had made it plain it was *Cynster* she'd chosen to seek help from.

A species of black fury had risen up and engulfed him. While still in its throes, he'd swallowed most of the bottle of whisky, then ridden out with his rifle—and nearly killed the very pigeon he planned to pluck!

*"Bah!"* He drained the glass, then emptied the dregs of the bottle into it. He stared at the empty bottle for several seconds, then pushed it away. "Perhaps I shouldn't have gone to the races last week." If, in a vain attempt to repair his losses, he hadn't gone to the race meet, he'd be several hundred pounds richer... well, less in debt. More to the point, he would have been watching his little pigeon; he would have known when she'd reached the end of her tether and could have smoothly stepped in to fill the position he'd worked so fiendishly carefully to create—that of manly defender of the weak little woman. The perfect position from which an experienced gentleman-rogue such as he could have further exploited the situation. Instead...

He ground his teeth. "Given how long she's held out, how was I to know the nitwit would reach breaking point last week? And then to cap it all by rushing to *Cynster* for help?" He imbued the name with all the loathing he could muster.

But Cynster had stepped in and, no doubt, was even now reaping the rewards that should have been Ramsey's. That he, Ramsey McDougal, had worked for. Although he hadn't dallied to find out, he assumed Cynster had rescued Niniver and was, even now, basking in the glow of being her hero.

It wasn't fair. Cynster didn't even need the money. Ramsey did.

Quite desperately.

Sipping the last of his whisky, eking out the last drops, he circled the question of what next. It was possible Cynster, being Cynster, was simply helping Niniver out of the goodness of his heart, as it were. Ramsey couldn't imagine behaving so himself, but he understood the concept. Noblesse oblige, and all that. He'd been born into similar circles, so he comprehended the notion but considered it vastly overrated. "However," he murmured, "that might mean that, if I simply hold off and wait, Cynster will take care of things and then return to his own interests."

Leaving the route to Niniver Carrick open once more.

That, Ramsey judged, was entirely possible.

Unfortunately, an essential element in such a plan was a commodity he was running short of—time.

If, as seemed likely, he couldn't afford to wait for

Cynster to withdraw, then…he would have to find some way to remove Marcus Cynster so that he could claim lovely Niniver for himself.

# *Eight*

*I nearly died this afternoon. And yet, thanks to Marcus, I'm still breathing.*

As late afternoon faded into evening, those words circled in Niniver's head, carried on waves of shock, amazement, and realization. Every time she remembered those last moments on Oswald's back, terror rose up as Death stared her in the face.

Then she would blink and realize that Marcus was still sitting beside her, his arm around her, his hand holding hers.

His warmth—contrasted by the icy water about her ankle—and the solid reality of his body against hers reassured her that she was, very definitely, still alive.

Time and again, relief poured through her, twining with heartfelt gratitude.

Ultimately, inevitably, the disturbing recollections subsided. Her mind moved on, and relief and gratitude were superseded by a broader comprehension, a deeper appreciation of life, of what it meant to be alive—as if the events of the afternoon had expanded her emotional horizons in every direction.

Finally, Marcus shifted and withdrew his arm from around her shoulders. She was about to protest the loss of his warmth, of his wordless comfort, when a sound at the door had her glancing that way.

Marcus rose as Hildy and Edgar entered. The pair had obviously conferred and come armed with what they'd decided she would need—a towel to dry her foot, a pair of knitted stockings, and a bandage to bind her ankle.

She let them fuss. Not only was it easier, but it was what they—not just Edgar and Hildy but the rest of the clan—needed; they needed to feel they'd taken care of her to whatever extent they could. While Hildy patted her foot dry and debated with Edgar how best to fashion their binding, Niniver wondered how many in the clan had, by now, heard the news. From what she remembered of the incident, the shot had come from the Carrick side of the road. The shooter had almost certainly been standing on Carrick land.

That said, she found it impossible to believe that said shooter was a member of the clan. So who could it have been? And what had driven them to it? Shooting her wasn't in anyone's best interests, not that she could see.

Marcus stood before the fireplace, his hands clasped behind his back, his gaze on Edgar and Miss Hildebrand as they tended to Niniver. Now that sufficient time had elapsed and his roiling emotions had settled somewhat, now that he could see with his own eyes that she had survived, that she was reasonably well—certainly not dying—he could more coolly and calmly recall, observe, and assess the incident, and its outcome.

One thing he would never forget was the way she'd clung to him after he'd hauled her from her saddle. When horror had stripped all the normal barriers of civilization away, and she'd looked at him… He'd seen her emotions, raw, real, and true, in her wide eyes.

Whether she consciously knew it yet or not, she trusted him. With her life, with her person. She'd turned to him and clung, and she'd known he would hold her. That he would protect her.

Just as he'd held her hand over the last hour, and she'd accepted and been reassured by his nearness.

The hurdle of gaining her trust—at least her unconscious trust—had been cleared.

And another hurdle had been cleared as well—the clan now saw him as a necessary hero, one who could and would protect their lady in ways they, individually and collectively, could not. Niniver herself had recognized that no clan member could have assisted her in dismissing McDougal. But he could, and he had. Likewise, enough clan members—Sean, Mitch, Fred, and doubtless others, too—knew that only a rider like him on a horse of the quality of Ned could have ridden Oswald down in time to save Niniver.

If he hadn't been the one with her, she would, at the very least, have been badly injured; most likely, she would have died.

And the clan would have been devastated, and soon it would have disintegrated.

He hadn't just saved her. He'd saved them, and they knew it.

Another hurdle well and truly cleared.

He hadn't expected to get so far so quickly, yet incidents seemed to be raining thick and fast. He had the sense—a hunter's sense—that there was some urgency to this affair; although he couldn't yet see from where the pressure was coming, he knew it was there.

Miss Hildebrand had brought flat-soled slippers for Niniver to wear. They'd removed her other boot, and she had the slippers on. Marcus had grave doubts about the wisdom of encouraging her to put weight on her injured foot so soon, but Edgar and Miss Hildebrand took her hands and drew her upright.

Marcus quit his position before the fireplace and returned to Niniver's side—just as, balancing on one foot, she accepted the canes Edgar had brought down.

The idea had been sound, but Manachan had been significantly taller than Niniver; the canes were the wrong length for her.

She tried to find a different way to hold them, but when one slipped from her grasp, causing her to list and put weight unexpectedly on her injured foot and she gave a sharp cry, Marcus waited no longer. He stooped and lifted her into his arms.

She blinked at him, then turned her head and extended the cane she still held to Edgar. "Perhaps tomorrow. I can almost use them as crutches."

Holding one in each hand, Edgar frowned at the canes. "I'll see what else I can find."

Ferguson had appeared and now hovered in the doorway. Marcus directed a look his way.

"Dinner is served, my lady. Sir. Miss Hildebrand."

"Excellent." Miss Hildebrand stepped back and waved at Marcus to lead the way.

He carried Niniver through the hall, down the corridor, and into the dining room. Ferguson held the chair in which she usually sat. Gently, Marcus set her down. She shifted, settling her skirts, then he eased the chair in for her.

Claiming the chair next to hers—now his customary place—he glanced up the table to the huge carver at its head. "You don't sit at the head of the table." His tone made the observation a question.

Flicking out her napkin, she shook her head. She glanced at the chair in question. "Perhaps one day I might, but...not yet."

Glancing across the table, Marcus saw that Miss Hildebrand was directing a look—a very pointed, meaning-laden look—at him. As Ferguson circled with the soup tureen and then they settled to sup, Marcus tried to imagine what, in Niniver's eyes, might preclude her from claiming...her father's place. Was that it?

As they ate their way through the four courses, he replayed her previous comments about her father's legacy, about how she wished to preserve it. He was fairly certain the matter of the chair was somehow connected with that.

Niniver and Miss Hildebrand chatted about the various errands Niniver had run in Ayr, leaving him free to follow his thoughts. To revisit and assess each little snippet Niniver had let fall through the prism of his instincts.

There was something there, something she hadn't yet told him—perhaps hadn't told anyone else—about the clan's situation. He was more than qualified to help her with whatever it was, but she would have to make the decision to tell him, to ask for his help in that arena, too.

He hoped she did, but he couldn't push. That much he understood and accepted.

It seemed that, just as he'd hoped—just as, in her usual nebulous ways, Fate had promised—there was more for him to do as Niniver's champion beyond the obvious aspects of the role. Protecting and defending her from physical attack was one thing, but there were other encroachments on her peace that rightly also fell to him to deal with. Or at least help with.

He slanted a glance at her, then looked further up the table at the empty chair.

Now there was a clear-cut goal. He would work until he saw her sitting there, secure in whatever way she needed to feel to fully claim her rightful place.

Dessert, a charlotte russe—apparently one of Niniver's favorites—distracted him; while she consumed the sweet concoction, her face lit with pleasure.

There was, he realized, no sign of lingering strain. She'd said that, as long as she wasn't standing on her ankle, it didn't hurt, and there was, in truth, no hint of pain in or around her eyes, much less about her luscious lips.

He was reminded again of the conundrum she posed. She looked like a porcelain doll—fragile, delicate, and easily damaged—but she was flesh and blood, and much stronger and far more resilient than she appeared.

Despite the trials life and the rest of her family had thrown at her, she hadn't broken yet. She hadn't even cracked.

Out of nowhere, Lady Osbaldestone's voice rang in his head, and he grinned at the aptness of her words.

Niniver caught his grin. She considered it, then she captured his gaze, briefly studied his eyes, and arched a brow. "What?"

His grin deepened into a smile. He held her gaze for a moment, then admitted, "I was thinking of how the grandes dames of London—specifically the arch-grande dame of them all, who I happen to know—would describe you."

She looked skeptical. "Do I want to know?"

Still smiling, he tilted his head. "She would say that you're 'made of stern stuff.' It's a compliment—and, from that particular lady, one of significant weight."

Faint color tinted her cheeks. "Why, thank you. I think." Immediately, she looked across the table. "Are we ready to retire?"

Miss Hildebrand confirmed they were. Still grinning to himself, Marcus rose. Niniver turned to him, but before she could speak, he stated, "No, I don't want to sit and imbibe—I'll come to the drawing room with you."

He and Ferguson eased her up from her chair, then he swooped and hoisted her into his arms once more.

Riding, acquiescent, in his hold, as he paced down the corridor, she sniffed. "I smell dreadfully of horse."

"So, no doubt, do I." He caught her eyes when she glanced at him. "Changing for dinner would have been difficult for you, and I elected to keep you company. As Miss Hildebrand hasn't complained, I believe we're excused."

She humphed but said nothing more.

He carried her to the sofa.

Niniver settled back against the cushions. To her surprise, but also her delight, Marcus went to the pianoforte and proceeded to entertain them. He really was an excellent pianist. She relaxed against the cushions and let the music wash over and through her.

Several pieces later, she realized he was playing by heart, and also from the heart—simply playing whatever piece his mind alighted on. There was strength in his music, and passion, and a sense of energy—of life. He played to exorcise his emotions and, in so doing, exorcised hers.

The tea trolley arrived, but he refused a cup and continued playing. She sipped, closed her eyes, and let the music speak to her and fill her mind.

By the time he finally reached an end—and his fingers stilled on the keys, the notes faded, and she opened her eyes and their gazes met and held—she felt a tangible connection. A link borne on his music, recognized by their senses, carried in that gaze, yet so real it impacted like a touch.

A caress.

He broke the connection and looked down. Then he closed the instrument and rose.

"Thank you, Mr. Cynster." Tugging her shawl about her shoulders, Hildy got to her feet. "That was an impressive performance."

Impressive, indeed. Niniver drank in the sight of him as he accepted Hildy's praise with a dip of his dark head, then he straightened and came toward her.

It was his focus as he looked at her that, as always, struck her. That thrilled her at some feminine level she was only just learning to recognize. To appreciate.

She was dimly aware of Hildy following him across the room.

"Are you ready to go up, my dear? I do think you would be wise to retire and rest that ankle." Hildy studied her, then glanced at Marcus. "Can you manage, do you think?"

Her gaze on Marcus's face—on his carefully guarded expression—Niniver replied, "I'll manage well enough, Hildy. You go up. Mr. Cynster and I will follow."

Suspicion bloomed in Marcus's eyes, and as she'd anticipated, he bent and, with senses-stealing ease, lifted her into his arms.

He nodded at Hildy. "If you would open the door?"

Hildy led the way from the room, up the main stairs, and around into the gallery. But when they reached the stairs that led to the next floor and her apartment at one end, she halted. "I'm sure Ella will be waiting in your room, so I'll bid you a good night, my dear." Hildy inclined her head approvingly to Marcus. "Mr. Cynster."

In unison, he and Niniver chorused a good night; she wondered if it was her imagination, but Marcus seemed a trifle disconcerted to be left alone with her in his arms.

She almost grinned. Silly man; everyone in the house trusted him. Most especially with her.

And they trusted her. The entire clan trusted her to make the right decisions. That trust was something she'd earned over the years, not just recently. And, tonight, she had every intention of making the right decision.

He carried her to her door. He paused before it, and she leaned down, grasped the knob, opened the door, and pushed it wide.

He strode in.

"Wait," she said, and he halted.

Stretching back, she caught the edge of the door and sent it swinging shut.

The soft thud and the click of the latch re-engaging reached them. As she relaxed back into his arms, he was scanning the room.

The lamp by the bed shed warm light through the room; it lit his face, and also revealed that there was no one else there. His dark gaze now openly suspicious, he looked down at her. "Where's Ella?"

"Ella never attends me at night, not unless I ring for her, and I rarely do." She held his gaze for an instant more, then tipped her head toward the bed. "You can set me down over there."

He looked around again, but there was no other option; setting her down on her dressing-table stool or the armchair by the hearth would be no help at all.

His jaw tightened, then he strode across the room, halted beside the bed, leaned across, and laid her on the covers, her head on the pillows.

She let him ease her body down, but she simultaneously curled the fingers of her right hand into the stock of his cravat.

He felt the material shift, glanced down, and froze. His hands still cradling her curves, he stared at her fist, locked about his neckcloth, then, slowly, he raised his gaze to her eyes. "Niniver—"

"Remember our earlier discussion about the price of protection?"

His jaw set. "That doesn't apply here."

She tipped her head, openly studying his face. "Well, I think it does, if anything more than before— and, really, you aren't all that good at lying." Each time he'd picked her up and carried her, he'd held her so gently, so carefully—with such rigid control that it had only served to highlight the fact that he'd really wanted to seize her. To crush her to him, rather than treat her like some delicate flower. She'd felt the tension thrumming through him, had heard it investing the music he'd played.

"But, regardless"—she locked her gaze with his—"I

wasn't talking about you. I discovered today that, quite apart from protection, cheating death has a price, too. And, for me, that price is claiming life." She knew exactly what she was doing. Using her hold on his cravat, using his strength and unbudging weight for leverage, she drew herself up until her lips were an inch from his. Her eyes still locked with his, she let her lips curve and softly said, "For me, the price is claiming you."

Lowering her lids, she set her lips to his.

For fully half a minute, he held fast against her, against the entreaty she pressed on him with her lips as well as her words—then he surrendered on a groan.

And seized control of the kiss.

As far as she would let him. She wasn't of a mind to allow him to think enough to make any honorable stand. To think enough to imagine that he knew better than she, and that this—all she intended—wasn't the right path.

It *was*, and she wasn't willing to listen to any arguments, not tonight. Today, she'd survived; tonight, she would live.

In that terrifying instant when she'd been sure she would die, she'd regretted every minute that she hadn't *lived*. She'd regretted, deeply, not seizing the chances that had come her way to explore life and living in all its varied aspects. But, most of all, in that instant of startling clarity she'd regretted not taking Marcus Cynster as her lover.

Tonight, that was her price—Fate's price, life's price, the price she would give and take, yield and claim, buoyed by relief, by joy, and by the unquenchable thirst for living that surviving had released inside her.

Their lips melded, tongues tangling and dueling as the heat between them grew. His lips were hard, commanding, demanding—demanding all she was only too ready to give. He claimed and possessed; she yielded and enticed. But they'd been this far before; tonight, she wanted more. Much more.

Tonight, she wanted all.

Still clutching his cravat, she fell back on the bed.

Instinctively rearranging his heavy limbs, he followed her down, ultimately ending stretched alongside her.

Their lips didn't part; the heated exchange abated not one jot.

Then he leaned over her, pressed her lips wide, and blatantly—so much more possessively—claimed her mouth. In response, she speared the fingers of her free hand through his hair; ignoring the tantalizing caress of his silky locks, she gripped his skull and kissed him back with everything she had inside her.

With her heart, with her soul.

With the *need* welling inside her.

And the kiss turned incendiary—an eruption of pure heat, the promise of a conflagration so intense it would consume her. That promise focused her wits, her senses, on him and only him; the world fell away, the room beyond the bed ceased to exist, and there was only them, sinking into the covers, locked together in an unrelenting drive to assuage a passion that was suddenly more powerful than them both.

Irresistibly compelling, the lure of his tongue heavily stroking hers captured her awareness, but then his hand cupped her breast, plumped, and squeezed, and she lost what little clarity she'd retained.

She wanted him, and he wanted her, and in that hour, in that place, nothing else mattered.

With single-minded determination, she set out to ensure that they got what they wanted. What they both needed.

She released her grip on his cravat and set her fingers to the folds. By touch, she drew the long pin free; without disturbing the communion of their mouths, she drew her hand from his hair, blindly managed to reanchor the pin in his lapel, then started unraveling the simple knot he favored—mentally blessing him for not indulging in any foolishly complicated style.

His hands stroked over and around her breasts; he seemed to know just where to press, where and how to caress to send her senses leaping. To have anticipation of his next touch prickling across her skin.

Breathing became a secondary consideration, and what breath she drew came via him. But while sensation held the ascendancy in her mind, she didn't care how giddy she grew—just as long as she absorbed every scintilla of his touches, every last tiny pressure.

He knew what he was doing; every caress was crafted and designed to heighten her awareness, to tighten her nerves one notch more. To open her eyes to the glory of this level of togetherness. This level of sharing. His hands sculpted her body; even through the fabric of her clothes, the heated hardness of his palms and fingers branded her, claimed her. With unrelenting focus, he devoted those moments to showing her—to laying before her the landscape of desire—and she committed herself to learning it all, the most avid pupil he would ever have.

Beneath his knowing hands, she responded, arching,

then gasping into the kiss as her body, unrestrained, answered his call. As she let her reins go, as she deliberately set herself free to experience and explore every path that with him she might find, she felt, sensed, *knew* that this—the sensual woman awakening inside her—was who she was meant to be.

That certainty, and the confidence it engendered, propelled her on. His cravat hung undone; slowly, she drew the long length free, then tossed it aside, beyond the bed. Need infused that building confidence and pushed her to act boldly, to unbutton his coat and his waistcoat and press both wide. Gripping the fabric, she raised up, pushing against him to wrestle both garments over his shoulders.

On a muttered oath, he pulled back from the kiss, from his absorption with her curves; with swift tugs, he freed his arms and, almost violently, sent the shed garments flying.

Delighted with the proof that he was as caught by the moment as she, she laughed.

His eyes trapped hers; his seemed to blaze. Then he caught her face between his hands and kissed her with enough passion to make her nerves sizzle as he tumbled them down to the counterpane.

Her hands flattened against his linen-clad chest. Even as she met and matched the fiery heat of his kiss, she shifted her fingers to the placket of his shirt. She continued to meet his passion with her own, with her flagrant and open desire, while her fingers deftly slipped button after button free...then she tugged the halves of the shirt wide and set her hands, palms flat, to his skin.

*Glory*. Eyes closed, she drank in the sensation of his

hot skin burning her palms. Then she sent her hands skating over his chest, his ridged abdomen, greedily feeling, sensing, touching, tracing—learning. Learning what she needed to know, to experience—the sculpted splendor of his chest, the heat and hardness of the heavy muscles banding it, the raspy brush of the crinkly black hair adorning his taut skin—and also exploring how her touch affected him.

He'd stilled, his breath coming in shallow pants. As if caught in a sensual web of her creation, he remained immobile as she experimented and discovered how grazing her fingertips across and around the flat discs of his nipples made him tense even more, how sweeping her hands, small though they were, across and down the heated planes made him shudder.

Made him close his eyes tighter and feel...

They'd both broken from the kiss, their senses shifting to focus on touch, on tactile sensation.

Marcus couldn't drag his senses from her snare. Couldn't drag in breath enough to clear his head, much less to care. In that moment, all he knew was an absolute, ravaging need to right the balance she'd tipped her way. He'd already opened her velvet riding jacket. While she caressed and explored his chest and shoulders, her touch laced with a heady blend of innocence and wanting, he set his fingers to the line of tiny seed pearl buttons that ran down the front of her blouse.

He doubted he'd ever undone buttons so rapidly. Normally he would have slowed the action to draw the moment out—to heighten anticipation, both hers and his. Tonight, he and she needed no further encouragement. He was already burning with a relentless desire to have her naked skin beneath his hands, to feel the fineness, the softness—to claim that much at least.

He couldn't think further than that. Not then. He couldn't, in fact, think at all.

She filled his mind, his senses; in that moment, she was the sum of his reality.

And she was wearing far too many clothes. Slippers. Stockings. Skirts. Petticoats. Underclothes.

He wasn't daunted, and neither was she. He tugged, and she obliged, then she turned the tables.

Lacings unraveled; material slid away, silk slithering over satiny skin before he whisked it free.

His boots hit the floor.

She wrestled him back, reaching to undo the fastenings of his breeches below his knees, then she fell on the buttons at his waist.

In shockingly short order, everything went flying. Everything except her bandage.

Everything else.

He hadn't expected that—hadn't anticipated her unrestrained ardor or his instinctive response.

He all but fell on her as she pulled him down.

Their bodies met, skin to scorching skin.

And they *burned*.

Without the slightest hesitation, they both plunged into the flames.

If he'd been able to think, he would have been shocked, but their greedy senses had run amok. He might have been able to exert some modicum of control over his own rabid recklessness, but containing hers—resisting hers—was the definition of impossible.

He caught her face, fitted his mouth to hers, and devoured.

She met him and matched him, urged him on—then she returned the pleasure, gave him back the heated pressure with a wanton abandon that left him reeling.

She—and their combining, escalating, incitingly competing passions—swept him up in an irresistible maelstrom of ravenous need. And with absolute abandon, she went with him, offering herself to him, to that soaring, swelling mutual hunger.

He closed his hand over her breast, and she gasped. He bent his head and drew the tight bud of one rosy nipple deep into his mouth and suckled hard—and she clutched his head to her and arched and moaned. His hands itched to stroke every inch of her silken skin, to learn every curve, every hollow; he allowed them to roam unrestrained, unrestricted, and she writhed and reached for him—gripping, demanding, devastatingly open in her wanting.

Her hair had come loose; as he laved her other breast, she thrashed her head, spreading silver-gilt tendrils across the pillow.

They'd left the lamp burning, and he was glad they had. That she'd initiated this without any thought—any need—for concealing darkness. His eyes drank in the sight of her, of her alabaster skin tinged with the rosy hue of blatant arousal.

From beneath her fine lashes, her eyes glittered, lit by molten passion.

He knew all too well where this was headed, where the road she and his own driving need had whipped them along would end, but he couldn't corral his wits long enough to think and decide if such a destination was good or bad.

Tonight, for good or ill, that decision wasn't his to make.

To discover that, in this sphere, there truly was a force strong enough to command him was, of itself, stunning enough to hold the inner him captive. To draw that inner man, the one cloaked in his sophisticated armor, well concealed behind his civilized façade, to the fore—to observe her, this precious woman, to consciously feel her temptation. To see her rising arousal, to view her escalating passion, to scent her need and sense her burgeoning desperation.

To revel in it all—to steep himself in her.

To draw all of her in like the finest elixir, to let her passion collide with his and bloom in an eruption of fiery heat. To let the flames sear him, to score his heart and scatter his wits until answering her call was the only impulse left in his brain.

They'd been writhing on the counterpane, him on top, her beneath, yet equally dominant—equally demanding. They'd already grown accustomed to the ineluctable delights of mutual nakedness; his hands had claimed every inch of her skin, and she'd been nearly as thorough in her exploration of him.

She'd been far more eager, far more ready to appreciate those delights than he'd expected. What remained of his rational mind was still vaguely stunned at how rapidly, how easily and effortlessly, they'd reached this point, yet his instincts had accepted—accepted and approved of her commitment, her single-minded focus—without a single qualm.

That deeper self within him knew she had it right.

That tonight was for this. That him and her coming together like this was meant to be.

He'd been trailing a line of open-mouthed kisses down and across her belly. He had a goal in mind, but she made a low noise in her throat, reached down, framed his face between her hands, and drew him up.

Urgently.

He allowed her to have her way; rising over her again, he let her press her lips to his, allowed her to kiss him—to press her passion on him—then he parted her lips and took control of the kiss and drank her in.

Perhaps she was right; despite her enthusiasm, he assumed this was her first time with a man, and what he'd had in mind might have been too much, at least to begin with. That could come later. For now...

She'd already shifted beneath him, parting her soft white thighs so that he lay between, his hips between her spread knees, the head of his erection just south of where they both, quite clearly, wanted it to be. Holding her to the kiss, he sent his fingers questing and found her hot and wet.

The feel of her plump softness so swollen and slick sent a surge of unbridled heat through his groin.

He found her entrance, circled it, and she groaned into his mouth. He kissed her more deeply, then pressed one finger deep, and she arched beneath him.

Quickly, he readied her; wordlessly—with soft moans, with lips and tongue, with imploring hands— she urged him on.

Then he drew his fingers from her, pushed her thighs further apart—and remembered.

Hauling back from the kiss, he looked down at her flushed face. Managed to force out the words, "Your ankle?"

Niniver opened her eyes. From a distance of mere

inches, she stared up at him. She could barely think, and he wanted to know… "It's fine. It's on the bed. I don't need it for this."

*Do I?* She couldn't imagine how.

Her very blood seemed heated, surging through her; in that instant, the only things she wanted—all she craved—was to be the woman reflected in his midnight-dark eyes and bathe in the flames of his desire.

She waited for no answer, no acknowledgement. Her fingers gripping his skull, she pulled his lips back to hers, then, beneath him, she wriggled and slid down the bed, widening her thighs to accommodate his hips.

His erection nudged into her softness, and she froze.

She could feel the blunt head abutting her entrance. Earlier, she'd caressed his length, had been fascinated by the strangeness of such baby-fine skin stretched over something so unforgivingly rigid and hard—and had fleetingly wondered how he would fit…

Everything inside her tightened, quivered.

He reached down. The unrelenting weight of his chest pinning her beneath him, he slid one large hand beneath her bottom, tilting her hips toward his. His other hand clasped one of her thighs, urging her to shift that limb higher and wider.

He kissed her. Suddenly, forcefully, he surged deep into her mouth and sent fire streaming down her veins. She gasped; all her senses switched to meet the sudden onslaught.

The long muscles of his back flexed, and he pressed in.

Pushed in, forging steadily into her body.

On a sobbing gasp, she clung, felt the pinch as her

maidenhead ruptured, but of much greater significance, at least to her reeling senses, was the incredible sensation of him filling her there—so hard, hot, so much of him.

She felt her body yield, second by second, inch by inch.

He didn't stop until he could go no further, until he was embedded to the hilt inside her.

Then he froze. His body was beyond rigid, held under merciless control. Muscles flickered; his grip on her curves tightened.

She sensed him drawing back from the kiss, but something in her rebelled at the notion of any separation. Tightening her grip on his shoulder and nape, she held him to her and, with her lips and tongue, drew him back…into an exchange that had altered.

Now he was inside her, now they were joined…the interplay of their mouths reflected that intimacy.

This, she realized, was what the word meant, this degree of glorious sharing.

She wanted more. She wasn't sure how to get it, but holding him to the kiss, she poured all her passionate desires, all her most ardent cravings into the exchange, and slowly, carefully, undulated beneath him.

At the cusp of the movement, she realized she could, and clamped her inner muscles around him, using them to caress that most sensitive part of him. Flagrantly encouraging him.

He shuddered.

Then he moved. Slowly at first, then, as she moved with him—as she matched her pace to his and urged him on—he swept her into the full measure of the dance.

Just as he moved in every other sphere, here, too, he moved with reined power.

He thrust deeper and deeper, and pushed her higher and higher, until every sense she possessed surrendered to the heat, to the flames that rose up and caught them.

The friction of his body on hers, in hers, was delicious. The surging weight of him moving upon her was her new definition of delight.

His lips remained on hers, his mouth fused with hers, and they shared every breath, every gasp, every groan.

Faster, harder, deeper; wordless but insistent, as her inner tension mounted she pushed him on, and he gave her all she asked for, every last iota of power she demanded, and she met him, matched him—gloried that she could.

That she could, indeed, be the woman she wanted to be—the woman she'd always sensed she could be in his arms.

Then tension spiked—and rose again, sharper, tighter, more acute.

And she needed yet more; she clung and gasped his name.

He responded by surging deeper yet, into her mouth, into her body. Their skins afire, their bodies slick, he pushed her on, up a peak composed of nothing but sensation.

One last hard thrust, one last tensing ratchet—and it felt as if a spring broke and flew apart.

Abruptly, the world fell away, and they were flying.

Into a cataclysm of sensation. Into a starburst of pleasure.

She shattered, and shards of ecstasy speared down every vein—then release, true release, hit her.

She was dimly aware that he went rigid in her arms, that his roar of completion was muffled by their kiss.

Then he slumped, and she held him.

Boneless and drifting on a sea of glory, she held him to her and listened to their hearts.

\* \* \*

Marcus returned to the land of the living by very slow degrees. Ultimately regaining sufficient wit to realize he was still lying fully atop Niniver—no doubt smothering her—he managed to summon strength enough to draw his hands from her lush curves and withdraw from her, then he slumped alongside her.

She didn't like him leaving her; even though she didn't waken, she made a grumbling sound and followed his movement, turning to slide her arms around his waist and rest her head on his chest.

Something in him tightened. Gently holding her to him, he pushed the covers, currently tangled beneath them, down, then drew them up over their cooling bodies. Reaching out, he turned down the lamp, then gathering her closer, settling her in his arms, he propped his chin against her head, closed his eyes, and let the moment draw him in.

Let himself wallow.

He must have sunk into satiated slumber. When he woke, the angle of the moonlight slanting through the window suggested several hours had passed.

She was sleeping soundly, a warm armful of feminine curves tucked against his side.

Exactly where she was supposed to be.

His inner self knew that without question, accepted it without quibble.

This was, he supposed, Fate at her finest.

Claiming Niniver in every way had been an intrinsic part of his ultimate goal. After the events of the day, he'd needed—with a compelling ferocity he did not, even now, fully understand—to have her beneath him, wanton and open, to hear her breathy cries of surrender as he buried himself in her body and made her his.

And he had. Now, she was his.

And, yes, he could see that that also made him hers.

It seemed a fair exchange.

So Fate in the form of some idiot with a rifle had pushed him into her bed, propelling them into intimacy. Thus succeeding in linking them irrevocably, because now more than ever he was never going to let her go.

Well and good. His next step along this ever-evolving path was, quite obviously, to get her agreement to marry him.

A proposal seemed...possibly too precipitate. While he would be happy to utter the appropriate words the instant she woke up, how would she respond to such a sudden offer?

Glancing down at her fair head, he frowned. He really had no idea what she would think if he uttered those fateful words now, immediately.

He had sisters. He had female cousins. He knew well enough that the customary male notion that if a well-bred virgin gave herself in passion, then she probably had marriage on her mind, while most likely true, was never a wise assumption to admit to. Even in the most straightforward circumstances, wise men trod warily around that point.

With Niniver, the circumstances were anything but straightforward. She assumed that her position as clan leader made marriage too risky, and he could see her point. Her stance was correct, were it any man but him.

He was no threat to her or her position. And he never would be.

For him, marriage to her would never be about that—about what she could bring him. First and foremost, for a man like him, marriage had to be about what he would bring her—namely security, protection, and help in easing life's burdens from her shoulders.

He knew his role.

But she didn't.

She thought he was like most gentlemen she knew, and he wasn't.

She was attracted to him, and she had wanted him enough to take him to her bed, although how much of the urgency behind her actions had been due to her near-brush with death he didn't know and couldn't guess.

More, she'd embarked on the engagement having already informed him of her decision never to wed, so although she might be happy to continue an affair, the passion they'd shared didn't mean that, overnight, she would change her stance on marriage.

Simply asking her to marry him now wasn't likely to yield the result he wanted. Worse, any too-precipitate declaration might work against him, painting him as a threat. He suspected that, no matter any private feelings, she was more than capable of banishing him for, as she would see it, the good of the clan.

The more he thought of it, the more it seemed clear

that proposing to her immediately would not be a wise move.

That didn't mean he had to wait overlong—just long enough to expand and ultimately correct her view of him and his expectations of their marriage.

His easiest way forward might well be to make her fall in love with him. His father and Thomas had achieved a similar goal, so that shouldn't be beyond him.

He spent the next half hour devising a strategy.

Gradually, sleep crept closer, luring him back to slumber.

As his mind started to drift, he remembered Mc-Dougal. He'd seen off the man in Ayr, and Niniver had made her preference plain. McDougal hadn't been happy, and he could have guessed they would be returning along the highway later that afternoon.

Could McDougal have been the one who had shot at her?

At her?

Or had McDougal shot at him?

The latter seemed a more likely possibility, yet surely such a suspicion was far-fetched.

Still, he knew McDougal hailed from the Highlands, and he had an excellent contact up there. Easy enough to ask for information.

He yawned and sank deeper in the bed. "Even if just for my own peace of mind."

He closed his eyes and let sleep drag him down.

# Nine

Hours later, Marcus was seated at the dining table, working his way through an extra-large helping of kedgeree, when Niniver breezed into the room.

She halted, and their gazes collided. For one finite instant, they both looked into the other's eyes, then she flashed him a brilliantly bright smile. "Good morning."

He inclined his head and murmured a more cautious "Good morning" back. From her wide-eyed look and that over-bright smile, she was skittish and unsure how to react. How to behave with him, now that they'd been intimate. He let his gaze skate downward. "How's your ankle?"

She appeared to be moving without restraint.

"Much better." She headed for the sideboard. "The binding helps. I can walk on it normally, and it doesn't hurt."

While she helped herself from the dishes arrayed on the sideboard, he addressed his attention to his plate. He'd forced himself to leave her clinging warmth and return to his room before she'd woken to spare her the inevitable awkward moment. Also to ensure she didn't tempt him to engage with her again. Now that he'd experienced the wonder, just the thought of the heated clasp of her body was enough to arouse him to a painful degree. When it came to her, to engaging with her, his will had been eroded and was now distinctly weak; if she pushed, if she demanded, he would follow wherever she led.

But protecting her was a task with many aspects, and one of those involved protecting her from unnecessary hurt, even if brought about by her own actions.

On top of that, he wasn't sure how she now viewed their activities of the night. For him, the heated moments had been more intense than any in his previous, rather extensive, experience. As she was his fated bride, he'd all but expected that; rather than being a surprise, the intensity had been a welcome confirmation. But she'd been a novice, and despite her passionate nature, untried; while he knew he'd pleasured her, he couldn't tell whether the reality with him had lived up to her expectations.

Some part of him was frankly aghast that he was even in the vaguest way doubting his own performance, and if she'd been an experienced woman, the notion wouldn't have entered his head. But she hadn't been experienced, so she would have no yardstick against which to measure the night—no previous standard to which to compare him.

As she approached the table, making for a place opposite him, and a footman stepped forward to hold her chair, Marcus studied her face, her features—and inwardly admitted he was nearly as uncertain over how to behave as she. Now she'd had a chance to think, to evaluate, had she enjoyed being intimate with him... or not?

He'd never in all his adult years suffered from such a lack of confidence. From such an excruciating vulnerability. With any other woman, the question wouldn't have been so important, yet with her, it was crucial.

It was also, he judged, not a question to which he was destined to get an answer anytime soon.

Niniver arranged her toast on her plate. She could feel Marcus's gaze on her face, but she didn't meet it. How did one interact with someone one had spent the night with, naked? She was certain he would know how to proceed, but she didn't. When she'd woken and found him already gone from her bed, from her room, she'd told herself the wisest course would be to assume that nothing in their outward behavior should change...yet now she was facing him across the dining table, she didn't see how that could work. Something fundamental between them *had* changed, and every nerve she possessed knew it.

"Here."

She glanced up. He was holding out the pot of marmalade. She reached for it. "Thank you."

Their fingers brushed. Instead of the sharp spike of skittering awareness she'd felt in days past, this time she felt a reassuring warmth. Setting down the jam pot, she drew in a deeper breath, then glanced from her plate to his. "Perhaps I'll try a little of the kedgeree." Now she thought of it, she felt ravenous.

He looked down at the small mountain he was intent on demolishing. "It's excellent. Your cook—Gwen, isn't it?—knows her kippers."

She wriggled her chair back, then rose and returned to the sideboard. "I gather she's partial to kippers herself, so she's very particular."

A minute later, she returned to the table, sat, and tried a forkful of the kipper, rice, and egg dish. Swallowing, she nodded. "You're right. It is very good. The seasoning's just right."

After a moment of watching her eat—was it her imagination, or was he faintly amused?—he murmured, "I gather Gwen makes kedgeree most mornings. Haven't you tried it before?"

Without raising her gaze, she considered, then replied, "I definitely ate kedgeree when I was younger, but I don't think I've tried it since Gwen became cook." She swallowed another mouthful and declared, "Hers is different."

He returned to eating. "I suppose each cook makes her own version."

"Well"—she waved her fork—"just think how much difference there can be in something as simple as scrambled eggs."

"True. I once had some made with truffles. Odd."

They continued trading stories of breakfasts they'd known; somewhat to her surprise, the moments passed more easily than she'd expected, and then they were rising from the table—and if she didn't yet feel confident that she'd found the right way to interact with him post-intimacy, she got the distinct impression that he, too, wasn't entirely certain of the reverse, either.

The latter observation made her a little less nervous. They walked side by side into the front hall. Again, her nerves no longer leapt at his nearness; instead, they seemed to hum, while her senses purred.

She forced her mind to focus—to remember what she needed to do that day. Halting, she glanced at him.

"I've estate business I must attend to. I'll be in the library."

He waved her down the appropriate corridor. "Lead on."

She did, and he prowled almost languidly in her wake. On reaching the library, she opened the door and headed down the long room toward the desk at the far end. How was she going to concentrate on the reports, accounts, and letters she had to deal with if he was hovering?

But how could she get rid of him? Did them being intimate give him new rights? Or, at least, new expectations?

She rounded the desk, halted before the old admiral's chair, and looked down at the plethora of documents arranged on the desk's surface, all awaiting her perusal. He'd prowled to a halt by the desk's side and was watching her and taking in the same sight, when a tap on the door he'd closed behind them had both of them glancing that way.

"Come."

At her command, the door opened, and Ferguson leaned in. "If you've a moment, my lady, there are several members of the clan who would like to speak with you."

She shook her wits to attention. "Yes. Of course." She debated whether to sit and decided against it. She was short enough as it was, and whatever her clansmen wanted to speak with her about, she'd do better standing. To Ferguson, who had paused as if to give her time to compose herself, she said, "Please show them in."

As Ferguson turned to summon whoever was waiting in the corridor, from the corner of her eye, she saw

Marcus move; he came further around the desk to halt a little way behind her left shoulder. His stance had altered from moments before; he was no longer relaxed, and somehow, he looked distinctly forbidding. Not quite projecting menace, but with an unsubtle promise that menace was only a blink away.

Before she could decide what she felt about that—about his clear signaling that he supported her—her attention was drawn to the men—a small procession of them—who came tramping through the library door.

Her instincts twitched as she saw who they were. Jed Canning was followed by his younger brother, Stewart, then came John Brooks, Ed Wisbech, Jem Hills, Liam Forrester, Martin Watts, Camden Marsh, and, bringing up the rear, Clement Boswell.

All the clansmen who had made her life a misery in recent months.

She fought to keep a frown from her face.

"Your would-be clan suitors?" came a deep dark rumble from behind her.

She nodded curtly but didn't glance around. He'd spoken too softly for anyone but her to hear. Ferguson had led the men in. They formed up in a loose line across the library, facing her down the length of the room. Sean followed Clement Boswell in, closed the door, then took up a stance before it.

She looked at Ferguson inquiringly.

"They want to tell you something." Ferguson looked at the line of men, all of whom glanced at him. Every last one looked supremely uncomfortable.

Then Liam Forrester lifted his head, cleared his throat, and stated, "We—each of us—wanted to say that we're sorry. For all the things we've done while, well, trying to get you to choose one of us." Carefully, he dipped his head. "We wanted to apologize and promise we'll never bother you again."

"Aye." Jem Hills was nervously clutching his hands. "We won't come singing beneath your window o' nights."

"Nor yet get into your flowers," Stewart Canning offered. "Not anymore."

"And me and Clem"—not to be outdone by his younger brother, Jed Canning spoke up, glancing at Clement Boswell, who nodded in agreement—"we want to apologize for scaring you with our fighting. We didn't mean to frighten you, nor say the things we did."

"We got carried away, like," Clement growled.

Unmoving and unmoved, Marcus listened as each of the men tendered their abject apologies to Niniver and promised never to, as they put it, bother her again. Well and good, but there was more to their embassy than that.

Every man, after tendering his apology, looked—pointedly—at him. Throughout the performance, Ferguson and Sean constantly looked his way, checking that he was listening and that he was hearing the real message they'd all come there to convey.

He did understand. They were stepping out of his path—resigning the field, as it were, to him.

They were also indicating in the clearest way they could, short of a verbal declaration, that they would support him in winning Niniver's hand.

All of which was heartening, encouraging, and also a trifle unnerving. He hadn't realized he'd been that transparent, but apparently his intentions regarding Niniver had been sufficiently well understood and, as happened within clans, promulgated widely. But what was most unnerving was that Niniver's clansmen would—quite clearly—now be watching, waiting, all but looking over his shoulder while he pursued her...

Jaw firming, he told himself that at least none of them would be getting in his way, and if he needed anything arranged, he had no doubt that all in the clan would now rush to aid him.

And, of course, she would no longer be distracted by her clansmen's antics.

All in all, it seemed that Fate had, again, moved to clear his route forward.

He ignored the prickle of wariness that tickled his nape and slid down his spine.

Niniver stood behind the desk, her gaze dutifully locked on her idiot clansmen, and fought to keep her thoughts from her face. With every bumbling apology, her heart sank lower. Blast them! Couldn't they have waited even a few more days?

She'd only just discovered—only tasted just once—the pleasures to be found in Marcus's arms, and here they were, systematically removing his reasons for remaining at Carrick Manor. For him to stay under this roof, so that he and she could continue to explore the landscape they'd discovered last night.

First, they'd driven her to frustrated distraction by their ridiculous acts, and now, when she'd finally managed to wring some good from the situation, here they were undermining her again!

*Aargh!* She felt like screaming, but of course, she couldn't. She had to keep her temper reined; she couldn't even snap at them.

The last to tender his full apology was Clement

Boswell, who admittedly had committed more sins against her than any of the others. Reaching the end of a lengthy recitation of his actions, Clement sent a commiserating frown along the line of his peers. "I knew as we never should have listened to that bloke."

The others nodded, most gloomily, some grimacing—clearly at their own foolishness.

"What bloke?"

The question from Marcus nearly made Niniver jump. So silent had he been throughout the performance that she'd almost forgotten he was there.

Clement directed a careful look up the room. "A swell—a gentleman, I suppose he was, a bit down on his luck. He used to drink regular at the inn in the village."

"Aye," Jed Canning said. "It were he gave us the ideas for how to approach you, m' lady." Jed shrugged. "Seemed a good idea to us to follow his advice, seeing he was a gentl'man and all, and more likely to know what you'd like."

Niniver was stunned. Before she could find her voice, Marcus asked, "What did he look like, this gentleman? Do you know his name?"

The men glanced at each other, then Jed looked at Marcus. "He was tallish, but not as tall as you. Browny hair."

"Brown eyes," Liam Forrester put in. "And his clothes weren't as nice—a bit shabby around the edges, if you know what I mean."

"Hazel eyes, really," Ed Wisbech said. "And the only name I ever heard was Doug. Mr. Doug, the barkeep used to call him, but he—the gentlemen—hasn't been around for the past few weeks."

Marcus had known the keeper of the village inn

all his life. If he needed further information—further confirmation—it would be easy to get. He nodded at the men. "Thank you. I believe I know who it was who led you astray. Let me know if you see him around these parts again."

"Oh, if we see him again, we'll be having several words with him ourselves, you may be sure." Clement Boswell cracked his knuckles meaningfully. Every one of the men looked like they'd have a few words to add to whatever Clement thought to say.

Marcus looked at Sean, then at Ferguson, and nodded. Sean stepped back and opened the library door. Ferguson waved the men toward it. With bows and gruff goodbyes to both him and Niniver, the men filed out. With final nods up the room, Sean and Ferguson followed.

When the door shut, Niniver swung to face him. "Ramsey McDougal?"

He met her gaze, saw the ire in her eyes. "So I would guess." His mind was leaping to several further conclusions, but of those he as yet had no proof.

Niniver had been searching his face—for some sign of what, he wasn't sure—but now she swung back to face her desk, surveyed the piles of papers upon it, then she pulled up the chair and sat. "At least they now know better than to follow McDougal's advice." She started shifting papers—then, as if she were speaking to herself, muttered, "Sometimes I wonder if I'll ever see the end of Nigel and Nolan's legacy."

Still standing where he'd been, to her left and a pace back from the desk, he heard the underlying frustration in her tone, and wondered...but until he had some greater right of claim to her confidence, he couldn't push for an explanation.

And from the glimpse he got of the set of her lips and chin, she wasn't about to offer one.

That there was something more going on, some deeper problem with the estate or the clan's finances—or both—seemed fairly certain, but he couldn't help her in that sphere unless she invited him in…

Was this a viable opening? An opportune moment to steer her toward the notion of marriage now that her clansmen had so clearly withdrawn from the lists?

He started to juggle ways of approaching the subject.

She slammed one paper down on a pile and grabbed up another, then made a disgusted sound. "Manure! Who would have imagined they could possibly get into a dispute over manure?"

Her rising tone, let alone the violence of her movements, bore testimony to her present temper.

Deciding that, after all, now was not the time to go down on bended knee, he murmured, "I've several letters to write. I'll be in the study."

"Hmm." She dipped her head to show she'd heard, but didn't lift her gaze from her papers.

Marcus headed for the door. Proposing could wait for a more propitious moment. Right now, he had the matter of McDougal to attend to, and for him, protecting Niniver would always come first.

\* \* \*

He returned to the library an hour later. Niniver was still sitting behind her desk, still poring over the papers spread over its surface.

She looked up when he shut the door. She watched

him walk down the long room. He wondered at the odd expression on her face, closed, tense, yet as if she were drinking in the sight of him…as if he'd be gone tomorrow.

No chance. He didn't know what might have made her think that, but he wasn't about to leave, and he wasn't about to be dismissed, either. Especially not after last night.

Halting before the desk, he held out two of the letters he'd spent the last hour writing; he'd already given the one for his family in the Vale to Sean to deliver. "I'd be grateful if you would frank these."

A slight frown still inhabiting her eyes—she'd been all but scowling at her papers when he'd walked in— she took the letters and scanned the directions. "Glencrae? He's a connection of yours, isn't he?"

"Yes. He married one of my father's cousins. They live in the Highlands."

She wrote her title across the corner, then looked at the second letter.

"The Hemmingses in Glasgow are Thomas's kin— connections of yours."

She humphed and wrote again.

"Thank you." He scooped up the letters and dropped them on the tray on the corner of the desk. The tray already contained several missives addressed in her neat, distinctly feminine script.

She'd looked back at the papers spread before her. Her expression… She almost looked defeated.

She started chewing her lower lip again.

Tamping down his instincts, which insisted he should outright demand to be told what the problem was, he hesitated, then walked to the nearest armchair, dragged it around, positioned it before the desk, and sat.

And waited.

Slowly, her gaze rose, until it fixed on his face. She continued to frown. She studied him for a moment, then prompted, "Did you want something?"

Several responses popped into his mind, but he squelched them. "Actually, I was wondering if you might want—or at least could use—something I can offer." His tone even, he continued, "I've worked with my father managing the Vale lands for the past ten and more years. I managed the estate on my own for nearly a year when my parents were traveling, before Thomas came. I now run my own estate. I know quite a lot about agricultural enterprises, especially those in this locality. I also have contacts in many levels of commerce." He tilted his head. Holding her gaze, studying the weary anxiety in her eyes, as gently as he could, he said, "You're clearly finding something difficult. If I can help, even if just as a sounding board, someone to listen to your ideas and concerns…" With one hand, he gestured. "I'm here. Use me."

Her frown slowly faded. She stared at him, clearly considering—transparently debating what she saw as a fairly momentous decision. As the seconds ticked by, he wondered yet again what on earth it was she was hiding. And if he had to guess, she was hiding it from everyone, and had been for some time.

Eventually, she drew in a slow, deep breath. Her gaze still locked on his face, she compressed her lips to a thin line…then she opened them and said, "When I first went through the estate's accounts after Nolan died, I couldn't understand why he was always so…

*exercised.* It seemed over every little thing, every tiny expense. Over his last months, he'd always seemed on the brink of…not so much rage as panicked desperation. I wasn't trained to know what I was looking at, but I do know my numbers, and I've lived on the estate all my life. So I had some idea, but everything about the accounts—the payments, the orders, the supplies, the yields—seemed, if not hugely prosperous, more or less what one would expect…"

Refocusing on his eyes, she held his gaze, then quietly said, "Those weren't the real books. Nolan kept the fake books here, in this desk, in case anyone came looking. The real accounts he kept in his room. When I found those and went through them—" She broke off and drew in another breath, using the moment to steady her voice. "When I finally understood the reality of the clan's situation… Suffice to say, I understood Nolan's panic."

"How bad was it?"

"As things then stood, the clan couldn't have seen out last year. I wondered if that was what ultimately drove Nolan into that chasm. He'd murdered to get the lairdship, but once he had it…he failed."

"Yet you've managed." Marcus paused, then asked, "What did you do?"

"I had money of my own—Papa's older sister was an eccentric, and I inherited her small fortune, and I also had some funds from Mama's family. I shifted most of those funds into the clan's accounts." She paused, then added, "No one knows, so please be discreet."

He nodded. "So your funds floated the clan through the immediate storm, but that's not what's worrying you now."

"No, it isn't." She looked at the papers covering the desk. "Now I'm worried that even putting *all* my funds in isn't going to be enough."

He didn't say anything for a long moment, but when she simply chewed her lower lip and volunteered nothing more, he leaned back in the armchair, balanced one booted ankle on his knee, and fixed his gaze on the bookshelves beyond her. "One thing my father drummed into my head—and the heads of all my siblings, the girls included—is that if you need help, you ask. That the old custom of trying to forge on and do it all yourself is not a strength, but instead a weakness." He paused, then went on, "The Cynster family is widely regarded as one of the wealthiest and most powerful in the country—and with good reason. And part of that reason—the true source of the family's strength—is that neither its wealth nor its power flow through just one man, or even one branch of the family tree. For instance, my uncle's the duke—so if you have a political or government-based problem, he's the one to ask. He and my aunt, the duchess—her contacts are as extensive and as powerful as his. But if you have any question about orcharding, it's my father's cousin Spencer Cynster you appeal to. For horses, there's no authority better than Demon Cynster and his wife, Felicity. For investments of the financial variety, it's Rupert Cynster. For any type of jewelry or antiquity—or even a house—it's Alasdair Cynster you ask. And so on."

Shifting his gaze back to her face, he went on, "The thing is—you ask. If you have a problem that touches an area you aren't an expert in, you ask someone who is—and even if they don't know the answer, they'll know someone who does." He nodded at the letters he'd dropped on the tray. "I wanted to know more about Ramsey McDougal, so I asked. I wrote to Glencrae, because McDougal is from the Highlands, and Glencrae is a Highland earl and well placed to learn what I need to know—namely why the scion of a Highland laird is lurking in, of all places, Ayr. McDougal's been in the vicinity for more than three years, and that in itself is strange. He has no local connections that I know of—which is the purpose of the second letter. The Hemmingses will know if McDougal has legitimate business interests in or around Ayr—or if they don't immediately know, they'll know who to ask to find out."

He paused, then added, "It hasn't escaped my notice that Ayr is a considerable way from the Highlands, and with all the ships coming and going constantly from the harbor, it also has a ready-made escape route."

She blinked. "You think McDougal's...what? A criminal?"

"Perhaps not quite that. But, as you noted, he was a crony of your brothers, which does not suggest that he's an upstanding citizen."

She grimaced and looked down at her papers. "No, indeed."

"However, to return to my point—that's the way a large, powerful, and successful family works. We ask each other for help, and help is always forthcoming. A family who understands that their true strength lies in assisting each other is the most powerful clan around."

She raised her gaze and met his squarely. "I don't have that sort of family."

"No. But I do." He held her gaze. "And you have me."

Did she? Niniver looked into his eyes and saw the

same steady, unwavering strength she always associated with him staring back at her. For a silent minute, she held his regard and let herself acknowledge that he was suggesting she ask for his help. She didn't need to beg but simply ask. And if she did, he would help her.

She'd already told him so much, why not the rest? And if, as he'd suggested, he could help her? Then for the good of the clan, she should take him up on the offer.

Which, she had to admit, was a very neat piece of rationalization, even for her.

Yes, she was close to reaching the end of her tether. Yes, she was almost to the point of grasping any lifeline she could find, yet in telling him the real source of her anxiety, wasn't she also trying to tie him to her? To keep him there—to give him a reason to stay? A reason that might work to hold him at the manor for the foreseeable future so that she and he could continue their liaison?

That was what she wanted; there was no question in her mind about that.

When he'd come in and then sat in the armchair, she'd been sure he'd come to tell her that, as she no longer needed his protection, he was leaving and returning to Bidealeigh.

Instead, here she was, being tempted—by him—to appeal to his protective, champion-like streak again.

Yet he was inviting her to ask, and he seemed to enjoy the challenge of helping her. Cast in that light, her manipulation was actually mutually beneficial…

She looked down. Selecting from the various piles, she picked up two sets of papers. "As far as I can tell, it's the balance of things that's going to make keeping the whole enterprise afloat seriously difficult."

He took the reports she handed him. While he glanced at them, she clasped her hands on the desk, and proceeded to describe the clan's financial problems as she saw them—something she'd shared with no one else.

The relief…was enormous.

He asked questions, and she answered. Now she'd opened the floodgates, she saw no reason to try to restrict the flow. If he could help her, if he would help her, then it behooved her to share all she knew.

At one point, she admitted, "Part of the reason I was so annoyed with my would-be clan suitors was that I was struggling with all this for the clan, and they seemed intent on making my life harder."

He grunted understandingly, then asked about the crop yields.

They went through everything. He queried the need for several payments, but when she explained, he understood. She was relieved to discover that he *listened* to her and took in the substance of what she tried to convey. Like her father—but unlike her brothers—he seemed to understand the need to take into account the people involved, and that, at its core, a clan was about its people. Ultimately, he agreed with her assessment that she'd already cut every expense that could be cut without damaging the clan itself.

But his probing didn't end there. At his suggestion, they separated all the threads of the estate's business dealings and evaluated each separately. That involved pulling out all the current ledgers, as well as the ledgers from the past several years for comparison. He fetched two other tables from the other end of the library and set them to either side of her desk so they could spread out the documents and still see everything.

Ferguson looked in to ask about luncheon. She directed him to bring in a cold collation, and she and Marcus ate and drank as they worked.

As the afternoon wore on, between them, they drew up charts of expenses and income for each clan business, then focused on those areas where, in the short term, the former exceeded the latter. Ultimately, Marcus pushed everything aside bar their charts and, sitting in the armchair he'd pulled up to the front of the desk, drew a timeline, once again showing expenses and income, week by week.

Sinking into her admiral's chair, Niniver leaned on the desk and peered across it as he wrote. His scrawl wasn't as legible as her writing, but it was mostly figures; she could make it out.

Finally, with a flourish, he circled three payments. "There." He sat back, stared at the timeline for several seconds, then raised his gaze to her face. "Those are your problem payments. By the end of the year"—he pointed to the figure at the bottom of the sheet—"you'll be ahead—not by a lot but by enough to be comfortable. Enough to take the clan through into next year, and through the next season, and things should get better after that."

She drew the sheet around and studied it. The payments in question were large—larger than any extra funds she could lay her hands on. She grimaced, but recalling his earlier admonition, she looked at him and asked, "So how do I get around these three problems?"

His lips curved in fleeting acknowledgment, but

then he sobered. "As I see it, you have three options. You could approach a bank or an investor for a loan. You could mortgage clan land, even just a part of it. Or..."

Marcus paused. He knew better than to suggest she accept a loan from him or his family; every clan had its pride. But he seriously doubted a bank would grant a loan to a clan with a lady at its helm, and mortgaging was problematic, given they were talking of clan lands. He focused on the sheet covered with his scrawl, currently in front of her. He frowned and held out his hand. "Let me see that again."

She handed over the sheet.

He ran his eye down both columns, noting the flow of the figures. "If, in the end, you come out ahead, then it might just be possible to alter the *timing* of your payments to keep the clan's head above water, so to speak." He grimaced at the sheet; he'd used the collated figures to compile it. "We need to go back to our earlier calculations and figure out what goes into each of these payments, and whether some can be split into smaller amounts stretched out over longer periods."

She didn't understand at first, but once he showed her what he meant, she threw herself into the arduous chore of breaking up all the amounts they'd previously consolidated. He worked on the expenses; she tackled the income.

Another hour ticked by. Ferguson supplied them with tea and thick slices of fruitcake, which they absentmindedly consumed. They brushed crumbs from the desk and continued scribbling. She'd stated that she knew her numbers; as he glanced over the figures she supplied, he was impressed by her accuracy. She was a great deal more reliable than his brothers.

The afternoon was sliding toward evening when, finally, they packed away the account ledgers, tidied the piles of notes, and at last laid out their assembled summation of the projected incomings and outgoings, broken down into individual payments week by week.

Marcus placed his palms on the desk, leaned on his braced arms, and scanned the figures. Niniver came to stand beside him; biting her lip, she did the same.

Slowly, something that felt very like triumph bloomed inside him. He forced himself to check twice more before he raised her hopes, but yes, the way was there. "You can do it." Glancing sideways, he met her gaze. "If you tell these four merchants"—looking back at the papers, he pointed to four names, accounting for four large payments over the year—"that the clan wishes to set up a monthly account, with a regular monthly payment, you'll even out the payments sufficiently to never be short of funds."

Looking down at the sheet, at the names, she frowned. "Will they agree?"

"Yes, they will." Straightening, he grinned. "They actually prefer such arrangements, because it makes them feel more certain that they'll be getting paid, and in reliable, regular installments, which helps them with their cash flow. However, while it means the clan will be making the earlier payments before the money actually needs to be paid, by the time you get to August"—he pointed at their sheet—"and later here, and here, then the clan is actually in arrears, but only for a short time—just for that month—but the merchants don't see that as a problem because they have their monthly payments in place."

He paused, then said, "They get security and certainty, and you get around your three difficult times." Glancing at her again, he studied her face. "By doing that, arranging that, you can steer the clan safely through this year."

Her gaze locked on their analysis, she sank slowly down into the chair behind the desk. He rounded the desk and sat again in the armchair facing it.

Eventually, she raised her gaze to his face, to his eyes. The cornflower blue of her eyes was hazed with emotion.

"Thank you."

There could be no doubt of the gratitude behind the words. She looked down at their papers—at what amounted to a rescue plan.

He knew the clan meant a great deal to her, that she took her position as elected leader very seriously—indeed, to heart. Yet this...beneath her words, in the depth of the relief emanating from her, he sensed... some deeper level of commitment.

"Niniver?" He didn't know how to ask, had no idea what it was he was sensing, but he had to know. If something existed that affected her this deeply, he had to know what it was. When she raised her gaze and again met his eyes, he made a vague gesture, encompassing everything they'd been working on for the better part of the day. "Why?"

Somewhere in the depths of her quiet self, there was some reason, some answer to that question—he felt sure of it.

She studied him for a long moment. A full minute

ticked by before, her voice low, she said, "On the day my father was buried, I lingered, just for a moment, before I turned from his grave."

He remembered. He nodded.

"I…" Her gaze grew distant, and she frowned. "I suppose you could say I understood him—certainly better than Nigel, Nolan, or Norris ever did. Much better than he understood any of us." She drew a long breath, her gaze still far away. "I knew he'd been murdered, and I knew even then that under Nolan, things wouldn't go as they should. Not as Papa would have planned, much less wanted."

She paused, and he sensed her focus turning inward.

Then she went on, "I know he never really saw me, that he would never have imagined I could ever accomplish anything for the clan. Yet when I stood looking down at his grave, I felt… I suppose you could say that I truly felt what it means to be a Carrick."

She refocused on Marcus's face and went on, "I made a vow that day, to Papa and to all the Carricks who had gone before, that I would do everything in my power to right any wrongs done by my brothers, and that I would restore the clan to prosperity, come what may."

*That* was what had moved her to selflessly shift almost all of her funds into the clan accounts. What now pushed her to make things right, regardless of any cost to her.

Her jaw firmed, and she tipped up her chin. Marcus didn't need to hear her say "I see that vow as a sacred one, an unbreakable obligation to my father and to the clan, and I will do everything I must to see it through" to know that that was true.

Her gaze had grown almost challenging—as if she thought he might scoff or make light of her commitment.

Nothing could be further from his thoughts, from his instinctive reaction. Meeting her gaze, holding it, he inclined his head. "Thank you for telling me. It makes it easier to understand what you want to do." Easier to know how to help.

The knowledge also left him, again, with a sense of discovering an even greater depth to her. She didn't just have facets—she had layers of facets; he wasn't sure a lifetime would be long enough to discover and explore them all. But reinterpreting all he'd seen of her in light of her vow…he could now understand the unrelenting focus she'd brought to restoring the Carrick clan, could now see from where her indomitable will sprang.

Commitment was something he understood. To say he was impressed by hers would have been a gross understatement. Every time he thought he saw and understood her, that he'd taken her full measure, she revealed another element of her character that didn't just appeal, but reached to his soul and resonated so truly, with such clarity, that he understood what it meant to be smitten.

The gong to remind them to dress for dinner reverberated through the house. They both instinctively glanced toward the door, then looked back at each other—then they lowered their gazes to the plethora of papers still lying all around them.

"We should put these away." Rising, she picked up their analysis—the outline of their plan to rescue the clan.

Pleased she'd said "we" and not "I," he rose and reached for a stack of notes. "Keep those pages where you can readily consult them and keep track of the amounts as they come through."

She nodded and slid the papers into the top drawer of the desk, then joined him in tidying the room.

# *Ten*

When and how was he going to ask her to marry him?

As night closed in around the manor, Marcus stood at the window in his room, idly looking out while reviewing the events of the day. With respect to getting to some suitable point when he might with reasonable hope utter the words "marry me," the day had been a case of one step forward, closely followed by one fractionally shorter step back. Yet despite the frustration, he felt he'd made progress. She'd finally trusted him enough to share the reality of her problems regarding the estate, something she hadn't shared with anyone else.

The knowledge that he'd gained her confidence and had succeeded in helping her chart a way forward had warmed him through the evening—one spent in easy conversation over the dinner table, followed by entertaining themselves in the drawing room with music from Miss Hildebrand, from him, and from Niniver.

And Niniver had started to relax; her smiles had come more readily, more naturally, as spontaneous expressions of happiness. The songs she'd chosen had reflected her improving spirits. He'd noticed that, and so

had Miss Hildebrand, although unlike him, she hadn't
known what had caused the change. Again, he'd felt as
if his halo was glowing; easing burdens from Niniver's
shoulders was a role he intended to permanently claim.

On top of that, the acceptance implied by her telling him of her vow over her father's grave had further
raised his hopes. More, learning of that vow and understanding her unwavering commitment to it had only
drawn him even deeper under her spell.

Putting family—or clan—above oneself to the point
of personal sacrifice was a warrior's code, yet one some
women shared. In Niniver, the propensity seemed an
integral part of who she was. He now knew her well
enough to harbor no doubt that she would strive to the
nth degree to fulfill what she viewed as a sacred obligation. She was the opposite of those who took—as
Nigel, Nolan, and even Norris had. Instead, she gave.
And gave.

That was one reason—almost certainly the principal
reason—why she was so highly regarded and innately
trusted by her clan; they saw her as their savior, and in
that they saw her clearly. And her propensity for giving without reservation was, clearly, destined to be one
aspect of his future role. Protecting her from giving to
the extent of exhausting herself, of running down her
personal resources to nothing. Wise warriors knew to
conserve enough strength to fight another day, but as
far as he'd seen, Niniver had no inherent limits. She
would give until she dropped. Or until someone hauled
her from the fray.

His role, obviously.

In some ways, that was what he'd done today, and
it had felt…perfect.

So the day had been far from a waste, yet he had still to reach a viable position from which to ask for her hand.

A light tap fell on his door, then it opened.

Niniver walked in.

Despite the gloom—he hadn't lighted any lamps—she saw him immediately. She closed the door, then walked—boldly, with very clear intent—toward him.

His thoughts scrambled. In a fleeting flash of insight, he realized that a large part of the uncertainty that had him still dithering over when to ask her for her hand owed its genesis to his expanding view of her. The more he saw of her, the more fascinating she became—the stronger, the more challenging—and the more clearly he perceived the befuddling contradiction between her fragile outward female form and the fiery passion and steely will within.

Each day he spent with her only deepened his understanding of what an unexpectedly complex and rivetingly powerful female she truly was—and would become.

And…he wanted her to love him. Not just need him.

The realization struck him—not as a shock, not as a result of anything outside him, but as a tide welling from a source he'd only just discovered inside him.

He could hardly be surprised. He was a Cynster, after all.

But what if he proposed, and—given her commitment to the clan, given her vow to her father—she felt obliged to accept for the good of the clan, rather than because she wanted him, desired him—loved him—in the same unrestrained and unconditional way he now wanted, desired—and, yes, *loved*—her?

She halted before him and, through the shadows, looked into his face.

Given her attraction to him, he'd assumed that gaining her agreement to marry him would be a simple matter. He could almost hear Fate laughing.

Her eyes searched his, then she raised a hand and laid her palm on the center of his chest.

His muscles leapt, arms instinctively tensing to rise and reach for her. Ruthlessly, he clamped down on the impulse.

But she sensed it. Her lips lightly curved, feminine confidence blooming. "As you're staying—"

"There is no price to be paid for my help this afternoon."

The statement was categorical, his tone almost harsh.

Tilting her head, Niniver searched his eyes, his face—what she could see of it in the dim light. Everything she could sense confirmed that he wanted her as much as she wanted him.

She'd paced—quietly—in her room for the past fifteen minutes, wondering...then she'd taken her courage in both hands and come tapping on his door. Given all she could sense, just from the simple contact of her hand on the top button of his waistcoat, of the passions rising to swirl around and between them, she was very glad she had. "I wasn't thinking in such terms. After last night, as you are still here... I assumed you would come to my room. To my bed."

His eyes, even darker and more fathomless in the night, remained locked on hers. "It's customary, through the evening, for a lady to give a gentleman some sign."

"I didn't know—I don't know how such things are done." She lifted her shoulders fractionally. "So I came to you." When he didn't respond, she went on, "I want more—more of you, of us. And you want the same."

She'd decided, and she was determined to seize every moment granted her, to claim every minute, every night, to extend their liaison for as long as she could. "Is there any reason we—you and I—can't simply be as we wish? Do as we wish? Here, together—just us?"

It was as if those words released something in him. She all but felt his rigid control waver, then fall.

"None at all." His arms rose, coming around her. His hands spread over her back. "And I definitely want more of you."

She stretched up as he bent his head. Their lips met, touched, brushed, then melded. She parted hers, and he entered, confidently claiming with a languid ease that somehow increased her anticipation.

Coming up on her toes, she met him, matched him, drew his tongue deep, then sent hers questing. Knowingly letting her own passions rise, sliding one hand up over his shoulder to cup his nape and anchor her, she kissed him back—and slipped the top button of his waistcoat free.

Tonight, she wanted more than to simply follow his lead. Tonight, she wanted to explore, to learn more—not just of him but of herself. She wanted to be, to live as the woman she'd discovered through the previous night she could be—the woman she became in his arms.

Getting him to shed his coat and waistcoat wasn't that hard; when she tugged, without breaking the kiss, he obliged and shrugged out of both garments and tossed them at a chair.

Then his hands were on her, tracing her curves, more demanding. Commanding.

She consciously let go and let the tide of compulsion that rose between them have her, take her, sweep her up and on.

He was adept at managing buttons and laces, his fingers swift and sure. She sent the fingers of one hand sifting through the dark silky locks of his hair, while with her other hand, she undid, one by one, the buttons closing his shirt.

Their lips parted only just long enough to allow them to draw fractured breaths before engaging again. Hot and slick, their tongues dueled, and her attention vacillated between the heated engagement of their mouths, the inciting pressure of his hands as he kneaded her breasts, and the enticing planes of his chest that she was intent on uncovering.

Heat rose and swirled, flames of desire licking, tempting. She felt that ineluctable warmth rise through her, urging her on, wanting more—a deep-seated needing.

A marrow-deep yearning.

But this time she knew satisfaction would come, that they would in the end reach that point of indescribable repletion. While the intensity of need remained, the compelling urgency still thrumming through their veins, the beat was less frenetic, the rhythm more steady and assured—much less desperate.

This time...they could take whatever time they wished, he and she both, to absorb every last nuance. As she couldn't know for how long he would remain—

how many days and nights their liaison would stretch for—she'd resolved to make every second count.

Then his shirt hung open; she laid her hands on his skin and claimed.

And he let her. Let her fill her senses with his body, with the heat and the promise inherent in the heavy bones and defined muscles while, garment by garment, he divested her of her clothes.

And she helped him out of his.

Soon, he was gloriously naked, but she wore many more layers. Yet not even her hands caressing his jutting length succeeded in diverting him from his purpose; if anything, the flames simply leapt higher, and he worked even more diligently to free her laces.

Her light corset hit the floor, then her chemise joined the rest of her clothes and she stood naked before him—except for her garters and stockings. When dressing for dinner, she'd removed the binding about her ankle; the joint hadn't troubled her all day.

Modesty had been for the night before; tonight was for fascination.

For an intent and a focus that was absolute, that fixated them unrelentingly, unwaveringly, on each other.

For five thudding heartbeats, they stood bathed in stark moonlight, viewing each other, each possessively cataloguing. Each equally greedily drinking in the promise.

Her mouth had dried; anticipation tightened her nerves.

He exhaled and went down on both knees before her. He cupped his palms about her ankles, then ran his hands upward, hot palms gliding over the backs of her calves, through the sensitive hollows behind her knees, and up, until his fingers touched her garters. With slow, controlled, caressing touches that made her shake, he undid both garters and, with fingertips trailing over her skin, rolled down her stockings.

One hand gripping his shoulder, she lifted one foot, then the other, allowing him to draw the stockings free. He sent them to join the pile of her clothes on the floor.

He sat back on his heels. Naked in the moonlight, like a dark god he looked up at her. Then he reached for her, closed his hands about her hips and drew her closer. "Come here."

She let him draw her nearer, shifting her feet to either side of his knees, as he seemed to wish. She caught a glimpse of his lips curving in a smile that looked expectant and hungry, then he leaned in and pressed a hot, wet, open-mouthed kiss to her navel, and she gasped.

He licked, laved, and set about tasting her. Tipping back her head the better to breathe—not that it seemed to help—she shifted her hands from his shoulders to his head, and held him to her.

His head dipped lower. His lips and questing tongue blazed a trail downward.

As he continued to weave his sensual magic, her breathing fractured and grew increasingly harried.

Then he was nuzzling the apex of her thighs. His tongue delved, sensation speared through her, and she barely swallowed a shriek. *"Marcus!"*

"Hmm."

That was the extent of his verbal response. His intimate explorations continued, deepening and expanding; he lifted one of her thighs and draped her knee over his shoulder, opening her to him, to his expert ministrations.

He licked, lightly suckled, probed...until she was breathless, and witless, and close to collapsing with unadulterated pleasure.

The intensity of her spiraling need shocked her, but she wasn't about to deny herself—or him—this. Rather than retreating, she embraced the moment, the experience in all its glory, with an abandon that rose from her soul. From her need to be this woman—vital and vibrant, and fully engaged with life.

Fully and intimately engaged with him.

Securely supported by his hands locked about her hips, tilting her and lifting her softness to his ravaging mouth, she surrendered, gave and took, and with her fingers gripping his skull, she held him to her and urged him on.

The flames within her surged, then roared; passion erupted and spilled down her veins.

And with every long, raspy lick, every scalding suckle, the conflagration only grew.

She felt her nerves begin that telltale coiling, and yet, yet...

It took several seconds for her to define what was not quite right. To realize that she wanted, with an unforgiving craving, to have him inside her.

Summoning every last ounce of her remaining will, she curled her fingers in his hair and tugged. She couldn't find words enough to demand.

But he understood. Perhaps he felt the same. Setting her on her feet, keeping his steadying hands on her hips, he rose.

If the steely rod of his erection was any indication, he wanted what she did, every bit as urgently.

His face was graven, the austere planes etched with

passion. His gaze, dark as the midnight sky yet ablaze with heat, locked on her face.

Her hands tensing again on his skull, she moved into him—as he drew her closer.

Their bodies met, heated flesh to burning skin. He bent his head and she stretched up, and their lips, their mouths, fused again.

Hotter, more urgent, more desperately intimate, the kiss seared.

She felt his hands ease down and slide around, then he gripped and raised her. Instinctively, she parted her thighs, clamped her knees to his flanks—and then he was lowering her. She gasped as she felt the engorged head of his erection breach her entrance. He lowered her further, fraction by fraction, and forged steadily in.

Filling her.

She lost the last of her breath on a gasp as he seated himself fully within her. The sensations... She clung to him, to the kiss, as tactile stimulation overran her mind.

But then he raised her—until she almost protested, expecting to lose the thrilling sensation of him buried so deeply within her, but at the last moment, he reversed direction and lowered her again—and she realized, accepted, and let the flames rage.

He raised and lowered her, and she clung and they burned, the heat of the engagement beyond scorching. She concentrated on using her inner muscles to caress him—and was rewarded with the sound of his fracturing breathing, with the tightening of his grip on her bottom, and the feel of his muscles turning to steel.

Yet although the shifting of his chest against her swollen breasts was another senses-stimulating rasp, she craved his weight—and with him, in this sphere, she'd given herself permission to demand all and everything she wanted.

Dragging her lips free of their kiss, she panted, "The bed."

From under heavy lids, his eyes touched hers. He held still for an instant, then, still holding her, he turned and walked to the bed.

The shift of his erection within her as he paced across the floor made her moan.

He reached the side of the bed, but instead of laying her down upon it, he turned and sat. Grasping her thighs, he rearranged her legs so that she straddled him. His gaze, the smoldering dark of his eyes half hidden by his long lashes, locked with hers. He eased his grip, and his large hands traced upward, cruising over her hips, up the planes of her back to her shoulders, then he slid his hands down her arms and fell back on the bed.

She tipped forward and caught herself with her palms on his chest. Bracing her arms, she blinked down at him as her body adjusted to the new position, to the altered angle. The feel of him high within her impacted even more strongly on her senses.

For a second, she closed her eyes, absorbing the reality, then she looked at him, licked her swollen lips, and managed, "Now what?"

He held her gaze. "Now you ride."

When she stared at him, unsure, he grasped her hips and raised her, then let her slowly sink back of her own accord... Her lids lowered, weighted by sensory pleasure, but she saw him close his eyes, clearly involuntarily. Instinctively, she tightened about him, and a guttural moan slid past his lips.

She didn't need further encouragement or instruction. She'd ridden all her life; she quickly learned the knack of rising and sinking down—it truly was like riding. And this time, the reins—their reins—were entirely in her hands. She experimented with pace, with angle and pressure.

He reached up and captured a breast in each hand, kneaded, then plucked her nipples.

When, eyes closing, she gasped and writhed, changing the way she rode him, he grunted and stroked the tightly furled buds again.

Heat flared, and the now-familiar flames rose up, licking over her flesh and his, leaving them dewed with the sheen of desire.

She gloried in all she felt, in the repetitive penetrations of the thick rod of his erection, the clamp and release of her sheath about his iron length. Most of all, she reveled in the urgency that built and built between them, that had his hips lifting to meet hers in an impossible-to-control response.

His hands fell from her breasts to her hips. She leaned forward and rode harder. Her hair flailing about her shoulders and flicking again and again across his chest, she whipped them both on.

All too soon, she'd reduced them both to desperation.

To where they had to have more, and more, and more. To where their senses were screaming and their nerves were so tight that just one more ratcheting turn would shatter them.

And then they were there—flying apart as the force of their mutual passions flayed them.

As sensation exploded in a supernova of pleasure and ecstasy claimed them.

She screamed, soft and breathless; his fingers digging into her hips, he held her down and groaned loud and long as he shuddered beneath her.

Her spine, all her bones, turned to jelly. Her strength drained away, and she slumped upon his chest.

Marcus raised his arms, wrapped them about her, and held her close. He listened to her gasping pants, to his own tortured breaths. Heard their hearts thud in unison.

Completion had never been so acute—so earth-shatteringly intense.

So meaningful.

So binding.

He held her and, eyes closed, let his senses absorb *everything*. Let them catalogue the glory of this reality, of their joined and sated state. Let his mind revisit the journey from the time she'd walked in and reached for him, and their lips had met—every little touch, every caress, every shared look.

The taste of her still lay like ambrosia on his tongue—heady, addictive. The velvet softness he'd licked now clasped his member while the satiny softness of her breasts and belly lay like a sensual blanket over him.

She'd stated that she wanted him, that she wanted more of what they'd shared the night before. In falling in with her plans, he'd hoped to gain some insight into how she felt about him, not just in this sphere but on a broader emotional plane. He'd hoped to get a glimpse into her heart, to learn if he'd made any inroads there—if she might have started down the road to loving him.

He'd looked, he'd watched, yet all he'd seen was

her unshielded and unrestrained embracing of physical pleasure with him. She was breathtakingly open in letting her delight and her appreciation show, yet of her heart, he hadn't caught so much as a glimpse.

He had no idea whether he'd even touched her in that way, whether any of what they'd shared had made any impression there.

She gave a little shiver; their bodies had started to cool. He lifted her from him. Together they wrestled the covers down, crawled beneath, then slumped once more into each other's arms.

Lying on his back with her cradled against his chest, he breathed deeply, letting the scent of her, of their lovemaking, sink to his bones—a reassurance on that level, at least. As satiation rolled over him, he wondered, fleetingly, how he was ever going to learn what dwelled in such a heavily shielded heart.

He fell asleep still wondering.

Niniver listened as Marcus's breathing slowed; she listened to him slide into sleep—and marveled at the emotional tide that rose within her. The feeling—the raw emotion—was so much more powerful than she'd ever imagined such a feeling would be.

She knew what the feeling was, knew what powered it, what fueled and governed the overwhelming, almost smothering sensation as it gripped her lungs and tightened about her heart.

But she forced herself to accept and not react. To simply let the feeling rise and wash through her.

One day, most likely soon, he would deem her safe and wish to return to his life at Bidealeigh. And when he did...she would have to smile lightly and let him go. She could not cling. She could not—would not ever—

let him see that her heart had become so deeply ensnared, so irrevocably enamored. It wasn't his fault that he was the one and only man who had ever truly seen her, who had ever appealed to her in a physical way.

She'd begged for his help, and he'd undertaken to protect her from external threats. From the first, she'd understood that it was her duty to protect her heart. That she hadn't done so had been her own decision, one she'd made with full knowledge of the consequences. It would be fundamentally wrong to try to bind him to her because of her own waywardness. And in recompense for risking her heart, she'd already gained more than a reasonable reward. Yes, her heart would ache after he left, but if she hadn't grasped the nettle and pushed to explore intimacy with him—the one man she could imagine exploring intimacy with—she would never have known the wonders she'd already experienced.

And she would never have known what it was to love, either.

To love and lose—hadn't someone written that to do so was better than never to love at all?

Whoever it was, they'd had it right.

And along with the welling warmth in her heart, she was also truly grateful for all he'd shown her, revealed to her, of herself. Of the woman she'd always suspected lay within, but who she'd never let out before—had never been able to allow to fully manifest.

With him by her side, every day, every night, she was gaining more confidence in being that woman. And that was making her stronger, ultimately better able to care for the clan.

Lulled by the waves of warmth lapping about her,

drawing her senses toward sleep, soothed by the thud of his heart beneath her cheek, her mind drifted, imagining…recoiling and rejecting.

She knew what sort of man he was. She had to make sure she never let him guess how she felt about him. She had to cling to her pride and keep her guard well up—because the very last thing she ever wanted to face was to have him offer his hand and his name because he felt he had to, because of honor or social pressure.

She couldn't bear that.

Eyes closed, she reached inside and touched the golden warmth that now lived inside her—the source of those overflowing feelings.

She would know it, explore it, even revel in it, but she would keep it close—close enough that he would never guess.

\* \* \*

"Damn!" Ramsey McDougal shut the door of his room. He walked to the chair beside the table and slumped into it.

He stared into space for several seconds, then glanced at the latest bottle of cheap whisky sitting by his glass on the table. He debated, but didn't reach for the bottle. He needed a clear—clearer—head.

Leaning his forearms on the table, he tapped the fingers of one hand on the surface.

He was running out of time.

"I knew it would come someday, but three weeks?" His whisper echoed in the sparsely furnished room.

His most pressing creditor had hunted him down— or rather, the man's lackeys had. The pair had cracked their knuckles menacingly while informing him that he needed to repay his sizeable loan—with interest—in just twenty-one days.

He didn't have the money. He had less than a guinea to his name.

After several minutes of blankly staring into space, he straightened and reached for the bottle. He poured himself half a glass, then recapped the bottle, lifted the glass, and, narrowing his eyes, sipped.

He continued sipping as his plan for financial relief took shape in his mind. He'd long ago realized that, for his purposes, Niniver Carrick was his best bet. "I wouldn't have to marry her inside the three weeks—the announcement of an engagement will be enough to hold the vultures at bay."

He didn't particularly want to return to the area so soon. If at all possible, he would prefer not to cross paths with Marcus Cynster—at least not unless he, rather than Cynster, was calling the shots.

Yet given the connection he'd seen between Cynster and Niniver, could he afford to waste even a day?

He swallowed a mouthful of the rough whisky, ignoring the nasty burn. Then he curled his lip. "Do I really care if Cynster tempts her into his bed?" The answer, in reality, was no. He cared nothing for Niniver herself, not in the greater scheme of things. She was pretty enough to excite his interest sufficiently that bedding her would be no hardship, but whether she was a virgin or already well broken in, he didn't care. "Just as long as it's me she ties the knot with, that's all that matters."

Gradually, the facets of his plan took shape, sliding into place one after another until he had something that resembled a workable whole.

He drained the glass, swallowed, and grimaced. "It might be a touch harebrained, but harebrained worked for Nolan. Even if he lost his wits later, his plan worked perfectly."

Ramsey didn't intend to lose his wits. Features set, he reviewed the plan, then nodded. "Wild and unexpected it might be, but that's probably what I need to win against a Cynster."

# Eleven

Marcus was waiting for Niniver when she appeared in the dining room the next morning. He intended to open a new front in his campaign. Despite the nebulous urgency he still felt over gaining her agreement to wed him and his resulting impatience, he was too experienced to cram his fences. He smiled and inclined his head to her. "Good morning."

"And good morning to you." Her smile sunny, her mood transparently bright, she went to the sideboard.

When she turned and came to the table, he rose and drew out the chair beside his.

She accepted the invitation with an openhearted smile, one of such ease, of closeness and unconscious trust, that he felt something inside him swell.

After settling her, he resumed his seat. He'd already finished eating; he reached for his coffee cup. "What are your plans for the day?"

She glanced at him, and her smile faded. She hesitated, then asked, "Do you need to return to Bidealeigh?"

Lowering the cup, he shook his head. "The staff know what they're doing, and there's nothing I need to preside over at the moment. And if anything crops up, they know where to find me." He smiled easily and waved one hand. "If there's any subject on which you'd like assistance or advice, consider me at your disposal."

She debated for only a second. "There's a new company that has contacted us, wanting to buy our goat hides to make gloves—I haven't met their representative before. I wouldn't mind... Well, I would appreciate your presence and any insights you might have as to any deal we might discuss. And later, I have a meeting with the local agent from Carter Livestock. In the past, they've taken our excess cattle at a reasonable price, but according to Rafferty, the agent, the prices are well down this year."

Marcus arched his brows in surprise. "I haven't heard anything about prices being down."

Niniver's chin firmed. "Indeed. I'm not at all sure I believe him. Then again"—she shrugged—"who knows?"

His face hardening, he inclined his head. "When is your first meeting?"

She glanced at the clock on the sideboard. "Not for another hour. Just enough time to have breakfast and check on Oswald. I told Sean I'd look in on him."

\* \* \*

They returned from the stables, where Oswald appeared to be reveling in all the extra attention occasioned by his injured flank, and stepped into the side corridor in time to hear voices in the front hall. Ferguson and some other man.

"That must be the man after our goat hides." Niniver tweaked Marcus's sleeve. "Let's go this way."

She led him via the servants' corridors to the service door toward the end of the library. She quietly opened the door and went in. Marcus followed and shut the door. She went to the desk, sat behind it, then quickly neatened the piles of papers.

Marcus's gaze remained on her for several seconds—she felt the warm weight—then he walked to one of the nearby armchairs, picked it up, carried it back, and set it to the side of and a little behind the desk.

He straightened as Ferguson knocked.

"Come," she called.

Ferguson looked in, smiled to see her—and Marcus, too—ready and waiting, then he announced, "Mr. Quinn from Waltham and Sons, my lady." He stepped aside and held open the door.

A short, rather rotund individual, conservatively attired in a jacket of subdued tweed, with thinning brown hair and round spectacles perched on the bridge of an undistinguished nose, came into the room. He walked with an almost mincing gait.

She rose. "Mr. Quinn." She indicated the chair facing the desk. "Do sit down."

Mr. Quinn advanced. His gaze moved from her to Marcus, then back again. A puzzled frown overlaid his expression. "Good day, my…er, lady."

She smiled politely and sat.

When Quinn again looked his way, Marcus inclined his head and, his expression uninformative, sank into the armchair; from the corner of her eye, she saw him arrange his long limbs in an elegant sprawl, entirely at his ease.

Quinn, in contrast, rather stiffly subsided and sat very upright in the chair, then placed his leather satchel across his knees.

She clasped her hands on the desk and regarded him

levelly. "I gather you have a proposition concerning goat hides to put to the clan, sir. If you would outline your interest, perhaps we can do business."

Quinn's expression grew uncertain. "I...ah." Fleetingly, he glanced at Marcus, then refocused on her. "I was hoping to speak with your...husband, perhaps? With the laird of the clan?"

Marcus stirred, drawing Quinn's attention. "Lady Carrick is formally the Lady of Clan Carrick. It is she you need to see." He caught Quinn's gaze. "She you need to convince of the value of your proposition."

"Ah." Quinn blinked, several times. Then he drew in a breath and, looking again at her, dipped his head. "My apologies, my lady. I wasn't aware. I hope you will excuse my clumsiness—it was entirely inadvertent, I assure you."

Marcus decided that, appearances aside, he approved of Quinn. Not many men would have moved so adroitly to retrieve their position.

"Apology accepted, sir." Niniver waved at Quinn to continue. "If you could explain your company's interest in our goats? I admit we haven't previously been approached about their hides."

"Indeed? Well, Waltham and Sons is keen to establish new sources of supply. The company..."

Marcus listened as Quinn explained his company's position in the world of glove manufacture, and their consequent interest in the Carrick goat herd, small though it was. When the fussy little man realized that Niniver not only knew which breed the Carrick flock was comprised of, but also the exact number of animals raised and slaughtered each year, he grew positively eager. Marcus hid a smile; from his attitude,

Quinn was now seeing Niniver not as any delicate and fragile lady, but as the owner of a goat herd he and his company would very much like to be able to buy from.

When it came to discussing the details of the putative deal, Niniver needed no help—and Quinn was no longer in any danger whatsoever of dismissing her or her acumen. A certain amount of haggling ensued. Marcus was quietly amazed at the price Niniver finally persuaded Quinn to agree to—per goat. The arrangement struck appeared pleasing to both parties; from Niniver's perspective, it would ensure a very welcome addition to the clan coffers this year, and in the years to come.

With his business successfully concluded, Quinn packed up his satchel, then rose and, beaming, held out his hand. "It's been a pleasure doing business with you, Lady Carrick."

Niniver rose and briefly shook his hand, then Quinn nodded amiably to Marcus, and turned for the door.

Marcus fell in at Quinn's heels and showed the man out. Closing the library door, he reflected that, despite her stated wish for support, in dealing with Quinn, Niniver had needed no help.

Her next visitor, however, was of a very different stripe. Fifteen minutes after Quinn had departed— minutes Marcus and Niniver had spent reviewing the state of the goat herd and discussing the potential for expanding it—Ferguson knocked and, after being commanded to enter, he opened the door and announced, "Mr. Rafferty from Carter Livestock, my lady."

Marcus uncrossed his legs and rose. Niniver came to her feet more slowly; one glance at her face, and he got the distinct impression that she didn't like Rafferty.

Again, her instincts were sound. Although they'd never met, Marcus recognized the man; his father had long ago pointed him out as one agent a wise man wouldn't trust. Tall and originally of rangy build, Rafferty was now expanding about the middle, yet he walked with a confident swagger, and his eyes were hard.

"Mr. Rafferty." Niniver's tone held a touch of imperious distance. She waved to the chair Quinn had vacated. "If you would be seated."

She sat, and waited only until Rafferty's breeches touched the chair's seat to state, "I've reviewed the prices we've received from Carter Livestock over the past several years. I understand you wish to lower them."

Although they'd never been introduced, Rafferty recognized Marcus, which left the agent uncertain how to proceed. He studied Marcus, once again seated at his ease, from under lowering brows. "If I may make so bold, sir, I've always dealt with a Carrick with regard to the Carrick cattle. I understand that Lady Carrick is now head of the clan."

"Indeed." Marcus smiled with an amiability that did not reach his eyes. "As you so rightly note, I'm not a member of the clan, but in this, you may consider me"—he vaguely waved—"her ladyship's assistant."

Rafferty nearly choked trying to smother his snort. But after a second's debate, he transferred his gaze to Niniver.

She caught his eye and arched her brows. "Mr. Rafferty—I'll be frank. I see no reason to lower the price the clan will accept for our animals. There has been no change in commercial conditions. If Carter Livestock cannot come up to our mark, then we will need to find some other company to deal with."

"Oh, you won't do that." Rafferty leaned back and tucked his thumbs in his waistcoat pockets. "I can assure you that you won't find any other company willing to offer as much as me and Carter Livestock—that's why your dad did business with us for so long. And as for reasons—well, the market's next to flooded, isn't it?" Without pausing for any response, Rafferty rolled on, elaborating on what he insisted was a glutted market.

When Niniver gave no sign of weakening, much less collapsing and begging him to take the clan's cattle at the low price he repeatedly stressed was the very best any agent would offer, Rafferty grew increasingly belligerent.

Marcus tensed, but held himself back. Niniver's expression had grown stony and remained unyielding.

Finally, his gaze locked on Niniver's face, Rafferty leaned forward, gripping the front of the desk as he concluded, "So, you see, you really should accept my price." He searched Niniver's face. "So do we have a deal?"

Niniver looked him in the eye. "No."

Rafferty blinked, then he surged to his feet and leaned threateningly over the desk. "What—"

Quicker than thought, Marcus was on his feet. "Rafferty." He didn't need to lower his tone to menacing; it was already there. When Rafferty glanced his way, he continued, his voice even, his diction precise, his gaze locked on Rafferty's flushed countenance, "The Lady—that's Lady with a capital L—said 'no.'"

For an instant, Rafferty glared at him; unmoved, Marcus stared steadily back.

Niniver looked from one to the other; when it came to intimidation, Rafferty was significantly outclassed. She allowed the stand-off to continue for a moment more, then she rose, drawing Rafferty's attention. "Thank you, Mr. Rafferty. Should the clan decide to continue our association with Carter Livestock under the terms you've outlined today, we will be in touch."

Rafferty blinked. He looked from her to Marcus. Then he straightened and tugged his waistcoat into place. "I can tell you, you won't get any better price—"

"Thank you, Mr. Rafferty. You've made your position quite clear." She stared evenly back at the man—something she found relatively easy to do with Marcus standing beside her. She nodded in curt dismissal. "Good day, sir."

Rafferty had no choice but to grit his teeth, turn on his heel, and stalk to the door. He opened it and walked through, leaving the door swinging.

Marcus stirred, then ambled down the room. He shut the door and prowled back to the desk.

She blew out a breath and sank into her chair. "Dreadful man."

"Indeed." Marcus halted. He reached out and pulled the chair he'd used back around to face the desk.

Once he sat, she met his eyes. "I haven't heard even a whisper about the price of cattle falling, have you?"

He shook his head. "And I certainly wouldn't trust Rafferty's—or, indeed, Carter Livestock's—word on the matter."

She sighed and looked down. After a moment, she

asked, "Do you know of any other agency we might approach to sell our cattle?"

She glanced up and saw his gaze grow distant, but then he refocused on her face. "If I were you, I'd write and ask Thomas. Two years ago, and I would have been certain who was best for you to deal with, but since Thomas married Lucilla and came to the Vale, I've been working exclusively with sheep. However, I did hear that Thomas found some new and better avenue for our herd, and from memory, your herd, although smaller, derives from much the same stock as ours."

She nodded. "Yes, they're much the same." She considered, then opened a side drawer and drew out a fresh sheet of paper. "I'll write to Thomas." Picking up a pen, she continued, "I've a suspicion Rafferty will be back, and I would so like to be able to tell him we're sending our cattle to someone else."

Marcus grinned. He watched her bend over her letter and decided the morning had gone rather well.

\* \* \*

After an uneventful afternoon and evening—and a far from uneventful night—Marcus succeeded in tempting Niniver to take out her pack of deerhounds and go hunting through the hills with him.

Just him. They didn't need anyone else—an arrangement she'd agreed to quite happily.

As they tramped over the rough grasses of the lower slopes and passed into the shadows of the taller trees, he allowed his mind to apply the right word to his actions. Wooing. Perhaps not in conventional style, but wooing nevertheless.

Wooing Niniver.

He glanced at her as she strode beside him. She was

looking down, watching where she placed her feet. She'd worn a heavy twill skirt, with a simple jacket over her blouse. Like many local women—ladies included, for practicality's sake—she wore trousers beneath her calf-length skirt and petticoat. Her riding boots showed beneath the hems and reminded him of her injury. "How's your ankle holding up?" They'd left the horses in the last of the paddocks and had been tramping for twenty minutes at least.

"It's completely recovered." She raised her head and shook back her hair. "I didn't wear the bandage at all yesterday, and I didn't feel the slightest twinge."

The words had barely left her lips when she stumbled.

He swooped and caught her in one arm. Holding the rifle he was carrying to one side, he pulled her upright against him.

She exhaled in what sounded like a long-suffering sigh. Then she wriggled.

He eased his hold enough to allow her to turn in his arm and face him.

She looked into his face, then she patted his chest. "It's all right. Just a rock sliding beneath my boot, and it wasn't even the same leg."

He knew his face had set in grim, rather skeptical lines.

She studied his eyes, then smiled, stretched up, and planted a light kiss on his lips. "I'm perfectly all right. Now let me go, and let's move on."

He humphed and complied. They'd brought five hounds with them, selected after some deliberation from her pack. Two were her strongest dogs, one was a promising younger dog, and the last two were bitches, sisters from her air-scenting family.

The hounds had come to mill about them, as they usually did, wanting to know what was going on and be a part of it. Once he'd freed her, Niniver shook out her skirts and gave the hounds the order that sent them back into a scouting pattern. Then he and she walked on.

They walked and tramped, scrambled up several narrow valleys, and steadily climbed higher into the foothills. It was the end of the recognized season for roe deer does; they sighted several red deer, but as they'd left the boundaries of the Carrick estate behind and were therefore on Crown land, they complied with the recognized prohibitions, restrained the hounds, and let those deer go.

It had been late morning when they'd left the horses. When they reached the upper limit of the tree line and stepped out into an expanse of wind-ruffled grass, Niniver tipped her head back and studied the sun. "It's well after noon. Let's stop for our picnic."

Marcus had been looking around. "There's a brook nearby—I can hear it."

Niniver gave her bitches an order. The pair raised their heads, sniffing the wind—then both turned and looked down a slight slope.

"Very neat." Marcus resettled the hunting bag he'd carried slung over one shoulder. "Let's see if they're right."

She snorted. "Of course they're right."

And so it proved. She set off in the direction the hounds had indicated and, at the base of a nearby dip, found a tiny brook running along a stone-strewn bed.

They spread the canvas Marcus had carried rolled up and lashed to the base of the hunting bag. He set the bag on the canvas, and Niniver busied herself unpacking the repast Gwen had provided. Local cheese, freshly baked bread, slices of ham, and pieces of roast fowl—chicken, partridge, and guinea fowl—plus egg sandwiches and cucumber sandwiches. There was a stoppered bottle of ale for Marcus, and one of the cider Niniver favored. There were also bones and hard biscuits for the hounds.

As she turned to distribute the largesse to the dogs, Marcus let himself down beside her. "A repast fit for a king and his hounds."

She turned to him and arched a brow.

He grinned. "And, of course, his queen."

*His* queen. She held his gaze and wished the midnight blue of his eyes wasn't quite so impenetrable, yet his expression remained lighthearted, easygoing, with nothing to suggest that he'd meant anything by the possessive pronoun…even though something in the way he'd said it had sent a ripple of awareness through her.

Letting the point slide, she looked into a side pocket of the bag, then reached in. "Peaches, figs, walnuts, and apricots, too." She displayed her finds, then laid them down with all the rest. "Where to start is the difficulty."

He unstoppered the bottle of cider and handed it to her. "With whatever your fancy favors."

Again, she detected an undercurrent of…suggestiveness in his tone. She glanced up and caught the watchful gleam in his eye. She smiled, inclined her head fractionally, and reached for the cider. "Indeed. That's an excellent place to start." Raising the bottle to her lips, she sipped.

He chuckled and reached for a chicken leg.

They ate in companionable silence. The shallow dip they were in was more a dimple in the side of the hill; the ground fell away beyond its lip to reveal a wide and distant view stretching all the way to the Rhinns of Kells. It was immensely pleasant sitting in the sunshine, feeling the warmth seep into her shoulders, hearing the soft snuffles as the dogs, satisfied with their snack, settled to doze in shaggy heaps around them.

She hadn't thought it likely, but between them, they ate everything Gwen had packed; the result of outdoor exercise, she supposed.

Replete, she sighed, then stretched out on her back and stared up at the nearly cloudless sky.

After several moments, Marcus shifted the empty pack, then he stretched out his long legs and lay down beside her, close enough that the shoulders of their jackets brushed, but otherwise not touching.

"I shouldn't lie here too long, or I'll freckle."

He laughed softly. "I hate to tell you, but you already have several freckles across the bridge of your nose."

"Thank you. I needed to hear that."

"Actually," he continued, as if she hadn't spoken, "I rather like them. I find myself unexpectedly partial to the sight."

And what was she supposed to say to that? Instead of attempting any reply, she closed her eyes, drew in a long breath, and slowly exhaled. "I'd forgotten what it's like—to spend the day just walking, without any real purpose. Without needing to do anything. I'd forgotten how much I enjoy it—how...restful this truly is. Thank you for suggesting it."

Without looking her way, Marcus reached over

and closed his hand around hers, raised it, and gently brushed a kiss to the backs of her fingers. "Believe me when I say that the outcome has been entirely my pleasure."

He was somewhat surprised by how true that was. How deep and real that pleasure. Knowing that, in arranging for this day's excursion, he'd succeeded in giving her a respite from her cares...warmed him in a way he'd never quite felt before. Intertwining their fingers, he lowered their hands, then simply lay beside her and, as she was, stared up at the endless blue of the sky.

It was tempting, in the drowsy haze induced by a full stomach and the lazy warmth of the sun, to contemplate kissing her—and then exploring what other delights the day might provide—yet...there was something to be said for keeping the day on this plane, one of simple pleasures.

He was conscious, again, of giving weight in his mind to her standing, to her position. They were in the open, and anyone—some of her clansmen out enjoying the day as they were—could wander by. In planning and plotting, in weighing his options and considering what actions he might take, he was somewhat surprised that the habit of considering how any action of his might impact on her standing as clan leader had so quickly become all but instinctive. If not his first thought in any situation, then certainly his second.

Given the position he coveted—that of her husband—falling into that habit was both reassuring and wise. He would always need to tread carefully around her, wary about damaging her standing with others. As he'd done with Quinn and Rafferty. He hadn't stepped in—effectively stepped in front of her—until Rafferty had crossed the line and become an overt threat.

Truth be told, he'd felt rather proud of his restraint.

He needed to absorb at the deepest level, to have his instincts comprehend and accept, that his role was to support her, not direct her. To shield, but not isolate.

To leave her with her will, her determination, and her dignity intact, to allow her to lead and act, and never to corral or hold her back.

His father had learned the knack, and his brother-in-law was walking the same path, too. In his case... The truth was he'd been born and bred to do this. To, as many men of their class would see it, play second fiddle to a lady.

His eyes drifted closed; his lips curved. His grand-mother Helena had had it right. For men like them, playing consort to a woman took more self-confidence and masculine strength than simply being a dominant male.

To men such as him, dominance came easily, while recognizing, respecting, and accommodating a lady's strength was a challenge.

One he felt he was meeting.

Minutes later, Niniver sat up. "If we remain here, I'll fall asleep, and then I'll burn."

"In that case"—he sat up, too—"let's get on."

The dogs roused and shook themselves. Niniver flicked the canvas free of crumbs, then folded and rolled it up, and handed it to him. Other than the empty bottles, there was nothing of any weight left in the bag. He slung it over his shoulder, shifted it so it hung at his back, out of his way, then he picked up the hunting rifle he'd borrowed from the rack in the manor's game room.

Niniver whistled the hounds into formation. He joined her, and they walked back through the trees and headed down the ridge, circling back toward the horses.

They tramped downward by way of narrow valleys they hadn't used on the way up. And saw no sign of the elusive roe deer.

He kept a close eye on the hounds. The simple pleasure of the day should have been reward enough, yet... As they started down another narrow fold in the land, he murmured, "I'm going to feel quite lacking if we return to the manor with nothing to show for the day."

Niniver glanced sidelong at him, then shifted her gaze back to her hounds. "It was a lovely day, regardless. No one will think—"

The dog in the lead halted. Head up, he looked to their left. Over a lip, the land fell away, and the trees grew more thickly. Whatever the dog had sensed, she couldn't see it.

The pair of bitches joined the lead dog, both scenting the air...both also froze, focused on the thicket.

Without a word, Marcus shrugged the bag from his shoulder and held it out to her. She took it, then watched in silence as, using the hand signals she'd trained the dogs to obey, he chose the lead dog and the oldest bitch to go with him, instructing the other three hounds to stay with her.

Then he angled toward the thicket and stalked, soundlessly, into the trees.

She waited. A minute ticked by, then she heard a panicked crash, almost immediately followed by the sharp retort of the rifle. Another, slower, set of crashing noises followed, and then all fell silent.

She crouched and called the three remaining hounds

to her, distracting them while she unlaced the rolled canvas from the hunting bag. Then she hefted the bag over one shoulder and, with the canvas in her hands and the hounds eagerly crowding near, went into the trees.

Marcus had brought down a nice-sized roe deer doe; he was trussing the dead animal's hooves when she reached him.

She'd long ago accepted that, as the deer were plentiful and people had to eat, taking the occasional animal was no crime against nature. She also recalled that Marcus, along with his family in the Vale, followed a rigid code regarding the taking of life on The Lady's lands.

He glanced up when she halted beside him. Seeing the canvas in her hands, he nodded. "Thank you. Can you help me roll her up?"

Between them, they wrapped the deer in the canvas, leaving the trussed legs, front and rear, free.

"Does your cook know to use all of the kill?" Marcus asked.

She nodded. "We follow the same creed as in the Vale." Now she thought of it… Straightening, she frowned. "That must hail from times past, when there were more links between the manor and the Vale." She met Marcus's eyes. "I know Algaria was a connection of Papa's, so there must have been a closer link between the households at some point."

"Perhaps." He bent and hoisted the animal so that the body lay draped across his shoulders, with the trussed legs hanging to either side; he gripped the lashed hooves, shrugged the body into position, and held it there. "But more likely, it's because the manor lands, and even the land we're on now, all lie under The Lady's rule."

She bent to pick up the rifle; he'd already ejected the spent shell and had, no doubt, pocketed it. "How do you know? About the manor lands being under The Lady's rule?"

He met her eyes. A second passed, then he said, "I can feel it." He turned and started to walk back through the trees to the path they'd been on.

She followed. When they were once more pacing along, slower now that he was carrying the dead weight of the deer, she asked, "Feel how?"

He thought before he replied, "I'm not like Lucilla. She... It's almost as if she can open some sort of direct channel to The Lady. For me, I have to be walking the land to sense Her. She's a presence—like when your senses tell you someone is watching, only in the case of The Lady, it's not watching so much as *being*."

"Can you sense that—Her—when you're riding?"

"Yes, but less certainly."

There were times she forgot that he was somehow connected to the land. It was all a trifle mystical, yet The Lady's power seemed so rigidly benign, she saw no reason to fear it—indeed, to do anything other than welcome it. She and the clan could use all the help they could get. "Even Papa..." She realized she was speaking her thoughts aloud, but when Marcus glanced at her, she continued, "I don't think he *believed*, as such, yet he was always very...respectful of anything to do with The Lady. I remember him saying that he saw no reason to get on Her bad side."

Marcus snorted. "That sounds like Manachan."

Memories of her father rolled over her—not the

more recent memories of the few years before his death, but memories from her childhood, when he'd stood, a larger-than-life figure, all but filling her world.

She felt Marcus's gaze touch her face more than once, but he said nothing more, and neither did she. They walked down to where they'd left the horses. Marcus tied the deer to the rear of his saddle, then he lifted her to her saddle; she called the hounds as he swung up to his. Then they turned their horses' heads for old Egan's farm.

* * *

The following day, Marcus accompanied Niniver on what, she'd informed him, was a regular and routine ride about the estate.

He'd been quietly pleased that she'd invited him to go with her. He would have ridden out with her regardless, but not having to insist that he couldn't protect her if he wasn't with her had been a boon. Especially as formulating any coherent explanation of who he might be protecting her from was no longer as easy as it once had been.

Her would-be suitors from within the clan, those whose actions had originally driven her to seek his help, had openly ceased their pursuit of her. And although all the clan elders had been as concerned as he over the shooting, no trace of the shooter had come to light, and it was increasingly looking as if it truly had been a stray shot from some errant hunter.

All of which suggested that there wasn't any real and present threat to her, and therefore nothing against which she needed his protection.

That didn't mean he would—or, in fact, could— countenance her riding about the estate alone.

They rode east from the manor, then circled south, halting along the way to speak with any men they saw in the fields, and stopping at the various farms and cottages.

He followed Niniver inside the homes, ducking under the lintels to stand behind her shoulder. It rapidly became apparent from the quick, covert glances cast his way that the clan members—like the clan elders—saw his hovering presence as a clear indication of his interest in her.

Well and good, but luckily for him, as Niniver chatted and talked, she remained transparently oblivious of the expectations he saw so clearly in all her clan members' eyes.

When they called at Egan's farm—this time to actually go into the farmhouse and not just the barn-cum-kennels—he discovered the old man lived with his daughter, her husband, and their two sons, one of whom was married and whose wife had recently given birth to twins.

A twin himself, he felt a tug of connection. But when the mother—who clearly knew Niniver well—pressed one swaddled bundle into Niniver's arms, he had eyes and senses for no one and nothing else.

Niniver's expression as she smiled down into the baby's face, as she laughed and let the infant bat at her curls, held so much love and devotion it literally stole his breath.

The sight held him transfixed.

And in that instant, he saw precisely why the clan had elected her as leader. Contrary to what she thought, it had nothing to do with her family name, but had everything to do with her capacity to care. With all her heart, with all her soul.

He'd already noted that she was one of those who gave to others gladly, who more or less lived to do so. What he saw revealed now, as she jiggled the baby in her arms and, smiling like a madonna, cooed softly and made the child gurgle and smile, was a quality of unconditional love he'd seen in no other, a sight that shook him to his soul and left him humbled.

He closed the distance between them, drawn by some invisible force, wanting, without knowing how, to touch that shining joy.

She glanced at him, smiled, and he felt as if that golden glory spilled onto him.

Fearing that his overwhelming fascination would be showing in his face, he forced himself to look down at the baby.

"Here."

Before he could stop her, Niniver was unloading the infant into his arms. As a recently minted uncle, he knew how to hold the child and instinctively did, cradling the bundled form in his arms.

The proud father drew near and stroked the child's cheek with a blunt but gentle finger. "Real little terror he'll be, no doubt."

Somewhat to Marcus's surprise, he found himself responding; within seconds, he'd become a part of a humorous joint attempt at predicting the future for the two babes.

As a well-known twin, he was appealed to for advice, first by Niniver, and then by the parents, grandparents, and great-grandparents. He and Niniver were offered and accepted tea and scones, but then, clearly reluctantly, she dragged herself—and him—away. But as they rode on, side by side through the sunshine, he knew the interlude was one he would never forget.

The thought of Niniver with his son in her arms, smiling at the child just like that...

Three of Ned's long paces, and he pushed the conjured vision deeper into his mind. They had a lot more riding yet to do.

As they circled the manor, halting at each clan family's home, Niniver felt a degree of relief as it became increasingly clear that Marcus's interest in their engagements was genuine—that he wasn't simply following at her heels because he felt obliged to. As they rode between farms, she wrestled with the question of how she might inveigle him to stay, to remain at the manor so their liaison could continue.

They'd only just become lovers, and she felt there was so much more she'd yet to learn, to experience, to know. She wanted as much as she could seize—of him and of them being together. But for that she needed him to stay, and now her clansmen had withdrawn their suits, and she knew of no others of Rafferty's ilk she was likely to have to deal with...

A possible answer slid into her mind as they drew rein outside the Bradshaws'. She put it from her while they were greeted by the burly farmer and his wife, and they chatted about the prospects for the harvest. Bradshaw was one of the clan elders and spokesman for the clan's crop farmers. His support within the clan was crucial, and she had always been surprised that he'd thrown his considerable weight behind her.

Given the financial shoals she was navigating in trying to keep the clan's finances above water, Bradshaw was someone whose reactions she noted more carefully than most.

But when they left, he returned her parting admonition that he should let her know if there was any farm matter with which she could help with a grave nod. "You take care of yourself, too, my lady. Don't think we don't appreciate all you do."

Bradshaw transferred his gaze to Marcus and nodded in farewell.

Wheeling Oswald, she saw Marcus incline his head in reply, then he turned Ned and, side by side, they thundered back toward the manor.

It was nearly time for luncheon, so they didn't dally, which gave her time to think.

When they slowed to enter the stable yard, she caught Marcus's eye. "I haven't been approached recently by any of Nigel and Nolan's friends." She fought to keep her eyes innocently wide. "I was wondering if McDougal will spread the word that I'm out of mourning, or will he keep it to himself, do you think?"

Marcus blinked, but she'd timed the question so that the appearance of Sean and Mitch and the fuss of halting, handing over reins, and waiting for Marcus to lift her down—something she quite looked forward to now, and which was quite the best consequence of her wrenched ankle—negated any chance of an immediate reply.

Thus giving the seed time to sink into Marcus's mind.

Once they were free of the horses and walking toward the side door, she slanted a questioning glance his way.

His expression was impassive, as difficult to read as

ever, but as his gaze met hers, it felt dark and stormy. "I wouldn't like to guess what a man of McDougal's ilk might do, but"—he opened the door for her—"no doubt we'll see."

She stepped into the house, and he followed.

*We'll* see. She felt her spirits rise.

He closed the door and fell in beside her as they walked down the corridor toward the front hall and the dining room beyond. Looking down, a slight frown on his face, he said, "Since seeing you in Ayr, McDougal hasn't made any attempt to contact you. Perhaps he's taken the hint. However, if I recall correctly, there were other cronies of Nigel and Nolan's who have shown an interest in you."

He glanced at her, and she nodded decisively. "Yes. Several. At least three came around. I avoided their calls by clinging to the excuse of mourning." Briefly, she glanced at him. "But I can't do that any longer. If they call, I'll have to see them. Most are sons of well-connected local families—refusing to meet them would be seen as a slight."

Marcus looked up as they reached the open door of the dining room. He waved Niniver inside, and hoped his response to the suggestion of her being forced to entertain Nigel and Nolan's dissolute friends was sufficiently well concealed. "Let's see what transpires. I'm sure if any of them arrive and find me here, in residence, they'll reassess any notion they might be entertaining of pressing their attentions on you."

And if they didn't, he would be only too happy to explain matters.

His lips curved as he followed Niniver across the room and drew out her chair. She'd just handed him another reason to press his own suit as fast as he dared, plus the perfect counterargument should she question his continued presence by her side.

*  *  *

On the evening of the following day, Marcus walked behind Niniver and Miss Hildebrand as they made their way back to the drawing room after dinner. Life was good. The only thing that could make his day better was if Niniver would agree to marry him.

He was starting to view his campaign of wooing her as a matter of weaving multiple threads with which to link her to him. Their day out hunting had drawn them closer on a personal level; today, when she'd retreated to the library after breakfast to deal with the financial accounts and a missive from the clan's bank, he'd presumed on her earlier trust and had followed. He'd had to employ a little subtle encouragement, but he'd been rewarded by her, initially tentatively—almost as if she'd thought *she* was the one presuming—asking for his opinion. He'd given it, and when she'd relaxed and grown more open and encouraging in return, he'd added his advice.

They'd spent all day in the library with the accounts. He'd learned a great deal more of the details of the clan's finances—and had ended even more amazed that a gently bred young lady with no formal training in estate management, much less in dealing with finances, had been able to comprehend the intricacies and achieve so much.

Every time he learned more about her, he grew yet more…fascinated, intrigued, but also respectful and proud.

He'd managed to have a quick word with Miss Hildebrand before Niniver had joined them in the drawing room before dinner. Now, reentering the drawing room, Miss Hildebrand made straight for the pianoforte. "You need some gaiety after all your hard work with those accounts, my dear. I'll play, and I'm sure Mr. Cynster will be happy to oblige and partner you." Miss Hildebrand drew in her voluminous skirts and sat on the piano's bench. She opened the instrument and looked up, her gaze limpidly innocent. "A waltz, I think?"

"Indeed." Marcus halted beside Niniver. As she turned to him, he bowed, then offered his hand. "If you will grant me the honor of this dance, Lady Carrick, I will count myself forever in your debt."

She laughed, but readily laid her fingers across his. "I'm not at all sure, Mr. Cynster, that you have that right." As he drew her into the curve of his arm and she laid her small hand on his shoulder, the blue of her gaze deepened. "For all of these past days, it is I who am forever in your debt, and if you wish to dance, then I'm more than delighted to be your partner."

He stepped out; holding her gaze, he whirled them down the room. At the far end, as he slowed to turn, his eyes still locked with hers, he said, his voice low, just for her, "These moments are not about payment, recompense, or even reward. For me, moments like this, and those we'll enjoy later in the night—all those moments when we laugh and enjoy—have nothing to do with anything beyond ourselves. Beyond you and me enjoying ourselves, enjoying each other. Enjoying being together."

Niniver studied his eyes, his expression, and saw nothing but complete sincerity. And when she thought back over the past days and nights, she had to admit that for her, too, those moments of sheer enjoyment, of simple pleasures, of intimate delight, had been… just that. Moments when he and she had *shared* the pleasure, the experience. And that sharing had only heightened the joy.

He whirled them back up the room. His eyes still on hers, he tilted his head slightly. "Please tell me you feel the same."

There was nothing flippant or flirtatious in his tone; indeed, it hinted at vulnerability. She let puzzlement show in her eyes. "I do feel the same." After a moment, she confessed, "I'm not used to having anyone with whom to share anything, let alone the moments we've been sharing. That's partly what makes me… sometimes unsure." As they swept through another turn, she briefly waved between them. "I'm not even used to having a partner to dance with."

His lips curved at that, and she sensed—indeed, felt—him relax. "In that case"—he fleetingly grinned, and in the next second, stepped out with even greater energy—"we should make the most of this."

She smothered a tiny scream; she felt like she was flying. As if previously he'd held back, but now they were waltzing free.

Hildy noticed and played even more vigorously.

Soon, Niniver was laughing, and so was he.

She let him whirl her on, giddy with a species of effervescent delight, and gave herself over to simply enjoying, to sharing the moments freely, openly, without restraint.

And if, in some dark corner of her mind, caution raised its head, she—as she had ever since she'd initiated their intimacy—pushed it back down with the admonition that, given that their liaison would inevitably end, most likely sometime soon, it was only sensible to seize and embrace every moment of wonder and joy that came her way—every minute of those simple pleasures he and she delighted in and shared.

\* \* \*

Hours later, Marcus lay on his back in Niniver's bed, with her a warm bundle snuggled against his side. Satiation lay heavy upon him, a relaxation so deep it reached to his marrow. But before he succumbed to sleep, the nebulous sense of needing to press ahead and secure Niniver's hand pushed him to reassess yet again. Could he ask her now? Had he waited long enough?

Had she fallen in love with him yet? At least enough to agree to wed him?

He felt he was operating on borrowed time, yet he wasn't entirely sure why. The pressure from her clansmen had vanished, along with all potential threat from them. As for any threat posed by Nigel and Nolan's friends, that would evaporate the instant she agreed to marry him. Without being overly cocksure, he doubted any local gentleman would seek to tread on his or his family's toes; once their engagement was announced, she would be shielded from such men.

He had to confess he was somewhat surprised that Ramsey McDougal hadn't spread the word that she was out of mourning. That would have effectively declared open season on her...which perhaps explained why McDougal had kept mum. If he still had designs on her himself...

Despite the grip satiation had on him, he felt himself tense. He hadn't yet heard from Glencrae, but even letters took time to travel that far. And Dominic might not have known enough himself, might have had to send deeper into the Highlands for information... It could be days yet before Marcus heard back. Days before he could weigh the issue properly and decide if McDougal warranted a private visit.

After all he'd seen and learned over the past days, he wasn't above a little direct intimidation.

He remained astounded by what he'd seen in the clan's accounts—the degree to which, courtesy of her brothers, Niniver had been pushed financially, yet she'd never given up, and had struggled, above all, to meet the needs of the clan.

By hook, crook, and, in many instances, sheer bloody-minded stubbornness, she'd pulled it off.

As far as he could tell, she would soon be out of the woods with the estate. It would take years before the clan was anything like financially strong, but she'd kept their collective heads above water, and the clan was almost on a stable footing once more. If no other financial problem threatened, she would lead the clan onto the road to prosperity, thus fulfilling the essence of her vow to her father.

If she married him, then not even any financial threat would deflect the clan's march toward better times, because as her husband, he wouldn't allow it. He could, and would, ensure that any lingering weaknesses were shored up, either via advice and guidance—or, if necessary, through direct financial aid. But he wasn't going to allow consideration of his value to the clan to figure in any way into her deliberations to marry him—not if he could help it.

Not if he could outweigh and overwhelm all such thoughts with something more powerful.

With love.

Better than most men, he knew what it was, but not even he fully understood it.

Unlike most men of his acquaintance, he was attempting to invoke love, to establish it and use it to his advantage—to help induce her to marry him. He was willing to commit wholeheartedly to loving her if only she would love him in return.

Yet he still couldn't tell what she thought—what she was feeling.

Whether she loved him or was merely delighted to be engaging in an affair with him.

He'd never tried to read a woman's mind before, had never had occasion to need to. Now...

Actions spoke louder than words. He knew that was true, so...

If that was true, then given the tenor of their engagements over the past nights, culminating in the interlude tonight, she had to be, if not already in love with him, then on the cusp of it. Or so he judged.

Every night they came together, their connection—the way they spoke to each other with lips and tongue, with touches and caresses, and ultimately with their bodies—deepened and expanded, becoming ever more powerful, and also more nuanced.

More a communication in a language they were both still learning, still exploring the limits of what they could say—of what that particular language allowed them to reveal, to share.

It was both exhilarating and frightening, in the way the best adventures were.

And they were in it together, adventuring together; he didn't doubt that.

Tonight, they'd reached a level of openness—of emotional exposure and unfettered sharing—that had left him wrung out on every level, yet at the same time, more deeply fulfilled, more buoyed and awash in emotional glory than he'd ever imagined he could be.

Without restraint, she'd shared herself, not just her body but, as he'd sensed it, her heart, and he'd matched her through every gasp, through every moan. They'd been together in every sense, on every plane.

She had to love him—at least enough.

Enough for him to ask for her hand.

He let that conclusion drift through his mind to see how it settled.

Almost, but not quite. Yes, it was time he took the plunge, set himself at the final fence and threw his heart over, but there was one last thing he should do to set the stage. One last thing he could do to shore up his chances of hearing her say: I will. I do.

# Twelve

"I was wondering..." Marcus caught Niniver's eye as he rose and drew out the chair beside his at the dining table. He waited until she sat; when she glanced at him inquiringly, he resumed his seat, picked up his fork, and poked at his kedgeree. "I should drop in at Bidealeigh—just to check that there's nothing I need to attend to there—and I wondered if you'd like to ride over with me?"

*Just to check...* Niniver swallowed the protest that had leapt to her tongue, along with the imminent smothering disappointment, and smiled with, she hoped, enough genuine delight to hide her immense relief. "Yes, of course. I'd love to." Her smile turned to a silly grin that she seemed incapable of muting. Switching her attention to her own mound of kedgeree, she added, "I haven't any meetings today, and with all the accounts done, there's no reason I can't take the time. And I haven't been to Bidealeigh—well, to the Hennessy farmhouse as was—since old man Hennessy grew so cantankerous. Well, except when I came to call on you, that is." She was babbling, but she was so happy she didn't truly care.

He wasn't leaving. That was all that mattered. She

didn't need to know why he still felt he needed to continue at the manor; as long as he intended to return with her and remain for the immediate future at least, she was content.

She didn't want to end their liaison, not when there was so much she'd yet to learn. Last night, she'd felt as if, together, he and she had teetered on the brink of some fabled wonder.

It gripped her so hard, so unrelentingly, the glory that together they gave birth to. She couldn't bear to lose it—not yet.

She made short work of her breakfast. Raising her teacup, she sipped, then swiveled in her chair to glance out of the window. "It's another fine day—not that we're riding far."

"I thought, if you have the time, that we might go a touch further and check on my hounds." He pushed away his empty plate. "I should give them a quick run, too."

She swung to face him. "I'd like that. I haven't seen your pack—not since that time we met up on the ridge, and even then you only had a few dogs with you."

"I don't have as many as you do." He leaned back in his chair and, over the top of his coffee cup, met her eyes. "I've concentrated on only two breeders and brought in sires from outside."

She didn't have to feign her eagerness. "I would love to have a chance to look them over. Who knows? Perhaps we should consider crossbreeding?"

"I wouldn't mind seeing if either of my lines have any of that air-scenting ability."

She nodded. "We'll assess them." She set down her

cup and pushed back from the table. "I need to change. Shall I meet you in the stable yard?"

He smiled. "I'll have the horses saddled and waiting."

She knew she was beaming brightly—positively radiantly—as she left the dining room and walked quickly through the front hall and back up the stairs. On reaching her room, she shut the door, then, buoyed on a wave of happiness, she spun and waltzed her way across the room to her armoire.

Laughing at herself, she pulled the double doors wide, reached in, and drew out her riding habit. She tossed the heavy skirt with its matching under-trousers and the fitted velvet jacket onto the bed, then crossed to her chest of drawers to find a suitable blouse.

Quite why she was so happy she didn't know. But happiness was an emotion she hadn't felt for so long that it seemed like a minor miracle to have it return, and in such overwhelming fashion.

He and their liaison—all they shared, not just through the nights but through all the hours of the days, too—made her happy.

Made her heart light, made it sing.

Made her believe in life again—that there would be good times as well as the bad, as well as the times of struggle and worry.

Swiftly climbing out of her morning gown, she donned her chosen blouse—one with ruffles that made her feel extra-feminine. The trousers and skirt took a few minutes more, then she shrugged on her jacket. She found her boots, toed off her house slippers, and sat to pull the boots on.

Struggle and worry had been all she'd known for

the last several years, concern and anxiety, even desolation, devastation, and fear.

Now...while she knew problems still remained, that there were hurdles yet to be overcome, she felt...empowered. Uplifted and so much more confident that, come what may, she would find her way through.

That she would save the clan and fulfill her vow to her father.

She stood, stamped her feet to settle the boots, then quickly checked her hair—already in a sufficiently tight bun. Then she swiped up her riding gloves from the top of her bureau, opened the door, and headed for the stairs.

Another day of learning more about Marcus. Another day of learning more about herself and about all life had to offer her.

Smiling, she clattered down the stairs.

* * *

"So when *are* you going to pop the question?"

Marcus raised his head and stared, stony-faced, across Ned's back at Sean.

Sean shrugged. "The clan's been talking—she is our lady, after all. So we want to know."

Marcus looked down and cinched Ned's girth. His first impulse was to tell Sean—and the clan—to mind their own business, yet they had supported him... If Niniver were in his shoes, she'd probably think the question entirely reasonable. "I want to give her time to get to know me better, rather than appear too precipitate. Ladies like to be wooed."

Sean snorted. "You'd know, I suppose."

Marcus bit back the reply that he'd never wooed any lady before—no need to point out that he was a novice in that sphere. Although he hadn't discussed marrying Niniver with anyone, he wasn't surprised that the clan was watching—and, apparently, taking a close interest; why else had they moved to clear his path of her would-be suitors? And he fully expected the clan as a whole was, by now, aware he was sharing their lady's bed. In local terms, that called for a handfasting at the very least, which, for the likes of him and Niniver, meant a betrothal.

They'd been saddling and bridling Ned and Oswald in the cleared space just inside the big stable. Sean checked Oswald's scarred flank, then turned the bay and started leading him to the open stable door. "Just as long as the knot gets tied—and soon."

Grasping Ned's reins, Marcus led the big gray in Oswald's wake. "I assure you, it will be." Perhaps later today, after he'd shown Niniver over Bidealeigh. After he'd impressed on her the material assets he would bring to their union and, perhaps, tempted her with his hounds—maybe then he'd put his luck to the test.

He knew why he'd decided to take her to Bidealeigh; the depth of their sharing last night had left him feeling that the moment to ask her was almost upon him, and he needed the reassurance.

The fact that he did was a niggle in his mind.

Leading Ned, he followed Sean and Oswald into the stable yard.

A sunny smile on her face, Niniver was walking their way. Seeing Sean with Oswald, she waved him to the mounting block to one side of the yard and changed direction to join them there.

Marcus halted Ned, set his boot in the stirrup, and swung up to the saddle. Only as he settled and lifted the reins did he realize he'd missed the chance to lift Niniver to her saddle. Watching her scramble up, then settle her boots and skirts, he inwardly shrugged; they were, no doubt, past the stage of needing to seize every chance to touch.

"Right, then?" Niniver called across the yard. When he inclined his head and waved her toward the stable yard gate, she started Oswald walking. "It's faster via the path through the fields. You lead—I'll follow."

"All right." He swung Ned's head for—at least as the horse thought of it—home. As he set off, Ned's big hooves clattering down the drive, with Oswald's hooves striking in counterpoint close behind, Marcus realized his own inner compass had already shifted; for him, Bidealeigh was no longer home.

\* \* \*

The ride from Carrick Manor to Bidealeigh, especially through the fields, didn't take long. Throughout, Niniver kept Oswald a length behind Ned. When they crossed the highway, Marcus glanced back, and was surprised to see that, far from being sunny and happy, Niniver's expression was closed, almost bleak.

He'd never previously felt his heart plummet, but in that instant, it did—and he had no idea why, because the instant he caught her eye, she brightened and flashed him a brilliant smile.

He smiled back, then had to face forward. As he and Ned soared over the next low stone wall, he told himself there was nothing to worry about; she must have been thinking about some business matter, something she and he hadn't yet dealt with. He would find out what it was later, and they would sort it out. No insurmountable concern, and no real difficulty between them.

They rode into the yard before Bidealeigh's stable. Johnny came walking out. His face lit with a smile when he saw who it was. "Good day to you, sir. It's good to have you back."

Marcus reined Ned in. "I'm only back for the day, so if there's anything you need me for, come up to the house later."

"Och, aye—all's well." Johnny dipped his head to Niniver. "I won't be needing to trouble you."

Marcus swung down from Ned's back, handed the reins to Johnny, and turned—to see Niniver slide from Oswald's back to the ground. It was a practiced maneuver, one she could patently accomplish with relative ease, yet recently she'd been waiting and allowing him to lift her down.

With a smile, she held out her reins to Johnny. "Thank you," she said as he took them.

Then she turned to survey the house—all without meeting Marcus's eyes.

Johnny led the horses away. A graveled path led from the stable yard over clipped lawns to the narrow front porch.

Marcus walked up to Niniver.

As he drew level, she glanced briefly his way and waved toward the house. Her lips were curved, but, again, she didn't raise her gaze to his eyes. "Shall we?"

"Indeed." He went to take her hand, but she started forward.

He fell in beside her, and she made a production of drawing off her riding gloves. It gave her an excuse to look down, and with the difference in their heights, that effectively hid her face from him.

As they walked toward Bidealeigh's front door, Marcus felt a chill touch his soul.

What the devil had gone wrong?

He had no idea, but clearly, something had.

But he couldn't fix whatever had gone wrong without knowing what it was.

He had to trust her to tell him—eventually. They'd already got over that hurdle. She'd trusted him enough to tell him about her private vow to her father; surely, once she'd assimilated the ramifications of whatever the issue was, she would tell him. She knew he would move heaven and earth to help her, so...

There was nothing he could do but wait.

And not push.

Her confidence would always have to be given freely; it would always be hers to give. Her right; her choice. Even once they were married...it would still be her decision.

Just another little challenge in being the husband of the lady of a clan.

He was, he told himself, up to it.

They stepped onto the porch and he reached past her to set the door swinging wide. "Welcome to Bidealeigh." The words felt stiff and formal.

She inclined her head and walked into the front hall. "Thank you."

Mrs. Flyte came bustling up from the kitchen. "Oh, it's you, sir. Welcome home." Seeing Niniver, Mrs. Flyte smiled and bobbed a curtsy. "My lady." Mrs. Flyte glanced at Marcus. "Will you be wanting anything, sir?"

"Ah—not at the moment." He glanced at Niniver, but she was, apparently, studying the paneled walls; she gave him no sign. "We're here for the day. Perhaps, after I check my correspondence, we might have some tea." He looked back at Mrs. Flyte. "In the living room, I suppose."

"Indeed, sir." Mrs. Flyte nodded approvingly. "Just ring when you're ready, and I'll bring in a tray." After another bobbed curtsy, she retreated down the long flagged corridor.

He turned to Niniver. "My letters will be in the study. I'm not sure how long it might take to deal with them. Do you want to wait in the living room, or—"

She tipped her head down the corridor. "I'll wait in the study."

He led her down the corridor and held open the door to the comfortable room he'd made into his study. Roughly rectangular, it wasn't that large. Bookshelves lined the three inner walls, playing host to a selection of account ledgers as well as various treatises and volumes on sheep, crops, cattle, and, of course, hounds. Half the outer wall was taken up by a wide window with a pretty view to the south. An Oriental rug covered most of the floor. A typical gentleman's desk stood before the window, facing the door, with two large armchairs on the rug before it. He followed her inside and shut the door.

She went straight to the window. "I didn't realize you had such a fine view."

"The house is on the side of a ridge—the elevation helps." He waited, but when she said nothing more, just stood before the glass looking out, he rounded the desk, drew out the chair behind it, and sat.

None of the correspondence lying piled on his blotter was urgent, and the pile didn't contain any missive from Glencrae, but dealing with everything presently on his plate seemed wise; if he asked Niniver to marry him later in the day and she accepted, he expected to be distracted for the next several days.

After sorting through the pile, he glanced at her. Arms crossed, she hadn't moved from her position before the window. He hadn't thought the view that absorbing, but although he waited, she didn't seem to feel his gaze, didn't turn to meet it.

Looking back at the letters, he opened the first, then settled to work his way through them.

Eventually, Niniver quit her stance by the window and drifted about the room—instantly capturing his awareness. He forced his eyes to remain on the reply he was writing, but his attention kept shifting to lock on her.

Finally, he pointed to the bookshelf to the right of the desk. "The books on deerhounds, and other hounds, are over there."

"Ah. Thank you." The first words she'd uttered in what felt like ages. She crossed the room, halted before the bookshelf, and tipped her head to read the spines.

He forced his wayward wits back to the task before him.

Eventually, he sealed the last missive and dropped it on the pile for Flyte to post.

"Would you like me to frank those?"

He looked up to see Niniver, a book open in her hands, looking his way. If she franked the letters, Flyte could just drop them in the bag. "If you would."

She closed the book, returned it to the shelf, then

crossed to stand before the desk. He handed her a pen and shifted the inkwell so she could reach it. She dipped, and wrote neatly across the corner of each envelope, then handed the pen back to him. "There." She straightened.

His gaze on her face, he tried to catch her eyes. "Thank you."

She nodded rather soberly. "And now," she said, her gaze still not quite meeting his, "I rather think I'm ready for some tea."

He rose and crossed the room in her wake; reaching past her, he opened the door, and she stepped through. She walked briskly down the corridor and into the living room at the far end, giving him no reason to touch her by way of guiding her.

He followed her into the room and went to tug the bellpull, and tried to tell himself that her actively asking to take tea was a good thing—an improvement, a sign she was possibly getting ready to share what was so dominating her mind. Yet to his senses, the gap between them seemed to be widening from a fissure to a chasm.

Niniver sat in one armchair. He took the other. They waited in silence; she studied her hands. Then Mrs. Flyte bustled in with the tray.

Niniver looked up and smiled easily—normally. At his housekeeper.

Balancing the tray on one hand, Mrs. Flyte tugged one of the low tables over and set it before Niniver. "I'll just put the tray here, then, shall I?"

"Thank you." Niniver watched Mrs. Flyte lower the tray. "I heard your daughter and son-in-law have just had twins. You must be delighted."

Mrs. Flyte straightened, her ruddy face breaking into a beaming smile. "Oh, we are, indeed! Such a thrill. Lots of twins hereabouts these days, it seems, but such a joy to have them."

"Was it a girl and boy?" Niniver reached for the teapot. "I didn't hear."

"Two boys. And the families—all of us—couldn't be happier." Mrs. Flyte clasped her hands over her ample waist. "We're all in something of a tizz, of course. No one on any side has had twins before, and we weren't expecting the pair of them, you see. Why—"

As Mrs. Flyte rattled on, with barely a glance his way Niniver handed Marcus his cup. He accepted it, and she picked up the cup she'd poured for herself, sat back, and, with her eyes fixed encouragingly on Mrs. Flyte's face, sipped.

Marcus listened to Mrs. Flyte respond to Niniver's artfully posed questions. Contrary to the immediate evidence, his housekeeper wasn't a garrulous sort; it was Niniver's questions that were drawing her out.

He tried to eat a slice of Mrs. Flyte's fruitcake. He was sure it was up to her usual exemplary standards, but today it turned to sawdust in his mouth. He set the plate with the crumbled remains back on the tray.

Not that either woman noticed his sudden and unusual lack of appetite. They were entirely engrossed in a discussion of the challenges in rearing twins.

He was a twin. His parents were the parents of twins, and so were his sister and brother-in-law. He was the uncle of twins. Yet neither woman thought to appeal to him.

Had circumstances been otherwise, he might have thought Niniver engaging so animatedly with Mrs.

Flyte was a good thing. As it was, he knew very well that the principal reason she was talking to his house-keeper was so that she wouldn't have to talk to him.

* * *

Niniver had had no idea that her heart could be dashed, battered, and pummeled to this extent. But she didn't have time to dwell on that now. Now, she had to get through the day with some semblance of dignity.

The difficulties that posed demanded she focus every particle of her awareness on achieving that end. Ruthlessly, she corralled her wits and kept them away from her surging emotions. Not now. Not yet.

Later.

When she had time to deal with her hurts, to lick her wounds and tend to her shattered heart.

She had no idea how she was going to cope with spending an entire day with Marcus at Bidealeigh, but she would. She had to. It wasn't his fault; he'd agreed to protect her from external threats, but it had been her duty to protect her heart.

It had been *her* decision to take him to her bed, to initiate their liaison. Her decision to set aside that self-preservatory duty and allow—indeed, to fight to permit—the connection between them to grow and expand.

She'd knowingly taken the risk that this—or something like it—might happen.

Now it had, she couldn't blame him for her hurt—couldn't hold him responsible for it.

By the time she'd extracted every last little detail about Mrs. Flyte's new grandchildren from the house-keeper, she'd finished her tea, and so had Marcus.

Mrs. Flyte blinked when she saw the empty cups on

the tray. "My goodness—I have run on. Well, I'll take the tray back with me, if you're done?"

When Marcus nodded an assent, Niniver smiled and added hers, and Mrs. Flyte hefted the tray and left.

Niniver watched her depart, and waited; she could feel Marcus's gaze on her face, but didn't turn to meet it. After the tea, she felt a touch more fortified; she could manage this.

"I had thought, perhaps, to show you around the house."

She should have seen that coming, but she'd had no time to plan. What to say? She glanced briefly his way, but let her eyes rise no higher than his lips. "Have you concluded your business?"

His lips tightened. After a moment, he said, "I should speak with Flyte, and with Earnest, my foreman. That won't take long in either case, but Earnest won't be back until lunchtime, so…" He paused, then went on, "I thought we might have a light luncheon here, and then visit the hounds before heading back to Carrick Manor."

Even in the circumstances, that wasn't a bad plan. She inclined her head. "Very well. So that leaves us with"—she swiveled to look at the clock on the mantelpiece—"about an hour to fill?" Again, she glanced at him.

He nodded. "Roughly an hour. So what would you like to do? A tour of the house, or…?"

She couldn't imagine keeping her composure through any house tour; quite aside from the corridors being so narrow that they would leave her too aware of his presence—of a body she now knew intimately, hers to touch if she wished—what if he showed her his bedroom?

"Actually, I would prefer to walk around the house—to better appreciate the setting and the views."

He studied her; she continued to look his way and didn't try to hide her face. She knew he would read nothing in her features; the past years had taught her how to hide her feelings behind an impenetrable façade. She hadn't been using that shield with him recently—indeed, she might not have ever used it with him at all—but it was the only way she would get through the day, and she'd fixed it firmly in place. Calmly, coolly, she arched her brows. "Shall we?"

His jaw set, his lips forming a thin line, but he dipped his head in agreement and rose.

She didn't wait for him to offer his hand. She came to her feet and led the way from the room.

\* \* \*

They walked around the house, pacing slowly as Niniver scanned the surrounding landscape, pausing now and then, presumably to admire a particular view. Or simply to waste time. Marcus watched her, wondering if he dared take her arm…but he no longer felt he had the right.

She'd pulled away. Without a word, without any hint of a reason, much less an explanation.

He couldn't think past the turmoil in his mind, could barely breathe past the constriction in his chest.

His hands in his pockets, he trailed after her and said nothing.

Luncheon proved a painfully quiet meal; although the cold collation Mrs. Flyte supplied deserved to be appreciated, neither Niniver nor he seemed to have much appetite.

Conversation was nonexistent. She continued to

avoid his eyes. Yet when he sent his senses questing, she didn't seem upset.

She no longer seemed *anything*. He couldn't read her emotions at all, and her expression, while in no way blank, gave no hints as to what she was feeling. Her face had become a pretty mask, one that told him nothing.

The close connection they'd shared, the ready and open communication, had vanished.

Its absence left a hole in his soul.

The realization staggered him, and he brought up his own mask, his own opaque façade.

They left the dining room and the farmhouse and walked back to the stable yard.

The mounting block wasn't really high enough for her. She had to allow him to lift her to her saddle, yet when he did...she might as well have been a pliable doll. He sensed no response at all.

The ride to his kennels, which were situated a short distance from the farmhouse in a protective dip in the land, gave him time to think. To finally step back from the building panic and look at what might have brought about such an absolute withdrawal.

That morning over breakfast, she'd been bright, breezy, and openly happy. She'd been eager to accompany him to Bidealeigh. Admittedly, she hadn't waited for him to lift her to her saddle, but the mounting block had been right there; her hopping up and scrambling into her saddle was surely more an indication of her eagerness to get on than anything else.

That eagerness had evaporated on the ride over the fields; by the time they'd reached Bidealeigh, she'd pulled back. From that point on, step by step, she'd retreated to a point where, it seemed, she was beyond his reach, physically and emotionally.

As if they were distant acquaintances, not lovers.

So what had happened on the ride to Bidealeigh? He hadn't been aware of any interruption or intrusion, but he'd been in the lead and hadn't been able to see her—not until they'd reached the highway, and by then she'd started to put up her walls.

Whatever had occasioned her retreat had occurred between the manor and the highway. Had nearing the highway triggered bad memories of her near-brush with death?

Why such a memory might cause her to cut the connection between them he couldn't imagine, but he couldn't think of anything else that might be behind her reaction. So what could he do to reach across the gap, to reassure her and draw her back to him?

The instant they walked into the kennels, he knew he'd found his route to salvation. He led her to the pens and introduced her to his hounds. Gaining confidence with each animal he presented, he told her of their pedigree, and how each performed while stalking and hunting.

And she started asking questions.

Which he promptly answered.

With every question she posed, he relaxed a trifle more; the connection between them was still there.

Then he led her to the breeding bitches and the puppies.

As the puppies gamboled and tumbled about her feet, Niniver laughed. She'd meant to keep her distance, to remain aloof even here, but how could she? Not in this setting. With every overenthusiastic lick, with every soft *whuff* from the bitches themselves—as if inviting her to share their pride in their offspring—she felt the walls she'd erected about her heart melt.

She sat in the straw and let the puppies have at her, ruffling their fur, tugging their ears and tails. Glancing up, she saw Marcus leaning on the pen gate and watching her. She saw the intent focus in his dark eyes, but couldn't prevent her lips from curving, couldn't stop her eyes from openly meeting his. "They're lovely. Such a gorgeous brindle. And so healthy and playful." She rubbed the tummy of one demanding shaggy lump, and the pup wriggled in ecstasy.

Looking up again, she saw Marcus hesitate, then he offered, "This is the bitch I thought might have some of the characteristics you look for in air-scenting."

She glanced at the bitch. The hound currently had her head down on her paws and was drowsily watching her pups crawl all over Niniver's lap. "Let's see whether the pups show any signs before disturbing her."

For the next half hour, she tried the pups with the easy, gentle tests she'd devised to point her toward the air-scenters in her own pack. Sure enough, at least three of the female pups showed some ability to follow a trail through the air.

Marcus had remained outside the pen—for which she was grateful; it really wasn't big enough for both of them and the hounds—but she could sense his interest and his growing excitement. It mirrored hers. Glancing up, she tipped her head toward the bitch. "Do you know her pedigree offhand?"

He rattled it off, going back generation by generation. She matched each sire and bitch to those she carried in her head for her own prized air-scenting family. "*There's* the connection!" With triumph coursing through her, she caught his eyes. "Four generations back—which almost certainly means it truly is a trait and not just an aberration."

"Indeed." Marcus looked at the bitch, who, intrigued by the new games her pups were playing with the humans, had stood and stretched, and now came closer to investigate. "She's been grumpy whenever I try to get her away from her pups."

Niniver scrambled to her feet. "It's too early yet."

"And she's getting on. This will be her last litter." Marcus swung open the gate. As Niniver stepped out, he tipped his head further along the pens. "But I have her eldest daughter further down. She has a litter that's a bit older, and she'll let us separate her from them."

"Excellent." She couldn't hold back her enthusiasm, and she didn't try. What was happening between them outside the kennels wasn't his fault; there was no reason to deny them this simple enjoyment of a shared passion.

They first tested the other litter of pups, and at least two females showed definite signs of air-scenting. "These tests are very rudimentary," she said, "but I've found they're strongly indicative."

Then they took the bitch out of the pen, and led her outside into the training arena. Having been cooped up with her brood, the hound was very ready for a game.

Fifteen minutes later, Niniver couldn't stop beaming. "Oh, yes!" She all but cheered as the hound performed the last test as if she was a homing pigeon. "She's definitely got the trait." She glanced at Marcus as he called the hound to heel. "You said you had two breeding lines. What about the other one?"

"They're a completely different line, from a Highland breeder. But we can test the females, if you like. If air-scenting is a defined and rare trait, I would expect them to be air-scenter null."

"Let's see."

The afternoon was waning by the time they'd verified to their own satisfaction that the females of his Highland-sourced breeding line displayed zero affinity for air-scenting.

Marcus's small kennel staff—two brothers—had come in and watched for a while, before heading off to a small room at the end of the kennels to make up the hounds' evening meal.

Returning the last hound to its pen, Marcus swung the gate shut and latched it. Niniver came to stand alongside him, still smiling as she peered over the high gate at the hound. "It's all right. You're still a good hound."

He smiled—easily and spontaneously—and it was such a relief, he turned to her as she turned to him.

They were suddenly close. If he just dipped his head...the impulse to kiss her surged inside him, so potent and powerful he was about to yield—

Her eyes flared, and she sidestepped away from the gate.

Away from him.

He slammed a mental door on instinct, on the nearly overpowering urge to seize her and haul her back. To kiss her...into submission.

Jaw tightening, he turned and looked toward the kennel's doors. He couldn't look at her, couldn't think of anything else to say except "Let's go."

Without another word, he stalked out of the kennels to where the horses waited. She walked quickly in his wake. He halted at Oswald's side. Without allowing any sign of reaction to show, he lifted her to her saddle.

Then he caught Ned's reins and swung up to the gray's broad back.

One glance at Niniver's face showed her features had set, and her mask—that god-awful screen he couldn't see through—was back in place.

They turned their horses' heads to the west and he led the way—back to Carrick Manor, the place he now desperately wanted to call home.

\* \* \*

They clattered into the manor's stable yard all too soon. Too soon for his emotions, scored and raging, to have settled.

He drew rein, and Ned, infected with his mood, stamped and tossed his head.

Niniver rode straight past and on to the spot closest to the house. She reined Oswald in, freed her feet from the stirrups, and slid to the ground.

Her expression remained uninformative. Without a glance Marcus's way, she tossed the reins to Mitch as he came running up. She didn't wait to see if he caught them, just started striding for the side door. "I've some letters to write." A vague wave directed the comment at Marcus. "I'll see you at dinner."

Still mounted, he stared after her.

So did Mitch and Sean; the latter had come to hold Ned's head.

Jaw clenching, Marcus dismounted.

The side door shut.

Sean and Mitch turned to look—pointedly—at him.

Marcus handed Ned's reins to Sean.

Sean took them. "Trouble in the wooing department?"

Gritting his teeth, Marcus headed for the door. "You could say that." He reached the door, hauled it open, and stalked after Niniver.

# Thirteen

Marcus had intended to follow Niniver, but on reaching the library door, he hauled back on his reins. The library was her bolt-hole. Barging in after her and making her feel that she wasn't safe even there...

Swallowing a growl, he stalked on down the corridor and took refuge in the study. He flung himself into the chair behind the desk. After a moment of unfocused brooding, he sent his mind back to the beginning of the day—when she'd seemed so happy, so bright and breezy. But on the ride to Bidealeigh, something had changed.

He spent the next hour reliving every subsequent minute of their day, trying to tease out some clue as to what had made her pull back so very definitely—how, why, any hint at all.

When the dressing gong sounded, he still had no idea what was going on. He rose, quit the study, and headed for the main stairs, but then his feet slowed, and he halted outside the library door. He considered the closed door, then grasped the knob, silently eased the door open, and looked down the long room.

Niniver wasn't there. She must have already gone upstairs.

At least it seemed she would be joining him for dinner.

He continued up the stairs to his room. Once inside, he stood still and listened. Faintly, the sounds of movement and quiet female voices reached him from the room next door.

Reassured at some level he didn't entirely understand, he changed, replacing breeches and top boots with trousers and shoes, his hacking jacket and shirt with a fine linen evening shirt, a striped silk waistcoat, and an evening coat. Unknotting the loose neckerchief he'd worn through the day, he reached for a crisp, white cravat.

Despite the intricacies of tying the cravat, his transformation didn't take long. He could still hear movement next door; Niniver had yet to go down.

He debated, but if he could hear her, then she could hear him. He decided that, in her present state, she might prefer not to run into him in the gallery. Regardless, he would rather be in the drawing room when she appeared. Making no effort to tread softly, he left the room, walked around the gallery to the head of the stairs, and went down.

In the drawing room, he took up a position by the mantelpiece, his gaze fixed on the drawing room doors...then decided that might appear too intimidating. He sat in one of the armchairs before the hearth, crossed one leg over the other in an effort to appear relaxed, and waited.

Miss Hildebrand appeared first. He rose; when she greeted him with her customary approval and an easy smile, he managed a smile in reply. After she'd settled on the sofa and he'd resumed his seat, she asked after his and Niniver's day. By reciting the bare facts, he avoided lying, even by implication, although, of course, Miss Hildebrand assumed Niniver had enjoyed herself.

She had while they'd been in the kennels, but then she'd abruptly pulled away again. He didn't think she'd enjoyed the strained feelings and fraught atmosphere that action had evoked any more than he had.

Miss Hildebrand glanced at the open drawing room door, then mentioned a story in the news sheets in which she thought he might have some interest. They chatted about local matters in a rather desultory way, while both continued to glance at the door.

Finally, they heard Niniver's footsteps cross the hall tiles and she appeared in the doorway, a vision in pale blue silk. She looked at him, then she glanced at Miss Hildebrand. "I'm sorry I'm late—I got distracted."

He rose, his gaze on Niniver's face, but she didn't glance at him again.

She'd halted just inside the doorway.

Ferguson appeared behind her. "Dinner is served, my lady."

"Thank you, Ferguson." Niniver swept her gaze from Miss Hildebrand over Marcus. "Shall we?"

He moved to assist Miss Hildebrand to her feet and gave her his arm. Niniver led them from the room, remaining just far enough ahead that there was no opportunity for him to suggest she take his other arm, as she had on previous evenings.

After settling Miss Hildebrand in her chair, he circled the table to sit in his now customary place beside

Niniver. She'd beckoned a footman to hold her chair for her and was already seated.

As he sat, he noticed Miss Hildebrand looking from him to Niniver; from her concerned expression, it seemed she'd detected the estrangement between them.

But Niniver blithely stated, "We had a lovely day at Bidealeigh." Flicking out her napkin, she looked at Miss Hildebrand. "Did anything of note happen here while we were away?"

He'd expected the conversation over the dinner table to be somewhat stilted. Instead, Niniver chatted—if not brightly, then at least with great glibness—about this and that, household matters, clan matters, directing her comments more or less exclusively across the table to her old governess.

Two courses came and went.

From her increasingly troubled glances his way, Miss Hildebrand had realized that Niniver was avoiding engaging with him; she made several valiant attempts to include him in their discussions, but in each case, Niniver quickly steered the conversation elsewhere. He didn't really mind; he felt no burning desire to discuss household or clan matters. He needed to speak with her about them—him and her and them together—and that would be very much better done in private.

At the end of the meal, he remained at the dining table to give her a chance to relax for a few minutes without the need to feel on guard against him. That she was on guard against him was no longer in doubt; when she'd pushed back from the table and he'd risen to pull back her chair, she'd tensed.

Wary, watchful—oh so very much on guard... against him.

He found that pill difficult to swallow.

A tot of neat whisky would, he hoped, help. It certainly couldn't hurt.

When the footmen retreated and Ferguson set the tray with the decanter and crystal glasses before him, the butler murmured, "What happened?"

Marcus reached for the decanter. "Damned if I know." He poured a restrained two fingers into a tumbler. He restoppered the decanter and lifted the glass. "But I intend to find out."

"Good." Ferguson hesitated, then added, "We all think that you and Lady Carrick...it would work."

Marcus tipped his head in acknowledgement—in agreement. "I've been working on convincing her of that, but then something interfered, and I haven't yet figured out what." He sipped, then lowered the glass. "But I will."

Ferguson nodded. "I'll leave you to it."

He departed, and Marcus sat back, sipped, and waited.

He returned to the drawing room just ahead of the tea tray. The conversation lagged. That said, he was grateful—and he was sure Niniver was, too—that Miss Hildebrand didn't suggest music, or—even worse—dancing. They drank their tea, then Niniver made a comment about being tired, and they all rose and climbed the stairs.

As usual, Miss Hildebrand parted from them in the gallery, patently still laboring under the misapprehension that Niniver's maid was awaiting her mistress in her bedchamber.

Niniver watched Hildy climb the stairs and fought to keep her senses calm, to keep her breathing even and her pulse from racing—yet every iota of her awareness was locked on the man standing, dark, silent, and powerful, by her side.

She needed to get safely into her room, but rushing—even walking too quickly—down the corridor would be a mistake. She knew better than to attempt to flee a predator, and her senses were informing her—half in breathless appreciation, half in breath-bated trepidation—that at that moment, with respect to her, Marcus was every inch a predator.

If she could just avoid engaging with him for a few minutes more…

That was what she wanted, wasn't it?

Turning from the stairs, she continued strolling at a normal social pace along the gallery. If she'd had the decision to make again, she wouldn't have insisted he occupy the room next to hers.

They drew level with his door. She was about to glance his way and wish him a good night when she felt his fingers lock like a steel manacle about her wrist.

He swung her to face him and stepped toward her.

She instinctively backed; heart leaping, lungs seizing, she locked her gaze on his face.

Using his body, he herded her until her spine hit the wall. He flattened the palm of his other hand against the wall by her head and leaned in. Her free hand rose, hovering between them, but she didn't push him away.

He was suddenly so very close; she sensed him all around her, his masculine strength a warm yet immovable wall surrounding her. Still holding her other hand, his long, strong fingers twining with hers, he lowered his head and met her gaze eye to eye.

The light cast by the wall sconces wasn't strong enough to illuminate his dark eyes, but she could feel his midnight gaze—and something in her refused to look away. But...

*Don't do it. Don't spoil it. Don't speak and bring everything between us to an end.*

The words tumbled through her mind, a senseless plea, even while her starved senses reached for him.

His chest swelled, then he demanded, his voice low and so tightly controlled that his tone almost grated, "What the devil happened?"

*I heard you and Sean. I know...*

What she knew, what she now understood, was there, all too clear in her mind, but the emotions that knowledge incited—betrayal, shattering disappointment, loss, grief, and heartbreak—rose up and obscured it. Rose up and choked her, and left her with no words to fling at him.

Ever since she'd learned the truth of why he was still there, with her, she'd tried to calm the torment inside her, tried to accept and step past her reaction so she could work out how to cope. So she could prepare herself for this moment and those to come.

She hadn't yet succeeded. Hadn't yet gained any effective distance. The turmoil inside still ruled her, and she had no rational, logical words with which to answer him.

All she had were her raging emotions.

And they were powerful enough to make her quiver with their pent-up force.

He was watching her intently, scrutinizing her face.

Whether he saw enough to guess her incapacity and the raging devastation she was wrestling with inside she didn't know, but something in his face altered and he softly cursed.

Then he bent his head and kissed her.

Kissed her as if he were starving for the taste of her—and, instantly, she was ravenous for him. She parted her lips on a needy, greedy gasp, unable to even think of holding back.

He plunged into her mouth and claimed—and a tide of yearning rose inside her.

*This.* She wanted this. This was what she craved—now and forever.

And if she couldn't have forever, she could at least have now.

Now. Tonight. And for however long she had until he said the fateful words and brought their paradise crashing down.

His lips ravaged hers, and emboldened, she met them and matched him. She kissed him back, as openly hungry and every bit as greedy as she sensed he was.

If she could keep him from speaking—if she could keep them both here, anchored on this plane of engagement—then she could fill her heart with this. With sensation and emotion and connection and glory.

She reached for him through the kiss—through raising her hands, placing her palms against his chest, then sending them surging up and over his shoulders. She came away from the wall and, spearing her fingers through his hair, stepped into him, coming up on her toes to press her own heated kisses on him.

He straightened; his hard hands spreading over her back, he urged her against him, then his hands swept lower. He grasped her derriere and molded her hips to his; she felt the iron-hard ridge of his erection pressing against her belly.

She opened her mouth under his and deliberately fanned the fire of their raging passions.

He pulled back on a gasp, muttered something unintelligible, then the door to his room swung inward and he swept her across the threshold.

And hauled her back into his arms. She went with alacrity, dimly heard the latch snick as their lips and bodies met again, and they plunged back into the flames.

She wanted him, and she didn't care what she had to give to secure her heart's desire. Their tonight was hers, and she seized the chance and him with utter abandon.

And he seemed to want her with the same intensity, the same reckless need.

The same fire.

Clothes flew, shed without the slightest inhibition. Onto the floor, on a chair—wherever they fell.

Her corset laces snagged, and he swore. She sent her fingers to join his, to desperately unravel the knots and strip the constriction away.

It fell, and she dragged in a huge breath, then his hands closed about her breasts, and she tipped her head back and moaned.

Hands splayed on his back, she clung as her senses rioted and her wits spun, and she gave herself up to the glorious pleasure of his ministrations. His fingers squeezed, tweaked, and her knees grew weak. He released one breast and caught her to him. While his other hand continued to flagrantly possess the ripe firmness of her breast, he bent his head and found her lips again, and he whirled them back into the conflagration of a kiss that poured molten heat down her veins.

She drank it in and wanted more. She wanted him— in the rawest, most intimate way. Nothing else could quench this ravening craving in her soul.

She needed to feel him deep inside her again, needed to revel in that sublime connection. Again. Now. One last time.

Her petticoats slithered down her legs. She stepped out of them and kicked the folds aside. As he reached for the hem of her chemise, she fell on the buttons at his waist.

They'd been circling, waltzing, toward the bed. Her thighs met the footboard as she slid the last button free, then caught and tugged loose the ties of his underdrawers. Before she could push both garments down his legs, he closed his hands about her waist, gripped and swung her up, and set her on her knees on the bed. Then he stripped her chemise, already bunched about her waist, off over her head.

Before she caught her breath or her balance, he turned, sat on the bed, and hauled off his boots. They hit the floor—first one, then the other.

Then he stood, stripped off his hose, trousers, and underwear, and turned to the bed.

He'd left no lamp burning in the room; the only light was the silver moonlight washing in through the uncurtained windows.

She'd seen him naked before, but only lying on the bed. Now…the silvery moonlight bathed his powerful physique, gilding the muscled contours, casting each fascinating ridge and hollow in shades of night.

In that instant, he was a god standing before her—a living, breathing manifestation of her dreams.

Before he could move, she held up a hand. "Wait."

He froze.

An amorphous, tantalizing sense of power flared and swirled through her. She clambered off the bed and stood naked before him. Her every sense had locked on him; she couldn't drag any part of her awareness from him, from his body. Reaching out, she touched her fingertips—just the pads of her fingers—to the heavy muscles banding his chest. Then, not knowing what drove her but confidently following the instinct, she walked slowly around him, letting those fingertips trail over his skin.

He tensed. His hands, until then lax by his sides, slowly closed into fists.

But he held still and allowed her the moment—a boon she appreciated and made the most of, letting her eyes drink their fill as she circled him. He was magnificent. And, transparently, in that moment—for tonight—he was willing to be hers.

Without restrictions, without reservations.

Yet very likely for the last time.

Recognition of that fact—of the outcome of what she'd learned—thudded, an insidious compulsion in her blood. Whatever she still wanted to know, to experience, she needed to seize the chance of now, and not hope for any other opportunity.

Certainty welled. As she ended her circuit of appreciation and came to a halt between him and the bed, she set both hands to lightly grip his sides, then she locked her gaze with his and simply said, "My turn."

Running her hands down his torso to his waist, to his hips, she sank to her knees. She might have been an innocent, but she'd never been a prude; she'd heard enough to know what she wanted. Bringing her hands inward, she grasped the rigid rod of his erection, lovingly caressed, then she bent her head and set her lips to the engorged head. And licked.

The short, shuddering, broken breath he dragged into his lungs had her lips curving. It was all the encouragement—the response—she needed.

She laved, explored with her lips and tongue, then she took him deep into her mouth and savored.

Marcus tipped back his head, closed his eyes, and fought to endure. The sophisticated man wanted to hold aloof, to simply wait her out, but as always, she'd sidestepped past his shields and called to, engaged with, the more primitive side of him. And that more primitive side, that fundamental part of him, wanted this—all of this. All he and she could share. His senses reveled in every lick, every suck; without conscious direction, he sank the fingers of both hands into her hair and guided her...

As ever, she proved an exemplary pupil. Too soon she had his balls on fire and the coiling tension ratcheting and spiraling—before he lost control, he pressed a thumb between her luscious lips and drew free of the silken haven of her mouth.

His muscles iron-hard yet tensed to quivering, as she smoothly rose—her small hands sliding up his burning skin—he swept her into his arms, all but tossed her on the bed, and followed her down.

Thought was far beyond him. As he fell on her and she seized him, she showed no sign of rationality, either.

Lips locked, mouths fusing, tongues tangling, their hands on each other, greedy in utterly wanton desire, they rolled and wrestled, savored and delighted, seized and surrendered.

Then he trapped her beneath him, hauled her thighs wide and, with one powerful thrust, joined them. A soft cry falling from her swollen lips, she arched beneath him, but then she clamped around him and held him, raised her lithe legs and wrapped them about his hips, and with a long undulation, she tipped her hips to his and urged him into the wildest of dances.

Together they surrendered to the compulsive beat, their bodies matching in instinctive harmony. And nothing else mattered; in that moment, there was only them—not her and him but them together—locked in the age-old dance. A dance not just of their senses, although those were fully engaged and all but overwhelmed, but of some deeper, more primal, more compelling force.

A force that rose between them, that flowed effortlessly as they joined, and linked them on some vital level that was more fundamental, more viscerally powerful, than anything else in life.

Eyes closed, lost in the raging beat, in the addictive heat, he felt the tension rising in them both—but he didn't want this, their dance, to end. Not so soon.

He buried himself inside her, then he held her to him and rolled to his side, and then to his back, raising her so that she straddled him with his erection still bathed in her wet heat.

Niniver gasped, planted her hands on his chest, braced her arms, and seized the chance he'd offered. With unrestrained abandon, she rode him, wild, free, untempered.

Tonight, she wanted everything—every ounce of sensation she could wring from the heated moments. His hands rose to close about her breasts, and he kneaded in time with her plunging ride.

She felt as if her mind was fully open, as if every last shield had been stripped away—as if sensation had taken her over and now ruled her, utterly and completely.

He came up on one elbow and set his mouth to her breast. One hard hand cradling the swollen mound, his fingers plumped her flesh, and his teeth grazed the distended peak, then he drew the aching bud into his mouth and suckled.

She cried out. Sliding her fingers into his hair, she held him to her and rode recklessly on.

Desire burned. Passion whipped. Ecstasy beckoned.

She hit the peak, all tension released, and she soared.

Shattered.

Her senses fragmented into shards of delight, and pleasure, sharp and bright, streaked down every vein. Then ecstasy bloomed, golden and irresistible, and engulfed her.

He held her still, tight upon him, until the last wave of her contractions faded, then he rolled and set her beneath him again.

She thought she was too limp, too wrung out, to match him again, but as he'd taught her over the previous nights, she was stronger than she thought.

Soon, her body was answering his call.

Soon, he was pounding into her, and she was clinging and glorying and urging him on.

This time, when the end came and took them from this world, the cataclysm was so powerful, it shook them to their souls.

They clung, holding fast as they whirled through the heat and the flames, as their passions, ignited, raged and burned, and consumed all they were. Until, at the last, all tension vanished, and they shattered and fell into the void—and ecstasy rushed in and filled them, remade, reforged, and held them.

They floated back to earth, their bodies slick and joined, their hearts thundering, their senses replete.

Filled with each other. Irredeemably linked, each to the other.

Satisfied, each in their own way, wrapped in each other's arms, they sank into satiation's sea.

* * *

He woke her in what he deemed to be the most appropriate way.

Dawn was a pearly glow on the horizon visible through one of the windows when, with the curve of her back to his chest, her bottom tight against his groin, he slid his aching erection into the slick, heated haven of her sheath.

And felt her wake.

Felt her, her senses, slowly rise, and her body gently clamp about him.

With his lips, he traced the shell of her ear, then murmured, "Don't move. You don't need to do anything but lie there and feel." Slowly, he drew back, then, just as slowly, surged in to fill her. Closing his eyes, his let his own senses quest. "Just lie there and let me love you."

He did just that, orchestrating the waves of pleasure to rise, then wash through them. Over and over, rising higher and higher, until, in the end, the wave reared insensibly high, crested, then crashed through them and swept them away.

To that shore only lovers could reach.

Where the thudding of hearts beating as one slowly ebbed, and ecstasy filled them with glory.

Minutes passed in unspoken communion, in the unalloyed joy of being one.

Slowly, slowly, they returned to the world.

Ultimately, although still drugged with satiation, he forced his mind to their reality. He still had no clue what had happened the day before, yet after the interludes of the night—interludes where they'd both knowingly and intentionally stepped beyond all shields and come together with a shattering lack of reservation, of any attempt to hold anything back—he couldn't doubt that she wanted him in precisely the same way he wanted her.

Meaning that, no matter that one part of his mind shied from simply stating the fact aloud, he loved her, and she loved him.

After last night—indeed, after all the last days, after all the complex, roiling mass of feelings they evoked in each other—there really could be no doubt of what linked them. Of what the force that drove them to cleave to each other was.

He also knew that he'd run out of time, that he had to speak now, that he couldn't afford to let her leave his arms, his bed, this room, before he'd reached across the chasm that had opened between them the day before.

He might not know, much less understand, what had caused it, but he definitely knew it was there.

Here, now, over the night, they'd been as they needed to be—together. He needed to speak and make sure that continued—that togetherness became their accepted state.

Although he'd withdrawn from her, he'd remained wrapped about her, his chest to her back, her bottom snug against his groin, his legs tangled with hers. As his mind assembled the required words, he decided the position was an advantage; with her held so close, he would be able to sense her reaction—and, possibly, not having the distraction of looking into her eyes might help him stay on course.

He mentally rehearsed various constructions, then settled on his approach. Refocusing his senses on her, he realized from the soft huff of her breathing that she was asleep.

He debated waiting, but…he knew the time was now.

Raising his head, he brushed a light kiss over her temple. "Niniver."

Niniver heard him call her. Bliss still held her; she didn't want to leave the realm of soul-deep pleasure to which he'd taken her. She wanted to cling to the connection—illusion though it might be—for as long as she could, but the pragmatic part of her knew what was coming.

Knew she had to let go.

Reluctantly, she let her senses surface. She blinked her eyes open as he said her name again. "Yes?" Her voice sounded low, husky. Along with consciousness, her emotions surged.

His lips caressed her temple. "We've been together for over a week. I've stood by your side and watched you deal with so much—with so many challenges. I took you to Bidealeigh yesterday so you could see what I have there—to underscore that I have land and, as you know, funds aplenty. And we deal well together, in the bedroom and elsewhere. We're complementary in many ways, and we share ideals and interests." He paused, then went on, "I want to marry you—I want you to marry me, to take me as your husband and become my wife. I want to stand by your side and protect you into the future. I want us to share that future."

She said nothing; she felt as if her heart was shattering.

"Please, Niniver, say you'll marry me."

His words were gentle, yet she was conscious of an underlying pressure—a compulsion she didn't understand.

Slowly, she filled her lungs, then she pushed back the covers, pulled out of his arms, swung her legs from his, and sat on the side of the bed. Without looking at him, she said, "I'm sorry, but no. I don't wish to marry you."

He—his entire body—went completely still; she would have sworn he'd stopped breathing.

Knowing she had to leave—now, before he recovered and argued and pushed—she rose and, ignoring her nakedness, walked to the haphazard pile of her clothes. Her chemise had fallen on top. She picked it up and drew it over her head.

"No?" Complete and utter befuddlement filled his tone.

She tugged down her chemise, then bent and swept up her clothes. Straightening, she set the pile on the end of the bed so that she could untangle her shawl from the heap. Her chin firm, without meeting his eyes, she said, "I never expected you to marry me. I took you to my bed, yes, but as my lover. I never said anything about marriage. I never wanted that—never wanted you to feel obliged to offer it. I'm sorry if others"—pulling the shawl free, she waved vaguely—"gave you the impression that I wished for marriage, that I looked for it from you or anyone, but I explained at the outset that marriage was not for me, and none of what's passed between us has changed my mind."

If anything, realizing that he—even he—had been compelled by the clan to offer for her hand had only convinced her even more immutably that never marrying was the right path for her.

She flicked the shawl about her shoulders. Honesty, and what remained between them, forced her to say, "I've enjoyed being with you—I've enjoyed all our hours together—but trapping you into matrimony was never my goal."

Briefly, she raised her eyes to his. Before her courage failed, she made herself say, "If you have any feelings for me, I would appreciate it if you left the manor as soon as possible."

With that, she picked up her clothes and, clinging to her dignity, walked to the door, opened it, and left.

Marcus came up on one elbow. He stared in utter disbelief as the door quietly closed. "What the...?"

He felt as if she'd hit him over the head with a brick;

his wits didn't seem able to re-engage. What had she said? That he'd felt obliged to offer for her hand? That others... "What others?"

Was she seriously trying to tell him that this—all of what had come to be between them—hadn't meant anything to her?

"Or at least not enough to get her to change her damned mind about marriage not being for her?"

Even after all his care over not stepping on her lady-of-the-clan toes? All his demonstrations that he could and would play second fiddle to her and not attempt to take control?

"Like hell." He tossed back the covers, leapt from the bed, and stalked after her.

It was too early for maids to be about, and there was no one else with rooms on that floor.

She'd closed her bedroom door; he flung it open and stormed inside. He shoved the door closed, then caught it before it slammed.

He turned to see her looking thoroughly shocked; he knew he was naked—he simply didn't care.

She'd swung to face him, her clothes still in her arms.

He transfixed her with a look and stalked toward her. He managed to say, reasonably evenly, "I believe we need to discuss my proposal."

Her jaw firmed. She tipped up her head. "No, we don't. Please leave."

"Not until I've explained a few points." He halted with her just out of arm's reach; she didn't relax, but neither did she bolt. She stood her ground, her eyes slowly narrowing. He battened down the feelings surging through him. "I don't know what you think I meant, but—"

Her eyes flashed. "I heard you."

"In that case, perhaps you'll explain why a perfectly normal proposal—"

"I didn't mean just now." She waved at the door. "Before! Yesterday."

He frowned. "What?"

She uttered a shaky, frustrated sound. She dumped her clothes on a chair, then faced him. Her eyes, normally a clear cornflower blue, were stormy. "I heard you and Sean talking in the stable yesterday morning."

He blinked and racked his memory for what they'd been talking about, what they'd said.

She saw and laughed humorlessly. "Sean asked when you were going to ask me to marry you." Her chin rose; her eyes grew colder. "I heard you agreeing to marry me to appease the clan."

He stared at her. "I *didn't*." Affronted, he raised his fists to his hips, then realized from her infinitesimal recoil that the stance was threatening. Forcing his arms to his sides, he locked his gaze with hers and poured every ounce of insistence he possessed into his tone. "That's not what that conversation was about."

Her lips and jaw set. Her eyes narrowed, and she pointed a finger at his nose. "I. Heard. You." She punctuated each word with a jab in his direction. "I *heard* the words come out of your mouth, and I heard what Sean said, too." She lowered her voice and mimicked, "Just as long as the knot gets tied—and soon." She switched back to her own voice to add, "And you assured him it would be!"

"Damn it!" Dropping his gaze, he raked a hand

through his hair. "Yes, he said those words, and so did I." Looking at her again, taking in all he could see roiling in the blue of her eyes, all he could hear in her anguished tone, he realized he was standing on very shaky ground.

He tried to calm down—and calm her down, enough for her to listen. "Niniver—I know the clan want me to marry you, but that isn't why I'm asking for your hand."

She laughed again, a scoffing sound that scored his heart. "Oh, *really*? Just how gullible do you think I am?" Her tone rose; her eyes darkened. Before he could respond, she locked her eyes with his and stated, "I trusted you." Her diction, her tone, made the words an indictment. "I let you close—I opened myself to you. And, yes, I *adore* being the woman I can be with you." She pointed at him again. "With you and only you."

As if she could no longer bear to remain still, she flung away, turning toward the window. "I don't expect you to understand, but I wanted to be that woman— the woman I can be if I'm free to be me, *all* of me. But from the first, I knew that our time together would be limited, that at some point you would return to your own life—" She broke off. Staring at the window, she went on, her voice lower, her tone darker, her words increasingly choked, "I never imagined that you of all men would allow the clan to pressure you into offering for my hand."

"Niniver—"

"No!" She glanced sidelong at him but didn't meet his eyes. "Just hear me out. Let me say this now, once, because I don't know if I'll ever be able to get through it again."

"You don't have to—"

"Yes, I do!"

When he remained silent, she hauled in another broken breath, and, head rising, stated, "I've always wanted someone, some man—father, brother, clansman, lover, it didn't really matter who—to see me for the woman I truly am. Not little Niniver, delicate and fragile, not Niniver, the lady of the clan—so busy fixing everyone else's problems she never has time for her own. I wanted someone to see *me*. And to want *me*, whether as friend, daughter, lady, lover, for the woman I truly am."

Clenching one fist, she set it to the center of her chest. "The woman I am inside. The woman I *want* to be—and could be, if only someone I trust would believe in me."

She hauled in another tortured breath. He wanted nothing more than to go to her and fold her in his arms, but...

She glanced fleetingly at him. "I had no idea I would feel like this—so devastated and hollow inside. I really don't know what you think you can explain. I know what I heard. I *know* you're only asking me to marry you because you feel you should. I—" She paused to drag in a breath that shook.

Instinctively, he stepped toward her, one hand rising to touch her arm and gather her to him. To comfort her.

"No!" She stepped away. "Please." And this time, the word was an outright plea. "I don't want to discuss this any further. Please, just go."

He was struggling to make sense of her words, let alone her emotions, while simultaneously awash with and sinking beneath his own. When he didn't immediately react, to his surprise, she came at him, waving him back, then with both hands pushing him back, as, step by stumbling step, he gave way—as he let her have her way...

She bundled him out of the room. She caught the door—and finally met his gaze. Her eyes were luminous, swimming in tears. "Please." Her voice was almost guttural. "Just go."

Her tears held him immobile; the pain he glimpsed behind them flayed him.

He'd never wanted to hurt her—how had things come to this?

She swung the door shut.

The latch clicked, then he heard the lock fall into place.

For a second, he simply stared at the panels. Her emotions had cut open something inside him; he felt as if he was bleeding feelings.

So many feelings were pouring out, he felt dizzy.

He set one palm to the door's panels, then gave in to instinct and leaned his forehead against the cool wood.

Beyond the door, he heard her sniff, then she started to almost silently weep.

The sound cut at him.

He'd felt her devastation, her grief; he knew they were real.

He wanted nothing more than to comfort her—his instincts were howling for him to do so—but she didn't want his comfort.

She didn't want him.

He knew her reasons were wrong, that her conclusion was wrong. He'd understood what she'd said. None of which explained why she would think he—as she'd put it, he of all men—would bow to the coercion of her clan. He'd seen her—but, it seemed, she hadn't seen him.

*I love you. That's why I'm asking—that's why I want you for my wife.*

She said she wanted someone to believe in her, but she hadn't believed in him.

So…what now? He forced air into his lungs, tried to think—and realized that was a lost cause. Not here. Not now.

She wanted him to leave, had begged him to do so. And he needed to get far enough away from her to see them—both him and her—clearly.

So he would go—for now.

He stalked back to his room, opened the armoire, hauled out his bag, and tossed it on the bed. Stopped to think—should he take all his clothes, or…? He needed fresh clothes anyway.

His emotions were roiling so close to his surface he couldn't focus on any rational point for longer than a second.

By the time he'd washed, dressed, and packed, he'd managed to think enough to convince himself that what he was doing—his present retreat—was the right move for him—for them—at this time.

He picked up his bag and quit the room, leaving the door swinging wide. He went down the stairs quietly; it was still very early, and he didn't need to see anyone, to have to explain anything to anyone.

He wasn't of a mind to waste any more time, yet he sensed she would allow him only one more chance—and that only because he intended to insist and would not accept anything less. When next he approached her—when next they spoke—he would have to get it right. He would have to have all his arguments assembled and in order if he expected to succeed in convincing her—Niniver, the stubborn—to change her mind.

# Fourteen

He rode hard and fast down the Carrick Manor drive.

When he'd gone into the stable to saddle Ned, Sean, who lived above the end of the stable, had heard him and come down to see what was going on.

Sean had approached as he'd slung Ned's saddle across the gray's broad back.

He'd silenced the other man with a single dark glance.

Sean had held up both hands placatingly and, wisely, said nothing. But he hadn't gone away.

Finally, while cinching the girth strap, he'd ground out, "I'm leaving—for one day. Twenty-four hours. Then I'll be back to pick up where I've left off."

He'd paused, then added, "She overheard us—you and me—talking in here yesterday morning, and she's misinterpreted and got upset. She needs a day to calm down and think things through. I would strongly suggest that all of you endeavor not to react or bother her in any way." He'd grasped the reins, planted his boot in the stirrup, and swung up to the saddle. He'd looked down at Sean. "And for God and The Lady's sake, *don't* say anything to her about me or marriage."

Warily, Sean had nodded. "All right. We'll see you tomorrow, then."

Marcus had clattered out of the stable without a backward glance, and sent Ned racing down the graveled drive.

The pounding thud of Ned's hooves, the power in the big horse's stride, soothed his still-roiling emotions with the illusion that he was actively doing something.

He was, in fact, doing the only thing he could at that point—retreating to fight another day. To regroup before a more definitive assault.

As he neared the highway, he glanced right and left and, as he'd expected, saw no one.

Vividly, he recalled his and Niniver's ride of the day before. By the time they'd reached the highway, he'd known something had disturbed her, but earlier in the stable yard, she'd concealed her reaction to his and Sean's words sufficiently well that it hadn't occurred to him that the incident that had caused her to pull back had, in fact, happened there.

Even had he known she'd overheard them, he wouldn't have imagined she would interpret their words as she had. Yes, the clan was eager to have him offer for her hand; her clan folk weren't stupid—or blind. That didn't mean they were the reason he wanted her to wife.

He should have simply told her that he loved her.

Hindsight was a wonderful thing. Unfortunately, he needed to have told her that earlier—before she'd overheard his and Sean's conversation. If he uttered the words now, she would think he was merely saying what he thought would sway her.

That he didn't truly mean it.

He still couldn't think clearly, yet despite the turmoil in his mind, one point was growing increasingly clear. He was going to have to find some way of convincing her he loved her.

Some way well beyond merely saying the words.

He and Ned reached the end of the drive; he didn't slow but rocketed across the highway. He let Ned soar over the low stone wall and race on into Bidealeigh lands.

He would spend the day in the quiet of the farmhouse, doing ordinary things and letting his mind settle. Then he would plan.

And then, tomorrow morning, he would return to Carrick Manor and reopen his campaign.

One aspect he hadn't questioned, hadn't even bothered to reassess, was his commitment to having Niniver as his wife. He wasn't giving up—on that, on her, on them; him leaving was, purely and simply, a tactical retreat.

\* \* \*

Ramsey McDougal sat his horse in a concealing copse by the side of the highway.

He'd pulled up at that spot, one that gave a long view over the Carrick fields to the manor, to reconsider his plan yet again.

Then, amazingly, he'd seen Cynster ride out. It was ridiculously early, yet the man had been riding hard.

Ramsey had remained very still and watched. A curve in the drive had afforded him a clear view of Cynster's face.

The man's expression had been set, hard—unforgiving.

Cynster had swept on, his big gray pounding down

the drive. Ramsey had watched as horse and rider raced across the highway, leapt the stone wall, and continued on. From their direction and the bag strapped to the back of Cynster's saddle, it appeared Ramsey's rival had taken himself off.

"Well, well, well." Ramsey sat his horse for several minutes while he digested what Cynster's departure implied, and what that might mean for him.

He'd come prepared to put his plan into action, but it was a risky venture—there was no doubt of that. But if Cynster had taken himself off of his own accord, then perhaps Ramsey wouldn't need his plan after all.

He looked down the drive to the distant manor, but it was still very early. Nudging his mount out of the gloom, Ramsey pushed the horse to a canter and continued on his way to Carsphairn village.

\* \* \*

That afternoon, Niniver sat at her desk in the library and tried to make her mind take in the figures and words she was reading. The clan's agent in Dumfries had written to say that he'd managed to get a better price than expected for some sheep they'd sent for sale. Given the state of the clan's coffers, given her recent experience with Carter Livestock, that was good news.

She could barely raise energy enough to register the fact.

To her surprise, no one had mentioned Marcus's absence. The lack of comment had been so pervasive she'd concluded that he must have said something to someone before he'd left—something that explained his leaving. She'd tried to imagine what story he might have spun, but that had only exacerbated the headache that had plagued her since morning.

Since that fraught scene in her bedroom, after which she'd spent a good hour weeping.

She hadn't wept since her father had died, but discovering that Marcus was no better than her other suitors and having to break with him had left her feeling equally distraught, and even more alone. Even more hollow inside.

He'd only been staying at the manor for nine days, yet it seemed much longer. Despite the fact that, other than him, everyone else in her life was still there, she felt his absence in the same way she had her father's—as if him going had left a gaping hole in her soul.

If anything, with Marcus, the feeling was sharper, more acute. The emptiness felt that much bleaker.

She was staring at the letter on the blotter before her, still not truly seeing it, still not taking in its import, when raised voices from the direction of the front hall dragged her from her fruitless reverie.

The voices—one was Ferguson's, the other some other man's—came closer. She couldn't make out their words, but it sounded as if Ferguson and the man were arguing as they came down the corridor.

Then the door opened and Ramsey McDougal strode in.

He saw her and smiled brilliantly. "There you are, my dear! I knew you couldn't really be immersed in business on such a lovely day."

It was a lovely day? She glanced at the window and confirmed the sun was shining. The sight did nothing to thaw the ice inside her.

She looked back and saw Ferguson, who had followed McDougal in, direct a stern and thoroughly disapproving glare at the younger man. "I explained to Mr. McDougal that you were occupied, my lady."

Ferguson looked somewhat rumpled, as if he'd attempted to physically prevent McDougal from disrupting her peace and had come off second best.

"Thank you, Ferguson." She didn't dismiss Ferguson; she didn't trust McDougal further than she could throw him, which equated to not at all.

For his part, Ferguson directed a look up the room at her, and when she didn't give him any sign to withdraw, he tugged his coat into place and took up a stance by the still-open door.

Reassured, she shifted her gaze to her unwelcome visitor. He was strolling up the room toward the desk, his expression set in lines of amiable geniality, but his gaze was too sharp, too intent, as he scanned the room as well as her with a frankly proprietorial gaze.

One that set her teeth on edge. Her mood darkened; her temples throbbed. "What did you wish to see me about, Mr. McDougal?" She kept her tone level, but there was no hint of warmth or welcome in her words, just crisp businesslike interrogation.

McDougal focused on her and smiled far too smoothly. "I've come to pay my respects, my dear—purely a social call. Given my long friendship with your brothers, I feel the least I should do is offer my arm, in whatever capacity you need it. I was shocked to hear that the clan has saddled you with such a heavy responsibility." He glanced frowningly at Ferguson. "Dashed unfair, if you ask me. But"—McDougal swung his gaze back to her—"should you need any advice, I'll be happy to assist. You can count on me."

He reached the desk and halted in front of one of

the armchairs before it, transparently waiting in the expectation of being invited to sit.

Niniver leaned back and studied him. Given his comments about her assuming the leadership of the clan, it seemed clear McDougal saw her as a sweet-faced, delicate chit of a girl, unsophisticated and naive. She didn't normally go out of her way to correct such assumptions, not in those outside the clan; she never knew when outsiders underestimating her might prove useful. But with McDougal…

She held few illusions about what sort of man he was; even if she hadn't had Marcus's antipathy to color her view, her own instincts had her seeing McDougal as a toad—regardless of his slick exterior, he was ugly and possibly poisonous.

More, had Marcus been at the manor, she seriously doubted McDougal would have attempted to force his way into her presence—he probably wouldn't have dared darken the manor's door.

However, now he was there…

"Mr. McDougal. I have, as it happens, a bone to pick with you—rather a large one."

"Oh?" His brows rose in feigned innocence, but she could see in his eyes that he was rapidly reviewing his actions and wondering what she'd learned.

"I believe, sir, that over the past weeks, you've been encouraging some of my clansmen to actively vie for my hand, thereby creating considerable difficulties for me and my household."

His eyes widened—this time, she judged, in honest surprise. "Ah." For a split second, he was at a complete loss—unsure whether to deny all knowledge—then he spread his hands in a "what would you have me say?"

gesture and smiled ingratiatingly. "I admit, my dear, that in my wish to gain your favor, I attempted to cast myself in a better light through comparison with your clansmen. I had hoped you would assess what they offered you, and thus, when I approached you, you would view me and my devotion to your well-being in a more appreciative light." He assumed an expression of contrition she knew to be utterly false. "I had no idea your clansmen would be so gauche as to cause any serious problems, and can only throw myself on your mercy." He met her eyes, his expression earnest. "I assure you that causing difficulties for you was never my intent."

She eyed him without expression. Not his intent? How had he expected to convince her of his "devotion to her well-being" if he hadn't intended to paint himself as saving her from the difficulties her clansmen had caused? As matters had transpired, those problems had sent her to Marcus, instead.

She continued to regard McDougal with, if anything, increasing animosity, leaving him unsure what to attempt next. Before he could decide, she stated, "Regardless of your intentions—which I would still question—you have caused me and my clan a great deal of unnecessary disruption. Given your behavior, given your friendship with my brothers—which is *not* an association likely to inspire my confidence—I am not inclined to view you with anything other than suspicion and disdain." She looked him in the eye. "I do not trust you, sir, and that is not likely to change. There is nothing for you here, and so I will bid you a good day."

McDougal had paled. His smile vanished; a muscle in his jaw ticked. "Surely you can give me an hour of your time. Give me a chance to explain."

"I have no interest in your explanations, sir. And, as you can plainly see"—she gestured to the letter on her blotter and the numerous others awaiting her attention—"I have business to attend to." She looked down the room. "Ferguson—if you would show Mr. McDougal out?"

McDougal's mask slipped; underneath, he was livid. If they'd been alone, she felt certain he wouldn't have accepted her dismissal; even now, he glanced at Ferguson and thought about pressing her.

But Ferguson looked McDougal in the eye. And waited.

McDougal regained control of his features, but his face remained flushed. Stiffly correct, he bowed to her. "As you wish, Lady Carrick. I hope we meet again in different circumstances."

His clipped accents made it plain that the circumstances he wished for were ones where she would be forced to pay him the subservience he believed he was due.

She watched him walk back down the room. He passed Ferguson and, without looking back, continued out of the door. Ferguson tracked him with his eyes, then turned and followed, pulling the door closed behind them.

Niniver stared broodingly at the door. She'd told McDougal the truth; she didn't trust him. She certainly didn't like him. But was he truly all that much different from the others? From all the men who had, in one degree or another, come to pay court to her? They all saw her as a pawn—as something to be won, then used, and ultimately discarded. Something—not someone.

A lady of a clan, not a woman. Not one of them had been interested in her as herself.

She'd thought Marcus had been different, but… She frowned and tried to focus on how Marcus had interacted with her—had it been different with him or not?—but her feelings, her still too-raw emotions, rose up and derailed her thoughts.

She didn't want to sink back into those feelings; wallowing in them did nothing but drain her, mire her, and prevent her from moving on.

Her gaze fell on the correspondence awaiting her attention. Lips twisting wryly, she sat up and smoothed out the letter from the agent in Dumfries. She needed to reply. She needed to pick up the pieces of her life and stop mooning over what might have been.

Marcus had been gone for less than a day, and already the first irritating male had arrived.

The stray thought made her grimace.

But she'd got rid of McDougal by herself; she hadn't needed Marcus to protect her.

Just as well, because he wasn't there.

She was alone again—and even if it felt as if she was more alone than she had been before, that was an illusion. She needed to get back to how she'd been before—before she'd risked asking Marcus for help, before she'd knowingly risked her heart.

She drew out a fresh sheet of paper, set it on her blotter, then reached for her pen. She started writing her reply to the agent; when she reached the end, she signed it *Niniver, Lady Carrick*—then paused.

Who was Niniver, Lady Carrick? Who was she now? Looking inside, she realized she wasn't the same young woman she had been ten days ago.

If she'd been faced with McDougal ten days ago, would she have dealt with him as expeditiously? With the same inner confidence that had allowed her to comprehensively dismiss him?

She'd long ago learned the wisdom of being honest with herself; it seemed that the past nine days had changed her. She was stronger, more confident, more assured. Less malleable, more openly assertive.

She stared at the letter, then raised her gaze and looked unseeing down the room. Whatever else she might lay at Marcus's door, her more certain strength was due to him, too.

After a moment, she shook aside her thoughts; they'd grown hopelessly tangled again. She only had to dwell on him for a second, and emotions overwhelmed her mind—emotions powerful enough to drown all rational thought.

"I need to be Lady Carrick." She looked at the letters spread before her. Lips setting, she reached for the letter knife.

\* \* \*

Later that evening, Niniver sat in her customary armchair in the drawing room, her knees crossed, one foot idly swinging, and wondered how much longer it would be before Ferguson arrived with the tea tray. She had no idea how she'd previously filled her evenings, but she was perfectly sure she'd never felt this…disengaged. This bored, this disinterested, so entirely at loose ends.

So missing the presence of a man who hadn't been a part of her life just ten days before.

After sending Ramsey McDougal on his way, she'd managed to make a reasonable attempt at, as she now thought of it, "being Lady Carrick." It was odd; she'd never previously thought of herself as "Lady Carrick," but now she'd commenced using the title as her focus, she was starting to feel as if she truly was working her way into the role.

She was starting to *see* herself as the lady of the clan.

To be conscious of the changes in herself as she… grew.

If having to deal with McDougal had led her to greater self-awareness, to a clearer appreciation of herself, perhaps he'd been a blessing in disguise.

She nearly snorted.

Hildy had, as usual, joined her for dinner. They'd eaten for the most part in silence. Niniver couldn't remember what topics they'd previously used to fill the time—or if, pre-Marcus, they truly had been that silent.

She had a sneaking suspicion the latter was true, and it was purely the last days that had made her aware of it.

The minutes ticked by, and she let her mind return to the minor irritation of trying to remember where she'd left her favorite ribbon, with the small cameo she'd attached to it that morning. She'd worn the ribbon looped about her throat through most of the day, but while she'd been working in the library, she'd taken it off; when she'd leaned forward, head bent over her letters, it had felt as if it was choking her.

She'd thought she'd left it on one corner of the desk, but later, when she'd looked for it, she hadn't been able to find it. Of course, then she'd doubted her memory, and now she truly wasn't sure where she'd left it. She made a mental note to tell Mrs. Kennedy to ask the maids to keep an eye out for it.

Finally, Ferguson arrived with the tea tray. Hildy

poured, they each consumed their usual cup, then they rose and headed for the stairs. In the gallery, Hildy paused by the attic stairs. "Good night, my dear. Sleep well."

"And you. I'll see you tomorrow."

They parted, and Niniver made her way to her room. She went in and shut the door, and felt grateful when the peace and silence of her own private space closed around her.

Without haste, she undressed, donned her night-gown, and got into bed. Lying back on the pillows, the covers drawn to her chin, she stared at the ceiling. She noted the moonbeams dappling the dim expanse, set dancing by the breeze rippling through the leaves of the trees through which the moonlight lanced.

She had, she realized, reached a level of calm, had achieved some degree of mental clarity. She could think, if not specifically about Marcus himself—one subject still too fraught with emotion—then at least about herself. She needed to think about what she did next, about how she wanted to go forward. About which direction she wanted to steer her life in.

About the new and stronger self she sensed emerging from the chrysalis of her younger, less sure, more self-conscious past.

Marcus might be gone, their liaison ended, but her time with him—his time with her—had changed her. Had started her down, not a different path, but perhaps the next path for her.

While with him, through being with him, her eyes had been opened to the woman she could be; the woman she became when in his arms—that woman truly did reside inside her. That same strength, and boldness, and the ability to act decisively and shape her own life—those characteristics, freed by her time with him, remained.

Looking back, looking inward, it seemed as if, up to ten days ago, she'd lacked some essential confidence, and asking for his help—and the days and nights they'd subsequently spent together—had provided that vital element, and freed and strengthened the woman she truly was.

The woman she needed to be.

The woman she wanted to be.

This new her, the woman she could feel herself growing into, felt right. With every step she took further into the transformation—with every action, such as dismissing McDougal, when she claimed and used her new inner strengths—she felt more sure, more established. More truly herself. As if she was standing on increasingly solid ground.

The change in her was real. The transformation was real.

She drew in a deep breath and, her eyes still fixed unseeing on the ceiling, held to her new strength, her increasing inner calmness, and let her mind shift to him.

She tried to see past the clouds of her emotions. Although they seemed to be settling, all she could sense beyond them was a gaping void. And, sadly, that was real, too.

She'd risked her heart, and he'd taken it. And there was nothing she could do about that.

\* \* \*

Marcus sat behind the desk in his study at Bidealeigh and stared broodingly at the letter spread open on his desk.

He'd spent the day immersing himself in reconnecting with his staff and ensuring everything on the estate was running smoothly. He'd kept himself busy and his mind engaged, and let his emotions and impulses settle.

He had come in from working with his hounds at dusk and found the letter waiting. He'd read it, then had washed and dined before bringing the letter with him to the study to reassess and make his plans for the morrow.

After a moment, he raised the crystal tumbler he held in one hand and took a long sip of the very finest malt whisky the Scottish Highlands produced. Whisky that, as it happened, came from the same source as the disturbing letter.

Dominic, Earl of Glencrae, wasn't one to mince words. He'd written that Ramsey McDougal had been banished from his ancestral lands—an act that, for those of the Highland clans, spoke volumes in and of itself—because he had sought to force a marriage with a neighboring laird's daughter by attempting to rape her. He hadn't succeeded only because the girl's brothers had arrived in time to save her.

Apparently, McDougal hadn't been pensioned off. He'd been summarily thrown out, and his family had disowned him.

Dominic advised that, should Marcus discover Ramsey McDougal hanging around the area, Marcus not wait for McDougal to give him an excuse before running him off.

His gaze on the letter, Marcus sipped again. He'd already decided to return to Carrick Manor first thing in the morning. He would have only one task when he got there—convincing Niniver to accept him as her husband. As he would not be letting her out of his sight until he did, she would be safe from McDougal and anyone else. But as soon as he had a chance, he would speak with Sir Godfrey Riddle, the local magistrate, and see what could be done about moving McDougal on.

No wonder the man had chosen Ayr as his base. With all the ships in the harbor, if anyone came after him, he could flee to anywhere in the world.

Dismissing McDougal from his mind, Marcus refocused on his major goal—his principal, dominant, and, until he achieved it, only goal: Convincing Niniver to marry him.

Now he'd drawn closer to her, now he'd seen and understood all the pressures bearing on her, the demands her position made of her, he fully comprehended on every level why Fate had linked them.

Him being her husband was the right role for him, and for her. And being his wife was a position she, too, needed to fulfill her.

All well and good. He now needed to meet the challenge of convincing her that she could trust him in the role—more specifically, he had to get her to see that she already did, that she'd already taken all the necessary steps. All he had to do was get her to acknowledge that.

How was a stickier question.

It hadn't escaped him that he'd fallen into the same trap—or was it a necessary pattern?—that his father and Thomas had. He'd left the woman who would be his wife. Admittedly, he hadn't wanted to, and he would be riding back tomorrow, yet it seemed that leaving was some peculiar rite of passage Fate forced them to go through in forming this most vital of relationships.

Perhaps because riding back was, in truth, an unvoiced declaration, to themselves if to no one else.

Riding back signaled that they'd made their decision, that they'd irrevocably cast their lot—that they'd committed to the path of standing at their lady's side and weren't about to be refused or turned away.

Commitment. Riding back screamed commitment.

And he was already impatient for the dawn.

Lips twisting in self-deprecation, he thought back to their parting that morning.

After a moment, he drained his glass, then set it aside.

Why hadn't he told her that he loved her?

It was the simple truth, and the words weren't that difficult to say.

Such a declaration, so powerful in its simplicity, would have stopped her in her tracks. It would have obviated her sense of betrayal, and would have allowed him to reach her. They could have talked.

Better still if he'd told her earlier, instead of...

He forced himself to face the unpalatable truth—that he'd been coward enough to want some reassurance that she loved him back. That cowardly need of his was what had really been behind his wooing of her. It hadn't been for her so much as for him.

And, as usual, Fate had seen through his ploy, laughed, and tripped him up. In no uncertain fashion. If he'd taken his heart in his hands and just asked her—taken the risk rather than putting it off to woo her first to gain some reassurance—she wouldn't have overheard anything to give her the wrong idea of why he wanted to marry her.

Now she'd had that idea planted in her mind, he would have to work even harder to get it out again.

And there was no way to attack the issue other than directly. With no more obfuscation, no more trying to shield his heart.

He'd seen the pattern often enough—with his parents, with Lucilla and Thomas, with so many other Cynster couples. Many tried resistance at first, but that was always a lost cause, and he wasn't in any mood to senselessly waste more time.

Since returning to Bidealeigh, his sense of time running out had only grown more acute.

So tomorrow morning, he would return to Carrick Manor, and once there, he would—verbally, metaphorically, and in every other way open to him—lay his heart at Niniver Carrick's dainty feet. And he would leave it there, where it belonged.

She'd owned his heart for years, but—out of a misjudged notion of protecting her—he'd never let her know.

And if she didn't love him in the same way?

Too bad. He would work, and strive, and simply be there, protecting and caring for her, until she did.

# Fifteen

Niniver woke to the dawn chorus, with the word "real" circling in her mind. The mists of sleep still clouded her thoughts; drowsy, not yet truly awake, she let her mind wander.

It returned, unerringly, to the moments, the minutes and hours, she'd spent with Marcus. There, in her bed. In the house, on the estate.

Shared moments, shared experiences, shared pleasures.

Shared joy.

*All those things had been real, too.*

The acknowledgement, that understanding, sank deep to where her emotions dwelled.

After a moment, she frowned and opened her eyes. She stared across the room.

*Real.* How could that be? She tried to reject the notion, to think of reasons to negate it, to prove it untrue...

"Damn!" No longer the least sleepy, she turned onto her back. "But I heard him. And Sean."

But did the clan wanting him to marry her mean that that was the reason *he* wanted to marry her?

*I know the clan want me to marry you, but that isn't why I'm asking for your hand.*

"Oh, my God." He'd told her he had another reason, but she'd heard his words as merely the obvious argument against her truth—the obvious way to insist that what she'd overheard hadn't meant what she'd thought.

She'd assumed he'd been pretending, that any reason he advanced would be fabricated to suit, to get her to agree to marry him. She'd been convinced he'd been about to swear he loved her, and she would have been forced to fling that back at him as a lie. Knowing it to be a lie.

But what if he'd told the truth, and he really did want to marry her? Not because the clan wanted him to, but for some other reason?

She'd trusted him. Initially instinctively, but her instincts hadn't been wrong. And in all those areas in which she'd trusted him—blindly for the most part, instinctively and completely—he had never let her down.

There really was no reason to start doubting her instincts now. No reason not to continue to trust him—to continue to accept that he wouldn't knowingly, intentionally, do anything to hurt her.

That was one truth she needed to own to: She did, still, trust him implicitly, and he'd given her no reason to change her stance.

But him wanting to marry her for some reason other than the clan's expectations didn't mean that he loved her, either.

She liked having him beside her. She enjoyed his company as much as she enjoyed having him as her lover. She felt more secure and simply safe when he was with her, and more able to deal effectively with all she needed to do for the clan.

But she didn't need a wedding to secure all that.

Yet she was fairly certain that was the price he would ask for and expect her to pay.

She didn't want to risk a marriage, not even to him, but she didn't want to lose him either, not if she didn't need to.

In this case, consideration of what was best for the clan didn't help. If his reason for wanting to marry her was one she could accept, then the benefit to the clan of having him as her husband was potentially enormous, quite aside from any question of the succession.

And if his reason wasn't one she could stomach, then the clan would be better served if she remained unwed.

It all came down to *why* he wanted to marry her.

And if—aside from all clan considerations, as a woman rather than as a lady—she truly wanted to marry him.

For the past year, she hadn't thought of herself, of her personal wants and needs. Her responsibilities had claimed her, and they had been so demanding that her stance of not marrying had been more or less dictated, clearly mandated as her correct path.

Now…if she was to lay aside the mantle of the clan and let herself—the new, stronger, more assured self she was growing into—decide, then… "If he loves me, I would marry him tomorrow."

She knew very little about love, about what it was, or how to recognize it. Her mother had died when she was very young, and she retained only a vague memory of her uncle and aunt, Thomas's parents. She had no real guide, yet she'd always sensed that, for a woman, love was the ultimate protection in a marriage.

Love, if he offered it, was the one inducement that would clear the way for her to take his hand.

Of course, if he loved her, he would want her love in return, but that was a simple matter. She'd loved him for years, and if he loved her, she would have no qualms over admitting that.

*If he loved her.*

How was she to find out if he did?

Somewhat to her surprise, the answer popped into her head on the heels of the question. Admittedly, the suggestion came from that newfound self of hers, but that was only another reason to embrace it.

Tossing back the covers, she rose and crossed to the washstand. Smiling to herself, she poured water from the ewer into the basin. The old Niniver would never have had the confidence to do what she was about to do.

She wanted to know, so she would go and ask him.

*Do you love me?* Four simple words on which their futures hung.

She trusted him enough to feel certain he wouldn't lie to her. And she now trusted her own instincts well enough to feel confident she would know if he tried.

They would settle this today, this morning, face to face.

Setting down the ewer, she felt a bolstering certainty she was starting to associate with being on the right path rise inside her. *Carpe diem.* Slipping her hands into the basin, she splashed water on her face.

\* \* \*

Marcus was at the breakfast table in the small parlor when Mrs. Flyte came in, a frown on her normally cheery face.

"Mindy just found this on the front porch, sir." She offered Marcus a small, lumpy, sealed packet. "Right by the front door, it was. No idea why they didn't knock, and Flyte says as he's seen and heard no one since we came downstairs."

Marcus took the packet. "Thank you."

Mrs. Flyte bobbed and left.

Marcus examined the crude packet—a sheet of paper folded over something squashable and sealed with a blob of wax. His name was scrawled in a masculine hand across the front. Turning the missive over, he slid his fingernail under the seal, broke it, then shook out what the packet contained.

A ribbon with a small cameo attached fell onto the tablecloth, along with a folded note.

He hadn't seen the cameo before, but the ribbon... he recognized that instantly. He'd seen it gracing Niniver's throat several times. He set down his fork, picked up the note, unfolded it, and read:

*I have her. If you want to see her again, come to the old lead mine where the gantry still stands. Come alone. Don't speak or alert anyone. You are being watched. If you make any attempt to raise the alarm, you won't see her alive again.*

*Come alone. Come now. Or you will never see sweet Niniver again.*

Unsurprisingly, the note was unsigned.

Marcus studied the writing, and thought of the letter on his study desk, the one from Glencrae.

Was this McDougal at work?

He'd already packed his bag and left it by the front

door. He'd already sent word to Johnny to saddle Ned and have him ready.

How closely was he being watched?

Did he dare leave a note, one for Johnny to deliver?

Did he dare alert Flyte and assume that when he, Marcus, left to go to the mine, any watcher would follow him?

He sat at the table for several minutes more, but, in the end, he rose, went into his study, and left the letter from Glencrae, the note from Niniver's kidnapper, and her ribbon and cameo lined up on his blotter. He wouldn't—couldn't—do anything that might increase the risk to her. But if anything happened and he didn't return, the desk was the first place his father or brothers would check.

Then he left the study, closing the door behind him, and called to Mrs. Flyte that he was off for a ride and would be back for his bag later.

Pulling on his riding gloves, he walked out of the house. Johnny had Ned waiting. The groom looked at him curiously when he didn't return the lad's smile, but as he swung up to Ned's back, he had no space in his mind for anything but the driving urge to find Niniver and get her back.

Whether it was Ramsey McDougal who had kidnapped her, or someone else, mattered not one jot.

Someone had seized her. His first step was to get her back.

Vengeance would come later.

Tapping his heels to Ned's sides, he set off for the old lead mines.

\* \* \*

Deserted long ago, the old lead mines lay to the north of the Carrick estate. The land belonged to the Crown, which meant no one tended it, and the area around the mine workings was now thoroughly overgrown.

For Marcus, as for most males who had grown up in the locality, throughout childhood, the mines had exerted a near-hypnotic tug, and even though they'd been forbidden from venturing into the area, of course, they had. That said, it was more than a decade since he'd last been near any of the mines.

Exactly how many mines there were, he didn't know, but there was only one with a gantry still standing over the entrance. The gantry had supported wheels to help haul the buckets of ore back to the entrance from the tunnel that led deep into the hillside.

It took him more than fifteen minutes to reach that mine. The entrance was an arched hole carved into the side of a hill in the lee of a rocky outcrop; immediately before it, the rusted gantry listed, framing the hole. Above the mine's entrance, the hillside rose toward the ridge of one of the rocky spines that stretched outward like gnarled fingers from the range to the west.

Although overgrown by tussocky grasses, the track leading to the mine was still discernible. It led to a small, still reasonably clear area before the mine's entrance, but, all around, the trees and bushes had crowded in.

There were umpteen places for a watcher to hide.

Marcus rode in a wide arc around the entrance, but all he spotted was a single horse, tethered to a tree not far from the mine. A man's saddle. There was no sign of any other horse or carriage, but Niniver was such a lightweight, she could easily have been brought there by a man on a horse.

It didn't, however, appear likely that she'd come there of her own accord, under her own steam.

He tried not to think of what might have happened, yet the unthinkable prospects urged him toward the mine. He rode Ned up the path and dismounted before the mine's mouth. It was dark inside, but there was light coming from somewhere deeper down the tunnel. "Niniver?"

He wasn't surprised when nothing but silence answered him.

Feeling decidedly grim, he looped Ned's reins and tied them to the saddle. Although obstreperous and fractious, Ned was attached to him; the horse might wander, but he wouldn't go far, and he would always come to Marcus's whistle. And if something happened to Marcus, Ned wouldn't let any other person near him. He might, eventually, take himself back to Bidealeigh, or perhaps the manor stable, but he wouldn't let anyone else take him—except Lucilla, who shared the ability to lure the big horse to her hand.

When Marcus pushed Ned away from the mine entrance, the big horse harrumphed, but then ambled off to graze.

Marcus faced the mine. Head tilted, he listened, but still heard not a single sound. Straightening, he walked into the darkness.

Almost immediately, he had to stoop to keep his head clear of the tunnel's ceiling. The tunnel led deeper under the hill, and as he'd thought, there was a light—a lamp, given the steadiness of the glow—

somewhere around the first bend, where the tunnel swung to the left.

Given the pervasive silence, which suggested that nothing was occurring at that moment, he paused to allow his eyes to adjust. As soon as he felt confident he could see where he was putting his feet, he headed down the old tunnel.

It was crudely constructed, hewn from the rock with picks and shored up by heavy timbers. He reached a narrow constriction just before the bend. He stepped through, then walked around the bend—only to discover the lamp was further away still, around another bend that curved to the right.

But the light had strengthened. "Niniver?"

He quickened his pace and rounded the next bend. A lamp stood to one side of the tunnel. Swiftly, he looked around, then he paced to the far side of the pool of light, but there was no one and nothing else there.

Just the lamp...

*Crack!*

Wood splintered. He looked back toward the entrance.

*Crack!*

Stone groaned.

He swore and raced back, past the lamp and around the second bend. He flew back along the next section and around the first bend—he cleared it in time to glimpse a shadowy figure, silhouetted by the daylight spilling through the mine's entrance, bring a massive sledgehammer down on the wooden support above the narrow constriction.

With a deafening roar, the tunnel's roof caved in.

Marcus flung himself back around the bend. He

stumbled and sprawled full length. Rocks flew and bounced. He covered his head with his arms and drew his legs up. He tried not to breathe as choking dust enveloped him.

Finally, the thunder of rocks falling faded.

Slowly, he raised his head. He blinked his eyes open, but he now lay in deep darkness. The gust of air caused by the rock fall must have blown out the lamp. Carefully, he straightened his limbs, then pushed himself up until he was sitting. Cuts, bruises, and scrapes he definitely had, but nothing seemed broken.

From somewhere beyond the cave-in, he heard, "Excellent!" Ramsey McDougal's voice echoed eerily. "Goodbye, Cynster. I doubt you can hear me, but in case you can, I suppose I should thank you for taking the bait and showing up so promptly. And if you are alive, let me save you some time—I checked, and now that this tunnel is blocked, there's no way out. So I'll leave you to ponder your sins. Meanwhile, I'm off to take your place. One way or another, Niniver Carrick and all she brings with her will soon be *mine*."

Marcus didn't respond. He listened as McDougal's footsteps retreated up the tunnel.

Then came silence.

It was broken by another long, tortured creak of stone.

Marcus frowned; now that his eyes had adjusted to the deeper gloom, the dark wasn't pitch black. But it should have been. There was light coming from somewhere, and this time, it was coming from the direction of the entrance.

Slowly, he got to his feet. Rocks and rubble had spilled around the bend. He scrambled over them and around the bend, and found himself facing a wall of jumbled rock. It filled the space where the tunnel had narrowed—but there *was* a small gap, high and to his left. The wooden support to the left of the constriction had remained in place, and a section of the upper support was still attached to it.

Relief flooded him. He hadn't realized he'd been holding his breath until the vise about his lungs released. He drew in a breath, careful to avoid breathing in too much dust. Quickly, he ran his gloved hands over the rock wall, testing, pushing.

The wall was much thicker to his right, where the supports had completely given way. There was no possible chance of digging his way out on that side. But to his left…the base of the wall was thick, but at the very top left, he pushed, and sent a small avalanche of loose stones and one hand-sized rock rolling back along the tunnel.

He started pulling and pushing away the rocks, working to make the small hole larger.

Another deep, aching groan, followed by two others, spurred him on. The tunnel's partial collapse had weakened the entire structure; from the sound of the protesting stone, the whole tunnel would all too soon cave in.

He didn't waste his breath swearing.

Grimly, he pulled and pushed at the rocks and rubble. But after the first few rocks, the first few inches, the newly formed wall grew much thicker, and he had to remove a lot more rock to widen the hole by even an inch.

He didn't slow. He couldn't give up—wouldn't give

up. Quite aside from wanting very much to live, there was Niniver still to be saved.

Ramsey McDougal had been banished for trying to force a marriage by attempted rape. Niniver didn't know that. She had no reason to suspect McDougal of such foul intentions.

Neither did any of her clansmen.

He had to get out, get free, and get to her, because if he didn't save her, he didn't know who would.

\* \* \*

Niniver clattered into the stable yard at Bidealeigh with five of her hounds trotting at Oswald's heels. She'd brought the hounds in case she needed an excuse to have ridden that way.

As matters had fallen out, she'd managed to leave the manor without Sean or any other of her clansmen tagging along as guardian. All three stablemen had been in the rear paddock, along with both stable lads, tending to a horse giving birth. Niniver had been able to slip into the stable, saddle Oswald—not an easy feat—then lead him out to the mounting block and ride away across the fields without anyone noticing. She'd stopped in at old Egan's farm to pick up her escort-cum-excuse, then ridden straight for Bidealeigh.

Now she'd made the decision to ask Marcus whether he loved her or not, she was hell-bent on doing so as soon as she could.

His groom dashed her hopes. "Mr. Cynster rode out not long ago, my lady."

"Oh." She frowned. "Do you know where he went? Will he be long, do you think?"

"I didn't hear where he was headed, but he rode off that way." The lad pointed to the northwest. "I don't

think he'll be long. I heard Mrs. Flyte say that he was
headed back to Carrick Manor, and that he'd left his
bag all packed by the front door and said he'd be back
to pick it up."

"Ah." So he was already intending to return to her?
That sounded promising. "Perhaps I'll go in and leave
a message." An encouraging one.

The groom held Oswald while she dismounted.

"I won't be long." She gave the hounds the order
to sit and stay. They obediently sat, but whined as she
walked away.

Reaching the front door, she tugged the bell chain
and heard a distant jangling. A minute later, Mrs. Flyte
opened the door.

The housekeeper's face lit at the sight of her. "Lady
Carrick." Mrs. Flyte opened the door wider. "I'm afraid
the master's just ridden out, but he did say he'd be
back." The housekeeper glanced down to the side, to
where Marcus's bag sat waiting. "Was Mr. Cynster expecting you, my lady?"

"No, he wasn't. I was out riding with my hounds,
and just thought to stop by." Niniver started pulling
off her gloves. "I'd like to leave a note, just to let him
know I called."

"Yes, of course, my lady." Mrs. Flyte stepped back.
Niniver walked into the small front foyer. Mrs. Flyte
closed the door, then waved her down the corridor toward Marcus's study. "I'm sure Mr. Cynster won't
mind if you use his desk. He keeps paper in the top
drawer to the right."

"Thank you. That will be perfect."

The bustling housekeeper opened the study door and
waved Niniver in. "If you'll excuse me, my lady, I've a

pot on the stove that needs stirring. Flyte's gone off to market, and the maid's gone for the day, so I'm the only one here, but please call if you need anything else."

Niniver nodded. "I doubt I'll be long."

Mrs. Flyte bobbed, then hurried off down the corridor to the kitchen. Niniver glanced around the study as she walked to the desk. Tugging off her second glove, she halted before the desk and looked down—at her favorite ribbon, carefully curled and placed to one side of the blotter.

Frowning, she picked it up. "But...how?" She twined the ribbon through her fingers, feeling the familiar silky weight, then checked the cameo; both were, indeed, hers.

Staring at the ribbon, she cast her mind back; she'd chosen that ribbon to wear yesterday morning because it was her favorite and she'd needed cheering up. *After* Marcus had left. She knew she'd been wearing the ribbon through the morning and had taken if off sometime after luncheon.

How had it come to be on Marcus's desk?

Focusing on the desk, she realized that the ribbon had been the third item left displayed on the blotter, with the other two items, letters, turned so they faced anyone who came into the room—more or less inviting whoever approached to examine them. The letters had been lined up to the left of the ribbon—one an elegantly written missive, the other a short note.

She picked up the first letter and read it. The "Glencrae" scrawled at its end told her who it was from, which strongly suggested the information contained within it was accurate. Which went some considerable way toward explaining why neither she nor, quite obviously, Marcus had trusted Ramsey McDougal.

Setting down the letter from Glencrae, she picked up the short note.

As her eyes traversed the few lines, her blood ran cold.

By the time she reached the note's end, her heart had stopped. "It's a trap."

A trap for Marcus.

For a moment, her wits whirled in panic, and her heart lurched and started to race, but then she drew in a deep breath and held it. She willed herself to calm, anchored herself in her new, stronger, woman-who-was-taking-charge-of-her-life persona.

Marcus had walked into a trap—knowingly. He'd suspected it was a trap—witness the two letters and her ribbon left as evidence—yet he'd gone regardless, and from what Johnny and Mrs. Flyte had said, he hadn't taken the risk of alerting anyone.

She'd come there intending to ask if he loved her, yet who needed words when faced with these actions?

He'd gone to save her—he would always act to protect and defend her.

And whoever was behind this—Ramsey McDougal?—had known to use her to bait his trap. Had known that she was Marcus's Achilles' heel, because of his devotion to her.

Because he loved her.

She needed no more evidence or proof.

"What I need to do now is to rescue *him*." He'd said he wanted to share a future with her. They couldn't do that if he died.

She set the note back down with the letter, and left

her ribbon there as well. Then she whirled and walked quickly out of the room and down the corridor to the kitchen. "Mrs. Flyte."

The housekeeper looked up from the pot she was stirring. "Yes, my lady?"

Niniver drew in a breath and, as calmly—as commandingly—as she could, said, "I believe Mr. Cynster is in grave peril, very possibly in peril of his life. He's gone to a rendezvous thinking some kidnapper is holding me hostage, but clearly, I'm free and perfectly all right. He's gone to one of the old lead mines—the one with a gantry still standing. Do you know which one that is?"

Mrs. Flyte's eyes had grown rounder and rounder. "Oh, dear me!" Forsaking her ladle, she wiped her hands on her apron. "I'm sorry, my lady, but I've never been about the old lead mines. I know whereabouts they are, but nothing about the mines themselves."

Niniver grimaced. "I'm the same." While all the local boys had grown up in and around the mines, few girls had ever ventured into the dirty places. "Perhaps Johnny will know."

But when Mrs. Flyte hauled her pot off the stove and they went out to the stable and inquired, Johnny shook his head. "I'm sorry, my lady, but I wasn't born in these parts. The master brought me here from north of Ayr, because I'm good with horses."

Niniver didn't like her chances of finding Marcus if she had to ride around the whole of the area dotted with the old workings. Her hounds, sensing her mounting anxiety and impending distress, pressed close, the two bitches leaning against her legs and pushing their heads under her hands.

Abruptly, she focused on them. "Of course." She looked up at Johnny. "Some of my hounds can air-scent. Did Mr. Cynster ride out on Ned?" When Johnny nodded, she said, "Quickly—bring me Ned's blanket."

Swinging to Mrs. Flyte, she said, "Mr. Cynster brought the clothes he wore over the past days back yesterday. Have you washed them yet?"

"No, my lady. I have them in the laundry. Mindy will be in tomorrow to do the washing."

"Excellent." Niniver grasped Mrs. Flyte's arm and squeezed imploringly. "Please fetch one of Mr. Cynster's shirts—one he's recently worn. His scent will be on it and with luck"—she looked at her hounds—"my hounds will be able to track both him and Ned."

"But you can't go on your own, my lady." Mrs. Flyte looked shocked, then her face fell. "Flyte's not here and the other men are in the far fields, way over to the east, today."

Niniver was already shaking her head. "I can't wait for them to be summoned." She didn't know from where the certainty sprang, but she knew she had to go and find Marcus *now*.

That she had to find him soon.

That this was one challenge she had to meet if she wanted the reward of a shared life with him.

Johnny came out carrying a heavy horse blanket. Niniver nodded at the railing. "Leave it there for the moment, near the hounds, and go and saddle a horse for yourself. I need you to take a message to the Vale."

Turning back to Mrs. Flyte, she gripped the woman's arm and steered her back toward the house. "I need that shirt. While you fetch it, I'll write a note to Marcus's parents, and my cousin, Thomas, and Marcus's sister.

I'll tell them what I think is going on, and where I'm going, where I'm sure Marcus is—I'll suggest they follow me there, or perhaps check at Carrick Manor on the way."

If the person behind this was McDougal, then *she* was his ultimate target, and this ploy was designed to get Marcus out of McDougal's way...and possibly also give McDougal either excuse or bait to get her to agree to his demands. Either way... "I think the perpetrator, believing me to be at Carrick Manor, will go there."

She released Mrs. Flyte and led the way into the house. She was starting to get an inkling of what McDougal's plan might be. "I think Mr. Cynster will have been trapped in the mine. Pray to heaven and The Lady that he won't yet be dead." Whether it was wishful thinking, an inability to believe otherwise, or something more accurate, she felt sure, somewhere inside her, that Marcus was still alive. "But the man behind this doesn't know I'm here and that I already know where Mr. Cynster has gone. I don't think he—the perpetrator—will still be at the mine when I get there."

She strode toward the study, planning aloud as she went. "If I can't free Mr. Cynster myself, I'll ride to the Bradshaw and Canning farms—they're closest, and have men who'll be able to help."

Pausing in the study doorway, she glanced at Mrs. Flyte. "I need that shirt."

Mrs. Flyte bobbed a curtsy. "Yes, my lady." With no further protestations, she hurried down the corridor.

Niniver marched into the study, crossed to the desk, and sat behind it. She found paper and a pen with a reasonable nib, and quickly wrote a note—she only had time for one—simply listing what had happened that she knew for fact, what she believed had happened to Marcus, and what she proposed to do.

She spent no time in making it neat or even composing full sentences. She wrote her name at the bottom, then blotted and folded the sheet.

As she rose with the missive in her hand, Mrs. Flyte appeared in the doorway clutching one of Marcus's shirts.

"Excellent." Niniver walked quickly to the door. She took the shirt. "When Mr. Flyte or any of the men return, please ask them to hold the fort here, pending further orders from Mr. Cynster."

Mrs. Flyte wrung her hands. "I do hope he's all right, my lady. Those mines are so old, and they always were said to be treacherous."

Niniver refused to let her mind dwell on the dangers. Pulling on her riding gloves, she made for the front door. "I'm sure Mr. Cynster will send word once we have him free."

She walked swiftly to the stable, with Mrs. Flyte trailing behind.

Johnny stood outside, the reins of a good-looking hack in one hand. "I figured Mr. Cynster would want me to take one of the faster horses."

"Indeed." Niniver handed him the note. "The butler at Casphairn Manor is Polby. Give that into his hands, and tell him it's from me, that Mr. Marcus is in danger, and that letter needs to get into the hands of either Lord Cynster, Lady Cynster, Mr. Thomas Carrick, or Mrs. Carrick immediately."

Johnny tucked the missive into his breeches pocket while reciting her message verbatim.

She nodded. "Good. Now go!"

Johnny swung up to the saddle and urged the big horse down the drive.

Niniver turned to her hounds. She dragged the horse blanket from the rail and presented it to all five hounds with the order to take the scent. Then, while Mrs. Flyte helped by tying the blanket to Niniver's saddle, Niniver called the two air-scenting bitches to one side and gave them Marcus's shirt to fix on.

Then she returned to Oswald, thrust the shirt into her saddlebag, led the big horse to the mounting block, and scrambled into the saddle.

Mrs. Flyte looked up at her. "I hope you find the master and that he's all right. Take care, my lady—and good luck!"

Niniver nodded. She called the hounds to hunt and set Oswald to follow their lead.

As she rode along a track leading, as Johnny had predicted, northwest across the Bidealeigh fields, she finally allowed herself to think of what she might find when she reached the old mine.

She imagined McDougal, assuming it was he, would have knocked Marcus out, tied him up, and hidden him in the mine. That seemed the most likely scenario. She refused to let her mind dwell on any other—not until something worse presented itself. She would deal with anything worse when she came face to face with it.

The dogs were running freely and holding direction for the area in which the old mines lay.

Niniver encouraged them and urged Oswald on. And silently prayed.

# Sixteen

Marcus shut his ears to the moaning and groaning of the rock all around him and doggedly pulled stone after stone out of the wall between him and the tunnel's entrance. Every now and then, grit and dirt drifted down from the ceiling—harbingers of the collapse yet to come.

He didn't want to die. He kept scrabbling and hauling, but it was slow going. He'd managed to widen the hole, initially smaller than his fist, to the size of a large pumpkin, but the gap was still nowhere near big enough for him to crawl through; at present, only his head would fit.

This was one time broad shoulders weren't going to be an advantage.

He had no idea how much longer he had before the tunnel caved in completely. Whether he'd be better off accepting his fate and spending his last moments making peace with God and The Lady.

But he couldn't believe this was how his life was meant to end. Not when he had so much yet to do. Like telling Niniver he loved her. Like protecting her from McDougal and his ilk.

Just the thought of what fiendish scheme McDougal

might, even now, be setting in motion was enough to make him clench his jaw and redouble his efforts.

He had to get out, not just for himself, but for Niniver, too. He had to get to her in time.

The dust in the air made breathing difficult. He paused to assess the size of the hole—still not big enough.

A familiar click of nails on stone reached him.

Hounds?

Angling his head, he peered through the gap toward the entrance.

And saw several deerhounds milling. The hounds saw him and woofed, then a sharp command rang out and the beasts drew back.

Marcus filled his lungs and was about to call out when Niniver came rushing into the tunnel. "Marcus?"

She saw the wall of jumbled rock. "Oh, no!"

"I'm all right," he called. Another horrendous groan sent a curtain of fine stones raining down between them.

"Thank God." She started to cough; ducking her head and covering her nose and mouth against the dust, she hurried to the wall.

"Niniver—no! Get out of here." He renewed his efforts to widen the hole, dislodging the tumbled rocks as fast as he could.

She ignored his order. On reaching the rock wall, she ran her gloved hands over its face, then stood on tiptoe and, through the gap, glared at him. "No. I'm not leaving you here. Keep digging."

She started to pull at the rocks, too, flinging the smaller ones aside, tugging to free the larger ones.

The groaning in the tunnel seemed to deepen. Dust

and fine grit was falling almost constantly. Stone cracked and fractured, slivers plinking on the tunnel floor.

His gloves were ripped. He kept pulling rocks away, but it took too long to gain even an inch.

"Niniver—*please*." He put every ounce of pleading he could muster into the word. "There's no point in both of us dying."

She didn't look up from her efforts to loosen a larger rock. "If you die, I die, regardless of whether I'm in this tunnel or not." She gave a soft grunt as she hauled the rock free. "So *stop* arguing. Just keep digging."

He heard the building panic in her voice, but he also knew her stubbornness. And her indomitable will.

He surrendered and frantically hauled stone after rock from the jumbled pile. "I love you."

"I know."

He blinked, then shook his hair out of his eyes. "You do?"

She waved briefly. "Well, why are you here?" She yanked a stone free and sent it spinning behind her. "You thought McDougal had kidnapped me, and you came to save me even though you knew it was almost certainly a trap."

"He had your ribbon."

"I think he stole it."

He braced and heaved, hauling a huge rock from the barricading wall. "If we get free—"

"*When* we get free." Cupping her gloved hands, she tumbled the loosened rocks toward her. "Speaking of which, can you get out, do you think?"

He paused to visually measure the hole. "Not quite yet."

The words had barely left his lips when, from above their heads, there came a horrendously loud, long groaning moan—followed by three sharp, staccato cracks.

They froze. Everything seemed to still.

He felt the shift in the atmosphere. "The tunnel's going." He looked at her. "Get out—now! Go!"

"Not without you!" She all but launched herself through the hole and grabbed his hands. "Come on! *Try!*"

The hole came to barely mid chest and was not as wide as he was. But he set his lips, clenched his jaw, freed his hands from her clasp, and hoisted himself up. Bracing his boots on tumbled rocks, he thrust his arms through the gap first, then twisted and shifted, making his shoulders as narrow as possible as he tried to angle himself through.

Niniver grabbed his hands. She wasn't going to leave him. Wasn't going to let him be taken from her.

She locked her fingers around his wrists and pulled with all her might as he wriggled and inched through.

About them, stone and rock rained down. At the edge of her vision, she saw a crack appear in the rock wall beside them.

The air seemed to shiver, and the floor quaked.

The tunnel, the whole hillside, groaned like a tortured being.

He was edging forward, but it was a horribly tight fit. She heard his clothes rip, heard his labored breathing, but his shoulders were nearly through.

Ignoring the grit in her throat, she dragged in a huge breath, set her boots against the rock, and hauled back with her full weight.

He grunted, twisted, then his shoulders came free.

He pulled his hands from her grasp, flattened them on the surrounding stone, and levered his lower torso, then his hips and legs, out through the jagged hole they'd created.

He tumbled free, landing in a sprawl on the tunnel floor.

She seized his hand. "Get up—get up!" With her other hand, she gripped his elbow and hauled, and he clambered to his feet. "Come on!"

She pushed under his arm, anchoring it over her shoulders. She looped her other arm around his waist. Larger and larger rocks were raining down; she prayed none would knock them out as together they pushed into a staggering run.

Faster and faster, they raced toward the tunnel mouth.

Behind them, the ceiling fell.

The roar was like an ungodly lion on their heels. Dust billowed out and in front of them, almost obscuring their vision, but the light of the world beyond the entrance beckoned them on, growing larger as they neared.

Marcus sensed the change in the air pressure as the tunnel gave way behind them, as section after section progressively collapsed, coming up fast on their heels. Rocks spilled to either side of them; several bounced past them and out of the tunnel mouth.

They had several yards yet to go when he saw the entrance to the tunnel start to buckle and sag.

He dug deep and sensed Niniver do the same.

With the last of his strength, he caught her to him and dove out of the entrance.

They passed through it and into the sunshine. He twisted and they landed wrapped together, skidding further away from the tunnel mouth as the ungodly roar reached its apogee—then the entire hillside slumped, filling in the tunnel, sealing it forever.

The roar cut off, replaced by a series of grumbling rumbles; gradually, the echoes faded. The sounds of falling rocks, of rocks settling, grew fewer, then ceased.

For a moment, their ears rang with the sudden silence, then the sounds of a bright spring morning in the countryside rushed in and engulfed them.

He rolled over to lie flat on his back and stared up at the blue of the sky—and gave heartfelt thanks that he could see it. And that Niniver was there, warm and alive, by his side.

He sensed her turn toward him. Shifting his head, he met her eyes. Dust and fine grit coated her bright hair and had laid a fine film over her alabaster skin, but her eyes were still bright, still so very blue. A scratch marred her forehead, but that was the only damage he could see.

She studied his eyes, then her gaze drifted over his face. Raising a hand, she lightly touched his cheek. "You're scraped."

He felt his lips curve. "All over. But I'll live." He caught her eyes as her gaze returned to his. Then he captured her hand, raised her wrist to his lips, and placed a kiss on the fine skin below the edge of her glove. Entirely sober, he said, "I wouldn't have made it out if you hadn't come, and then stayed to help. Thank you—by which I mean thank you for being stubborn enough to ignore my orders and not leave me."

Her lips curved in response, but her eyes remained

steady on his. "You've rescued me in various ways over the last days. And you were trapped because you came to rescue me again." She held his gaze, then softly—almost wonderingly—said, "You walked into what you knew would be a trap because you love me." Before he could respond—before he could agree—she added, "And I love you. So"—she rolled onto her back and stared upward—"I had to come to rescue you, too, because how could you rescue me in the future if I let you die here?"

He wasn't so battered that he didn't recognize a deflection when he heard it. "You love me?"

She sighed, then shifted her hand to twine their gloved fingers. "I always have." She paused; he glanced at her and saw she was frowning slightly. "In fact, I can't recall a time when I didn't love you. Even when we were children, you were that boy from the Vale, the one I couldn't stop staring at whenever you happened to be in sight."

He humphed and looked upward, then admitted, "I knew you lived at Carrick Manor, that you were there, but I didn't really notice you until around the time of your father's death."

She humphed. "You were a boy. Boys don't notice girls until, one day, they do."

He chuckled wryly. "I have a twin sister, remember? I always noticed girls, and I assure you Lucilla and my girl cousins ensured that I never thought of females as a lesser species."

"Hmm. Then perhaps it's your sister and cousins I should thank for you being as you are." She turned her head and met his gaze. "You've always seen me for what I am. You know that just because I'm physically delicate doesn't mean I'm incapable or unable."

He looked into her eyes. "You are one of the most able women I know, and I know quite a few."

She held his gaze, then she rolled to her side and came up on one elbow; leaning over him, she gently framed his face with one gloved hand and pressed her lips to his.

He savored her lips. Tasted the rosy curves, and the lingering tension inside him unraveled. He sighed into the kiss.

Raising his hands, he gently held her as that first kiss became several, as they explored anew, claimed again, and gloried in the simple exchange.

And the underlying intimacy.

Then soft noses nuzzled them, and on a laugh, they broke apart.

The hounds had crept near; they softly whined and pushed closer yet, shaggy bodies quivering and tails waving, wanting to be part of the fun. Laughing, Niniver sat up and pushed them away. "No—that's enough." She glanced at him. "I wouldn't have found you so quickly—wouldn't have found you in time—if it hadn't been for them."

He frowned and sat up. "How did you know to track me at all? Did someone from Bidealeigh alert you— no. There couldn't have been time." Ignoring the many twinges, and the sharper pains from various gouges in his flesh, he got to his feet.

"I arrived at Bidealeigh not long after you'd left. I'd brought the hounds in case I needed an excuse." Looking up, she met his gaze. "I was coming to ask you if you loved me. I realized I hadn't given you a chance to explain, and that just because the clan wanted you to marry me, that didn't necessarily mean that was the reason *you* wanted to marry me."

"The clan's approval is purely fortuitous. In the circumstances, their approval helps, but what the clan wished for never featured in my reasons." He held her gaze. "I'd intended to return to Carrick Manor from the moment I left—I only left because you begged me to. I was about to return, but then I got McDougal's note."

She nodded. "I saw your bag and realized that you didn't intend to back away from what we had—from what we'd found. So I asked to leave a note for you, and Mrs. Flyte showed me into your study. I found my ribbon and read the letters you'd left on your desk." She looked at him. "So it was McDougal? He seems the most likely culprit."

"It was definitely him." Marcus felt his face harden as he recalled the moments after McDougal had made the tunnel collapse. "He was so sure he'd buried me and that I wouldn't survive, he spoke to me."

She snorted. "Gloatingly, I suppose?"

"Indeed." He dusted himself off, then examined his clothes. Ripped in many places, they were beyond repair, but would do for now.

Still sitting, Niniver ruffled the hounds' ears. "I didn't know which mine to come to, but they tracked Ned and brought me straight to him. And the air-scenters confirmed you were inside."

"Speaking of Ned, we should find him and head back to Carrick Manor." He held out his hand to her; when she grasped it, he pulled her to her feet. "From what McDougal said, I assume he intended to make straight for the manor and you."

"Only I went to Bidealeigh, looking for you." She beat at her clothes, brushing away the dirt as best she could.

Her heavy riding skirts and velvet jacket were dust-covered, but otherwise unharmed. "You'll do. And I'll pass muster until I can get a change of clothes. For now—" He broke off and whistled. When Ned and Oswald both came trotting up, he met her gaze. "We need to get back to Carrick Manor—"

"And then," Niniver said, steely determination ringing in her tone as she grasped Oswald's reins, "we need to catch Ramsey McDougal and put an end to his schemes."

* * *

Assuming McDougal would be at the manor, they exercised due caution as they neared. Niniver led the way along a track that followed the fences of the rear horse paddocks. Approaching from that angle, the bulk of the stable and the old barn screened them from all but the attic windows; as it was now late morning, it was unlikely any of the staff would be in their rooms to spot incoming riders and carry word downstairs.

The mare all the stablemen and stable lads had been tending when Niniver had left had completed the task of birthing her foal; she now stood in the paddock closest to the stable, her gangly foal on wobbly legs by her side.

Fred was perched on the rail, watching the pair. As Niniver and Marcus neared, Fred grinned and dipped his head to them. "We wondered where you'd got to, my lady."

"I had business with Mr. Cynster." She reined in.

As the hounds clustered around, noses poking

through the rails to scent the mare and foal, Fred got a better look at her, then he looked at Marcus, and his eyes flared. "Heavens be! What happened to you two?"

"It's a long story, which we'll no doubt be telling everyone soon." His expression hard, Marcus glanced toward the stable. "But first, is McDougal here?"

Fred's eyes narrowed. He swung around and jumped down from the fence. "If you mean a gentl'man claims to have been one of the young masters-that-were's friends—the same one who called yesterday and saw Lady Carrick, and that Ferguson followed out and made sure left the manor—then yes. He arrived 'bout half an hour ago. Last I saw, Sean was walking his horse in the yard."

"That's him." Niniver exchanged a glance with Marcus, then looked at Fred. "Can you open the stable's rear door for us?"

Grim-faced, Marcus nodded. "Let's get out of sight, find out where McDougal is and what he's doing, and then decide what to do."

Fred swung open the stable's rear door, and they walked their horses into the dimness. The hounds followed. Niniver and Marcus dismounted as Mitch came up. "Cor, what happened to you two?"

"Later," Marcus said. "First, we need to learn if McDougal is still inside, exactly where he is, and what he's doing."

Mitch went out to the stable yard and called Sean in. All Niniver had to do was tell the three stablemen that McDougal had tried to kill Marcus by pretending he'd kidnapped her, and that McDougal was intent on forcing her to marry him so he could gain control of the clan, and the three would have done anything she wanted.

Mitch went inside to ask about McDougal.

Meanwhile, to reduce the chance of McDougal riding off, Sean unsaddled and unbridled McDougal's chestnut and turned the horse into a stall at the far end of the stable.

Mitch returned with Ferguson.

Niniver waved aside Ferguson's questions before he could ask them. "We'll explain all later. For now, we need to know where McDougal is and what he's doing."

Ferguson blinked but responded to the command in her tone. "He asked to see you. I showed him into the drawing room and went looking for you. When I asked Sean, he said Oswald was gone, so I told McDougal you'd gone out riding. He thought about that, then asked to leave you a note. I showed him to the library— I wouldn't have left him, but he all but ordered me out." Ferguson tipped his head at the house. "He's still there— I left a footman outside the door to let me know the instant he's finished and ready to leave."

"We don't want him to leave." Marcus met Niniver's eyes. "McDougal's dangerous, and not just to you and me. We need to end this now."

Niniver thought quickly; as far as she could see, the only actual evidence they had that it had been McDougal who had trapped Marcus in the mine and left him to die was Marcus's recognition of McDougal's voice. She didn't know what influence McDougal's family could bring to bear, but they'd already managed to get him free of one major charge, even though they'd subsequently banished him from their lands. Measuring her words, she said, "I want McDougal behind bars where he can't harm me, you, the clan, or anyone else ever again. So"—she glanced at her clansmen—"I want to give him the opportunity to tell me—us—more. We need to encourage him to give us enough evidence to ensure he can't escape."

Returning her gaze to Marcus, she stated, "I'm going to go in and change." She glanced at Ferguson. "I want you to go in and tell McDougal I've returned, that I'm changing and will join him shortly." Imagining their meeting, she added, "Leave him in the library—I'll speak with him there."

Marcus straightened. "Not alone."

A glance at the others' faces showed that they all agreed. She couldn't help a small smile, but she inclined her head. "Not precisely, but to him, I'll appear to be alone. I want you—all of you—to be in the corridor, listening at both doors—the main one and the one at the far end. Get Hildy, Mrs. Kennedy, and Gwen, too. I want witnesses to whatever he says, but he won't speak freely if anyone else is in the room. If I walk in, and you all creep up quietly, there's no reason he'll suspect you're there. Once he says enough, you can all come in, and we'll hold him until the authorities arrive."

Marcus's gaze hadn't left her face; she could read his indecision in his eyes. He knew her plan was the most straightforward and, most likely, would succeed; against that, should McDougal realize and try to seize her to use as a hostage...

Holding Marcus's gaze, she said, "It's the best way."

His lips twisted in a grimace and he lowered his gaze—to the hounds sitting and lying about her feet. "Take the hounds in with you." He raised his eyes to meet hers. "I agree that getting more evidence against McDougal will make dealing appropriately with him much easier, but you need some level of immediate protection against him, and the hounds will give you that."

She nodded eagerly. "That's an excellent idea. I'll take them all with me—he's not to know I don't often have them inside the house. And the clicking of their claws will mask any sounds you and the others might make."

In light of Marcus's addition to her plan and his subsequent backing, the other men agreed, and they immediately put the plan into action. Niniver called the hounds to heel, and with Ferguson and Mitch, went into the house.

After ensuring McDougal was still in the library, Mitch returned to the side door and beckoned the others in; they left the stable lads guarding the horses with strict instructions to make sure McDougal didn't try to take one and escape.

When Marcus, Sean, and Fred joined Mitch in the side corridor, he murmured, "Happy as a grig, McDougal was, to hear that Lady Carrick had come home and would soon be down to meet with him. He's settled in the library, like she wanted."

Ferguson met them at the head of the corridor that ran along the side of the library. "I'd swear the bastard was going through the estate's accounts when I went in."

Marcus's smile was openly predatory. "Let him dream. It won't be for long."

Two minutes later, Niniver came hurrying down the main stairs, the hounds moving in a fluid pack around her. She turned into the corridor, and Marcus saw that, in addition to changing into a day gown of pale blue, she'd washed her face and made an effort to remove all signs of her having been in the mine.

She saw him noticing and flashed him a quick smile. To him and the others, she whispered, "Ready?"

They all nodded. She moved past them and led the way down the corridor; the hounds, thrilled to be allowed to remain with her, trotted happily to either side and behind her. The men followed, keeping to the runner and endeavoring to walk silently.

As they neared the main library door, over Niniver's head, Marcus glimpsed Miss Hildebrand, Mrs. Kennedy, Gwen, and one of the older maids creep out from the side corridor and take up position, listening at the service door at the other end of the library.

Niniver reached the main door. She grasped the doorknob, turned to briefly meet his eyes, then she opened the door and, with her usual calm assurance, walked inside.

She left the door swinging, and with the hounds pushing in behind her, that no doubt seemed natural.

Marcus took up station by the hinged side of the door, with Ferguson, Sean, and Mitch crowding close on the other side. Through the narrow gap between door and frame, Marcus could see McDougal seated in Niniver's chair behind the desk.

The bastard had, indeed, been going through the estate's accounts, but with Niniver's entrance, he quickly shut the ledger he'd been reading and got to his feet.

"Good morning, Mr. McDougal." Niniver's frosty tones confirmed that she, too, had noted McDougal's previous occupation. She halted in the middle of the room. "I have to own to surprise that you've called again—so soon after yesterday. I had thought I had made my disinterest in further acquaintance with you quite plain."

McDougal's smile was a combination of smugness and ingratiation. "Indeed, you did, but, today, I'm here on a mission of mercy. I rather think you'll be grateful that I've seen fit to disregard your words of yesterday and come to tell you of the grave tidings I bear."

Niniver maintained her icy demeanor but played along by looking faintly uncertain and a touch uneasy. "What grave tidings?" With a flick of her fingers, she signaled the hounds to sit.

"I'm afraid it's about Cynster." McDougal made an effort to school his features into an expression of somber concern.

Niniver had to wonder if McDougal thought she really was gullible enough to believe such a patently insincere pretense.

Soberly, McDougal shook his head. "He's been badly injured and is asking for you." He fixed his gaze on her face. "I offered to come and fetch you." He waved at the desk. "As you were out, I was writing you a note. But they—those tending him—say you must come immediately if you want to see him. I don't wish to upset you, but no one knows how much longer he has."

She could readily imagine how she would have reacted to that news if she hadn't ridden to Bidealeigh that morning; she would have panicked, and putting aside her dislike of McDougal, she would have gone with him, focused only on reaching Marcus. She hauled in a breath; the emotions welling as she realized what might have been made it believably unsteady. "Where is he?"

"At the inn in the village."

A place she would have no hesitation in accompanying McDougal to, but the rooms above the inn could be reached via an outside stair. With the landlord busy in the tap downstairs and his family busy in the kitchens, those rooms might well be the perfect venue for what she had no doubt McDougal had in mind. She asked, "He's at the inn?"

McDougal nodded. "In one of the rooms above it."

She frowned. "His family?"

"The landlord sent word. They should be with Cynster by the time we get there." McDougal came around the desk.

The hounds sat up straighter, sidling to place themselves between him and her. His gaze drawn to them, McDougal halted, then he met her gaze. "We need to go immediately. Cynster was in a bad way when I left. He might not survive much longer."

"Actually, McDougal, I'm perfectly all right." Marcus walked into the room. His gaze on McDougal, he arched a brow. "How are you?"

Niniver had glanced at Marcus. As he halted by her shoulder, she looked back at McDougal—in time to appreciate his goggling, open-mouthed, horrified stare.

McDougal bolted—to the French doors to the terrace and the lawn beyond. The doors were open; he pushed them wide and charged through.

The hounds had leapt to their feet. Fleeing before sight-hounds turned anything into prey.

Niniver gave the hounds the order to pursue. All five

flew through the open doors, leapt the terrace balustrade, and streaked over the lawn.

They brought McDougal down two-thirds of the way across the clipped expanse.

The hounds were trained to hold, but not bite. McDougal thrashed, trying to push them off, but he was no match for five well-trained deerhounds.

Marcus waved Niniver through the French doors, then followed her out. The others poured into the library and trailed after them as, side by side, she and he went down the terrace steps and strolled unhurriedly across the lawn.

Niniver suspected everyone was enjoying the sight of McDougal being subdued by the hounds.

When they reached him, he was being held facedown with two hounds sprawled across his back, while another two beasts had caught his sleeves in their teeth and were holding his arms down on the grass, spread wide. The remaining hound paced before him, watching for any attempt to flee.

McDougal had surrendered and lay still beneath them.

"Call them off." Marcus waited until Niniver gave the command, then reached past the hounds, grabbed McDougal's collar, and hauled him to his feet.

He swung McDougal to face him—and smiled. "In case you think you're going to talk your way free..." He plowed his fist into McDougal's face.

Bone crunched. McDougal staggered.

Marcus released him. McDougal's eyes rolled up, and he collapsed on the lawn at Marcus's and Niniver's feet.

Sean, who had halted to one side, looked down at

McDougal with open disgust, then he shook his head. "You shouldn't have hit him so hard. Now you can't hit him again."

Rubbing his knuckles, Marcus studied McDougal and reluctantly concluded that the man really was unconscious. He shrugged. "There's always later."

Sean tilted his head, considering. "True enough."

Marcus looked at Niniver, then reached out and took her hand.

She gripped his fingers and raised her gaze from McDougal's sprawled form to Marcus's face.

For a long moment, he simply let his mind and his senses drink her in—her ethereal beauty and those fabulously alive, cornflower-blue eyes. Let his soul acknowledge what she truly was to him, all she represented.

Her gaze was steady on his, and he sensed she was doing much the same.

Then her fingers tightened, and she squeezed his hand, then she looked at the others now crowding about—the clan members who'd been in the corridor to bear witness to McDougal's perfidy now joined by the rest of the household who, drawn by the commotion, had come pouring out through the library.

Niniver drew in a breath through suddenly tight lungs. "I have an announcement to make." Everyone looked at her, including the man by her side. Raising her head, she continued, "Mr. Cynster and I intend to marry—" She added the words "sometime soon," but those were drowned out by the cheers, clapping, and congratulations that rained down upon them.

She turned to Marcus to see how he'd reacted to her taking the initiative.

He met her gaze openly, and all she saw in the midnight blue of his eyes was warmth and approval.

All she saw was love.

His long fingers shifted about hers, then he raised her hand and—gently, lingeringly—kissed her fingers. "Thank you."

Her heart swelled. "No—thank you. For seeing me, and believing in me, in who I really am, and for loving me for myself. For giving me the chance to grow into who, with you by my side, I can be."

His smile was everything she wanted it to be. "You were always Niniver—you always had this strength." He drew her to him, and she rose up on her toes as he bent his head, and they kissed.

And the crowd about them whooped, clapped, and cheered, and the hounds yipped and danced around them.

# Seventeen

Niniver quickly discovered that declaring that they would marry had been the easy part. Taking the next steps while simultaneously dealing with the matter of Ramsey McDougal and his attempted crimes was considerably more complicated.

Yet having declared their intentions, she felt increasingly impatient to get matters moving in an altarly direction, and with Marcus beside her, she felt as if she could conquer the world. She wasn't inclined to waste the feeling.

After ensuring McDougal, now groaning and holding his jaw, was adequately contained behind a locked door in the cellar, she and Marcus returned to the library. A quick canvass of their options suggested that, if they wished to resolve matters expeditiously, they needed the support of several others.

"But first," Marcus said, looking down at his ripped and dusty attire, "I need to wash and change into something presentable."

"We need to send word to your people, too." She explained how she'd left things at Bidealeigh. "Mrs. Flyte will be anxious, and Flyte will be, too, when he gets back." She outlined the information she'd sent with Johnny to the Vale.

Marcus nodded and reached for paper and a pen. "I'd better send a note post-haste to the Vale to tell them we're all right and they don't need to hurry—and to break the news of our betrothal."

"Can I suggest you refer to it as 'our impending wedding'?" When he met her eyes, she shrugged. "If we're aiming for expeditious, it seems wise to start out as we mean to go on."

He grinned, dipped the nib in the inkwell, and started writing. "That the pater and Thomas aren't here already suggests that they—and Mama and Lucilla, as well—have been out." He paused, rereading what he'd written. "They'll most likely return home for luncheon. Shall I tell them to call here afterward?"

"Yes—we need your parents, at least, and Thomas, too, I think."

After he finished the short statement to his family, she added a few lines to Thomas, and they dispatched Sean to carry the missive to the Vale. With that taken care of, Marcus sent Fred with a note to his staff at Bidealeigh, with instructions to return with the letters and ribbon from his study desk, as well as his packed bag.

They then turned their sights on summoning the local magistrate, Sir Godfrey Riddle. With Marcus's assistance, Niniver composed a carefully worded note declaring that they had apprehended a felon and had evidence to lay before Sir Godfrey; they asked him to call that afternoon, as well.

Fred returned with Marcus's bag. Marcus briefly left her writing while he went upstairs to wash and change out of his ruined clothes. He returned as she was sealing the note to Sir Godfrey. She put it into Mitch's waiting hands; he saluted them both and left.

Then Ferguson looked in to announce luncheon, and they repaired to the dining room, where Hildy joined them. Up to that point, neither Niniver nor Marcus had explained to any of the clan just what had happened before they'd returned to the manor, dusty, scratched, and bruised. Prompted by Hildy's excited questions, Niniver realized that the easiest way to eliminate speculation was to tell their tale to the entire household, and then let them spread the word.

One thing a clan excelled at was spreading information far and wide.

She explained her thoughts to Marcus. He nodded. "Good idea. Otherwise, we'll end up repeating the tale again and again, and it'll evolve into something even more fantastic." He smiled at her. "It was fantastic enough, but not something I think either of us need to relive more than necessary."

Looking inward, she realized that was true. While the relief of getting him out alive, of surviving herself, was precious and intense even in recollection, and that euphoric relief was indeed a feeling she would always hold in her heart, the gut-wrenching anxiety preceding it, and the horror she—and she was sure Marcus, too—had experienced when it had seemed they might not get out in time...she didn't need to revisit that more than once. Or twice, given they would have to relate their story to his family and Sir Godfrey later.

As soon as they'd finished eating, she asked Ferguson to summon all the staff currently at the manor. Although he did his best to hold to his usual impassive butler's mien, like everyone else, he seemed unable to stop smiling.

With Marcus and Hildy, she repaired to the drawing room. She sat in her usual armchair. Rather than sit in its mate across the hearth, Marcus took up a position beside and a little behind her chair, one boot propped on the fender, one arm elegantly resting on the mantelpiece.

The household filed in, all eager to hear their tale. She directed the older women to take the seats, while the men and the younger maids stood all around. When everyone was there, she glanced up at Marcus. "You start."

He met her eyes, nodded fractionally, then looked at the assembled crowd. "I was about to leave Bidealeigh this morning, intending to return here, when my housekeeper handed me a note found on the front step." He continued, relating what he'd done. Niniver broke in to explain how her favorite ribbon with her cameo attached had vanished the day before, presumably from the library, sometime after McDougal had called on her there.

"I thought I saw him slip something into his pocket when he turned away from the desk," Ferguson said. "But I couldn't think what he might have taken."

She nodded. "I'm sure that's where I left it, but it wasn't there later." She glanced back at Marcus.

He took up the tale. "So I rode out to the mine—the one where the gantry still stands." Most of the local males knew where that was; heads nodded around the room.

She sat back and listened. Although Marcus's words were matter-of-fact, given the connection between them, she could easily place herself in his shoes; knowing how she would feel if it had been him supposedly kidnapped and she the one walking into the mine, hoping to find him, she could appreciate his emotions, the raw intensity of all he'd felt.

After he described how McDougal had knocked out the tunnel supports—"I suspect he'd already weakened them"—and then related McDougal's words to him, the men in the clan shifted, restive and restless, wanting vengeance.

Marcus looked down at her. "I noticed there was a small gap left in the upper left corner, where the fallen rock hadn't quite filled the tunnel. I started digging there."

At his nod, she cleared her throat and looked around at the faces. "I'd decided to call at Bidealeigh this morning, not knowing that Mr. Cynster was intending to return. Sean and the others in the stable were out in the paddock tending to a mare, so I saddled Oswald and rode out. I stopped at old Egan's place…"

As she went through the steps and stages that had led to her walking into the old mine and finding Marcus trapped behind the rock wall, she realized this was an excellent way of rehearsing what they would need to tell the others—Marcus's family, Thomas, and Sir Godfrey—when they arrived.

Both she and Marcus trimmed their tale to the essential facts, leaving out much of the drama, the moments of near-horror, and the consequent elation. As they neared the end of the story, with her hounds bringing down McDougal on the lawn, she recognized that telling so many of the clan in this manner was also the right path to putting the episode behind them all in the cleanest, neatest, most final way.

When the tale was done and everyone had finished exclaiming, she concluded, "We—Mr. Cynster and I—have told you all this so that you've heard it from our lips and can pass it on to others in the clan, along with the news that we are to wed, as soon as we can make the appropriate arrangements."

The household clapped and cheered again, then, beaming with delight, everyone filed out, already chattering and certain to spread the news to all their kin just as soon as they possibly could.

Marcus crouched by Niniver's chair. When she looked at him, he met her eyes. "That went well, I think."

She nodded. After a glance at the retreating backs, she murmured, "I honestly can't remember the members of this household ever smiling so much."

He felt his lips curve. He didn't tell her that she, too, was smiling, and had been consistently smiling for longer than he'd ever seen her smile before. Rising, he tugged down his waistcoat, then a movement outside caught his eye. "Ah—we have visitors. And it appears that my family took my assurance that there was no further danger to heart. They've even brought the babies."

Indeed, barring Annabelle, still in London, Marcus's entire family had come—his parents, his younger brothers, plus Lucilla and Thomas and their twin daughters, Chloe, the elder, and Christina.

Catriona, Lady Cynster, led her tribe up the porch steps to where Marcus and Niniver waited. His mother halted before them and studied them, then she smiled, spread her arms wide, and embraced them. "My dears, I am so very *very* pleased for you."

Lord Richard was at his wife's heels. As Catriona released them and stepped aside, Richard swooped in to plant a kiss on Niniver's cheek. "Welcome to the family, my dear. We're a rambunctious lot, but you'll get used to us."

Richard's smile took all threat from his words. Niniver found her usual shyness, her customary uncertainty in social situations, evaporating. She watched as Richard met his eldest son's eyes and grinned. He held out his hand. "Welcome to the club. Now you'll understand all the mutterings Thomas and I share."

Marcus laughed. He slanted a smiling glance at Niniver. "Oh, I think I understand some of those already."

Then Lucilla was there, and Thomas, too, each holding one of their baby daughters. Moments later, Calvin and Carter joined the group. Niniver expected to feel overwhelmed, but Marcus's hand found hers, his fingers twined with hers, and she found that relaxing, smiling, and letting that rambunctious warmth wash over her wasn't so difficult.

They were still standing on the porch when the clatter of hoofbeats coming up the drive had them all looking out. Sir Godfrey rode up on a good-looking chestnut. Sean appeared to take the horse. After dismounting and handing over the reins, Sir Godfrey strode toward the steps. He halted at the bottom and looked up at all the faces. "Well! This looks like a family gathering."

"It undoubtedly is, Godfrey, dear," Catriona said, "but I understand that there is, indeed, a felon around here somewhere."

"Ah, well. That's all right, then." Sir Godfrey started up the stairs. "But what's the occasion?"

Marcus told him. Sir Godfrey was fulsome in his compliments to them both. "Excellent match, what? Yes, yes—very appropriate in so many ways."

"Please"—blushing, Niniver waved to the open door—"do come in and sit down."

"Indeed." Marcus ushered his mother, sister, Thomas, and the babies forward. "We've a story to tell, and it's just as well you've all come—we can tell you all at once."

Everyone found themselves seats in the drawing room. Niniver sat in her usual armchair, while Catriona took the armchair opposite, and Lord Richard assumed a mirror pose to Marcus, standing behind his wife's chair with one arm propped along the mantelpiece. Thomas and Lucilla sat on the sofa, each holding one of the babies. Calvin and Carter fetched straight-backed chairs and set them beyond the end of the sofa, facing the fireplace, while Sir Godfrey took the armchair opposite the sofa.

"Well, then." From beneath his bushy eyebrows, Sir Godfrey looked at Marcus. "Might I suggest you start at the beginning, wherever the beginning might be?"

Marcus paused, then drew Glencrae's letter from his coat pocket. "In reality, the beginning lies some years back. I had reason to wonder why a man like Ramsey McDougal was hanging around Ayr, as he has been for several years, so I wrote to one of our cousins in the Highlands—the Earl of Glencrae—and asked what he knew of McDougal." He unfolded the letter and read the earl's reply aloud.

Sir Godfrey humphed. "I've wondered, too. I've run

across McDougal from time to time socially, and he always struck me as a shady character. Not quite up to snuff. Seems we were both right to view him askance." Sir Godfrey fixed Marcus with a shrewd eye. "I take it McDougal is the felon you've summoned me here to deal with?"

Marcus nodded. "McDougal is presently residing in the cellar, behind a stout locked door. To explain, it seems that McDougal had designs on Niniver—on marrying her, one way or another, and thereby assuming control of the Carrick fortune and also the clan estate." Steadily, step by step, Marcus outlined what they now knew Ramsey McDougal had done.

At every revelation, Sir Godfrey halted Marcus's recitation and asked what evidence existed as proof, what witnesses they might call to attest to the truth of what they believed had happened. For all his bluff geniality, Sir Godfrey was an exceedingly shrewd man; as the tale of McDougal's perfidy continued, it was plain he was taking in every fact.

When Marcus described what had occurred when he'd responded to McDougal's note and gone to the old lead mine, Niniver noticed a change in all the members of his family. An increased tension in the men, a heightened alertness in Lucilla and Catriona. Thomas looked grim, and even the twin babes had locked their wide gazes on Marcus and looked unwontedly serious.

Eventually, Marcus paused and looked at Niniver. She met his gaze briefly, then took up the tale, explaining how she had gone to Bidealeigh, realized from the letters and ribbon Marcus had left on his desk what had happened, and set out to find Marcus.

Lucilla and Thomas, and Marcus's brothers, were intrigued by her description of how she'd used her hounds and their peculiar talents to locate him.

Then Marcus took back the reins and filled in the rest, glibly passing over the more emotionally fraught moments by sticking to the bald facts.

When, between them, he and she gave a verbatim account of what McDougal had said when she'd returned to the library and found him looking through the estate ledgers, Sir Godfrey snorted. "A bad egg, through and through, and not even very clever about it." He eyed Marcus and Niniver. "I take it you have others who overheard?"

She nodded. "Several clan elders, and also my old governess, Miss Hildebrand."

Marcus described the final scene.

"Aha!" Sir Godfrey grinned. "So he ran, did he? Excellent. That's the best admission of guilt there is." He glanced at Richard, then at Catriona and the others, then Sir Godfrey looked at Niniver. "My dear, I believe we can settle this quite quickly, especially given I have three local landowners present—Lord Richard and Lady Catriona, yourself, and Mr. Cynster. If I might speak with your clan members—those who overheard what McDougal said—then I believe I can reach a summary judgment and take McDougal off your hands."

"Our butler, Ferguson"—Niniver looked at Marcus and he moved to tug the bellpull—"will arrange for you to speak with whomever you wish."

Ferguson duly arrived, and with a few quick words, all was arranged. Sir Godfrey rose and arched his brows at Lord Richard. "Richard, Marcus—and perhaps, in the circumstances, you might come, too, Thomas?" To

Niniver, Sir Godfrey said, "As McDougal's principal target was you and the clan, then it might be best were you not present at the questioning, but Thomas can represent the clan at one remove, so to speak."

"Yes. Of course." If Marcus was to be present, Niniver had complete faith that the full truth of McDougal's machinations would be exposed.

"Besides"—Sir Godfrey's eyes twinkled as he turned away—"I rather think you have a wedding to organize. Excellent entertainments, Cynster weddings."

With that, attended by his selected group of gentlemen, he followed Ferguson from the room.

"Well!" After settling Christina in her arms, Catriona, her green eyes alight, looked from Niniver to Lucilla, then back again. "I rather think Godfrey's correct. We need to make plans. Have you and Marcus decided when you wish to marry?"

Niniver blinked. "We had thought…as soon as possible?"

Catriona widened her eyes, plainly considering, then she smiled. "Indeed—why not? So…" She looked inquiringly at Niniver. "The first thing we need to decide is *when* 'as soon as possible' actually is."

Niniver inwardly braced, expecting to feel overwhelmed. Instead, although Catriona and Lucilla had plenty of opinions and ideas, which they freely shared, both deferred to her—and, more, encouraged her to offer her own views, her own wishes and inclinations.

"Your wedding is *your* day, my dear," Catriona decreed. "From morning to night, *you* get to choose."

Somewhat to Niniver's surprise, both Marcus's brothers—Calvin, an elegantly sophisticated young gentleman-about-town, and Carter, the youngest of the brood, a budding artist and a rather quieter and, Niniver judged, more sensitive gentleman—joined in, making just as many suggestions as Lucilla, although generally on different aspects of the day, such as how many guests might be accommodated in the small village church.

"If we managed for Lucilla's wedding, we'll manage with this one." Carter smiled encouragingly at Niniver. "And I'm getting the distinct impression that Niniver and Marcus would prefer a much smaller affair."

Remembering Lucilla's wedding—massive by local standards—Niniver glanced at Catriona. "I know there are a lot of Cynsters, but perhaps if we limit it to just family?"

Catriona smiled reassuringly. "That won't be a problem. We can let Marcus decide exactly whom of the family to invite, but we'll endeavor to keep a balance between the two clans, as it were."

They were all in agreement that banns should be read, and finally settled on a date nearly four weeks away.

"But that will give you time to get your gown made." Lucilla smiled. "Believe it or not, you'll find that absorbing, and very memorable." Lucilla tipped her head, studying Niniver. "Indeed, you're so very delicate, you're going to look like a fairy princess no matter what you wear."

"Hmm." Carter leaned forward, his gaze travelling over Niniver's face and figure, but in a distinctly academic way. "I could do some sketches—it might be fun."

Calvin laughed and ribbed Carter, but in a lighthearted, good-humored way, and Carter responded in kind.

Niniver felt as if she was whirling; her wedding—*her wedding*—was taking shape before her very eyes. And it all seemed so…effortless. She'd expected to feel pressured, to feel defensive and uncertain. Instead, she found herself relaxing into the easy camaraderie the Cynster siblings shared.

*So this is what it feels like to have a real family.*

It was so very tempting to let the sense of being a part of it sweep her away.

Then male voices sounded outside the door. A moment later, it opened, and Sir Godfrey led the gentlemen in. He smiled kindly at Niniver. "Well, my dear, that's done, and I'm satisfied. I believe I have enough sound evidence before me to pass judgment on McDougal and remove him from society, ours or anyone else's."

"However," Richard said, his diction crisp as he walked forward to reclaim his position beside Catriona's chair, "there is an issue, or so Marcus says."

Thomas returned to sit beside Lucilla. All eyes turned to Marcus as he shut the door and came forward.

He halted and met Niniver's eyes, then looked at his mother. "If Sir Godfrey convicts McDougal of attempting to murder me, then McDougal will hang."

Niniver felt an icy sensation brush over her nape. She couldn't have explained it, but something in her recoiled at the thought. It wasn't that she thought McDougal didn't deserve to hang; he'd nearly succeeded in killing Marcus, and she didn't want to think what he'd had in store for her. But…

Marcus met her eyes. "I don't feel a hanging is the right prelude for our marriage."

"Ah." Catriona was staring at Marcus. After a long moment, she said, "I have to agree." Looking up, she held out a hand to Richard; when he grasped it, she spoke, to him but also to them all. "As much as I would prefer to see McDougal removed from this world and thus denied any chance of harming anyone again, Marcus is correct. For him and Niniver to start married life with a hanging... The Lady wouldn't approve. She is life, not death. And while Marcus and Niniver might marry in a church, they are also marrying under Her aegis. They have both lived all their lives under Her hand, and they are both Her chosen, just as Lucilla and Thomas are—just as you and I are."

Catriona turned to look at Sir Godfrey. "Godfrey, I know such talk makes you uncomfortable, but in this, Marcus is correct."

"Entirely correct." Lucilla had closed her eyes. Now she opened them, met her twin's gaze, and nodded. "You're right." Lucilla glanced at Thomas, then looked at Sir Godfrey. "We have got to find some other way of dealing appropriately with McDougal."

Sir Godfrey frowned; in a lesser man, his expression might have been taken as indicative of inner squirming. "That's all very well, but as your magistrate, I'm bound to do my duty."

Calvin leaned forward. "Exactly what does your duty require in such a case?"

"I have to pass an appropriate sentence." Sir Godfrey grimaced. "And it needs to fit the crime—in this case, attempted murder."

"But," Calvin persisted, "'appropriate' is open to interpretation, isn't it?"

"Well, yes," Sir Godfrey admitted.

"So if we can devise a punishment that you could deem fitting, something other than hanging, that would be acceptable." Calvin raised his brows in question.

Sir Godfrey pursed his lips, then nodded. "Devise me a suitable punishment, and I'll agree not to hang the fellow."

Calvin smiled and shifted his gaze to his family. "Right, then. What can we come up with?"

In the end, it was Thomas who supplied the critical element—a description of a certain captain of a merchantman known far and wide as a man no one crossed. They elaborated on their scheme and, finally, convinced Sir Godfrey to declare that if McDougal accepted their alternative, he could escape the hangman.

"Excellent!" Catriona beamed upon her family and Sir Godfrey. "Now"—still smiling, she looked at Niniver—"I do believe we've earned our tea."

Niniver smiled back, Marcus rang for Ferguson, then Lucilla, Catriona, Calvin, and Carter refocused the conversation on the topic they transparently considered paramount—the arrangements for the next Cynster wedding.

\* \* \*

By the time the Cynsters left, Niniver felt as if she was floating, all but detached from reality. Sir Godfrey had taken his leave immediately following afternoon tea. He'd patted her hand and, beaming genially, had assured her that, between them, he, Marcus, and Lord Richard would attend to the matter of Ramsey

McDougal's fate, and she should therefore feel free to focus on her wedding without a care.

As she intended to do just that—to, in the matter of McDougal, allow Marcus to rule—she'd smiled prettily and bade Sir Godfrey farewell.

Standing beside her on the porch, Marcus had murmured, "He means well."

"I'm not fussed—at least, not over McDougal." She'd turned to study his face. "But when do you plan on breaking the news to him?"

"Later." Marcus had steered her back inside. "Once he's had a chance to contemplate the shadow of the hangman's noose."

They'd returned to the drawing room and immersed themselves in—wrapped themselves in—the warm gaiety generated by his family. As Lord Richard had warned her, they were rambunctious; Niniver eventually concluded that her waning shyness, at least with them, was an outcome of her growing confidence, of the effect Marcus had on her. Of the light in his eyes when they met hers, and the support she sensed coming unwaveringly from him—and the blatant possessiveness that underlay his protectiveness.

She saw the same complex intertwining of motive and emotion between Richard and Catriona, between Lucilla and Thomas, and felt…blessed.

This was, indeed, how Marcus and she were meant to be—how their lives would be from now on.

Ferguson had come in at one point, but to her surprise, it had been Marcus he wished to speak with. After Marcus returned, Catriona rose and shook out her skirts. "It's time to go home." She bent over her twin granddaughters, with one finger lightly stroked each delicate cheek. "They'll be getting fractious soon, and will want to be fed and then put to bed, so we'd better head back to the Vale."

In matriarchal fashion, Catriona gathered her brood and swept them out to where Sean and Mitch held their horses, and Fred held the curricle in which Thomas had driven Lucilla and the babes.

Niniver stood on the porch with Marcus and waved them all away.

"Ferguson came to remind me about the hounds," Marcus said.

"Heavens! I'd forgotten."

He grinned. "We've time enough to ride over to Egan's place and put them back in their kennels. They performed admirably today and deserve to rest in comfort."

"Indeed, they do." She glanced down at her gown. "But I'll have to change again—I can't ride in this."

The sound of wheels rolling on gravel had her looking toward the stable yard.

"I thought we might use one of your brothers' curricles. The hounds can follow a carriage just as well as a rider."

She blinked and straightened. "True."

Hildy appeared from the front hall. "Here you are." She held out one of Niniver's warmer shawls. "Ferguson mentioned you'd be driving to the kennels, and the sun's almost gone."

"Thank you." Niniver accepted the shawl and flicked it about her shoulders, then she smiled at Marcus. "It appears I'm ready."

"Excellent." Smiling himself, he offered her his arm,

then, with a nod to Hildy, led her down the steps. The hounds milled around them, ready to go home.

After helping her into the curricle, Marcus rounded it, accepted the reins from Mitch, then climbed up beside her. With a flick of the reins, he set the horse trotting. She checked that the hounds were keeping pace, then settled back to enjoy the ride.

Too soon, they reached Egan's barn and drew up outside. Marcus tied off the reins, then helped her down. She led the way inside and discovered that Egan had left food out for the five hounds. They fell on the bowls. While they ate, she glanced into the other pens; the rest of the pack had already been fed, watered, and penned for the night.

After returning the five triumphant beasts to their respective pens, she and Marcus quit the barn.

While he settled the heavy bar across the doors, she glanced at the nearby farmhouse. "I'm surprised Egan hasn't come out. Usually, given any reason at all, he'll be here."

"No doubt he's getting ready for dinner. Or he might already be eating it." Marcus took her elbow and led her to the curricle. "Perhaps we can come out tomorrow and work with the rest of the pack." He handed her up into the curricle.

"Yes—let's." She sat and settled her skirts and shawl. "Now I know air-scenting works and is useful, I'm even more determined to improve the trait."

Marcus climbed up, sat beside her, and picked up the reins. "What did you use as focus for them this morning?"

On the drive back, they chatted about the hounds,

but as the manor rose ahead, surrounded by its screening stands of firs, Niniver fell silent.

Marcus glanced at her; she was sitting with her hands clasped in her lap, staring at the house. "What are you thinking?"

Briefly, she met his eyes. After a moment, her gaze once more on the house, she offered, "I just realized where I was—where we were—just this morning. With me here alone, and you at Bidealeigh. Now…everything's changed." With another glance at him, she hurriedly added, "All for the better, but still…everything seems to have happened so very quickly."

"Are you feeling overwhelmed?"

"Not overwhelmed. More like swept away." She waved. "Into a landscape that so much resembles my dreams that I'm not sure I trust it to still be there if I close my eyes, then open them again."

He smiled. "I can assure you that I'm no mirage, and I have absolutely no intention of ever not being here, exactly where I am, by your side."

"I know." A second later, in a smaller voice, she added, "And I find that quite…staggering."

He studied her profile, then murmured, "Second thoughts?"

Her chin set, and she met his gaze, her blue eyes suddenly fierce. "Never." She studied his eyes. "But you must feel it, too."

He had to look at the horse. But now she'd mentioned it… He looked inward, then admitted, "Yes, and no. To me, it's more like everything inside me— so much that is the essence of me—was bottled up, held back behind a wall. And you coming to ask for my help was the crack in the wall that let everything out. It feels like I'm a river flowing freely again." He glanced at her. "If that makes any sense."

She held his gaze for a moment, then nodded and looked ahead. Seconds later, she said, "For me, it's more than being free. It's as if a door has opened, and I've stepped through into a realm of new possibilities."

The thought expressed, the concept given words, simultaneously set his heart winging and anchored him. If that was what becoming his wife meant to her… Contentment bloomed and spread through him.

He drove up to the front steps of the manor. Fred came running to hold the horse's head. Marcus descended to the gravel, then reached up and helped Niniver down. Winding her arm in his, he smiled at her. "Come."

He led her up the front steps and across the front porch. The twin doors opened wide as they neared.

Niniver gasped, but Marcus didn't stop. He led her on into the bosom of her assembled clan.

Clan Carrick had gathered. The elders had summoned the entire clan. The household had opened up the drawing room and dining room; together with the front hall, they formed a huge expanse that was large enough to hold everyone, from the old women in their chairs, to the babes in arms, and the children of all ages—Niniver glimpsed them all as Marcus led her through the throng, down an avenue created by the elders and their spouses. Everyone was not just smiling, but beaming.

The path through the throng ended at a small stepladder set before the huge hearth in the back wall of the front hall. Marcus helped her climb up; she turned on the upper step to face the multitude. The additional height meant that her shoulder was level with his eyes, and she could survey the assembled horde.

She looked at the sea of excited, expectant faces and didn't have any notion of what to say.

But, apparently, it wasn't her they'd come to hear.

Still holding her hand, Marcus turned to face the crowd, and all eyes swung his way. "Ladies and gentlemen, elders, and children of Clan Carrick." His voice rang clearly over the heads. He squeezed her hand gently, then continued, "Today, I give to you the same pledge I will shortly make to your lady before the altar in the village church." Turning to her, he met her gaze, and there was a wealth of emotions in his midnight eyes. "That I will honor, protect, and serve you until my dying day."

There was an instant of silence as the impact and meaning of the words spread out over the crowd, then a cheer rose—growing stronger and more tumultuous as voice after voice joined in.

The sound rolled on, but to Niniver, it dimmed as she looked into Marcus's eyes. As she saw the commitment, the devotion that knew no bounds, the unwavering resolution. She slipped her hand from his clasp, placed it on his shoulder, and leaned closer. "Thank you." With her other hand, she framed his jaw, then, in full view of her entire clan, she bent her head and kissed him.

The approving roar from the clan rattled the rafters.

* * *

After Niniver had shared their plans for their wedding day and they'd been congratulated by one and all, with their arms twined, she and Marcus strolled through the assembled throng. Ferguson, Mrs. Kennedy, and Gwen and her staff had organized a celebratory supper, and ale and ginger wine flowed freely.

People pressed Niniver's hand, smiled shyly at Marcus or wrung his hand, and rained blessings on them both.

"Wonderful, my dear!"

"Such excitement!"

"I never thought I'd live to see the day—and nor did many others in the clan."

"You've done right well for us, my lady."

"It's been too many years since the clan has celebrated anything at all."

That last comment stayed with them both.

Marcus's staff and his tenant farmers had been invited, and they had driven over to join the celebration. Marcus directed Niniver's attention to where several of his farmers were engaged in a discussion with several Carrick farmers, with their wives in a group, heads together, close by. "It's good to see them mingling. We'll have to discuss how to merge the holdings sometime." He glanced at her and smiled. "But not tonight."

Tonight… Hildy played the pianoforte, and people cleared a space in the drawing room, and Marcus drew her into his arms and they waltzed.

She was quite sure she was floating on happiness.

Eventually, others joined in. Later, she and Marcus took a turn at the pianoforte, with him playing and her singing—then others joined in and a choir formed, and they made music as the stars glittered in the sky.

As the evening rolled on, Marcus stayed by her side. Moving through the crowd, chatting and laughing, Niniver felt her heart swell—she had never felt so blessed.

She paused before the hall fireplace and looked

at the happy, beaming faces, heard the joy in everyone's voices. She caught Marcus's eye. "Someone said it before—it's been *so long* since the clan has celebrated like this."

He held her gaze. "This is our beginning. You committed yourself to leading the clan out of the wilderness—financially, yes, but money alone won't give a clan heart. Being financially secure is only a part of feeling prosperous. This"—with a wave, he indicated the gathering—"is equally important. This is your first step in drawing the clan together, into making them strong and whole again."

She studied him for a moment, then tightened her hold on his arm. "Not my first step—*our* first step."

The curve of his lips deepened. "As I'll always be by your side, I suppose that's true. Whatever road you take, I will be with you."

\* \* \*

Later, while Niniver was still engaged with the clan celebration, Marcus made his way down the cellar steps to the locked door behind which they'd deposited Ramsey McDougal.

Sean and Ferguson followed at his heels, but when Marcus turned the heavy key and swung the door open, both men hung back, clearly visible in the shadows and standing ready should McDougal make any attempt to escape, but at a sufficient distance to allow Marcus to be the focus of their prisoner's attention.

McDougal was sitting on the crude cot they'd placed in the small room. He didn't rise when Marcus walked in, just looked up with no expression on his face or in his eyes. No hope; no expectation.

Marcus halted and looked down at him.

After a full minute, McDougal said, "Come to gloat?"

"I'm here to lay out your options."

"Options?" McDougal laughed harshly. "There aren't any, are there?"

"Not in the normal way, no. If you weren't here, on The Lady's lands, you would be destined for the hangman. You stepped over a line in trying to do away with me."

"I didn't have much choice. It was that, or ruination anyway."

"We always have choices, and you're about to be given one now."

McDougal frowned. "Why?"

"Not because it was left up to me," Marcus dryly informed him. "But there are…forces that we in this area acknowledge, and there are consequences that flow from that. And one of those applies in this case. You might have tried to kill me, but if it hadn't been for you, Niniver and I might never have found our way to where we both belong. You were the one who pushed her into asking for my help. If you hadn't interfered and all but forced her into it, she might never have taken that step. You were the necessary catalyst that brought us together. Consequently, she and I owe you that much. So we've interceded with Sir Godfrey, and I'm authorized to offer you an alternative to the hangman's noose."

He paused, but McDougal was now listening avidly. "Please do note that convincing Sir Godfrey took the combined energies of my family. He was not happy, but he agreed to our request. This is, therefore, not an offer to refuse lightly—there is no other alternative but to hang."

McDougal made a get-on-with-it gesture.

Inwardly, Marcus smiled. "The alternative is simple. There's a Captain McPhee who sails out of Ayr. He captains his own merchantman and trades with the colonies. About a third of his crew are prisoners indentured under a particular scheme. Sir Godfrey has agreed that an acceptable sentence for your crimes is for you to be indentured to McPhee for a period of twenty years."

McDougal blinked. "Twenty years?"

Marcus caught his gaze. "That's shorter than the rest of your life."

His words struck home. McDougal stared at him as, slowly, the reality of the choice sank in.

McDougal shifted his gaze to the wall beside the door; he continued to stare unseeing.

Another minute ticked by, then Marcus prompted, "Well?"

McDougal swallowed. Without looking at Marcus, he replied, "I'll take it. I don't really have any choice."

Marcus didn't see any need to tell McDougal that the lack of choice, and losing a good portion of his life, were two of the arguments that had swayed Sir Godfrey. "Sir Godfrey will send constables to fetch you in the morning. Until then"—Marcus turned toward the door—"sleep well."

He was about to step over the threshold when some impulse had him glancing back. McDougal still sat on the edge of the cot, his expression lost and utterly bleak. Marcus found words on his lips; he let them spill uncensored. "No matter how things look, you've been given a chance—don't waste it."

With that, he walked out of the tiny room, swung the door shut, locked it, then handed the key to Ferguson.

Ferguson accepted the heavy key with a nod. "You've done your bit. Now leave the rest to us."

With a dip of his head in reply, Marcus started up the cellar steps—into the light, into the gaiety.

To his love who was waiting for him to return to her side.

\* \* \*

Niniver couldn't think of any more perfect way to end her day.

The clan celebration finally wound down, and the families piled into carts and drays and rattled away into a crisp, clear night.

Marcus was waiting to lead her upstairs. Hildy climbed the stairs alongside them but, as usual, headed up to her apartment with a cheery "Sleep well, my dears."

Niniver walked beside Marcus along the gallery toward their rooms. Her smile deepening, she glanced at his face, then caught his hand and drew him on—to her door, to her room.

She set the door swinging, then laughed as he twirled her through. She whirled, and he followed, closing the door before swooping to catch her and sweep her on. He halted by the window. He released her, framed her face between his hands, and tipped it up to his.

He looked into her eyes; his were dark, his gaze intense as it held hers. "I love you."

She closed her hands over the backs of his. "And I love you."

For one long moment, they listened and understood,

and gloried in the truth and unflinching reality of those words.

Then he bent his head and she stretched up on her toes, and their lips met.

Brushed, settled, then melded and merged as they slid into the kiss, and let it claim them.

Let desire rise up and wrap them in heat.

Let passion spark, then erupt into flame.

Let it take them, rack them, wreck and remake them.

They gave themselves up to the ineluctable heat, to passion's beat, to the driving urgency. To the bliss of their joining, of a connection strong and true that reached so much deeper than skin and touch, carried on sensations so much more intense than simple emotions.

They surrendered and claimed anew the connection that linked their souls.

Later, when they lay sated and spent in each other's arms, relaxed and floating on oblivion's golden sea, Marcus brushed his lips to her temple and whispered the words that, above all others, now ruled him. "I love you." Wonder, acceptance, and an evolving understanding colored the words.

Niniver's lashes flickered, then rose. Brilliantly intense cornflower-blue eyes met his. "And I love you in exactly the same way."

Marcus felt his lips curve. He shifted his head enough to touch his lips to hers, then lay back and closed his eyes. She was fairylike and fragile, delicate and womanly weak, yet even in the power of their love, she matched him. He harbored not a single doubt that in her he'd found his destiny.

His true and fated love, now and forever.

* * *

The following morning dawned bright and clear. When Niniver woke, late, courtesy of Marcus's idea of how best to celebrate the dawn—a ritual with which she had absolutely no argument—she discovered that he'd already risen and gone down.

No doubt he was famished; she certainly was.

After washing and dressing, she went down to the dining room and, sure enough, found him seated in his usual place, addressing his customary pile of kedgeree. She couldn't stop smiling inanely as she called a cheery "Good morning" and went to the sideboard to fill her plate. She felt ridiculously domestic—something she'd never really thought she would feel.

Marcus had grunted a reply, but when she turned back to the table, he rose and drew out—not her usual chair to his right, but the huge carver at the head of the table.

Her father's chair.

Her plate in her hand, she hesitated, staring at the ornate chair that had for generations been occupied by the head of Clan Carrick. Then she drew in a breath, raised her gaze to Marcus's—read the encouragement in his eyes. Ferguson was standing back by the sideboard, watching but saying nothing, yet...

She swallowed and walked forward. She set her plate down in the place at the head of the table, then drew in her skirts and sat in the chair.

Marcus pushed it in for her, then returned to the chair on her right.

Niniver looked down the table, then she looked at Ferguson. Then she reached for the teapot and poured herself a cup.

# Epilogue

May was blooming on the day they were married in the tiny church in Carsphairn village.

Every last man, woman, and child in Clan Carrick attended the simple service; even though the number of Cynsters and connections attending had been kept tightly controlled, the church was still packed. But it was very much a family wedding on both sides, more relaxed in tone and manner than Lucilla's grand wedding had been.

Niniver's gown, a frothy concoction formed of layers of ivory lace, was the perfect outfit for what she thought of as her fairytale wedding, and the cornflower-blue sapphires that were Marcus's wedding gift graced her throat and wrist, the ring glowing on her right hand, all echoing the hue of her eyes.

Lucilla stood as Niniver's maid of honor, and Thomas was Marcus's best man—the two had grown close over the years since Thomas had married Lucilla. The wedding party stood as ample testimony to the close connection that now existed and would continue to exist between the neighboring estates.

Norris had returned to give Niniver away. She'd been glad to welcome him home again, even if only for a short stay. Norris had, it seemed, found his niche in academia; he was more confident, more certain of himself, than Niniver had ever seen him. After several relaxed discussions between him, her, and Marcus, she no longer felt the need to feel anxious over Norris's ability to manage out in the world on his own.

Everything seemed to be falling into place perfectly; looking back, she could even bless McDougal and the clansmen he'd enlisted to pester her. If they hadn't, she might never have found her path to where she now stood, looking forward to a future with Marcus Cynster by her side.

He had always fascinated her, and during the service, from the instant she'd stepped into the church and seen him waiting at the end of the aisle, she'd had eyes for no other. He'd commanded her attention—and if the way his midnight gaze had rested unwaveringly on her was any guide, she'd commanded his. Which only seemed fair.

Then he'd placed a simple gold band on her finger, and her heart had soared.

Now, the music swelled, growing even more celebratory and triumphant as, with all the formalities finally concluded, they turned and, as husband and wife, started their walk up the aisle, into their joint future.

When they emerged from the church, it was to cheers from the crowd that had spilled onto the lawn ahead of them, to bright spring sunshine and a flirting breeze that scattered hawthorn blossoms over them— Nature's benediction.

Niniver gave herself over to the glory of the day, to the pride and possessiveness that shone in Marcus's eyes, and gladly went with him down the steps and into the milling throng to greet their guests.

In the center of the lawn, they came upon Lucilla and Thomas standing with several others of Marcus's family.

Niniver paused to give both Chloe and Christina, one in Thomas's arms, the other in Lucilla's, a kiss on their foreheads.

Marcus tightened his grip on her hand—she sensed in encouragement—as he drew her to face the others in the group, two tall gentlemen and a lady. "Allow me to introduce my cousins—I don't think you met them at Lucilla's wedding."

The taller of the gentlemen—a strikingly handsome man with black hair, aristocratic features similar to Marcus's, and distinctive pale green eyes—glanced sidelong at Marcus, his lips twisting cynically. "You mean you made sure we didn't meet her then, so we couldn't steal a march on you."

Unperturbed, Marcus arched his brows back. "It worked."

He turned to Niniver, but before he could speak, the gentleman smoothly captured her hand, bowed, and, as he straightened, smiled at her. "Sebastian, Marquess of Earith, my dear. Welcome to the family."

Niniver was suddenly very glad that she was safely married to Marcus. Even though Sebastian very correctly released her hand and she sensed no predatory interest, much less intent, and therefore no threat whatsoever from him, there was just *something* about him, some element in the aura that hung from his broad shoulders like an invisible cloak, that screamed to any female with operating senses: *Danger!*

Up until then, she'd considered Marcus to be supremely distracting, but her senses were informing her in no uncertain fashion that Sebastian, Marquess of Earith, was without question the most disturbingly attractive man she'd ever met.

Somewhat to her relief, once Sebastian had released her hand, he turned with a certain languid laziness to the gentleman standing beside him.

She lifted her gaze to that gentleman's face, and blinked. He, too, was exceedingly handsome—clearly that trait ran in the family; it was purely the fact that he was standing next to his brother, the marquess, that had kept her from noting him. That they were brothers was apparent; their faces held the same autocratic cast, even though the second gentleman's hair was dark brown and his eyes were a plain dark brown, too.

"Michael Cynster, my dear Niniver." The gentleman—Lord Michael, she realized—bowed as elegantly as the marquess over her hand. "And as Sebastian said, you're a very welcome addition to the family circle."

Standing opposite Michael, Thomas snorted. "Odd. I don't recall you expressing quite the same delight at my joining the Cynster throng."

Straightening, Michael arched his brows, but before he could respond, the dark-haired lady beside him—who had waited with what Niniver sensed was rising impatience—crisply put in, "That's because you're a male."

Locking eyes of the same strangely compelling pale green hue as the marquess's on Niniver's face, the lady grinned impishly. "We need more females of the right caliber to counter this lot—not more males of the same ilk. The Cynsters are all too good at breeding those."

Marcus, Sebastian, and Michael scoffed, but the bright-eyed lady paid them no heed. She took Niniver's hand, but instead of simply pressing her fingers, she stepped closer and enveloped her in a scented embrace. "Welcome to the family, Niniver. And if you ever need help, we'll always be here for you." She cut a laughing glance at Marcus as she stepped back. "And for Marcus, too."

Resuming her position beside Michael, opposite Niniver, the lady added, "Oh—and I'm Louisa, in case you hadn't guessed."

Niniver found it hard not to laugh, not to respond to the light in Louisa's eyes. "I had guessed, as it happens." Marcus had given her a list of his closest relatives, and she'd studied it in preparation for today.

"But speaking of ladies of the right caliber"—Sebastian waved to a group of three who were strolling up to join them—"here we have a situation of two against one."

Louisa glanced around, then shifted to make room. "But only one of said ladies is not one of us—and even she is the equivalent of a sister to you lot, and so no help. We need ladies able to take noblemen like you in hand."

To various dismissive snorts and a deep murmur of "only in your imagination" from Sebastian, the three newcomers joined their circle and were introduced as Prudence Cynster, a second cousin, Christopher Cynster, another second cousin, and Lady Antonia Rawlings, who was no relation at all but who had grown up with the Cynster brood.

Christopher proved to be a raconteur; he quickly had them all laughing.

As the animated conversations rolled on, Niniver realized that all the other ladies in their group were older than she, yet other than Lucilla, all were unmarried. She didn't think any of the others were quite thirty—she remembered hearing that Lucilla was the oldest female in that generation, and her new sister-in-law wasn't thirty yet—but for so many patently well-bred and well-connected young ladies to have reached their late twenties unmarried seemed distinctly odd.

She'd thought that, at twenty-five, she had already been on the shelf.

Standing beside Niniver and rocking Chloe in her arms, Lucilla noticed Niniver's puzzlement and, with typical acuity, correctly guessed its cause. Tipping her head closer, she murmured, "Most of the Cynster young ladies—and others, like Antonia, brought up in much the same circles—are having difficulty finding gentlemen able to accommodate their characters. In a way, it's the obverse of what Louisa was referring to—while our men are difficult to tame, our females are difficult to match."

Straightening, Lucilla met Niniver's gaze; her smile serene, she continued, "You were lucky—you found one of our males already predisposed and trained to share." She glanced at Marcus, then her gaze moved on to Sebastian and Michael. "Most gentlemen of such ilk don't, or won't. They need to be brought to it, and that's not an easy task, as Prudence, Antonia, and even more Louisa—and indeed, all the females of our generation—are discovering. For our generation, a successful marriage is going to be…perhaps not a bigger challenge than it was for our parents, but certainly a different one—a goal not at all easily attained."

Chloe caught one of Lucilla's trailing red tresses and tugged, demanding her mother's attention.

Noting the baby's stubborn expression, Niniver laughed.

A moment later, Marcus twined his fingers with hers, and they excused themselves and wandered on, tacking their way through the many other guests.

He took her on a circuit to pay their respects to his family's older generations. His grandmother was both kindly and terrifying; Niniver had no idea how the dowager duchess managed to be both simultaneously, but she left the old lady feeling relieved, but also as if the matriarch's patent approval had conferred a very special benediction.

As, arm in arm with Niniver, Marcus strolled through the crowd, none of whom showed any inclination to quit the gathering just yet, he looked about him with an ever-deepening satisfaction, not just in his own achievements but in hers, in theirs. Over the last month, he'd worked diligently alongside her to reorganize and reform the Carrick estate practices to make the most of the clan's lands, improve the clan's financial position, and bolster the health and welfare of the clan's people. For their part, the clan's farmers and elders had given them nothing but openhearted support; it was clear they were ready and willing to follow her into the next phase of rebuilding.

Although much of the funds flowing into the estate were coming from him, along with many contacts from him and Thomas, Marcus had made sure that it was Niniver who led—who made the final decisions, declared the changes, and drove their implementation. He might be beside her every step of the way, but she was the lady of the clan, and it was important for the future that her position remained not just clear but unequivocal.

The outcome of their labors lay all around them. He could see it, sense it, in the ready laughs and smiles, in the real joy buoying all the clan. His own people at Bidealeigh were slowly merging with the Carrick clansmen; eventually, at some point, they would come together as a whole.

That was still in the future, but for today...the uplifting swell of confident joy carried all before it.

"We've started, haven't we?" she asked. As he glanced down, Niniver looked up and caught his eye; her cornflower-blue eyes glowed with the same satisfaction he felt. "We've got ourselves and the clan moving together down the road to prosperity."

He remembered what she'd told him of her vow to her father. "Indeed, we have. We've reached that road and started down it, and we will keep marching on."

Her fingers tightened on his. Her eyes brimmed with love. "Together."

With his eyes, he gave her back the same emotion. "Together."

They held that shared look—basked in the promise of their love—for several moments, then they raised their heads and walked on.

\* \* \*

The crowd on the lawn was only just starting to thin when Niniver slipped away.

Leaving Marcus chatting about horses with Thomas, Sean, Mitch, and Fred, she circled back through the crowd toward the church, then slipped along its side into the graveyard.

Her father's grave lay under the shade of a tree just

bursting into full leaf. She halted at the foot and looked at the tombstone: *Manachan Randall Carrick, Laird of Clan Carrick*, with the dates of his birth and death beneath.

She remembered the day they'd lowered his coffin into the ground. Heard again in her head the words of the solemn vow she'd made.

Her eyes on the tombstone, she drew in a deep breath, then quietly said, "We're not there yet, but we've made a start. And neither Marcus nor I are the sort to back away from a challenge. We will see it through. We'll do whatever we need to do to move the clan forward, to walk the road to prosperity all the way to the end."

Tilting her head, she smiled softly. "You never saw me properly while you lived. I wonder if you can see me now you're dead? If you can… I think you would be proud of what I've done. And I think you'll be pleased by what's yet to come."

She stood looking at the grave for several seconds, then, still smiling, she turned and walked away.

Ahead, she saw Marcus waiting at the opening of the path to the graveyard. Smile deepening, she quickened her pace, the silk and lace of her wedding gown's skirts susurrating about her.

As she neared, he held out a hand.

Without hesitation and with welling joy, she laid her fingers in his and felt his close, warm and sure, about them.

His gaze on her eyes, understanding in his, he raised her fingers to his lips, brushed a kiss across her knuckles, then he wound her arm in his, turned, and led her on.

Into their future, one colored by the promise of hard work and commensurate satisfaction, with the certainty of shared joys and likely shared sorrows.

One that shone with togetherness, with yearning, with happiness.

A future that glowed with love.

Behind them, the graveyard quieted. The tree over the grave of the last laird of the Carricks quivered in a sighing breeze.

Then all fell silent and still once more, somnolent in the sunshine and shadows, as peace, deep and profound, settled over the graves.

\* \* \* \* \*

For alerts as new books are released, plus information on upcoming books, sign up for Stephanie's private e-mail newsletter, either on her website or at:
**eepurl.com/gLgPj**

Or if you're a member of Goodreads, join the discussion of Stephanie's books at the **Fans of Stephanie Laurens** group.

You can e-mail Stephanie at **stephanie@stephanielaurens.com**

Or find her on Facebook at **www.facebook.com/AuthorStephanieLaurens**

You can find detailed information on all Stephanie's published books, including covers, descriptions and excerpts, on her website at **www.stephanielaurens.com**

*For action, adventure and romance on the high seas, don't
miss Stephanie Laurens's exhilarating new series*

## THE ADVENTURERS QUARTET

*The voyage begins in 2016!*

*'Stephanie Laurens' heroines are a marvellous tribute to Georgette Heyer'*
—Cathy Kelly

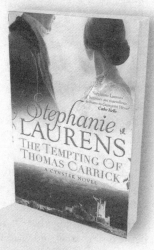

Strong-willed and passionate Lucilla Cynster is the last woman Thomas Carrick wants to ask for help, but when events take a disturbing turn on his family's estate, he is faced with no choice but to do exactly that. Will he be able to ignore the bond that seethes between them?

# Where Cynsters gather, love is never far behind

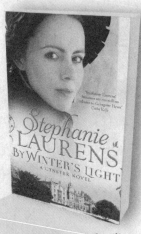

It's December and six Cynster families come together at snow-bound Casphairn Manor to celebrate the season in true Cynster fashion.

The festive occasion brings together Daniel Crosbie, tutor to Lucifer Cynster's sons, and Claire Meadows, widow and governess to Gabriel Cynster's daughter —and the embers of an unexpected passion smoulder between them.

However, once bitten, twice shy. Claire believes a second marriage is not in her stars. Until catastrophe strikes… Will Claire learn that love—true love— is worth any risk, any price?

**HARLEQUIN®MIRA®**

www.mirabooks.co.uk